FROZEN TUNDRA

FROZEN TUNDRA

Rick Shefchik

NORTH STAR PRESS OF ST. CLOUD, INC.
St. Cloud, Minnesota

Acknowledgements

Thanks again to Dan Kelly for his sharp editing eye and sharper sense of storytelling. Thank you to Dr. Paul Weatherby for his technical advice and longtime support and encouragement. Thanks to Chuck Laszewski for the lore and for Lambeau. Thanks to Jim McCarthy for his faith and hard work.

ISBN: 0-87839-359-5
ISBN-13: 978-0-87839-359-6

First Edition, September 1, 2010

Printed in the United States of America

Published by
North Star Press of St. Cloud, Inc.
P.O. Box 451
St. Cloud, Minnesota 56302

www.northstarpress.com

For Claire,
who has helped me immensely with every manuscript,
and will someday write brilliant books.

ONE

Snow swirled like a white dust storm across the two-lane highway, obliterating the center line and hiding oncoming cars until just before their pinprick headlights zoomed past Joe Horvath's Tahoe. He held his speed at forty, squinting through his ice-crusted windshield to make out the numbers on the mailboxes. The farmhouse he was looking for had been described to him as a typical rural Minnesota two-story with white wooden siding, set next to an old wooden barn, faded to gray. A crumbling tile silo would be next to the barn. A detached four-car garage and a large, tan pole barn should stand back from the road, with several smaller outbuildings scattered on the property.

He'd found the county road he was looking for and knew he was close to the right farm. The property bordered the St. Croix Wild River State Park—a perfect spot, he'd been told, protected from the curious and the uninvited by a dense, state-owned forest.

Horvath was one of the uninvited.

He slowed down when he spotted a cluster of cars at a farmhouse, set back almost a quarter-mile from the road. These weren't the older cars often seen scattered around on rural spreads, kept for parts or just rusting away in the weeds. These were mostly newer cars and SUVs, like Horvath's Tahoe. He could still see the indentation of tire tracks on the driveway, and the cars were only lightly snow-covered. Recent arrivals.

He stopped at the mailbox, got out of his SUV and brushed away the snow that covered the numbers: 32233.

This was it.

Horvath got back into the Tahoe and pulled the roll of cash from his jacket pocket, thumbing through it one more time. He had about ten thousand dollars— mostly in hundreds, with a few tens and twenties. He then took the Smith & Wesson 4506 semi-automatic from his glove compartment and put it into the shoulder holster inside his fleece vest. Under his heavy parka, the gun wouldn't be noticeable. He knew he wouldn't be the only one packing.

He put the SUV in gear and drove up the driveway, then turned it around so he was facing the road. He got out and trudged through the snow toward the farmhouse.

Horvath was a stocky man in his early fifties, with thin, graying hair clipped close and a darker moustache that he trimmed neatly every morning. He knew how to dress for days like this: thermal underwear, snowmobile pants, flannel shirt, fleece vest, parka, Thinsulate gloves, and a fleece hat with earflaps. It would be warmer once he got inside, but he could always drop the parka. Experience had taught him that you can never be overdressed for a December day in this part of the country.

He skipped the farmhouse. The action wouldn't be there. It would be in the barn, or the pole building. More vehicles—luxury cars, pickups with toppers, commercial-style vans with no writing on the side panels and no rear windows, and several SUVs with metal cages in the rear cargo area—were parked behind the house, at least two dozen, and he counted plates from five different states.

Horvath walked to the barn and stopped to listen for sounds inside, but heard nothing over the whistling of the wind. He looked through a window next to the sliding double-wide door, but it was too dark inside to see anything. He pulled on the sliding door and made an opening big enough to slip through. He slid the door shut behind him.

It wasn't much warmer inside the barn, and there was no illumination except for the dim gray light that came through the ground-level windows. As his eyes adjusted, he could see a long table to his left piled with thick chains, weights, and straps. Next to that, along the side wall, was a small treadmill, and in the center of the room was a hub with wooden spokes that extended outward, like the harnesses for a carnival pony ride. To his right he saw a hunk of some kind of animal hide, or flesh, hanging from a metal pole. The barn smelled like spoiled meat.

He turned to go back out to the driveway when he saw another hand grasp the edge of the door from the outside and yank it open. The inside of the barn became brighter.

"Help you?"

The first thing Horvath saw was the shotgun barrel, and then he saw the dog.

Horvath squinted at the man holding the shotgun, trying to make out his face against the white background outside. He had a week's worth of beard visible under his fur-lined bomber hat, and wore a stained gray barn jacket with rips in the sleeves. His blue jeans were tucked into dirty Sorel boots. The shotgun was crooked in his right elbow—not pointed directly at Horvath, but close enough.

In his left hand, the man held a rope attached to a shivering, steaming, bloody dog. The white and black dog's front legs dangled off the ground; its back legs were limp. There was a pink trail in the snow next to the man's boot prints. The dog's eyes were open but glassy and unfocused. Its muzzle was ripped apart, with a chunk missing that exposed its upper right teeth and gums. The left side of the dog's head, from nose to eye socket, looked like fresh hamburger. There were open, bloody stumps where the dog's ears had once been, and fresh, deep gouges up and down its neck, shoulders, and legs.

"I was looking for the fights," Horvath said. It sickened him to see the maimed dog, and he couldn't betray his disgust.

"I don't know you," the man with the shotgun said. Vapor from the cold air escaped his mouth with every word.

"Reggie told me about it. He gave me directions."

"Reggie Clark?"

"Yeah."

"He's over there, in the pole barn with the others." The man gestured to his left with the barrel of the shotgun.

"With all the snow, I couldn't tell where to look . . ."

"Yeah."

"Are you Dillon?"

The man nodded. "This is my place. What's your name?"

"Fred Thurston."

"Okay. Reggie said you'd come. How much did you bring?"

Horvath reached into his pants pocket and pulled out the wad of bills. He thumbed it for Dillon. "Ten grand."

Dillon stepped aside slightly and waited for Horvath to leave the barn and head to the pole building. The prospect of another gambler with a big roll seemed to overcome any suspicion the man might have had about Horvath.

"Did I miss much?"

"Just this piece of shit getting his face chewed off." Dillon lifted the dog by the rope. It whimpered, the sound muffled by the blood in its throat and the choking rope. "Cost me seven grand."

Horvath nodded and stepped past the man out into the driveway. He saw the bloody trail that led to the pole barn. It was already beginning to drift over. Horvath owned hunting dogs—well-trained black labs that did what he told them to do. They were loyal and affectionate. He punished them if necessary, but he was never cruel to them. Any man who would treat a dog the way Dillon treated that pit bull was no man at all.

He was halfway across the driveway when he heard the shotgun blast. After taking a moment to let the anger that swept through him pass, he wiped the freezing drips off his moustache, spat into the snow, and walked to the pole barn door.

A stench of blood, wet dog, beer and sweat hit him as he walked in. Two rows of fluorescent lights attached to the support beams inside the aluminum-sided pole barn threw bright light on the men—thirty or so—who surrounded the plywood ring in the center of the building. Horvath understood now why he hadn't heard anything over the howling wind—the interior walls were lined with triple layers of pink fiberglass insulation to muffle escaping sound. A makeshift bar was set up on a folding display table near the rear of the barn, with an array of liquor bottles and mixes, and two beer kegs under the table. The guy behind the bar was also serving hot dogs and bratwurst from a covered steamer on the table. The room echoed with laughter, curses, and fevered negotiation. Some of the men looked up when Horvath walked through the door, but they quickly went back to their conversations.

Two pit bulls were being washed in tubs outside the ring. Horvath knew the procedure was standard before each fight. This prevented their handlers from coating them with poison that could incapacitate or kill the other dog. The two dogs were not rookies. They had ugly, scabbed-over scars on their faces, necks, and legs. Despite the wounds, they were magnificent animals—eager and alert, with leg, hip, and shoulder muscles that rippled with each shift of their weight in the washtubs. One was all charcoal gray from the shoulders back, and all white from the shoulders to the face, except for a swatch of gray around his right eye. He looked as though he'd been held by the front legs and dipped into a vat. The other was mostly buckskin, except for the left half of his face, which was white. Both were jumping and twisting against their restraints. They knew what was coming.

Horvath walked up to an empty spot along the three-foot-high, twenty-foot-square plywood ring. He caught Reggie Clark's eye and nodded. Reggie nodded back, but showed no inclination to come over and talk. Clark was standing next to three other black men, one of whom stood almost a foot taller than the rest. Horvath recognized him instantly. So far, so good.

Horvath checked his watch. He had a half-hour to work with, an hour at best. He would have to endure at least one fight.

"Jag!" one of the handlers yelled at the buckskin-colored dog. He was leading it up to the scratch line on the near side of the ring. The other handler was a black man in a navy hooded sweatshirt that said AUBURN across the front. He seemed to know the guys Reggie was standing with. He gave them a thumbs-up as he positioned his gray-and-white dog at the other scratch line. Both dogs were straining to break free of their handlers.

"I like Coke," the man standing next to Horvath said. He smelled of whiskey and sausages, rather than cola. Horvath was puzzled—was the guy talking about cocaine? So what? Then he heard the black handler yell, "Coke!" at his dog, and Horvath understood. Coke was the dog. Horvath was being offered a bet on Jag.

"How much?" Horvath said.

"Six."

"Hundred?"

The man laughed harshly, narrowed his eyes. "Thousand."

"I don't like Jag that much. I'll do four."

"Sold. Let's see your money."

Horvath pulled four thousand off his roll and fanned it in front of the man, who seemed satisfied.

"You need some blow?" the guy asked.

"No thanks."

"Meth?"

"I'm good."

"Have a snort, then."

The man held up a flask, and Horvath took it. God only knew what kind of crap had been in this guy's mouth, but Horvath took a pull anyway. Brandy . Cheap stuff.

The buzz in the pole barn grew as the referee stepped over the plywood wall and walked into the middle of the ring between the two straining, salivating dogs. Spectators began shouting when the ref looked at both handlers and gave them the sign to release their dogs. He hustled back over the wooden barrier as Jag and Coke sprinted at each other, and the men around the ring released a collective, guttural roar. Horvath heard the dogs' teeth clash as they collided in the center. The cries from the crowd grew louder as the two taut-muscled animals—growling viciously—wrestled for position, chomping frantically at each other's necks, flopping and rolling in the dirt. They opened their jaws only to readjust their bites and sink their fangs even deeper into each other. Streams of red spurted from the wounds on the snarling dogs, dripped from their teeth, and splattered onto the plywood barrier. They rolled over and over in the blood on the floor from the previous fight, while their own fresh blood turned the dirt a deep, sticky purple. Horvath had to look away.

While the crowd was screaming and cursing at the two dogs, Horvath walked over to the tall black man.

D'Metrius Truman's peripheral vision apparently had not been affected by his time in federal prison. He sensed Horvath's approach and turned to face him.

"Yeah?"

"Listen to me," Horvath said. He looked up at the sculpted athlete while the men around them continued to howl at the dogs. "You have to get out of here—now."

"Why?"

Clark was keeping his back to their conversation. The rest of the spectators were gripped in twisted ecstasy over the sight of the dogs in a writhing tangle in the center of the ring, occasionally growling and whining, then shaking their heads from side to side to rip into their opponent's flesh. Still, Horvath spoke as quietly as he could.

"The feds are coming to raid. Tonight."

"Who are you?" Truman asked.

"I'm your last chance."

Truman's looked Horvath up and down.

"I ain't goin' nowhere," he said. He turned back to the ring.

"Nowhere but back to prison."

Truman man stiffened. Horvath could see he'd gotten his attention. Truman could play it as cool as he wanted, but he knew that if he were rounded up in another dogfighting sting, any judge in the country would lock him up for the maximum. The nation had been outraged that Truman owned a dog kennel in Alabama, where pit bulls were raised for fighting. His status as an All-Pro quarterback with the Minnesota Vikings hadn't helped him in the PR fight. If anything, it made everything worse. There had been no evidence that he had personally electrocuted, hanged or shot any of his dogs after they lost fights, but it was bad enough that it had happened on his property, at the hands of his friends and relatives. He was an instant pariah, the latest poster boy for all the outrages committed by professional athletes.

Truman's lawyers had argued that dogfighting was indeed horrible, but was a "sport" that Truman's father and uncles had engaged in—and taken him to watch— from the time he was a young child. It was the culture he'd been raised in, they said. Now he understood that it was vicious and barbaric, they said. He knew it was wrong, they said. The Alabama judge had been somewhat persuaded: five years, with a chance at parole after two. The public wanted more.

"You can't afford a second conviction," Horvath said into Truman's ear. "You'll never play football again."

"I ain't playin' now," Truman said. "I'm still suspended. And even if I wasn't, nobody would sign me."

"There's a job waiting for you, if we get out before the cops show up."

"I came with those guys." Truman nodded toward two men leaning over the barrier and shouting at Coke to get off his back and rip Jag's throat open.

"You're leaving with me," Horvath said. "Now."

Truman shrugged, but Horvath saw fear in his eyes. Maybe he did have something to lose. He was willing to find out.

The dogs were still growling and yelping, and the men around the ring were still screaming at them as Horvath and Truman walked, unnoticed, to the door. Truman, in a dark, three-quarter-length fleece-lined coat, with a black wool cap pulled down over his ears, put on a pair of leather gloves when Horvath pushed the door open. The snow was coming down in diagonal bursts and then swirling—a near white-out in the driveway.

"Do you have a gun?" Horvath yelled over the wind.

"Yeah."

"Give it to me. You can't be found with that here."

Truman put his hand inside his coat and gave Horvath the gun—a Colt 1911.

"Loaded?" Horvath asked.

"What do you think?"

Horvath ejected the full magazine into his free hand, looked it over, and put it back in. He racked the slide to put a round in the chamber, released the safety, and put the gun into his pocket.

When they reached the barn, the door slid open and Dillon emerged, shotgun still under his arm. He stopped to look at Horvath and Truman.

"Leaving kinda early," Dillon said.

"We gotta be somewhere," Horvath said. He put his hands in the pockets of the parka, nudged Truman with his shoulder and kept walking.

"Hold it," Dillon said. "Who the hell are you, anyway?"

He raised the shotgun parallel to the ground. Horvath turned, and, with his left hand, pointed toward the barn behind Dillon.

"Let's go back in there for a minute."

"Why?"

"This is why."

Horvath pulled Truman's gun out of his pocket in his gloved right hand and pointed it at Dillon's chest. Dillon started to aim the shotgun, but Horvath fired twice, dropping Dillon where he stood.

"What the fuck!" Truman shouted.

Horvath ignored him. He slid the barn door open a little wider, picked up Dillon's feet and dragged him through the entrance to a training wheel in the center of the room. He propped up the body, slipped one of the harnesses over his neck, and put another bullet through Dillon's forehead. Then he walked out of the barn and slid the door closed behind him. He took Truman by the arm and pulled him down the driveway toward his Tahoe.

"That asshole has murdered his last dog," Horvath said.

"But that was my gun!"

"That's right. And no one's going to believe you weren't here, or you didn't do this, if I turn you in. Now let's get the fuck out of here."

He pushed the remote entry for the Tahoe and climbed in the driver's side. Truman got in the passenger side, and Horvath turned the ignition. To Horvath's relief, the SUV started immediately. The wipers brushed off the accumulated snow from the front windshield. He'd have to stop somewhere to clear the back window. No time now. He put the Tahoe in gear, accelerated down the driveway, and executed a sliding turn to the right, heading north toward Rush City. He'd pick up the interstate there. Within minutes, Horvath spotted several plain black sedans going past them, heading south toward the farm. Feds.

D'Metrius Truman turned to look at the line of black cars, then snapped back and stared out the front windshield. He remained speechless as the snow swirled around the speeding SUV. Finally, just before Horvath turned onto I-35, Truman managed to form a question.

"Who in the hell are you?"

"I'll tell you all about it on the way."

"On the way where?"

"Green Bay."

TWO

The midafternoon sky over the Santa Catalina Mountains in Tucson was typically, brilliantly, blue, with a flat cluster of white winter clouds casting shadows on the jagged peaks. Sam Skarda pulled his rented Chrysler Sebring convertible into the driveway of the one-story adobe and tile-roofed house in the foothills, took his golf clubs out of the trunk and leaned them against the wall inside the garage. He walked into the house through the laundry room, calling Caroline's name when he reached the open foyer.

"Out here," she called, from the back patio.

Sam walked through the great room, decorated with southwest art and soft desert colors, and slid open the screen door to the patio. From the backyard of Caroline Crandall's home, the entire valley stretched out below. The growing city seemed to ooze like river silt around the foothills of the Santa Rita Mountains to the south, the Rincon Mountains to the east, and the Tucson Mountains to the west. It was a beautiful sight, especially at sunset. Sam never tired of it—nor of the sight just a few feet away. Caroline, in a white bikini with a wide-brimmed straw hat and a pair of sunglasses to protect her face, pruned branches from her lime tree. Her dark hair, normally shoulder-length, was pulled up into a loose twist behind her head. There was a glass of something clear and cold, with lime, on the table next to her.

She would have had a cigarette going in the ashtray the last time Sam visited, but she was keeping to her resolution to quit—made at least in part due to Sam's description of his father's unsuccessful battle with lung cancer.

The Roches' close-harmony version of "Good King Wenceslas" flowed from the outdoor speakers. Sam still wasn't used to hearing Christmas songs in the desert. Christmas was supposed to be cold noses, warm hats, snowmen, and frosted pine trees. Here in Tucson there was no snow—deep, crisp, or even.

"You like the Roches?" Sam said.

"Who?"

Caroline smiled at him when he walked over to her and leaned on the adobe wall that bordered her patio garden.

"That's who you're listening to."

"Oh. I just plugged your iPod into my stereo. Whatever you were playing before . . ."

"My Christmas playlist."

"I like it. Gets me in the holiday mood. Except for . . . what's the group that does 'Christmas in Jail'?"

"The Youngsters. Fifties doo-wop group."

"Real festive, that one."

"I can only take so much festivity."

"You must have a thousand Christmas songs. Why so many?"

"When we put our band together to play the police holiday party a few years ago, we wanted to learn some Christmas songs. I converted a bunch of my mom's old Christmas albums to MP3s. It kind of grew from there."

In fact, Sam had over two thousand Christmas songs loaded onto his iPod now. Sitting in his office in White Bear Lake, Minnesota, one day in late November, he'd turned the radio on to the oldies station that was playing non-stop Christmas music. By the next day, he'd heard Bing Crosby sing "White Christmas" four times. There was nothing wrong with the song per se, but after the third time he wanted to take out his Glock 23 and blow the radio through the wall.

Now he spent his free time in the office surfing for fresh holiday MP3s. As the collection grew, he'd begun doing Internet research on the songs' origins. Knowing a familiar song's backstory made it seem less like audio wallpaper.

He'd learned, for instance, that there really was a good King Wenceslas—except that he was the Duke of Bohemia, not a king, and he was so good that he was murdered in 929 by his envious younger brother. In 1853 an English clergyman named John Mason Neale wrote a children's song about the good, martyred duke, set to an older Swedish carol about the coming of spring. It became a Christmas classic, even though the "feast of Stephen" took place the day after Christmas, on St. Stephen's Day. Sam had ten versions of the song, including a mandolin instrumental version by David Grisman and a full-blown choir arrangement by the Harry Simeone Chorale.

He had only one version of "Christmas in Jail." No one could top the original.

"Where'd you play today?" Caroline asked.

"Silverbell. Couldn't get on anywhere else."

"Why don't you call one of the private clubs? Drop a few names."

"I hate doing that."

"Fine, be ethical. How'd you play?"

"I can't break seventy-five lately. Maybe it's these six-hour Sunday rounds. Or maybe I just don't practice enough."

"Maybe you need me to carry your bag again."

"Maybe you should play with me."

"Uh-uh," she said. "I'll play anywhere but in the desert. It just bothers me to see all the water they use to keep the courses green. If you want me to play with you, it doesn't have to be golf, does it?"

She took off her sunglasses and let her eyes graze from his chest and tanned forearms downward toward his belt buckle. He did his best to return the look—though he knew he still had too much of the straight-arrow cop in him to be a convincing playboy.

Sam had been in Tucson almost a week—the longest time he and Caroline had spent together since they'd met at the Masters. He'd earned a berth in the tournament by winning the U.S. Publinx while re-habbing a gunshot wound to his knee. Caroline was the ex-wife of one of Sam's college golf teammates, and she'd filled in as his emergency caddie at the Masters. Though he missed the cut, she became much more to him over the course of that week—including a target of a revenge-bent serial killer. Sam had been hired by the privacy-obsessed officials at August National to find the killer and prevent a mass murder at the tournament, but in doing so, Sam had put Caroline's life in danger. That violent Sunday at Augusta had earned Sam an elite position as a go-to private investigator for national sports figures, but it had upset Caroline deeply, enough to keep them apart for a while.

They'd both been busy—Sam making the transition from Minneapolis police detective to his own P.I. agency and Caroline getting about her new life as the ex-wife of a golf pro. She'd done well in the divorce. The house was not huge, but it had everything she wanted, and the location was spectacular. She'd found a job she enjoyed with U.S. Immigration in Tucson. She enjoyed working in her garden, and she was educating herself about Arizona's native flowers and plants. In the process, she'd become concerned about the desert's water usage issues—including the millions of gallons used each day to keep the state's golf courses from burning out and turning a most golf-unfriendly brown.

Sam and Caroline had been unsure how, or whether, their lives could fit together. Sam's base was in Minnesota, and his work always had the potential to be violent and dangerous. Caroline had lived all over the world as the daughter of a military man, then as an itinerant caddie, and finally as a PGA Tour wife, but Arizona was home now. It was quiet and predictable. Letting Sam get deeper into her life, she was letting his work in, too—work that was rarely quiet and never predictable. But they had to move forward or give up, and neither wanted to give up.

"Did you think about it?" she asked.

Caroline bundled a pile of lime branches together and carried them to a plastic waste barrel beside the house. She moved languidly, letting the sun play on her legs and shoulders. Sam knew she was doing a sell job, and she had his full attention.

"It?" Sam said, his eyes roaming up and down her tanned skin. "I'm thinking about *it* right now."

"Not *that* it," Caroline said. "About moving down here."

"Sure. I think about it a lot."

"And?"

"I don't know yet. What about you?"

"I can't move to Minnesota."

"Immigration has an office there. We've got all the illegals you could ask for."

"Sam, moving here makes sense. You could open an agency. Start another band. Play golf whenever you wanted. And be with me."

It was what Sam wanted. But . . . now? He'd just opened his office. His cop connections in Minneapolis and St. Paul had been vital in getting work—though his Augusta National connection was the reason he'd been getting sports cases. He supposed he could work out of Tucson, too.

He gazed out over the garden to the valley below and thought about leaving Minnesota. He'd been steadily losing his affection for winter. He'd given up skiing because of his knee injury. The aesthetic pleasure of a fresh snowfall evaporated in the morning as he shoveled out the end of his driveway after the plow went by. Yet this was the time of year—the Christmas music, the lights, the post-card views of snow-covered roofs and chimneys—that made him most sentimental about the place where he'd grown up. December always made him think of his father, the tough Minneapolis cop who'd flooded a skating rink in their backyard every winter to play pickup hockey with the neighbor kids. He wouldn't miss winter, but he would miss the people: his cop buddies, the friends he'd grown up with, his mother, who'd moved back home to Duluth, and his sister, who was raising three young hockey players in a St. Paul suburb. There would be trade-offs he wasn't ready to make yet.

The iPod was playing Kenny Chesney's "All I Want For Christmas Is a Real Good Tan," and Sam gazed at Caroline, lightly browned with tiny beads of perspiration glistening on her thighs, arms, and in the shaded valley between her breasts. The trade-offs suddenly seemed to tilt in favor of Tucson.

"I'd have to be back in Minnesota for the summer," Sam said.

"I don't like Tucson in July either."

"I'm not talking about a month. May to September."

"What about my job?"

"How much vacation do you get?"

"Three weeks."

"Can't you call in sick for a couple of months?"

Caroline made a face, crossed the patio to her rose bushes and began working on them with her pruning shears. She reached behind her and tightened the knot of her thick dark hair, to expose her neck and shoulders to the sun, while Sam admired her graceful curves. Sam wasn't ready to leave Arizona, but his return flight to Minneapolis, to his empty house, was booked for Monday. Maybe it was time to call a realtor and get his charming, three-bedroom arts-and-crafts bungalow ready to go on the market. He knew one thing—he didn't want to live alone anymore.

He walked back into the house, mixed himself a gin and tonic, and took out his cell phone. He had kept it turned off during his round; he couldn't stand it when people used their phones on the golf course. It was way up there on his list of major annoyances—just below car alarms.

He sat down on a stool next to the cooktop island and dialed the message-retrieval number for his office. He might as well find out what kind of work he might be returning to.

There were two messages. Both had come in Friday.

"Sam? It's me, Gretchen. Gretchen Kahler. So . . . how are you? I saw your name in the news again. First the Masters. Now that story with the Red Sox. I guess you've left the cops, then. Right? So, if I asked you a favor—I mean, I know I'm in no position to ask you for a favor, but . . .

"Well, look, let me tell you what's going on here. Maybe you know that I'm in Green Bay now. I work for the Packers—I'm the team doctor. Basically, I'm a general practitioner for the team—everything from nosebleeds to broken legs . . .

"I know this is getting long, but here's why I called . . . hold it, this . . ."

After that, there were a few sounds, some clicks, then silence. That was the end of the call.

Gretchen Kahler. Sam didn't think about her very often anymore, and that was a good thing. They'd almost gotten married ten years ago.

He stared at his phone, waiting to process the first message before going on to the second. He knew she'd wanted to go into sports medicine, but didn't know she was with the Packers. It made sense—she was originally from Eau Claire, Wisconsin, only a hundred miles from Minneapolis, but squarely in Packerland. It hadn't taken Sam long to find out that Gretchen was a sports-loving Cheesehead.

They'd met at a murder. Sam and his partner were the first cops at the scene of a shooting in an alley in South Minneapolis, and Gretchen had been one of the

EMTs who showed up with the paramedic unit. She'd caught Sam's eye right away. Short, athletic-looking, blond and in braids, quietly confident. The sight of a man with a hole the size of a peach in his chest didn't seem to faze her. She went about her business quickly and efficiently, and when she knew that the man was dead, she advised Sam to call the morgue.

The next time they bumped into each other on a case—a traffic accident at Lake and Hiawatha, where a woman had gone halfway through her windshield—he said hello to her, and she remembered him. He asked her what time she got off her shift, and she agreed to meet him for coffee.

She had a great smile when she wasn't working on injured or dead people—small, even teeth and a cute set of dimples. There was just a hint of red in her blond hair, the same with her eyebrows. She had some faded freckles, and her eyes were pale blue. Sam hadn't dated anyone seriously since college, but he wanted to date Gretchen. She was in the process of breaking up with another guy, she'd said. It might take another week or two, but she wanted to go out with Sam, too. She liked cops—some of them, anyway.

Gretchen gave the news to the other guy, but he didn't retreat gracefully. Eventually, Sam had run into him outside her apartment on his way to pick her up for a concert. Sam was not in his uniform. When the guy accused Sam of stealing his girlfriend, Sam tried to be reasonable. It was already over between the two of you, he'd said. The guy was drunk and took a swing at Sam. Sam dropped him with one punch.

"I don't think she wants to be friends," Sam had said. He stepped over the sprawled ex-boyfriend and went up to Gretchen's apartment.

They were together for two years. Gretchen was three years younger than Sam, but the age difference didn't matter. They were both becoming hardened by the work they did. There were times she got so absorbed by her job that Sam had to step in and insist they see a movie or go to a music club. They ate out often, because neither had time to learn how to cook anything more complicated than eggs. Gretchen spent much of her spare time going to the gym or training for 10-K races, while Sam played golf. She came out to the course with him a few times and showed talent for the game, but the pace of a round was too slow for her. She enjoyed his music, and was usually there when he played with Night Beat, the band he'd formed with some fellow cops. He wrote some songs for her and about her. She crocheted a guitar strap for him. When he was promoted to detective, she threw a surprise party for him at his house. His mother and sister were there, and both of them told Sam they liked her very much. He thought they would marry when the time seemed right.

Then Gretchen told him she was going to med school.

"That's great," Sam had said. "University of Minnesota?"

"No. Wisconsin."

"Wisconsin?"

He knew he should have seen it coming. She was young, ambitious, talented, and not ready to settle down. Not ready to become a cop's wife, to eventually stay home raising babies while Sam was out doing the things she had once done.

"I've always wanted to be a doctor—I know that now. I thought being a paramedic would be enough, but it's not."

Sam hadn't mentioned marriage. He didn't have to. Gretchen knew.

"I'm not ready, Sam," she said. "We both have too much to do now. Too much ahead of us. If we'd met a few years later . . ."

The night before she moved to Madison, they went out to their favorite Thai restaurant, and she cried. Sam wanted to, but didn't. Gretchen was on her way out of his life. He accepted it, hated it, and found ways to turn away from it. He had to; like the guy he'd left sprawled on the sidewalk in front of her apartment, he knew he and Gretchen weren't going to be friends. He wrote one breakup song about her, then put it away and never played it.

There'd been other women since, but no one important until Caroline. Hearing from Gretchen on his answering machine dredged up a tangle of old feelings, but he put them back in place before retrieving her second message.

"Me again. Sorry—bad signal. This is the thing . . . there are some strange things happening with this team . . . with management. I suppose you read that the Packers signed D'Metrius Truman. The commissioner has reinstated him, and he's probably going to start next Sunday. I know we're losing, and we don't have a lot of talent, but why do we need that kind of trouble? Management keeps bringing in these . . . thugs . . . who aren't good for the team or the community. It's almost like they want to turn the fans off, and around here, that's pretty hard to do. But I see it happening.

"And there's a deep split on the executive board. It's more than just a difference of opinion on how to run the team. Frank Janaszak—the team president—tells me some of the committee members want to sell the team. You know we're owned by the public, right? Frank and a couple of the others would never dream of selling, but there's lots of people out there who'd love to get their hands on the Packers. It would be a pretty cheap way to become an NFL owner, and this team could be a gold mine for someone. Frank's worried that at least one guy on the committee would do anything to steer the team into private ownership.

"I don't know . . . it feels like we're losing control of the club. Someone inside or outside of the organization is pushing us toward a cliff, and we don't know how to stop it. I told Frank I was going to talk to you. Could you call him? I tried to think of somebody else who could handle something like this . . . I mean, I know it could be weird between us . . . but this isn't about me. We're just worried about the team, where it's going, who's with us and who's against us. I told Frank you're good at this kind of thing. If we don't hear from you, I'll understand. But . . . well, anyway, thanks for listening, Sam. I hope you're happy. I'm . . . I'm doing okay. Talk to you soon—I hope."

She left her number, Janaszak's number, and said goodbye.

Of course he'd call. He had seen the story in the *Arizona Daily Star* that Truman had signed with the Packers, and he'd been surprised. Why would a 1-12 team bother bringing in a reviled character like Truman—especially one who hadn't played a down in more than two years? The Green Bay Packers now had the biggest collection of criminals in the NFL, and that was saying something.

What had Gretchen meant about "sell the team?" Unlike all other pro sports franchises, the Packers were owned by its fans, who held shares in the team. That wasn't likely to change. If anything, more cities were talking about following Green Bay's model, to eliminate the tired drama of an owner threatening to move unless the city or state coughed up more money. But Sam knew almost nothing about the Packers' bylaws or leadership structure.

All of that could keep. He had one day left with Caroline, and hearing Gretchen's voice had only reinforced how much he was going to miss her. It also reminded him that, no matter how certain he might be that he'd finally found the right woman, circumstances had a way of changing.

He picked up his drink and carried it out to the patio. Caroline was still working on the rose bushes, looking relaxed and goddess-like in the golden glow of the late afternoon sun.

"Nice ass for a border guard," Sam said. "No wonder so many people are trying to sneak in."

Caroline opened her eyes and replied without moving her head.

"I'm not a border guard," she said. "Get it right: I'm an intelligence research specialist for the Immigration Service."

"Let me take you to dinner. You can explain it all to me again over wine and steak."

"Let's stay home. I have two beautiful ribeyes in the fridge, and two ridiculously expensive bottles of Cabernet. Besides, where are we going to hear better music?"

Sam's iPod was playing "Christmas Time Is Here" by Vince Guaraldi. The impressionistic piano chords went well with the pink-and-turquoise desert sky.

"You like Vince Guaraldi?" he said.

"Who?"

Caroline put down the pruning shears, shook out her hair, and walked over to Sam. She put her arms around his neck and kissed him. Her back felt warm under Sam's palms as he pulled her closer to him. They kissed until the song changed to "I've Got My Love to Keep Me Warm" by Billie Holiday—written in 1937 by Irving Berlin, first sung by Dick Powell and Alice Faye in a film called "On the Avenue"— and Sam wanted to go into the bedroom. So did Caroline. They walked into the house. On the way to her room, Caroline asked Sam if he'd had any messages.

"Two," he said.

"Anything important?"

"Possible case in Green Bay."

"Who called?"

"It's . . . it was a woman I used to know. Gretchen Kahler."

"How well did you know her?"

"We were together a couple of years."

Caroline stopped outside her bedroom door and turned to look at Sam. She had the don't-bullshit-me look in her eyes, and Sam couldn't blame her.

"And she wants you to work on a case?"

"I haven't talked to her in ten years."

"Then why did she call you?"

"Probably because I was the first private eye she came to in her Rolodex."

"I don't like this . . ."

"I'll find out more about it tomorrow. Right now, I don't care about anything except you."

In her room, Sam untied the string behind her neck that held up her bikini top. He let the straps fall in front, and the top came halfway off, well below the tan line. Caroline put her arm around Sam's shoulder and ran her hand through his hair, which was now as almost as long as it had been when he was in college—not long, exactly, but enough for Caroline to grab a good handful. With her other hand, Caroline unbuttoned the two front buttons on his golf shirt, then pulled it over his head. As she did, Sam decided to stop waiting for gravity, and pulled down the straps of the bikini top. Caroline's white breasts spilled out, and Sam nuzzled them while Caroline unbuckled his belt.

Soon they were both naked in the middle of Caroline's bedroom, with sunset pouring into the room from above the crest of the Tucson Mountains, making a bright amber rectangle on the opposite wall. Sam ran his hands through Caroline's luxurious dark hair, down her rib cage, across her stomach and back up to her breasts.

Caroline let her head fall back as he gently caressed her nipples, and then took his arm and guided him to her king-size bed.

Sam slept for two hours afterwards, the effects of golf, the sun, the drink, and Caroline. When he awoke, he heard her in the kitchen, preparing vegetables to go with the steaks to the strains of "Happy Holidays" by Andy Williams—written by Irving Berlin for the show "Holiday Inn," in the key of F-sharp, the only key he knew.

Sam knew he should get up and help Caroline with the meal, but he remained in bed a few extra minutes, listening to the music and the ticking of the bedroom clock in the darkened room. He thought about the message from Gretchen, and he thought about going to Wisconsin. He didn't know how long he'd be gone, or when he could come back. If he did go, he didn't know how he was going to keep peace with Caroline.

He did know that sometimes, loving a woman wasn't enough to make it work.

THREE

Ed Larson had been to Doc Mueller's place on Lake Minocqua several times, but always in the summer, when the walleyes, northerns, muskies, and smallmouth bass were biting—and if they weren't, you just had a few beers in the boat and watched the clouds roll by. Minocqua was a pleasant, three-hour drive northwest of Green Bay, but it was a different story during a heavy snow, like the one now drifting across the highway in frozen streams of white.

Larson was second-guessing his decision to go ice fishing on Minocqua with his friend Mueller, but they were more than halfway there. It made no sense to turn around.

"Mind if I turn on the radio, Doc?" Larson said. "I want a forecast."

"More snow," said Mueller.

They were a mismatched pair. Dr. Karl "Doc" Mueller had the tall, bony build of an athlete, with a sharply defined facial structure and deep-set blue eyes. He wore his gray hair over the top half of his ears and onto his collar, but never shaggy—he trimmed it often, in a style he knew the ladies liked. Ed Larson was short and pudgy, with white hair that he tried to keep long enough on the sides to swirl across the top of his mostly bald head. He had a broad nose and round, reddish cheeks that made him the inevitable choice to play Santa Claus at the Packers' employee Christmas party.

Mueller was doing ten miles an hour over the speed limit in his four-wheel-drive Land Rover, even though the center line was rarely visible. He came up behind a snowplow and was forced to slow down for the fourteen-ton vehicle as it blasted solid sheets of snow and ice into the ditch while dumping sand in its wake. Each time Mueller edged toward the center to see if it was safe to pass the plow, the road curved or climbed a hill. Finally they hit a straight stretch of highway, and Mueller impatiently yanked the wheel to the left, into the oncoming lane. Larson couldn't see what was on the other side of the cloud of snow being kicked up by the plow's blade, and he wasn't sure Mueller could, either.

"What are you doing?" Larson asked. His fingers tightened on his seat belt.

"Passing this putz."

When they emerged from the billowing snow, the road ahead was clear, and Mueller glided back to the right in front of the plow. Larson knew it would have done no good to tell Mueller to be patient—that it didn't matter if they got to the lake five or ten minutes later. Doc's foot was always on the gas. He was a live-on-the-edge guy who always wanted to see how fast, high, and far he could go. It had worked for him for over sixty years, and his friends accepted that when they chose to hang out with him.

"This is just the weather we want," Mueller said. "We'll have the lake to ourselves."

"You sure the ice is thick enough?"

"It's thick enough, Ed. I called my bait-shop guy up there. Trust me."

Larson trusted Doc Mueller. Everyone in the Green Bay Packers organization did. Vince Lombardi himself had hired Doc Mueller as an assistant physician when he was just twenty-six, and he'd eventually risen to the position of team physician, a job he'd held for twenty-five years. He'd been a key component of the Packers' last Super Bowl win, keeping battered stars on the field when less skilled or more cautious doctors might have sent them to the hospital. Thanks to his talent, hard work, and loyalty to the team—other clubs had courted him over the years, but he'd turned down all offers—he was eventually rewarded with a spot on the Packers' seven-member executive committee, which made all the key decisions for the team. He was now vice-president, second in command to Chairman Frank Janaszak.

Ed Larson was the committee's secretary, and had served even longer than Mueller. He didn't resent the fact that Mueller was in line to become chairman. Janaszak's declining health would force him to step down soon. Larson was in his late sixties and didn't want to take on the pressure or the responsibility of being the man who ran America's only publicly owned franchise. Frank Janaszak had been brilliant at the job. Larson had no doubt Doc Mueller would be equally brilliant—in a very different, less conservative style.

Ed was semi-retired from the meat packing company he owned with his sons Andy and Chuck. He could get away for a couple of days in midweek for fishing if he wanted to. So could Doc Mueller. They went to all the games at Lambeau, of course, and sometimes Ed did road trips with his wife. Shelly Larson particularly liked going to shopping meccas like Miami, New York, and Los Angeles, but skipped the annual slogs to Minneapolis and Detroit. Mueller went on almost every road trip. He had been divorced for ten years and traveled where and when he pleased.

The truth was, the road trips weren't as much fun as they used to be—and neither were the home games. The Packers had finished last in the division two years running, and this season they had won just once. If their bad play held form, they were once again in line for the first pick in the NFL draft. High draft picks, however, had not been a path to improvement. Two years ago, their top pick demanded to be traded on draft day, saying he'd sit out a year rather than play in Green Bay. The Packers backed down, swapping first-round picks with the Eagles and ending up with a wide receiver who had world-class speed and hands made of cement. ("Jaymar Dukes looks and runs like Superman," wrote *Gazette* columnist Randy Joyce. "Too bad the NFL is using Kryptonite footballs.")

Last year's three-victory season had produced no help in the draft, either, because Florida State running back and Heisman Trophy winner Tyrone Givens also refused to sign after Green Bay drafted him first overall. "Too damn cold up there," Givens had said at a press conference arranged by his agent, Arnie Hollister. "I ain't livin' in an igloo for a team that don't win."

Givens held fast, and the Packers eventually traded his rights to the Raiders for a massive defensive tackle who blew out his knee in training camp. Now the Packers were in line to draft Southern Cal quarterback Dayne Collins, the consensus choice among scouts, general managers, and sportswriters as the obvious number-one pick—a guy who would definitely fill the void at a position that had killed the Packers since the Favre Era ended. But Collins was also going to be represented by Hollister, one of the toughest negotiators in the business. There was little chance that Collins would sign with Green Bay, either. He'd been quoted as saying he understood why Givens—the current favorite for NFL rookie of the year in Oakland—had chosen not to sign with a cold-weather team.

"I'm a California dude all the way," Collins had said. "I hate snow. If the Packers are smart, they won't draft me, because I won't play there."

Ed Larson couldn't understand that. He'd lived in Wisconsin all his life, taking over the meatpacking plant from his own father and growing the business to the point where his sons would be comfortable all their lives. And who wouldn't be comfortable in a safe, clean environment like Green Bay, Wisconsin? They had it all here: lakes, rivers, forests, hills, farms, and dairyland, and a city of 100,000 that offered anything a reasonable man could want. And if you couldn't find it in Green Bay, Milwaukee was 100 miles away, and Chicago less than a hundred more. He wouldn't have lived anywhere else for any amount of money.

If it weren't for the Packers' recent woes, he'd have said life was nearly perfect.

But all this losing bothered him. The Packers had finished last in their division a few times between the Vince Lombardi glory days and the Super Bowl teams of the late 1990s, but this seemed like more than a couple of off-years. By any honest evaluation, they were the worst team in football, something that couldn't be said about the Packers since the mid-1950s. There'd been mistakes in talent evaluation, they'd lost key veterans to retirement, they'd lost a good coach who left for more money and a more competitive roster, and they'd had no success with the draft or the free-agency market. They couldn't convince the top-quality players—the difference-makers—to come to Green Bay. Instead, they'd begun gambling on the dregs of the waiver wire—players who were considered too inconsistent, too violent, too much of a drug risk, or simply too crazy for other teams to take a chance on. Larson had talked to general manager Dick Jordan about the situation, but he always got the same answer:

"I've got no choice, Ed. The only guys with any talent who are willing to play here are the guys nobody else wants. Everybody else turns me down."

Inevitably, there'd been incidents. The most recent had occurred just last week, when LaBobby Suggs, a free-agent nose guard the Packers had signed in September, was arrested for a break-in and rape in West de Pere. It was the sixth time since training camp that a Packer had been arrested. Even for the NFL, that was getting to be a bit much. The Suggs story had been front-page news in the *Press-Gazette* for days, and the TV networks were sending reporters to Green Bay to find out what had gone wrong. "Trouble in Titletown" was the way ABC had framed their story; ESPN had gone with "Meltdown on the Frozen Tundra."

It was good to be getting away. Ed Larson hadn't been ice fishing for years, but he liked the idea of five or six hours in a fish house on a frozen lake, staring into a twelve-inch hole with a beer in his hand and no telephone, television or radio to remind him what a mess the Packers had become.

It would also give him time to straighten out Doc Mueller. For some reason, Mueller seemed obsessed with exploring the possibility of selling the Packers to a private owner. The idea had been kicked around for decades, but no one on the Packers' executive committee had ever seriously considered it. The Packers had 112,000 owners—ordinary people in Green Bay and all over the world who had bought unredeemable shares of the team for $100 apiece just to show their support and commitment to the Green and Gold. Green Bay was the envy of every city in America that had ever been blackmailed by an owner who threatened to move a pro team unless the city built them a new stadium or arena.

And now, for some reason, Mueller thought the Packers should consider going private, just like every other major sports franchise. Larson didn't get it. Nor did he want to.

T HEY WERE JUST TWENTY MILES outside of Minocqua now. Larson had planned to wait until they got their hole augered and their portable fish house set up, but he couldn't hold back any longer. He turned down the music on the radio and looked over at Mueller.

"Doc, I hope you've given up your idea about the team going private."

"It's not my idea, Ed. I've heard the idea floating around since I joined the organization. It's just something I think the committee should look at. Run the numbers, feel out the commissioner's office. We could talk to the investment bankers in New York—see what kind of money and interest are out there. I've already got a nibble from a buyer."

"Who?"

"Well, keep this to yourself for now. Purdy McCutcheon. Former college player at Georgia."

"Georgia?" Larson exhaled in disgust.

"Last guy cut by the Falcons back in '91."

"All the wannabes say that."

"He loves the game. He'd be a respectful owner. And he's black—that would be good for the league, and for Green Bay's image."

"You're pretty excited about this guy."

"It wouldn't have to be his group. I just think, under the circumstances, we'd be crazy not to look at this."

"What about our history?" Larson said. "These are the Packers. The Green Bay Packers. You want to throw away eighty years of public ownership?"

"If it doesn't work anymore . . ."

"I don't know where you get that. Who says it doesn't work anymore?"

"The numbers don't lie."

"Yeah, we're down. We've been down before."

"But what if a private owner—McCutcheon, for instance—came up with a plan to make more money than this team has ever dreamed of?"

"Money's just that, Doc—money," Larson said. "We've got something money can't buy. We've got pride. The Packers are ours, and if I have anything to say about it, they'll always be ours—not some corporate egomaniac's."

Mueller turned and studied Larson's face. In a way, Larson was the quintessential Packer—more than Curly Lambeau, Vince Lombardi, or Brett Favre. He was, after all, one of the town's last real meatpackers. Ed's father helped get Lambeau Field built back in 1956. In Larson's firmly set jaw and icy gray eyes, Mueller saw the determination of an entire community that could have lost its team a half-dozen times in the last century, but always found a way to stay in the big leagues, doing things their own way.

"You wouldn't even consider it?"

Odd, Larson thought—he sounded genuinely sad.

"No," Larson said. "Never."

"I'm sorry, Ed."

"No need to be sorry. Nothing's changed. Let's catch some fish."

THE SNOW HAD STOPPED FALLING when Mueller parked the Land Rover in the driveway of his cabin on the south shore of Lake Minocqua. The cabin was really a well-kept three-bedroom house, heated year-round, with a dock seventy feet from the back door, where Mueller kept his thirty-foot fishing boat tied up during the summer. Mueller pushed the automatic opener and pulled the SUV into the garage, parking it next to a dented Ford F150 pickup with a topper on the back.

"We're taking the old truck," Mueller said. "I've got the auger, the portable fish house, and all the gear in the back."

"You got beer back there, too?" Larson asked.

"Nope. We'll stop at a store on the way to the landing."

They got into the truck, which started up immediately when Mueller turned the key in the ignition. They were at the liquor store in less than five minutes. It was a one-story place with unpainted vertical wooden siding, neon beer signs in the windows, an Old Milwaukee promotional banner tied above the door ("Welcome Snowmobilers") and a Yamaha Nytro and a pickup truck parked in the lot. Larson started to get out when they pulled into the parking lot, but Mueller said, "You don't have to get out, Ed. I got this."

"I gotta pee."

"I don't know if they've got a can in there . . ."

"Public place. Gotta have a can."

Larson zipped up his bulky down jacket, got out of the cab, and walked ahead of Mueller into the store. A guy in a lime green-and-black snowmobile suit was making small talk with the clerk behind the counter. Larson asked if he had a bathroom, and the clerk pointed to a door next to a Miller Lite floor display. Mueller followed Larson inside and went quickly to the refrigerator section, where he picked out a six-pack of Leinenkugel bottles and brought it to the counter.

"Hey, Doc," the clerk said.

Mueller nodded at the clerk and handed him his credit card.

"We're heading out, Jim," Mueller said to the guy in the snowmobile suit. The guy nodded back to him.

The clerk looked up from ringing up the beer, stared a moment at his Arctic Armor bib and jacket and said, "I heard about that stuff. If you fall in, you float, right?"

"Yeah." Mueller looked over his shoulder and saw that Larson was coming out of the john.

"Good thing. Ice is still pretty thin."

"We'll be okay," Mueller said quietly. "I know a spot."

"Okay, then. But I wouldn't do any jumpin' jacks."

As they were leaving, the clerk called after them, "It'll be cold out there. You got something heavier to wear on your feet?" Larson wore a pair of heavy snow boots—warm enough for hours in a fish house, but Mueller had on a pair of slip-on duck boots. Mueller ignored the man and walked out the door.

FOUR

It was snowing when Sam's plane landed in the Twin Cities, snowing on the slow drive to his house, and still snowing when he called the Packers' administrative offices and talked briefly with Frank Janaszak ("Please, come to my office. I don't want to talk about this over the phone.")

It was still snowing the next morning when he got into his Jeep Cherokee and took off for Wisconsin. He'd been having second thoughts about his purchase of the Cherokee. He had the money, thanks to his last job in Boston, and the Minnesota winters almost demanded something that would get him through deep snow. But if he did move to Arizona, how often would he need the four-wheel drive?

By the time he crossed the St. Croix River, he'd lost all his reservations about the Cherokee. Cars, SUVs, and semis were strewn in the ditches along I-94, and it looked like the slow-moving system was going to be with him all across the state of Wisconsin. The 280-mile drive from Minneapolis to Green Bay took six hours, but the Christmas oddities shuffling through his iPod made the time go by faster: "Santa Claus Wants Some Lovin'" by Mack Rice, "Thanks For Christmas" by XTC, and "Reindeer Boogie" by Trisha Yearwood, mixed with some perennials like Bobby Helms's "Jingle Bell Rock" and "Christmas (Baby Please Come Home)" by Darlene Love. With more than 2,000 Christmas songs on the playlist, he was in no danger of succumbing to "White Christmas" fatigue.

He stopped once, for a hamburger and a bathroom break in Wausau. While kicking the snow and ice chunks off his mudflaps—fenderbergs, some people called them—he realized how willing he'd be to live without winter in the upper Midwest. Road salt was already eating away at his Cherokee. Back in Minneapolis, the alley behind his house and garage was nearly impassable because of icy ruts. If this snow kept up while he was gone, there would be cars buried by the plow in front of his house, and long lines of pissed-off people at the impound lot trying to retrieve the cars that were hauled away by the city.

He looked to the south and saw skiers on the slopes of Rib Mountain—a bizarre landform that looked like a goiter in the middle of rolling farmland. He'd been a decent skier before the knee injury—not good enough to race, but capable of handling any slope in the Midwest. He'd always planned to try skiing out West someday. That was before a street punk named Dantre Pierce shot him. He sold his skis a couple of years later and bought a new driver.

He wondered if Gretchen had heard about his gunshot wound. They hadn't exchanged so much as a phone call or a Christmas card since she'd gone to med school. He'd heard she'd gotten married. No kids, as far as he knew, but that could have changed. He was about to reopen a door he'd meant to keep shut—and would have, if she hadn't asked him for help. Life was full of surprises.

It was a little after three in the afternoon when Sam drove into Green Bay on Shawano Avenue. It felt like dusk. The snow had tapered to light flurries, but the streetlights were on, the plows were out, and the Tuesday afternoon traffic was inching along in the familiar funeral procession of a snow emergency. Sam had called Gretchen after talking to Janaszak and told her he would be in Green Bay late Tuesday afternoon. He knew her house was on the other side of town, near the university. At this pace, it might take him at least another half-hour to get there, so he called her on his cell phone. No answer. Maybe she was at work. He left a message that he was on his way. A minute later, his phone rang.

"Sorry I didn't pick up, Sam," Gretchen said. "I screen my calls now."

"Why?"

"I'll explain when you get here."

Gretchen's house—a two-story with a covered front porch and an attached garage—faced the street. There was a basketball hoop over the garage door—kids?—a large elm tree in the front yard that would shade most of the house in the summer, and two roof-sized pines sheltering the front steps. The driveway had been shoveled within the hour. Sam backed the Cherokee into the right side of the driveway, so he could blast out if the plow went by while he was inside. He had a one-night reservation at the Country Inn on Kepler Drive, a couple of miles away. The desk clerk had told him over the phone that the reservation could be extended until Thursday, but the room had been reserved months ago for the weekend. The Packers had a home game with Minnesota.

The front door opened before Sam reached the steps. Gretchen stepped outside, wearing a gray ribbed sweater over a white turtleneck. She took a look up and down the street, and then held the door for Sam to come in. She closed it behind him, locked it, and turned the deadbolt. They exchanged an awkward hug and then stood in her foyer, looking at each other for the first time in ten years.

"I hadn't realized how long it's been," she said.

"You mean, you didn't realize how much I've aged?" Sam asked, smiling.

Gretchen laughed. Her smile was apologetic. Her eyebrows arched and her forehead wrinkled—a dead giveaway that he'd understood what she was really thinking.

"No, no, you look great," she said. "You're obviously keeping yourself in good shape. Looks like you've been in the sun."

"I was in Arizona when you called."

"I just meant . . . I can see that your work isn't easy."

"Nice way of putting it. You really haven't aged at all."

Sam was telling the truth, and Gretchen knew it. Her hair was a little shorter than the last time he'd seen her, but there was no gray in the strawberry blond locks that she still wore in braids. If anything, she might have lost a little weight, but she looked as fit and energetic as ever. The only sign that time had passed was the beginnings of some lines at the corners of her eyes.

"I still work out a lot," she said. "Today was a great day for cross-country skiing. I try to get in ten miles on my days off. Hey, let me take your coat. Come in and sit down."

Sam noticed that Gretchen glanced out the window on her way to the closet. He followed her into the kitchen, where she poured Sam a cup of coffee.

"Still take it black?"

"Yeah."

Gretchen filled the teapot with water from the tap, put it on the stove, and turned on the burner. "I know you're still playing golf," she said. "How about the band—still together?"

"Mostly," Sam said. "Guys come and go, but we play once or twice a month."

"Good. I know how much that meant to you."

"You've got a nice place," Sam said, not knowing what else to say. It was a nice place. Gretchen had decorated it with a lot of homemade touches—pottery, tapestries, glassware, paintings—that she'd probably done herself. She'd always been artistic. After they'd broken up, Sam had mentally changed that to "arty."

"Is your husband home?"

Gretchen's expression turned serious. She pulled up a chair across from Sam's at the kitchen table and sat, running her hand down one braid and then flipping it behind her shoulder.

"He doesn't live here anymore. We're divorced."

Sam was surprised, and then wondered if he should feel that some form of payback had taken place. She'd walked out, assuming she'd find something as good or better than what they had, and it appeared she'd been wrong. It was amazing to him how quickly he could be drawn right back to the past, indulging old grievances he thought he'd put behind him. But ten years really was a long time, and his spiteful thoughts left almost as quickly as they had come. Sitting before him was a person he'd once loved, a person now in pain. Concern took over.

"I'm sorry, Gretchen. What happened?"

"He stopped growing. I stopped loving him. Then he threatened to kill me."

"Do you have a restraining order?"

"Yes, but you know how much good those things do."

Sam did know. For every abusive husband or boyfriend who obeyed a restraining order, there was another who ignored it. The cops would respond when called, but they couldn't stand guard. An abuser determined to get back at his wife or girlfriend couldn't be stopped.

"Do you have a gun?"

"No. I hate guns."

"When's the last time you had contact with him?"

"Talking to him? Probably a month ago. But I see him. He watches me. He drives by the house, walks around the atrium at Lambeau Field when I'm at work..."

"He's supposed to stay 500 feet from you, right?"

"Right. But he doesn't. I've called the cops, but he seems to know when to leave. I'm just afraid some night he's going to break in here. I haven't had any company since I got the restraining order, but if he sees your car in the driveway... but, look, that isn't why I asked you to come. Believe me, I can handle this."

"I've heard that a hundred times from women in your situation. Sometimes, they're wrong."

Sam almost added, "dead wrong," but checked himself. He didn't want to upset Gretchen any more than she already was. She knew she was in a bad spot—he could see it on her face. Maybe he could help her—if she'd let him.

"Let me tell you what's been going on with the Packers," Gretchen said. The tea kettle began to whistle, and she got up to pour the water into a cup with an herbal teabag.

"First, tell me if anybody in the organization besides Frank Janaszak knows you're talking to me."

"Just Frank."

"He's—what, the team president? Board chairman? I'm not quite sure how it works here."

"Yes, he's the president. He runs the team. He'd be like the owner on any other NFL team. He's also head of the executive committee. There are seven of them, and they vote on the big decisions. But when it comes to hiring a coach or a general manager, Frank is the final word."

"And he wants to see me because..."

"I told him I thought you could help us."

"What made you decide to call me?"

"We get the news in Green Bay, Sam. We heard about the Masters . . . about you handling that extortion case for the Red Sox. Frank was impressed."

"Are you two close?"

Gretchen colored a bit at the question, which surprised Sam. He hadn't meant it that way.

"I just really respect him, Sam. He's kind of a father figure for me. He's in his mid-seventies now, and he's had heart trouble for a few years. He's going to have to retire soon, and I'm dreading that day. He's been the best thing that's happened to this franchise since Vince Lombardi—or Brett Favre. To some people here, I'm the lady doctor. Not to Frank. He's always treated me like a professional, and like a friend."

"Why did you blush when I asked you about him?"

"Did I? Probably because of Scott. My husband. He thinks I've got a thing for Frank. He's accused us of having an affair."

"It's none of my business, but . . ."

"The answer is no. Frank's happily married to a wonderful woman. He has a great family. It's not like that at all. But Scott . . . well, he's not exactly rational when it comes to me. And Frank isn't the only one he's accused."

"We'll get back to Scott. What do you think is going on here?"

"I think Doc Mueller is plotting to sell the team."

"And who's he, exactly?"

"Dr. Karl Mueller. He used to have my job. Then they created a fancy title for him, and then elected him to the executive committee. He's got this superman image in the organization. He was a high school football and basketball star in Madison, played a couple of years as a wide receiver for the Badgers, and then went to med school. He hired me, but I think it was an affirmative action directive from the executive committee, or maybe just from Frank. We've never exactly hit it off, but that's not what this is about. He was the guy who survived the truck going through the ice on Lake Minocqua yesterday."

"Wait—what?"

"You didn't hear about it? It's been on the news all day."

"I was listening to music on the drive over."

"Figures."

"Who didn't survive?"

"Ed Larson."

Gretchen explained to Sam that Mueller had been raising the issue of private ownership for months, and the committee kept refusing to discuss it. Two of the committee members appeared to support him: Sherwood Talley, the committee treasurer and an executive with a Wisconsin bank chain; and Jerry Pritchard, owner of Green Bay's largest construction company. Frank's allies against a sale included Larson; Mike Henderson, who owned a cluster of GM dealerships in eastern Wisconsin; and Stephen Kleinschmidt, chairman and CEO of Green Bay Memorial hospital. Now Larson was dead, and his likely replacement—Convention and Visitors Bureau president Tom Boulanger—was thought to be sympathetic to Mueller's arguments.

"And what exactly are Mueller's arguments?" Sam asked.

"That the team is losing, the roster is full of bad apples, and good players don't want to come here because of the weather, our record, and our lowball offers. He says the only way to solve these problems is more cash. But we're the smallest media market in the league, and we can't go back to the city or the county and try to get more from the taxpayers. We already did that when we raised $250,000,000 to renovate Lambeau."

"So what's Mueller's plan?"

"Sell the team to somebody who'll pump money into it. Frank assumes Mueller would stay with the team in some executive position."

"But the fans don't want the team to be sold."

"If it helped us get better players, and get back to the playoffs, they might change their mind."

"What does Frank think?"

"Over his dead body."

"So, what's his plan to dig out of this mess?"

"He doesn't really have one. At this point, that's going to be up to the next president."

"And who will that be?"

"Mueller, probably. With Boulanger on board, Mueller will have a four to three majority, but he knows a narrow vote on something like selling the team would never fly with the community."

"Does the committee announce its vote totals?"

"No, but it would get out somehow. Nothing about the Packers can stay secret around here. When Frank steps down, if the next new committee member sides with Mueller, five to two would do it."

It still sounded iffy to Sam—but not iffy enough to dismiss out of hand. Public ownership of a major league sports franchise seemed like a quaint, twentieth-century notion when compared with the corporate culture surrounding the modern pro team. But could one guy—Mueller—grease enough palms, or eliminate enough human obstacles, to turn the Green Bay Packers into another private plaything? And even if he could do it, would Mueller be willing to kill somebody to make it happen?

"You think Mueller killed Larson?"

Gretchen sighed. "I wouldn't be surprised."

"Does Frank?"

"He's suspicious."

"How about the rest of the committee? The rest of the organization? The town?"

"Tragic accident," Gretchen said. She bounced the teabag in her cup a few times and took another sip. Sam sipped his coffee from a mug that looked like it had been hand-crafted in a pottery or ceramics class.

"What do the cops say up at Minocqua?"

"Same thing. The truck went into fifteen feet of water. Mueller said he tried to help Ed get out, but the cab filled up with water so fast, it was all he could do to get his own door open."

"Why didn't Mueller drown?"

"He was wearing one of those jacket-and-bib outfits that float. Besides, he's so athletic . . . he's the kind of guy who would make it."

"And Larson?"

"He was old and overweight. He was wearing a down jacket and heavy boots. He sank like a rock."

"Who pulled Mueller out?"

"Police rescue team. Some local on a snowmobile saw them go in."

It did sound suspicious to Sam, but only because he knew the background. If he'd been one of the cops on the scene, it never would have occurred to him that a guy would try to kill his fishing buddy by going through the ice with him in a truck. Even an ice fisherman couldn't be that nuts.

"And what about D'Metrius Truman? How does he fit into all this?"

"I don't know," Gretchen said. "But it helps prove Mueller's point that we have to take the dregs of the football world to try to compete with other teams. We're one and twelve. We haven't signed our first-round pick for the last two years. We're probably not going to be able to draft that Heisman Trophy winner from Southern Cal. He's already saying he won't come here. So we end up with guys who either can't play, can't stay healthy, or can't stay out of trouble."

"Do you get any say when they bring in a guy with injury problems?"

"We give them all physicals. I've advised against signing a half-dozen players that Dick Jordan ended up signing anyway. Then they break down, and there's not much I can do for them. They go on injured reserve, or we release them, and we bring in another one."

"Why does Jordan sign them?"

"Because he doesn't have anybody else to choose from. I don't blame him. There are millions of guys who can't play NFL football. He gambles on guys who can."

It was a mess. It was also apparent that Gretchen was taking it all very personally. Her chin rested on her palm, with her elbow on the kitchen table. There were frown lines arching across her forehead. She was as pretty as Sam remembered her, maybe even prettier. When they'd been together, Gretchen had always jumped from one goal to the next: hours in the gym, days reading new EMT training manuals, months taking craft classes, all those spontaneous outings on her bike or her skis. She hated weakness; she hated to ask for help. Now her workplace was in chaos and her home life had become dangerous and unpredictable. For the first time, Sam felt protective toward her.

A loud pounding that sounded like it was coming from the front door startled both of them.

"Gretchen! Open up!"

"Is that Scott?"

Gretchen nodded. She pushed her chair back from the table, glanced quickly at Sam, and opened up a kitchen drawer behind her.

"Don't," Sam said. He could see her hand closing around the handle of a knife. "I've got this."

Sam's Glock 23 was in the car, out in the driveway. Had he known about Krebbs before arriving, that wouldn't have happened.

"Would he bring a gun here?"

"I don't think so," Gretchen said. "Maybe. I don't know."

Not good enough.

"Who the fuck is in there with you?" Krebbs yelled. He banged the door again.

Sam glanced around and noticed the sliding door that led to the back deck. He put his jacket on and got up from the table.

"Don't let him in. Is there another door into the main level?"

"Just the garage service door. That's locked."

"Call 9-1-1, then go to the living room and tell him to go away. I'll go around the side. If we can hold him until the police get here, we can put him away for a while."

Gretchen nodded. She closed the kitchen drawer and dialed 9-1-1. Sam slipped out the sliding door, shut it behind him and took long strides through the knee-deep snow to the edge of the back deck. It would be quicker to reach the front door if he went around the house to the right, on the opposite side of the house from the garage.

"Get out of here, Scott!" Sam heard Gretchen yell from inside the house. "Leave me alone!"

"Who's in there?"

"None of your damn business!"

The snow was too deep to run through, and Sam's ankle-high shoes were filling with snow. He struggled through the drifts to reach the front of the house, and peered around the corner. The banging had stopped. Sam walked farther out into the front yard until he could see the front porch; there was no one there. He saw footprints in the snow leading around the garage, and Sam turned to retrace his own footsteps to the deck. Before he could round the back of the house, he heard the glass door to the deck slam open, and then heard Gretchen scream.

FIVE

Sam scrambled through the snow, up the steps to the deck, and ran through the open door to the kitchen. There was no one there, but he heard sounds coming from the living room. When Sam entered the room, a tall man wearing a leather-sleeved jacket and blue jeans was facing Gretchen, an arm chair between them. Krebbs was in an athlete's stance, feinting from one side of the chair to the other, trying to make a grab for her. He must have noticed Gretchen turn her head to look at Sam, because he was ready for Sam's charge. Sam got a hand on Krebbs's jacket, but Krebbs twisted away at the last second and put a couch between himself and Sam.

"This is the guy, huh?" Krebbs said to Gretchen. His lank blond hair hung in sweaty strands on either side of his face, and he had an untrimmed cop-killer goatee. His eyes were wild, the whites visible all around the dark-blue pupils. "Are you fucking my wife, pal?"

"Take it easy," Sam said. "You don't want this kind of trouble."

"No, *you* don't want this kind of trouble," Krebbs said. "Keep your filthy hands off my wife."

Sam made another run at Krebbs, but his knee had stiffened up from the awkward, lunging strides he'd taken through the snow. Krebbs dodged him and gave him a shove onto the stairs that led to the second floor. Sam landed clumsily, hitting his shoulder on one of the steps. The pain shot through him, and he was barely able to avoid a square hit to the side of his head when Krebbs kicked at him with his long left leg. The sole of his boot grazed Sam's temple, but he managed to roll down to the floor, grabbing Krebbs's planted leg and pulling him down with him. He landed two inconsequential punches to Krebbs's midsection, then they both got to their feet, holding each other by the shoulders and trying to free their hands to hit each other. Sam could smell the alcohol. Nothing worse than trying to subdue a jealous drunk—especially one who had a longer wingspan.

As Sam was trying to deal with the leverage problem, Gretchen rushed to them and shoved Krebbs as hard as she could toward the front door. He lost his footing and went down, slamming the back of his head against the door. Sam was about to pick him up and slug him, but Gretchen pushed him away.

"Get out of my house, Scott. The cops are coming."

"Your house? It's *our* house!"

"Not anymore. It's over. How can I get through to you? We're finished."

"Because of this asshole?" Krebbs got to his feet, his fists ready to have another go at Sam.

"I haven't seen Sam in ten years—until today. Go get some help, Scott. You're sick."

"Sick of *you*!" he shouted. Tears started streaming down his cheeks. Then he abruptly turned to the door, undid the deadbolt, and ran outside. Sam began to go after him, but Gretchen grabbed his sleeve.

"I don't want you involved in this, Sam. He's dangerous. He'd kill you."

Sam suddenly felt small, and he remembered that Gretchen had a way of doing that. He'd tried to protect her, and now she was protecting him.

"If we could have kept him here, the cops would have had him."

"For how long? And then he'd be out and looking for you."

Sam watched Krebbs's silver Chevy Trailblazer pull away, fishtailing up the snowy street. Still no cops. They'd arrive eventually.

He and Gretchen returned to the kitchen to wait. She closed the door to the deck, got out a mop, and cleaned the wet tracks Sam and Krebbs had left on the floor. Sam noticed her breathing was remarkably controlled, while he was still panting from the fight. Yet Gretchen's downcast, unfocused eyes gave her away. She was aerobically fit and emotionally undone.

They sat at the table over more tea and coffee, and Gretchen told Sam how she'd come to marry Scott Krebbs. They'd met at Madison while she was going to med school. He was part of a group Gretchen played soccer with on Saturday and Sunday mornings on one of the intramural fields. He was a physical education grad who'd come to Madison from Kenosha on a basketball scholarship, realized he wasn't good enough to be a starter, and transferred to U.W. Green Bay before his junior year. He was back in Madison taking graduate classes in phys ed when he met her.

"I was almost through with my studies, and ready for a relationship. He was a handsome, charming, athletic guy who seemed to have the kind of high energy level I was looking for. He was always up for a run, or a bike ride, or cross-country skiing. He was into all the action sports—soccer, basketball, touch football, softball, tennis . . ."

"But not golf."

"No," Gretchen said. She shook her head and smiled at Sam. "Definitely not golf."

"Did he drink then?"

"He liked a beer or two after a workout. But he kept his drinking to a minimum the first few years we were together."

Gretchen's residency was at Green Bay Memorial, and Krebbs got a job as an assistant basketball coach at one of the high schools. They reached a point similar to the place Sam and Gretchen had been: It was either time to get married or move on. They got married and bought the house. Gretchen kept her last name.

"The first year or two was happy enough, but when I got hired by the Packers, Scott began showing a side of his personality I really hadn't noticed before. He didn't like the idea of my being so immersed in a mostly male environment. He didn't like the idea that I was in the Packers locker room. He didn't like the idea that elite athletes were walking around naked and looking at his wife."

At first Gretchen laughed off his concerns, but eventually she came to realize how jealous he really was. There was a rookie cornerback from Montana State who needed an intense regimen of massage, whirlpool, and injections for a torn hamstring, and Gretchen found herself spending a lot of time helping the kid. He was a long shot to make the team in the first place, a free agent from a small conference who had nothing to fall back on if he got cut. Gretchen felt sorry for him, and talked about him a few times with Krebbs when she came home from work.

"One morning I came to practice, and the kid didn't show up for his therapy. Later that day I found out he'd been assaulted and badly beaten outside a bar the night before. He was hospitalized with a punctured lung from a kick to the ribs. The description of the guy who beat him was pretty basic: tall and white."

"You thought it was Scott?"

"He'd been out drinking that night with his friends. When he came home, I remembered seeing this funny, smug look on his face, as though he'd won some money or something.

"It terrified me that he might have been responsible for beating that rookie. I never asked him about it. That's when it started."

She'd somehow managed to convince Krebbs that it would be career suicide for her to get mixed up with a player. Then his suspicions turned to the coaching staff and the administration.

"Anytime I was more than a few minutes late coming home from a practice, he accused me of trying to hide an affair from him. It was worse when the team went on the road. He couldn't stand the thought of my being in the team hotel, just a door away from some horny coach or team executive. After the first season, he began booking his own flights to the cities where the Packers played, and stayed with me in my hotel room.

"I wouldn't have minded having him with me during the down time before and after the game, but we never did any sightseeing or went out to eat. He just kept me in the room, ordered room service and watched television.

"I couldn't live that way anymore. I asked him to go to counseling. He said I was the one who needed counseling and refused to go. I actually did visit a marriage counselor. He accused me of having an affair with him."

She uttered a short, mirthless laugh. "I mean, it would have been funny, if it weren't so awful."

"When did you decide on divorce?"

"A few months ago. He begged me to forgive him. He swore he'd change. And I gave him his chances. I didn't want to fail at this."

She stared into her teacup, unable or unwilling to meet Sam's eyes. He knew she was reading his mind: Why didn't you stay with me? This never would have happened to you. But he also knew Gretchen was too proud and too independent to ever look back at a decision and question herself. She'd done what was best for her at the time; marrying Krebbs had turned out to be a mistake, but not something she could have anticipated, and not something she was going waste any regrets over.

"Did he ever hit you?"

She shook her head quickly, looking down. A long moment later, she said, "No. He'd threaten to—you know, he'd pull his fist back, or he'd pick something up, like he was going to hit me with it, but he never did. I think he knew I'd hit back."

"That doesn't mean he won't. He's a big guy, stronger than you are."

"I know. Today was as bad as I've ever seen him. If you hadn't been here . . ." She caught herself, about to admit the situation was more than she could handle. "We would have had a brawl."

A brawl that Krebbs would have won. Sam was glad she was standing up for herself—proud of her, really. But it would be a deadly mistake if she thought her strength was an even match for Krebbs's jealous fury.

They heard the squad car pull into the driveway and two car doors slam. Rather than looking relieved that the cops had arrived, Gretchen sighed and got to her feet as though going to greet a vacuum cleaner salesman or a Jehovah's Witness.

Two uniformed Green Bay police officers introduced themselves at the door, and Gretchen invited them inside. Sam remained seated in the kitchen, knowing what to expect. He could hear one of them asking Gretchen questions, which she patiently answered. The other was probably looking around the living room for evidence of a violent struggle. Eventually, the cops walked into the kitchen. The male cop was round and double-chinned; the woman cop was tall with curly dark hair protruding from under her billed cap.

"I'm officer Jansen," the woman cop said. "This is my partner, officer Downs. Who are you?"

"Sam Skarda. A friend of Gretchen's."

"Boyfriend?"

"No."

"Then what are you doing here?"

"I just dropped in for a visit. I haven't seen Gretchen in ten years."

"Did that set off the hubby?" Downs asked Gretchen.

"I guess. He moved out a couple of weeks ago, but I know he drives by a lot. He saw Sam's car in the driveway . . . then he started banging on the door."

"Did you let him in?"

"No. I keep the doors locked."

"How'd he get in?" Jansen asked. "I don't see signs of forced entry."

"He came in the door to the deck."

"Thought you said you kept the doors locked."

"That was my fault," Sam said. "I went out the back way. I was going to go around to the front of the house and stop him from trying to get in, while Gretchen called the police. But he came around the other way."

"You shouldn't have gotten involved," Downs said.

"I used to be a cop. I've been at dozens of domestics."

"Used to be?"

"I'm a private investigator now."

Downs rolled his eyes and looked at Jansen.

"Just what we need, eh, Bev?"

Jansen ignored her partner's remark and said, "Where'd you work the job?"

"Minneapolis."

"What are you doing here?"

"Like I said, visiting Gretchen. She's an old friend."

This wasn't getting them anywhere. Krebbs was long gone, there were no overt signs of a break-in or a struggle, he hadn't actually laid a hand on Gretchen, and now the cops were hung up on Sam and what his role was in all this. Now he understood Gretchen's reaction when she heard the cops arrive. They were too late. Nothing they could do, except drag it out.

Eventually Sam and Gretchen convinced them that Krebbs had violated his restraining order and had left when he realized the police were on their way. The cops said they could pick him up—if they could find him—but Krebbs had lost his job at the high school, and Gretchen didn't know where he was living now. An apartment somewhere, but she didn't have the address or a phone number. The cops said they'd drive by Gretchen's house from time to time, and keep an eye out for Krebbs.

"It would be best for everybody if you stayed out of this," Officer Jansen said to Sam as they walked to the front door.

"I understand," Sam said. All too well.

Gretchen watched through the living room window as the officers got back into their squad car, backed out of the driveway and headed up the street. Then she walked over to Sam, put her arms around his waist and rested the side of her face against his chest. She wasn't crying, but she clung to him with the weariness of a boxer in the late rounds of a fight.

"I don't know how much longer I can take this, Sam."

She looked up at him. Her lips were parted, her eyes were moist, and Sam was sure she had never looked that beautiful in the two years they'd been together. He put his hand on her head and pressed it into his chest, with the other arm around her shoulders.

"I know you didn't ask me to," he said. "But I'm going to help you."

If I can.

Six

I t was a typical Tuesday night at the White House—blaring eighties' heavy metal on the sound system, thick cigarette smoke mixing with the clouds created by the fog machine, and a stripper named Barb Starr swinging around the pole with one hand while removing her top with the other.

The walls, what could be seen of them, were covered with plaques, posters, pennants, and autographed photos of Packers greats from the past. It wasn't the best collection of bar memorabilia to be found in Green Bay, not by the length of a Paul Hornung field goal, but it served the purpose. The Packers kitsch placed the White House squarely in the mainstream of right-thinking local establishments. There might be young women taking their clothes off here and displaying parts of their anatomy that only their husbands and gynecologists should see, but how about those Packers?

If you happened to be a Packers player, past or present, you drank for free at the White House. Everybody knew that. In return, the players tended to be generous with their tips. That way, owner Butch Grunwald didn't have to pay his dancers so much. Feature acts like Barb Starr could generally count on a couple of hundred bucks for a one-song lap dance with a current player. The old-timers were a bit more frugal, but fifty to a hundred was typical. The regular schmoes paid a flat twenty, and maybe tipped another ten. Barb made it a personal rule never to work in a city that did not have at least one pro sports franchise. Green Bay qualified, barely.

Barb's head was dangling behind her, her streaked-blonde hair brushing the stage floor and her nipples pointed to the ceiling, when she saw her ship come in the door that night. She recognized them immediately: Former Pro-Bowl cornerback Cornell Johnson, linebacker Jason Drabek, nose guard LaBobby Suggs, and new—and infamous—quarterback D'Metrius Truman. The usual buzz went around the room, as it did whenever Packers entered the place. Butch Grunwald went over to greet them, ushered them to the foot of the stage, introduced them to the guys sitting at the best table, and then convinced those guys to give up their table.

From that point on, Barb's show was directed at one table only. The rest of the crowd understood. They'd seen it before, and they all enjoyed watching a talented entertainer like Barb Starr shake her ample tits in the faces of guys they'd be cheering for on TV that Sunday. Butch put on "Start Me Up" by the Stones, and Barb went to the props she kept on hand for just such an occasion. She put on a Packers helmet and ran a green-and-gold Packers jersey slowly back and forth between her legs, bouncing up and down as though she were riding a horse. The place began to shake as Johnson and Drabek stood up and clapped along to the rhythm and Barb's gyrations. Truman and Suggs remained seated. Suggs was out on bail from his recent arrest, and was trying to keep a lower profile. Truman didn't want to be jumped by some animal-rights nut.

The headlines had been predictable: "Pack signs dogfight con Truman," "Past could hound new Packers QB," and "Can Truman turn these mutts around?" The local TV stations all wanted interviews, but at general manager Dick Jordan's suggestion, Truman had held a brief press conference in the Packers' Lambeau headquarters, once again expressing his remorse for being involved in dog fighting, and vowing to keep his nose clean and help return the Packers to NFL prominence. He took no questions.

That was good enough for most fans, though a vocal minority had picketed the Packers offices for several days, holding signs saying "Packers—Tackle Cruelty" and carrying pictures of mauled pit bulls. The prevailing sentiment, however, was that Truman should be given a chance to start over. He had paid his debt to society—a stiffer one, some noted, than was often handed out to thugs who used fists and weapons on humans. It didn't seem to matter to anyone in Wisconsin that he'd once been the star quarterback for the hated next-door rivals, the Vikings. All the Cheeseheads cared about were wins. It appeared likely that, if Truman played well and the Packers managed to win a game or two before the season ended, he'd be brought back next year—with the blessing of most fans.

That didn't make Truman any more at ease. When he and his agent, Michael Banks, had first talked contract with Dick Jordan, the bullet-headed former Packers tight end who'd been brought in to try to straighten out his former team, Jordan had told him, "D'Metrius, you'll be on a short leash here—and I used that term intentionally. If I hear even the slightest hint that you're hanging out with your old dog-fighting friends, you're gone. If you get in trouble with the police here in Green Bay, or on the road, you're gone. Drugs, guns—you're out of here.

"I still think you can help us win games, or I wouldn't have picked up the phone when Michael called, and I wouldn't have asked the league to lift your suspension. But you have to understand that I'm sticking my neck way out here. Frankly, if I could find somebody with half your talent, but a clean background, you wouldn't be here. And you won't be here if you fuck up. I don't need the ASPCA and the animal-rights people on my ass, with all our other problems. Stay out of trouble, play hard, and we both win. Go back to your old ways, you lose—and I'll still be here.

"Hopefully."

Truman didn't give a shit whether Jordan was back next year or not. He just knew that if the Packers cut him, his NFL career was probably over. Michael Banks was more optimistic, assuring him that somebody else would take a chance on him if it didn't work out in Green Bay. But if he couldn't play for a 1 and 12 team, who could he play for? His legs felt heavy during his first couple of workouts, his arm didn't have the snap it used to have, and he definitely tired more quickly than he had before being locked up. A prison exercise yard was no place to stay in NFL shape. Yet he had no doubt whatsoever that he could still play. The Packers were a horseshit team, but put D'Metrius Truman in an open field, with the option to run or throw, and he could still make things happen. He'd show them that on Sunday, and the Sunday after that—as long as nothing happened off the field.

He probably should have turned down the invitation to hit a few clubs with some of his new teammates, but you don't become a team leader by sitting in your hotel room studying the playbook. Football was only part of it; the other part was getting to know the guys, and that meant off the field. When Drabek suggested they go out for some drinks and laughs, Truman almost felt obligated to say yes. Blowing off your new teammates like that was a good way for word to get around that you were too good for them. Next thing you knew, your receivers were running the wrong routes and dropping passes. Your left guard and tackle were letting their guys get past them, and you were getting creamed from your blind side. He had a lot to prove to these guys, and it had to start with being social.

Barb Starr was being extremely social. She'd taken off the helmet and stepped off the stage as AC/DC's "You Shook Me All Night Long" thundered from the wall speakers, straddling Cornell Johnson's legs and shimmying her rack in his face. He let her know she was welcome to sit, and she sat. She puckered her lips, grabbed his head in her hands and kissed him, then lowered his head until his face was planted between her breasts, where she had a small tattoo of a butterfly. Truman heard the crowd begin to yell even louder, and assumed they were cheering for Cornell's close-up examination of Barb's cleavage. But then he realized there was a hand on Cornell's shoulder, and a guy standing behind him demanding attention.

"I don't give a shit how many interceptions you have," said the guy standing behind Cornell Johnson. "You don't come in here and suck my girl's tits!"

"Your girl?" Barb said. She tilted her head up to look at the guy, a burly biker type with a red beard, wearing a down vest over long-sleeved thermal underwear. "I don't even know you."

Cornell looked the guy up and down, and gave him a condescending smile.

"Unless you're name's Butterfly, I don't see no proof that she's your girl."

The bearded guy spun Cornell Johnson around in his chair and landed a fist in the approximate spot where Barb's left breast had been a moment earlier. Then chairs started scraping, people start yelling, and fists started swinging.

Some of the customers jumped on the biker. Some ran in to help him. LaBobby Suggs got up from his chair and first looked at the door, but seeing there was no quick escape, he did what he could to try to pull the biker off Cornell. Drabek jumped to his feet and started throwing punches at anyone who got close to their table, without bothering to find out whose side they were on. Truman backed up against the stage and raised his fists, ready to defend himself, but no one seemed to want to get mixed up with the dog-killer. His instincts told him to wade into the pile and do whatever it took to get Cornell out of trouble, but his head told him he'd be on the next plane out of town if he laid a hand on anyone. But when somebody hit LaBobby Suggs over the head with a chair, sending the big tackle to the floor in a heap, Truman knew he couldn't stay out of it. He began grabbing anybody who wasn't a Packer and throwing him aside. Truman was about to slug a stocky older guy who had grabbed his shoulders when he recognized him: Joe Horvath.

"Cops are on their way." Horvath was yelling over Barb's screams and the shouts of the battling players and customers. "Get out of here. There's a back way."

"What about the guys?"

"Suggs is fucked. Nothing you can do for him. Johnson and Drabek will be okay. You won't. Move!"

Truman was rarely indecisive, but he froze for a moment. What kind of a man walks out when his teammates are getting an ass-kicking? Then again, they wouldn't be his teammates much longer if he was fighting when the cops showed up. He looked back once more as Drabek picked up a guy and gave him a forearm to the mouth. Then he followed Horvath out of the bar.

Horvath clicked a button on his keyless entry as they hurried through the back parking lot, and Truman heard the *fwit* and saw the taillights flash on the Tahoe he'd been in when Horvath had driven him to Green Bay a few days earlier. Why was this guy hovering around him all the time? Then he heard sirens, and saw a pair of Green Bay PD squad cars pulling up to the front of the club. Truman could ask questions later. Best thing to do now was to get as far away from the White House as possible.

Too bad. He'd liked the looks of that Barb Starr.

They were half a mile from the strip club when Truman said, "How'd you know I'd be there tonight?"

"I know everything I need to know."

Horvath didn't look at Truman. They were headed toward the hotel where Truman was staying. The vapor lights overhead illuminated white snowflakes tumbling against the blackness into the slush beneath the Tahoe's wheels, and piling on top of the three-foot snowbanks that lined the streets.

"Who was that guy who jumped us?" Truman asked.

"How should I know?"

Truman didn't know the answer to that question, but he had his suspicions. He'd been to more nightclubs in more NFL cities than he could remember, and he'd seen lots of stupid fights that could have been avoided, but this one seemed more stupid and random than most. It was almost like the guy was just waiting for one of them to touch the stripper. So what? That's what you did at strip clubs.

"And why were you there tonight?"

"Look, you ask too many questions. I saved your ass—again. That's all you need to know. You should be grateful."

"Yeah, I should be grateful. You did save my ass—but for what?"

"You'll find out soon enough."

SEVEN

The bedside clock radio in his motel room awakened Sam at 7:00 a.m. He swung his legs off the bed, rubbed his eyes, stood, stretched—and winced. His left knee was stiff, as usual, and his left side was bruised from Scott Krebbs pushing him into the stairs at Gretchen's house. He went to the window and drew the curtain—at last, sunshine in Green Bay. Several more inches of snow had fallen overnight, but the front had passed through—which always meant clear and cold weather behind it. Sam watched a guy fumbling with his keys in the parking lot, vapor escaping his mouth and enveloping his head, and guessed that the temperature was in single digits.

". . . newstime is seven oh four, and it's four above in Green Bay," the radio announcer said. "Our lead local story this morning: more troubles with the law for the Packers."

Sam hobbled across the room and turned up the radio.

". . . fight at the White House gentlemen's club last night. Green Bay police say it took five squads to subdue the combatants, three of whom are current members of the Packers: cornerback Cornell Johnson, linebacker Jason Drabek, and nose guard LaBobby Suggs. For Suggs, it was the second serious run-in with police in less than three weeks. He was released on bail in November after his arrest in an alleged home invasion and sexual assault in West de Pere. Packers media relations director secretary Liz Graczyk said neither Coach Marv Ackley nor General Manager Dick Jordan would comment on the incident until all the facts were known.

"In other news, traffic accidents claimed two lives and injured more than a dozen on northeastern Wisconsin highways as another foot of snow made driving treacherous . . ."

Sam got into the shower. There was no doubt that something had gone seriously wrong with the Packers. Gretchen trusted Frank Janaszak. He was the place to start to start finding out why. Maybe it was all a series of unfortunate coincidences. Athletes were unpredictable—if they weren't, nobody would bet on the games. So was the weather. So was the public's taste. The Packers fans might be the least fickle fans in pro sports, but everybody had his limits.

That became even more obvious after Sam dressed and walked down to the motel lobby for coffee and a roll. He picked up a copy of that morning's *Press-Gazette* and saw two Packers-related stories on the front page. The first said that the team was having trouble rounding up enough volunteers to help shovel out the seats at Lambeau Field for that Sunday's game with Minnesota. The second was a piece by local sports columnist Randy Joyce, under the headline "This isn't working":

I hate to be the one to say it out loud, but somewhere deep in your Green-and-Gold soul, in that place behind the Boyd Dowler game-worn jersey and the Don Majkowski autographed wristband, you know it's true.

The Packers have officially lost their way. Jumped the Dolphin. Gone to Detroit in a handbasket. Call it what you will, but this is now, officially, a broken franchise.

I don't blame anyone in particular. I blame everyone. That includes you—you loyal, lifelong Packer backers who somehow allowed things to slide so far that the Pack has fallen and can't get up. You kept filling the seats, buying the gear, watching the games, calling the talk shows, reading the blogs, filling up the chat rooms, and convincing each other that because things have turned around in the past, they would turn around again. Well, guess what? The only turn this franchise is taking is for the even worse—if that's possible.

Do you need a recap? Seven wins in the last three years, and just three since the beginning of last season. That's about one win for every three arrests. Nice statement, guys. Maybe today's Packers fan isn't old enough to remember the Mossy Cade days, when one of our more clear-eyed politicians said, "Let's build the new prison across the street from the Packers' practice facility, so the players can walk to work." I for one am feeling nostalgic for those days. Who'd want to meet this current collection of Packers in a dark alley? Or on a lighted football field, for that matter. The Packers current motto: If you can't beat 'em, hurt 'em. And if you don't hurt somebody on the field, well, there's plenty of opportunities off the field.

But if the fans have accepted this collection of low-lifes as the representatives of our once-glorious Packers tradition, what about the executive committee? Hey, I respect Frank Janaszak and all that—great guy, loves Green Bay, brought the team to a couple of Super Bowls back in the Pleistocene Era—but his hands-off approach to running the team has run the team into the ground. The rest of the committee has followed Janaszak's hear-no-evil-see-no-evil approach for too long. As for the board of directors—what board of directors? A forty-five-member rubber stamp is what they've become. If Frank says it, it must be so. Time for beer.

Thank God for revenue sharing. As the Pack slips further and further behind the rest of the league in wins, talent, and franchise value, it's becoming clear that the only thing keeping us in the league is NFL Socialism. It's obvious now that we're the team Pete Rozelle had in mind back in the early '60s when he told the haves that they had to start sharing with the have-nots. Even so, teams like the Cowboys, Giants, Patriots—even Indianapolis, for Lombardi's sake—are much better run, and better financed, than the current Packers. We can only hope that someday football socialism will have the same effect that it does in the rest of the world: Make everybody equally miserable.

In the meantime, rumor has it that Janaszak will be stepping down soon. For his health. I say, why not today? Or, at the very least, the minute the clock runs out on this putrid season. It's no secret that Doc Mueller would take the job, and that he'd be good at the job. He's our last link to the Lombardi years, and he wouldn't be afraid to make bold moves and take some risks. I just hope the recent tragic accident up at Lake Minocqua hasn't taken the stomach out of the guy. Thank God he came out of that hole in the ice. Maybe it's a sign that he was meant to run this team.

Somebody has to.

Sam folded the paper and took a sip of his coffee. That column had been written before the bar fight. If Joyce was an accurate reflection of the town's mood yesterday, Frank Janaszak's morning was not going to be pleasant—and talking to Sam wasn't going to cheer him up. He took out his phone and dialed Gretchen's number.

"Everything peaceful at your place last night?"

"No sign of Scott, if that's what you mean. He usually gives it a couple of days before trying again."

"Did you hear the news this morning?"

"About the fight at the White House? Yeah. I've already talked to Frank. We've got an appointment with him in his office this morning. I've got to go over to the practice facility in about ten minutes, but I'll meet you in the atrium lobby at eleven."

"Atrium?"

"Oh . . . you haven't been to Lambeau, have you?"

"No."

"There's a complex of shops and offices on the east side of the stadium, connected by a covered atrium. Frank's office is on the fourth floor. You could get a beer at Curly's Pub while you're waiting for me."

"I'd be a little lonely in the bar at that hour of the morning."

"No, you wouldn't. Trust me."

Sam finished reading the paper, and then left for Lambeau, maneuvering the Cherokee slowly through the streets while listening to Merle Haggard's "If We Make It Through December" until he hit freshly plowed Lombardi Avenue. He could see the stadium from half a mile away as he approached. When he pulled into the east parking lot, his eyes were riveted on the twin twenty-foot bronze statues that guarded the plaza in front of the main entrance: Curly Lambeau—bareheaded, wearing a sweatshirt and holding a football in his left hand while pointing off into the distance with his right—and Vince Lombardi—wearing a topcoat and fedora, hands clasped behind him, gazing sternly forward as though he were witnessing an unpardonable breach of blocking technique.

The Atrium was four stories high and a good 200 feet across, with yard-line markers on the floor corresponding to the yard lines on the outdoor field next door. A green staircase twined around the elevator shaft in the center of the atrium floor, and supported the green walkways that connected each floor of the shops and offices to the stadium. The décor was vintage brick, with murals, banners, and photos on the walls depicting great moments and players in Packers history. A stairway led downstairs to the Packers Hall of Fame, and another led upstairs to Curly's, the pub named after the Packers' founder and first coach. Sam went up.

He walked into a sprawling sports bar with pool tables, dartboards, video games, and interactive football skills games. There were TVs everywhere his glance happened to fall—seventy or more, at least. The entire complex seemed like a pro football Disneyland. He half expected to see Disney World-style likenesses of Jim Taylor or Ray Nitschke wandering around offering to shake hands and pose for photos.

Gretchen was right: The bar was already crowded with people in green-and-gold Packers regalia, shopping bags from the Packers pro shop on the floor next to them, talking about last week's loss, the upcoming game with the Vikings, and what it was going to take to make their team competitive again. There was a smell of stale beer in the air, like a fraternity basement—as though the pub went through so much beer that they didn't have time to clean the tap hoses.

Sam pulled up a seat at the bar on the window side, and looked out at the east parking lot below. Beyond the lot, across Oneida Street, was the Don Hutson practice facility, where the team worked out during the week. A stream of cars was pulling in, and most of the people who got out were wearing heavy outdoor clothing. The volunteer shovel corps. Their numbers might have been down from previous years, but it was still impressive to see that many people willing to help clear the aisles for a 1 and 12 football team.

The bartender stopped by to ask Sam what he'd have. He took a quick look at the menu, which promised large portions of the usual burgers, fries, and sandwiches, along with quaint local fare like booyah, fried cheese curds, and a Titletown banana crème pie. Sam asked for a pint of Leinenkugel. He hadn't been hired yet; his gun was still in the Cherokee. By the rules he followed, that meant it was all right to have a drink—even though it was early in the day by almost anyone's standards, except for the Packers loyalists around him. A digital scoreboard-type clock near the interactive games was counting down the hours, minutes, and seconds to Sunday's kick-off: 109 H, 47 M, 38 S. Close enough to game time that the fans at Curly's were already getting prepared.

The four fans at Sam's right were talking about the team's latest problems.

"I heard one cop got sent to the hospital," said an unshaven man wearing a gold knit sideline cap with a white strip down the middle and a "G" on the front. It was frayed and soiled, as though he hadn't taken it off since the day he bought it.

The woman next to him wore a pink Packers baseball cap. "After the trouble LaBobby Suggs has already got himself into, you'd think he'd know enough to stay out of a place like that."

The man on her left was bareheaded and wore a green jacket with black sleeves and the logos of each of the Packers' Super Bowl wins on the left arm. "The problem is, these guys can't hold their liquor. Not like the old Packers could. Max McGee could've drunk this bunch under the table and still caught two touchdown passes the next day."

"Hell, I been to the White House plenty of times. Nothin' wrong with it. You just gotta behave yourself."

The woman on his left, with a gold Packers helmet pendant hanging from a chain around her neck, glanced at him disapprovingly, but didn't say anything.

"These guys can't do nothin' like the old Packers," the first man said. "If this keeps up, I'll tell my cousin he can keep his tickets for next year's game with the Lions. Why should I freeze my butt to watch a bunch of thugs lose to the goddamn Lions?"

"I'm waitin' to see how Truman pans out," the guy in the green-and-black jacket said.

"I'll tell you right now how he's gonna pan out—lousy," said the man in the sideline cap. "He's been in prison for almost three years. He can't play. Hell, Hornung was never the same after he had to sit out that year for gambling."

"Truman's younger than Hornung was," said the woman in the pink cap. "He was a great athlete."

"So was Hornung. It don't make no difference. You sit out that long, you lose it. I don't know why Jordan keeps bringing in these guys."

"What's he supposed to do, if our draft picks won't sign?" said the man in the jacket.

"I don't know," the man in the cap muttered. He finished his beer with a big gulp and pushed it toward the bartender. "I don't know how we put up with it back in the '80s when the Packers sucked, but this is worse. We ain't gettin' any younger, either. Somethin's gotta be done."

"Let me ask you something," Sam said. He leaned toward the four, who turned their heads in his direction. "Do you think a private owner could turn the team around?"

The four Packers fans looked at each other as though Sam had stepped out of a space ship. They seemed to find his question too amusing to laugh at.

"Private owner?" the man in the sideline cap said. "The Packers are owned by the public."

"I know," Sam said. "But what if the franchise was sold to some billionaire who would pump a lot of money into the team?"

"That can't happen," said the woman with the pendant. "Can it?"

"It could, I guess," said the man next to her. "But it won't. I mean, I don't think that would ever happen."

"I'd like to see the team get better, but an owner could move the team," said the woman in the pink cap. "That's too much of a risk."

"Now, wait a minute," the guy in the sideline cap said. "Think about it. You tie an owner to a fifty-year lease at Lambeau, something like that. You put in some kind of clause that says if the place is sold out for so many games, the lease automatically renews. They could never leave. Then you get a football guy to come in here to run the team, a guy who knows what he's doing, not like these morons on the executive committee."

"Doc Mueller could do it, if they'd make him president," said the guy in the jacket.

"Yeah, he could. But whoever it is, he's gonna need a lot of money, and spend it the way it should be spent, on smart draft picks and the best free agents. I think that would turn the team around, fast. I'm not saying we should do it, but I could see it bein' better than the way things are now. Did you guys read Randy Joyce's column today?"

The others nodded.

"Hell if he isn't onto something. This team's broken."

"Do you own stock in the team?" Sam asked him.

"Yeah, I got a couple of certificates framed on the wall in my rec room."

"Would you sell them back if the team decided to go private?"

"Right now, no. But another year or two like this, and I'd have to think about it."

"Who are you, anyway?" the woman with the pendant asked. "Where are you coming up with this stuff?"

"I'm from out of town," Sam said.

"No shit," said the man in the green-and-black jacket. The others laughed.

Sam smiled, then took out his cell phone and glanced at the time: almost eleven. He took a final sip of his beer, left a tip on the bar, and headed for the exit.

EIGHT

G
retchen was standing at the elevator doors in the center of the atrium when Sam came down the stairs from Curly's. She wore a green Packers windbreaker that said "Medical Staff" in small letters on the left side. Her hair was pulled back in a ponytail under a green baseball cap with a white "G" in the center. She looked as though she hadn't slept much the previous night.

"You all right?" Sam asked.

"Fine. Frank is waiting for us."

She pushed the button for the fourth floor when the elevator arrived. Since it was obvious she didn't want to talk about what had happened with Krebbs, Sam asked her if the strip club fight had had an impact in the locker room that morning.

"Marv pretty much ignored it. There've been so many incidents this fall that he doesn't know what to say anymore. We had a short staff meeting before practice. He told us not to talk to reporters about internal club business, and then we talked about Minnesota."

"Did you get a look at the players who were in the fight?"

"LaBobby had a pretty deep cut on his head from somebody hitting him with a chair. Drabek has a black eye. Johnson's hands are bruised and swollen. They'll all play on Sunday, if the league doesn't suspend them."

"That's a possibility?"

"You never know. The commissioner isn't happy about what's been happening here. Oh, I heard one other thing."

"What's that?"

"D'Metrius Truman was there last night."

"That wasn't in the news this morning."

"He got out before the police showed up."

"Lucky for him."

"Yeah, wasn't it?"

The elevator doors opened to the Packers' fourth-floor executive offices. Gretchen led them down the hallway to the receptionist area outside Frank Janaszak's office. The woman at the desk, wearing a gold blouse with the Packers "G" over the left breast, looked up and smiled.

"Hi, Gretchen," she said. "Frank's waiting for you."

The woman's smile faded as she glanced at Sam. He could read her thoughts: Who's this guy? More trouble, no doubt.

Janaszak's office looked out over the east parking lot and the Hutson facility. There was an autographed Packers helmet on his desk and two framed photos on the wall: Bart Starr sneaking across the goal line in the '67 Ice Bowl, with a ref holding up his arms to signal the game-winning touchdown, and Brett Favre racing to the end zone, helmet held aloft in his right hand, to celebrate a touchdown pass against the Patriots in Super Bowl XXXI.

Gretchen introduced Sam to Janaszak, who was lumpy, graying, and had the look of a politician the morning after being voted out of office. Janaszak sat down behind his desk, and Sam and Gretchen took seats facing him.

"I suppose you heard the latest," Janaszak said.

"I did," Sam said. "I also heard that D'Metrius Truman was at the club but got out before the cops showed up."

Janaszak looked surprised.

"Where did you hear that?"

"It's all over the locker room, Frank," Gretchen said.

"Terrific," the club president said. He leaned his chin on his arm and shook his head. "It's just a matter of time before the media finds out."

"You've got bigger problems," Sam said. "But first, I want to know why you asked me here, and what you want me to do."

Janaszak picked up the Packers helmet on his desk and turned it sideways, reading the bold Sharpie signatures. "Reggie White . . . Ray Nitschke . . . Bart Starr . . . Brett Favre . . . you know what these signatures represent, Sam?"

"Hall of famers."

"More than that. Excellence. The best the NFL has to offer. The stuff this league is built on. Can you imagine the NFL without the Green Bay Packers?"

"No."

"Well, try. Because that's what we're facing. If Doc Mueller gets his way, the Packers as we know them will no longer exist."

"So Mueller is floating the idea of the team going private?"

"It's past the floating stage now. He's actively campaigning for it. He's got a couple of friends in the press, he's got some powerful local business people behind him, and he's got three votes on the executive committee. One more season like the one we're having now, and he'll have a majority of the fans, too. Then it's a done deal."

"I take it you're not one of the votes."

"Never. Neither was Ed Larson, but you know what happened to him."

"You think Mueller killed him."

"I do."

"Why not go to the cops?"

"No proof. Besides, I think Mueller has cop friends I don't have. Unless we get this bastard dead to rights, this will turn into another ugly public spectacle that this team definitely doesn't need."

"And you wanted me because . . ."

"Because Gretchen said she knew you. She thought you could help us. She trusts you, and I trust Gretchen."

He gave Gretchen a tired smile, which she returned.

"You could get a local guy."

"I know David Porter at Augusta National. I know Lou Kenwood in Boston. They both recommend you. A local guy . . . well, let me put it this way: There are no disinterested parties in Green Bay, not when it comes to the Packers. We could use some outside perspective."

"How much time do we have?"

"What do you mean?"

"Do you fear for your life?"

Sam expected Janaszak to be surprised by the question, but he didn't show it.

"Do I think Doc Mueller would try to get me out of the way? Yes, I do."

"They say you might retire."

"I might. I should. My cardiologist tells me I'm working too hard, worrying too much, heading for trouble."

"He's right," Gretchen said. "I've given Frank several stress tests, and he's not doing real well. I've got him on digitalis."

"Gretchen's my personal physician now," Janaszak said. "I keep telling her she ought to get out of this football racket and make some real money in private practice."

"I'm not going anywhere as long as you're here," Gretchen said. "After that . . ."

"But if I leave now, they'll name Mueller team president, and he'll bring in another vote on his side. I have to stay."

"Does Mueller have a buyer in mind?"

"I have no idea. We don't talk much these days. That's something I want you to find out."

"What else?"

"Investigate the guy, quietly. Find out who his associates are, who he hangs out with. I mean, he knows everybody in Green Bay, but he's got to have somebody helping him put this play together. Somebody, somewhere, must know what he's up to, what his game is."

"Did you ever think about tapping his phone?"

"Actually, I did. Without specifically mentioning Doc, I asked our head of security if we could do that. He advised against it, and I think he's right. Let's keep this legal. I feel bad enough about this already. Spying on one of our own committee members—hell, I feel like the KGB."

"Anything else you want me to do?"

"Yes. There's something that doesn't feel right about our personnel decisions. I always trusted Dick Jordan, but he's assembled a roster full of thugs. I've wanted to step in, but Mueller and some of the other committee members keep telling me I'm not an expert in player personnel. I just know that our drafts have been terrible, and our free agents have been tougher off the field than they have been on the field. I still don't know whose idea it was to bring Truman here. If you can find that out . . ."

"Lots of teams go through bad cycles. Detroit was winless a couple of years ago."

"I know. But this has lasted too long to be just bad luck. Everything we've touched in the last three years has turned to shit, and the bottom line is, this town is about ready to sell. That can't happen."

"With all due respect, Frank, would private ownership really be such a bad thing?"

Janaszak got up from his desk and walked around to where Sam and Gretchen were sitting.

"Come with me. I want to show you something."

They followed Janaszak out the door of his office to the row of luxury suites on the east side of the stadium. Entering one, Janaszak walked to the Plexiglas window that overlooked the snow-covered seats and field. Below them, hundreds of people walked along the rows with shovels in front of them, moving the snow toward the aisles, where those piles were shoveled onto slides, and the snow then cascaded down to the floor of the stadium, where it was shoveled into waiting dump trucks.

"We pay these people just over minimum wage, and provide the shovels," Janaszak said. "They take time off from their jobs and their families to come here and help us. One guy comes up from Florida whenever we put out the call. We've always had more help than we could use—but not this year. Our ticket waiting list is getting shorter, not longer. We'll be sold out for Minnesota, but if the weather's lousy, we'll have empty seats. We haven't had empty seats since the '70s."

He turned to look at Sam, despair etched on his face.

"Private ownership might look like the answer, but it isn't."

"How do you know?"

"If this team had been privately owned, it would have moved to a bigger city after going broke in 1923. But that didn't happen, because Curly Lambeau and some local businessmen turned it into a nonprofit corporation and sold five-dollar shares of stock to the public. Same thing happened when the Packers hit hard times during the Depression—another stock sale in 1935 raised fifteen thousand dollars to keep the team here in Green Bay. The fans saved the team again in 1950 when they bought over one hundred thousand dollars' worth of new stock.

"It's the history of this franchise—the inevitability, you could say—that we'll hit bottom now and then. We won just two games in 1949 and 1953. In '58, the year before Lombardi took over, we won once. We had three-year stretches in the '70s and '80s when we averaged four wins. At any one of those times, a private owner could have—would have—said, 'We can't win here. The town's too small. Not enough radio and TV money. We're moving to St. Louis, or New Orleans, or Nashville, or Las Vegas.' It happened to all the other small towns that had NFL franchises—Canton, Racine, Duluth, Evansville—but it never happened here. Not yet, anyway. And I'm not gonna let it happen. We're not going to be the Los Angeles Packers."

Sam watched the volunteers lifting one shovel load of snow after another onto the slide beneath their suite. No one was leaning on a shovel or looking at their watch. They were working as hard as they would have to clear their own driveways after a blizzard. Despite current events, these Packers fans still felt pride of ownership.

"Could the shareholders block a sale?" Sam asked.

"No. The club can buy back the stock at a fraction of its face value. Only the forty-five members of our board of directors can stop a sale, and they almost always do what the executive committee recommends."

"Why do you think Doc Mueller would be willing to kill to put this team in private hands?"

"Honestly, I have no idea," Janaszak said. He sat down on one of the plush armchairs in the suite and gazed off into the bright-blue sky above the scoreboard at the south end of the stadium. "He's a Wisconsin native. He's been with the team longer than anybody. I just don't understand it."

"Maybe you're wrong. Maybe what happened at Lake Minocqua was an accident."

"I hope so. Go on up there. Talk to the cops. See what they say. I'll pay your standard rate, whatever it is, for as long as it takes you to find out what's going on."

"Okay. But before I go, I need to talk to your head of security."

"Why?"

"We've got to coordinate. I'll need to talk to players, maybe some coaches. I'm going to keep this as discreet as I can, but your security guy needs to know what I'm doing, and why."

Janaszak didn't say anything. He looked at Gretchen, then scratched his forehead.

"I wanted to keep this totally quiet," Janaszak finally said.

"That's fine. But if your security chief is even slightly competent, he's going to find out about me. We've got to bring him in on this."

"All right. Let's go back to my office."

They walked back to the executive suites, and Sam and Gretchen took their chairs again in front of Janaszak's desk while he stopped at the secretary's desk outside. Janaszak then entered his office and said, "He'll be up in a minute."

While they waited, Janaszak gave Sam some background about the rest of the executive committee: Woody Talley, the banker; Steve Kleinschmidt, the hospital administrator; Mike Henderson, the car dealer; Jerry Pritchard, owner of a construction company; and nominee Tom Boulanger, head of the Green Bay Convention & Visitors Bureau.

"Talley, Pritchard, and Boulanger would all vote with Mueller to go private," Janaszak said. "But a four-to-three split isn't good enough, and Mueller knows it. He's got to get at least one more vote."

"Yours?"

"Or Kleinschmidt's, or Henderson's."

"That's another reason I want to talk to your security guy. If you've got this figured out right, all three of you could be in danger."

"Here he is now."

Sam turned around and looked at the man who stood in the doorway. He wore a gray suit that fit him well, despite his stocky, muscular build. He had a neatly trimmed moustache and short-cropped salt-and-pepper hair. He looked all cop — maybe former FBI.

Janaszak gave a two-finger salute to the man in the doorway.

"Sam Skarda, this is Joe Horvath."

NINE

Doc Mueller was in a private card room at the Oneida Casino when he received a call on his cell phone. His hole cards were the ten and jack of hearts, and the eight and nine of hearts came out on the flop, along with the eight of spades. Two more cards to come. He had a good feeling about the queen or the seven, good enough to stay in. He didn't want to answer his phone, but only a handful of people had his number, and he couldn't afford to ignore any of them.

He glanced at the number, opened the phone and said, "Call you back in five."

"Another thousand to you, Doc," the dealer said.

Mueller took another look at his hole cards, and stared across the table at Bobby Steen, who'd just raised. Steen always wore sunglasses and a Packers visor when he played. Mueller hated that. If it were up to him, nobody would be allowed to wear shades or hats when they played poker. But it wasn't up to him—not here, anyway. He played house rules here. He'd always been treated exceptionally well by the Indian-owned casino, across the road from Green Bay's airport. The casino was a major sponsor of the Packers. In return for a generous line of credit, Mueller curbed his impulse to throw his weight around with the Oneidas.

Besides, he didn't really worry about a player who wanted to conceal his eyes. If the guy didn't trust his eyes not to give him away, he'd find another way to do it. A twitch. A tendency. The way he breathed. The way he sipped his drink. When he spoke, or why. Sooner or later, Mueller would get a read on him. And he was convinced that he could read Bobby Steen. There were two eights showing. That's what he had.

Mueller stayed in. The turn was the ten of diamonds.

"Doc, I hope you don't mind me askin', but how long were you in the water up there at Minocqua?"

Mueller studied the ten, then turned to the questioner on his right, Darrell Bergstrom. Like Steen, Bergstrom was a regular at these games, and he'd played enough hands of Texas Hold 'Em with Doc Mueller to feel like they were friends.

"About fifteen minutes," Mueller said.

"That's long enough to get hypothermia. I know, 'cause my cousin Jeff went through the ice on Winnebago a couple winters ago. They got him out after about twenty minutes, but he was in the hospital for a couple days."

"I was lucky, Darrell. The guy on the snowmobile showed up just in time. He called the sheriff, and the rescue team got there before I got hypothermia."

"Jeff almost died . . ."

"Yeah, I know it can be rough."

"At first he thought he was okay. He started feeling warmer, but that's a bad sign. His heartbeat and breathing slowed down. He got arrhythmia, they said—"

"Glad he's okay."

"—and it's hard to get that stabilized when your core temperature gets that cold. They had to—"

"Your bet, Darrell."

"Oh, right. Check. How thick was the ice you went through?"

"I thought it was six inches. Turned out to be three. There was a current we couldn't see because of the snow."

Mueller raised two thousand. Steen studied his hole cards for a few seconds, looked up at Mueller's impassive face, and matched the raise. He was bluffing. Wendell Cross, the fourth player in the game, folded.

"And the river," the dealer said.

The last card was the king of diamonds. No straight, no flush. Just a pair of tens—and the pair of eights that everyone had. He could fold. Probably should. But he was convinced Steen had nothing, too. Steen raised two thousand. It was a lot to bet on nothing. But Mueller already had six thousand in. He wasn't going to let Steen take his money without showing his cards.

Mueller first started gambling in junior high school—penny-ante stuff, poker games in the caddy shack at Maple Bluff Country Club and a buck or two with his pals on the heavyweight championship fights. He played poker with his high-school teammates. In college he ran the dormitory and frat house football pools. After his junior year at Wisconsin, when he figured out that he wasn't going to get drafted by the NFL, he started looking around at med schools. He wanted a break from the Wisconsin winters, a place where he could have a little fun when he wasn't putting in long hours in the labs or on the books. He ended up at the University of Nevada School of Medicine in Las Vegas.

It was there that Mueller discovered the restorative powers of a few hours at a blackjack table. He was usually smart enough to know when it was time to quit, and lucky enough to walk out ahead more often than not. When course work became dreary, Mueller visited one of the casinos and recharged himself.

He moved back to Wisconsin for his residency and concentrated on poker, winning often and nicely supplementing his lifestyle. When the Packers hired him,

Mueller slipped easily into the casual card-playing and golf-betting lifestyle of the young athletes he was with. He never worried about NFL security nosing into his gambling habits. He wasn't Art Schlichter—or Paul Hornung—with the potential to do something on the field to change a game's outcome. Even in the trainer's room, the league had strict rules about reporting and treating injuries so professional gamblers couldn't gain an inside edge on a team's roster decisions. Mueller scrupulously followed those rules. He was also careful never to take one of the players for too much money. Instead, he confined his high-stakes poker partners to the businessmen and boosters who wanted to hang around the periphery of a pro team. Some of those guys would almost rather have lost to the Packers' team physician than win against somebody else.

Over the years, though, things had gradually changed. The guys he played cards with now didn't enjoy losing, and Mueller wasn't so lucky as he used to be.

"I'll call," Mueller said. He pushed another thousand to the middle of the table. Steen turned over his hole cards—the queen and king of hearts.

"Kings and eights," Steen said. He reached for the pot. "Damn, I'm glad that king showed up."

Mueller pushed his cards to the dealer. It would have pleased him to tell Steen that he was a lucky punk whose sunglasses made him look ridiculous. Instead, he stood up, smiled, and drained the remainder of his scotch and water.

"I'll be back, fellas. I gotta take this call."

Mueller left the table and walked over to the waitress standing by the door. He put his empty glass on the tray next to her.

"Another one of these, Suzy."

"Right away, Dr. Mueller."

She walked out of the room toward the service bar, and Doc followed her into the hall, admiring the backs of her thighs, sheathed in opaque black nylon and supporting a fine, wiggling young ass under a very short skirt. When she rounded the corner that led to the bar, he pushed a speed-dial button on his phone and put it to his ear. Then he heard Horvath's voice.

"You win the hand?"

"No. Asshole got lucky. What's up?"

"We got trouble."

"What kind?"

"Janaszak hired a private eye."

"Shit. Who?"

"Guy from Minneapolis. Skarda."

"You know him?"

"Heard of him. He could be a handful."

"How tough would it be to get rid of him?"

"It's more than just him."

"What do you mean?"

"He's friends with Gretchen Kahler. She brought him to Frank."

"God dammit. Who else has Frank been talking to?"

"Nobody, as far as I know. He brought me up to his office today to meet Skarda. Said he didn't want anybody else to know what they were doing."

"What are they doing?"

"Investigating you."

Mueller was silent. He'd been prepared for Frank to fight back, but he didn't think he'd go outside the organization. Best-case scenario: The stress of trying to block the privatization vote would put him in the hospital, or kill him, and that would be that. Worst-case scenario: Frank would put up an emotional argument before the executive committee, he'd be voted down, and he'd shut up and retire. That would be messier, but Mueller knew he could survive it. He had the facts. He had the figures. He had the votes, or would have when the time came. Why was Frank dragging a detective into this? And what were they going to do about it?

"Look, Skarda has no dog in this fight. There are only two things that would keep him around if things got nasty: Money . . ."

"I think he's got money. He's worked for some top-shelf clients."

". . . and personal reasons. What kind of friends is he with Gretchen? They sleeping together?"

"I don't know, but I'll find out."

"She still with that nut-job husband of hers?"

"No. He moved out a few weeks ago."

"And how do you know that?"

"I know what I need to know."

"You think Skarda's an old boyfriend?"

"Probably."

"Then we can make trouble for her. He might decide it's in Gretchen's best interests if he leaves town. What's he doing now?"

"Driving up to Lake Minocqua tonight."

"What does he think he's going to accomplish there?"

"You know."

"We're okay. Believe me."

"I hope so."

The door behind Mueller opened, and Bobby Steen stuck his head out of the card room.

"You in or out, Doc?"

Mueller knew he should walk away. There was business to attend to. But he saw the reflection of himself in Steen's sunglasses, and behind those shades he knew that Steen was hoping he would throw some good money after bad. He'd show the punk.

"One second, Bobby," he said. Steen nodded, smiled, and let the door close. Mueller waited until he was sure Steen had walked back to the table before resuming the conversation.

"Did they get the stadium shoveled?"

"Yeah. About 250 showed up."

"How's it look?"

"Okay. Why?"

"Any ice left in the rows?"

"Sure. There's always some."

"Here's what's going to happen. Find someone you trust who wants to make a quick ten grand. Make sure he gets to Lambeau on Sunday about an hour before the game. He's going to have an accident."

"What kind of accident?"

"Slip and fall. He's going to step on a patch of ice under his seat, go down on his ass, get carted out on a stretcher, and he's going to find a personal-injury attorney. Somebody who wouldn't object to suing the Packers."

"Who you gonna find like that around here?"

"Our friend has a guy. But we need a lawsuit for at least five million, filed first thing Monday morning. I've got a chiropractor who'll swear the guy's back is permanently out of alignment. When the committee meets on Monday, I want the lawsuit all over the papers and the local TV stations."

"That'll be easy enough."

"We'll tell the executive committee that under the current circumstances, this kind of thing is bound to keep happening."

"You've got everything covered, don't you?"

"I thought I did. I didn't need this guy Skarda coming in."

"We'll handle him."

Suzy came down the hall with Mueller's Scotch and several bottles of beer on a tray. She smiled and said softly, "I put it on your tab, Dr. Mueller."

He winked at her, took the Scotch off the tray and took a sip.

"Nice work with that White House fight, by the way," Mueller said into the phone after Suzy had gone into the card room.

"Thanks. It almost got fucked up, though. I told Drabek to bring Johnson and LaBobby Suggs. But Johnson invited Truman."

"Truman was there?"

"I got him out before the cops showed up."

"That's too close. We need Truman around until the end of the season. At least until the next committee meeting."

"I know. I'll keep a closer eye on things."

"Do that."

"Any word from your friend?"

"He's pleased, so far. But now it's critical. There can't be any fuck-ups. If Skarda puts a few things together, he could stop this deal in its tracks."

"I'll get rid of him."

"One way or another."

"One way or another."

"I have to get back to the game. Call me tonight."

"Sure."

Mueller snapped his phone shut, took another sip of Scotch, and went back into the card room. He was down eight thousand. He couldn't walk away now—there were going to be expenses on Sunday.

"Gentlemen," he said, "let's play cards."

TEN

Sam left Lambeau Field and went west on Highway 29 to Wausau, then north on U.S. 51 to Minocqua. He listened to his Christmas jazz playlist—Duke Ellington, Vince Guaraldi, Dexter Gordon, Chet Baker—on the three-hour drive. He'd hoped the drive to Northern Wisconsin would be pretty, in a Christmas-card way, but instead it was drab, under overcast skies. The hardwood forests were stark and colorless, with abandoned birds' nests and stubborn brown oak leaves the only cover for the bare limbs. The sky was gray, the snow was white, the pines looked almost black—like looking at nature on a black-and-white TV. He couldn't keep his mind from drifting to Arizona, to warmth and color, to Caroline.

The road into Minocqua crossed a short bridge to the center of town, built on a peninsula in the middle of the sprawling lake. Sam pulled into the parking lot at the Minocqua Police Department just after four o'clock. Half a dozen cars were parked outside the modern, one-story building with the A-frame front entrance. The days were getting short. Even with the clear sky to the west, it would be dark in about half an hour. Sam hoped the chief hadn't already gone home for the day.

He was in luck. His boots dripped puddles of slush on the tiled lobby while the dispatcher-receptionist called the chief's office and told him a detective from Green Bay wanted to see him. She smiled at Sam and buzzed him through the outer door.

Chief Gary Weston was a fit-looking younger man with a thick head of light brown hair and a bit of gray in his goatee. He wore a short-sleeved blue police department shirt, open at the neck over a white undershirt, with an embroidered gold Minocqua P.D. badge over the left breast pocket and an American flag stitched onto the right upper arm.

He stood when Sam walked in and reached over his desk to shake hands.

"Skarda, is it?" the chief asked.

"That's right."

"And you're doing some investigative work for the Packers."

He pronounced the word "inVEStigative," rather than "investiGAYtive." That pleased Sam. Education didn't mean everything, but it was often a tip-off that things had a fighting chance to be done right.

"Yeah—about the accident last week, with Dr. Mueller and Mr. Larson."

"Okay. You're welcome to read the report. We did what we could—two officers on snowmobiles from our department, and the Oneida County water rescue team from Rhinelander. We were just too late to get Ed Larson."

"Were you there?"

"I got there just as they were pulling Doc Mueller off the ice."

"Do you know him?"

"Sure. Everybody around here knows him. He's had that place over on the point for thirty years."

"Where's that, exactly—if I wanted to take a drive by?"

Weston told him to drive south out of town, cross the bridge and take a left on Country Club Road. Mueller's place was on a dirt road that looped north of the golf course. He gave him the address, ending with the standard small-town assurance, "You can't miss it."

"Is he a good guy?"

"Yeah, he's a good guy," Weston said. "You know, he could get overwhelmed by people always wanting to talk about the Packers, if he let it happen, so he keeps kind of a low profile. I don't blame him."

"How do you know him?"

"Played golf with him a few times over at the country club. I've been in his boat a couple times."

"Did you know Larson?"

"No. Just of him. We all knew Doc brought guys from the Packers' executive committee up here from time to time. We don't bother them. Try not to, anyway."

"Tell me about the accident."

"What's this for—insurance claim or something?"

"Not exactly. We just want to know what happened."

"Well, like I said, it's all in the report. We got a call from a local guy that a truck had gone through the ice near the public landing at about one that afternoon."

"Who called it in?"

"Jim Escher. He was snowmobiling out on the lake."

"Any other trucks on the lake that day?"

"No. Couple of portable fish houses around the point, but people figured the ice was a couple days away yet."

"Not Mueller."

"No. Doc tends to trust his own instincts. He's been the first truck out there several years. I guess he thought it was safe."

"Why'd Doc make it out, and Larson didn't?"

"Probably because of what they were wearing. Doc had one of those new bibs that traps the air and floats. Everybody who ice fishes ought to wear one. But they're kind of expensive, I guess."

"Larson?"

"Down jacket and jeans. Big boots. When down gets wet . . ." He pointed toward the floor and whistled a descending note.

"Dumb mistake."

"You see it all the time."

"But Doc knew better."

"Well, he lives here. He knows how to take care of himself."

Sam almost asked the next, obvious question: Shouldn't he have taken care of Ed Larson, too? From the look on Weston's face, the point had already been made.

"What was Mueller doing when your officers got there?"

Weston glanced up at the clock, then turned with a slight attitude of weariness and pulled a report out of a file on the counter behind him. He flipped the top page, read down to the middle of the next page, and told Sam that Mueller had a set of ice-rescue picks—"the kind with the wooden handles, attached to each other by a rope." Rescuers found Mueller hanging onto the edge of the ice with the picks, which he later said he always kept in the cab of his truck.

"He only had one set?"

"That's what the report says," Weston said. He held it up as though offering to toss it across the desk, but then went back to reading it to Sam. The officer who wrote the report said Mueller told the rescuers he tried to give them to Larson, but Larson panicked and wouldn't take them. The truck sank shortly thereafter, and Larson was unable to get out. Mueller was not able to haul himself out of the hole with the picks because the ice kept breaking around him, but the picks and the suit enabled him to stay above water until help arrived.

"How long could he have lasted?"

"Maybe forty minutes. Hypothermia would have got him after that. But Escher saw the truck go in, so we got there within ten minutes."

"How deep was the water?"

Approximately sixteen feet, according to the report. County divers pulled Larson out of the water about forty-five minutes after the truck went down. The truck was hauled out of the bay the following day.

Sam had to ask his next question delicately. The only ones who knew why he was investigating the accident were Gretchen, Janaszak, and Horvath. The Packers were family to everyone who followed the team, which meant everyone in Wisconsin—and gossip about family traveled fast. He had to be able to trust that Weston would keep this conversation between them.

"Chief, if the two guys in the truck hadn't been with the Packers, would this accident have raised any red flags with you?"

Weston stared back at Sam. Then he broke eye contact, put his hands behind his head and leaned back in his chair, looking up at the ceiling.

"That's kind of an insulting question, if you don't mind my saying so," Weston finally said. "If you're asking what I think you're asking, I'm giving you a flat 'no way.' No one's dumb enough to pull a stunt like that. You want to kill a guy, there's lots of safer ways to do it, without killing yourself, too.

"Not to mention—this is a professional operation we run here. I don't care who was in that lake. If something looked wrong, we'd investigate. End of story."

Weston was staring at Sam again, tapping the mouse pad on his desk with his right hand and waiting for him to explain why he thought Doc Mueller would have wanted to drown Ed Larson. Sam wasn't going to do that.

"What kind of truck was it?"

"1994 Ford F-150. With a topper."

"They drive up here in that?"

"No. They came up in a Land Rover. They left it at Doc's place."

They looked at each other for a while without saying anything. Then Weston said, "That's not unusual. Easier to fit all the gear in the back of the pickup. Besides, why risk a $80,000 vehicle?"

Sam said nothing. He looked up at the white face of the clock on the wall to his left—same industrial model they'd had in the Minneapolis Police Department, with the red second hand. It was almost 5:00 p.m.

"Know where I can find this Jim Escher?"

"He's in the book. I can look it up for you."

"Is he a friend of Mueller's?"

"Like I said, almost everybody here knows Doc, one way or another."

Weston found Jim Escher's number and wrote it on a piece of paper. Sam took the paper, folded it, and put it in his pocket. He stood and thanked Weston for his time.

"I don't know that I helped you any," Weston said. "I just told you what's in the report."

"No, you helped a lot. Thanks again."

Sam dialed Escher's number when he got to his car. When a man answered, Sam identified himself as an insurance adjuster doing some follow-up work on the ice fishing accident. Could he come over and talk?

"What's your name?"

"It's, uh, Skarda. Sam Skarda."

There was a pause, and then Escher said, "I'm kind of busy."

"It'll only take a couple of minutes."

"No, I really can't. Sorry."

"How about tomorrow morning?"

"Look, I gotta go."

J IM ESCHER HUNG UP. Then he called Doc Mueller.

"Hey, that guy you told me about—Skarda. He just called."

Escher was standing in the living room of his year-round place, overlooking a bay on the southeast shore of Clear Lake. The clouds had moved out, and the sky was a flaming crimson to the west. It would be way below zero tonight.

"What's he want?" Mueller asked.

"He wants to come over and talk about the accident."

"What did you tell him?"

"Said I can't. Too busy."

"That wasn't smart. Now he thinks you're ducking him. He'll come over anyway."

"What should I say?"

"Nothing. You were just passing by on your sled. You called the cops. That's it."

"Maybe somebody saw me stop at the hole. Before I called it in."

"So what? You went to get help."

"Look, I don't want to talk to this guy. Maybe I should just get out of here till he leaves."

"He knows you're home. He'll just be more suspicious if you take off."

"I don't want to deal with this."

"Why? Don't you want your money?"

"Sure, I do. You said there wouldn't be any questions. All I had to do was keep an eye on the truck, then make sure you were okay after it went in, and call the cops."

"Well, I didn't know Janaszak was going to hire this guy."

"Who is he?"

"Private eye from Minneapolis."

"Hey, I didn't agree to fuck with private eyes. It was a simple deal. This ain't simple anymore."

"I'm sorry about that. Unforeseen development."

"So what should I do?"

"You could take him out."

"What do you mean—*kill* him?"

"You told him you didn't want him to come to your house. If he does, he's trespassing. You've got a right to shoot strangers who show up at your place, uninvited."

"I don't know . . ."

"It's in the fucking Constitution, Jim. You were cleaning your shotgun, you heard a noise at the door, you asked who was there, nobody answered, you were afraid for your life, so you defended yourself. He's licensed to carry—they'll find a gun on him."

Escher didn't say anything.

"I could find you another fifty grand."

"For killing a guy? Make it a hundred."

Now it was Mueller's turn to stop and think. It all depended on how determined Skarda was, and how strongly he suspected that the accident was a set-up. There was no way to know that, no way to know for sure what he'd do if and when he got to Escher's place—and no way to know for sure how Escher would handle things. If Skarda turned out to be a bulldog, a hundred grand was not too much to pay to get him out of the picture. Assuming, of course, that he could count on Jim Escher one more time. He sure didn't trust him to talk to Skarda.

"Look, Jim, just get out your shotgun and wait for Skarda. We'll take care of you, I promise."

"What does that mean? A hundred grand?"

"Yes. That's what it means."

S AM GOT JIM ESCHER'S ADDRESS from the local phone book, but had no idea how to find the house. The post office was closed, and he didn't think it was a good idea to go back to the police station to ask for directions. If Weston was still there, he'd probably strongly discourage a visit to Escher's place.

He headed north out of town on U.S. 51 and passed a Save More grocery store. Somebody in there was likely to know Jim Escher, or tell him how to get to the road where he lived. Sam pulled into the parking lot and walked in through the automatic doors, stepping through the pools of melting snow from the wheels of shopping carts. There were four check-out lanes, and only one was in service. The summer residents were long gone.

"Hey," Sam said to the long-haired teenage boy wearing a green apron by the register in the open lane. "I'm looking for Jim Escher's place. You know where that is?"

"Escher?" the boy asked. "I think he's a friend of my dad's. I don't know where he lives, though."

"I've got his address. 4121 Bass Lake Road. And I don't see a Bass Lake on my map."

"Oh, that's over on Clear Lake."

"No wonder I couldn't find it."

"Yeah, it gets kinda confusing around here, with all the lakes."

"How do I get over there?"

"Fastest way?"

"That'd be good."

"You stay on 51 going north to Highway 47, then take a right and go maybe two miles to Arbor Vitae. Take a right there, and keep going east. You run right into Bass Lake Road."

"Does that take me past Country Club Road? Doc Mueller's place?"

"No. Country Club's a dead-end. You gotta go back through town."

"Oh. Okay, thanks."

"Sure. Take care."

Good thought. Sam wasn't wearing his gun, but decided it would be a good idea to put it on when he got to Escher's place. If Escher were somehow involved with Mueller, a little precaution was in order.

Sam decided to look at Mueller's place first. He drove past the golf course, took the side road, rounded a curve, and came to a wooded hillside lot on a point looking north over the lake. If Doc Mueller had owned a place here for thirty years, the original cabin must have been a tear-down. The current two-story house had six-foot picture windows and a wrap-around porch, with a tuck-under two-stall garage. A boat and a snowmobile, both with black canvas covers, were parked beneath an overhang attached to an original wooden outbuilding. There was enough cut and stacked firewood beside the outbuilding to heat the house for five winters. There were no lights on inside, and judging from the snow in the driveway, no one had been here for several days.

Sam turned around and headed back out to the highway. He looped around the north end of the lake and got on Highway 47 going south. He turned onto Bass Lake Road and began looking at mailboxes for the number. The cabins all had driveways that led into the trees along the south shore of the lake, and would be shielded by foliage during the high season, but through the bare limbs in the dim light, he could make out the shapes of the structures. These weren't expensive year-round showplaces like Mueller's, or the other ones Sam had seen along the shore of Lake

Minocqua. Some looked like three-season cabins, while others looked to be modest two-bedroom homes. Most did not have lights on. The one that sat at the other end of the driveway at 4121 Bass Lake Road did.

Sam had half-expected Escher to run after hanging up on him. In fact, he'd have preferred it—it would have been further evidence that something wasn't right about this accident. The fact that Escher was apparently still home could have meant a few things: Escher didn't expect him to come by, Escher didn't have anything to hide, or Escher was waiting for him.

Sam continued past the house and turned around in the next driveway up the road. He cut his lights, drove back the way he'd come, and pulled the Cherokee off the road by Escher's mailbox. He reached into the back seat, opened his travel bag, and pulled his Glock 23 out of its holster. He inserted a magazine, racked a round into the chamber, and put the gun in the right pocket of his jacket. Then he pulled his black fleece cap over his ears, put on his gloves, and stepped out of the SUV, closing the door quietly behind him.

The lights were still on in the house, and a pale orange moon was visible through the bare trees to the east, catching some of the last light from the winter sunset. There was a detached garage with the door closed to the right of the house, with recent tire tracks leading into it, and a blue-and-black Yamaha snowmobile parked near the back porch. The snow crunched under the treads of Sam's slip-on snow boots as he walked up the driveway. When he neared the house, he slowed down and stepped more carefully.

INSIDE THE HOUSE, ESCHER was waiting, looking through the window from a darkened bedroom, loaded shotgun across his lap.

He'd seen Skarda's car go by the house, slow down, and double back with the lights off. He'd seen Skarda get out of the car and walk up the driveway.

He'd killed a man once before. If necessary, he'd do it again.

No one had found out about the first time. No one would. It had happened ten years earlier. He'd been deer hunting on state forest land near Antigo, planning to use a tree stand he'd built a few years before. But when he got there before sunup the day of the opener, there'd been another man in the stand. Escher told him to get out. The man said no. Escher said he'd built that stand. The man said it was on public property. No one owned it. He was staying put.

Escher was furious. He walked off into the forest but couldn't forget about the guy in his stand. Late that afternoon, he took off his blaze-orange jacket and hat, put them in his car, pulled on a camo jacket, and went back to that part of the forest. It was near dusk, and the guy was just climbing down from the stand. He'd taken only a few steps away from the tree when, from 200 feet away, Escher put a .30-.06 slug through the man's head. There was no snow on the ground, so there was no way to track Escher as he retreated to his car and drove off. The death was listed as accidental, from a stray bullet.

There would be no way to cover up killing Skarda, or to call it an accident when the buckshot-riddled body was found on the front steps of Escher's house. But he was in a tight spot, and Mueller was a smart guy. What he said about the Constitution, about protecting your property from a stranger, sounded right. How could Escher know who was coming to his house in the dark? He could say he'd been sleeping, and he heard something, someone, at the door. His shotgun had been lying on the table because he'd been cleaning it. He was scared, maybe a little disoriented because he'd just awakened. He gave Skarda a warning. Asked him to identify himself. Skarda didn't say anything. Turns out he had a gun. What was Escher supposed to do?

The more he thought about it, the more the idea of blowing Skarda's head off appealed to him. He could use a hundred grand. Really use it. He'd been out of work for three months, and he didn't think the lodge where he did maintenance work was going to hire him again next summer. He'd been caught charging gas for his own boat on the lodge's account. And that fifteen-year-old girl had complained about him peeking into her room, though the manager seemed to believe him when he denied it. He didn't want to move to the city, but if the lodge didn't want him back—they'd let him go two weeks before the season ended this year—he didn't know where else to look for work. He'd had to refinance the cabin last year, and he was two months behind on the payments for his snowmobile. The kind of money Mueller had promised would allow him to stay in his lake place for years. All he had to do was get rid of a nosy detective.

The bedroom was next to the lighted living room. Escher could see Skarda near the steps that led to the front door. Well, it was the back door, really. The front of the house, in Escher's mind, faced the lake. Who comes to a man's back door in the night? Escher stood up and walked out of the bedroom, positioning himself at the entrance to the living room, where Skarda could not see him through the window, but Escher could cover the doorway. *Come a little closer, you cocksucking private dick. Knock on the door. Come on. You'll get just what you're looking for. Just what I gave that asshole who took my tree stand.*

Sam didn't see a doorbell, but there was a brass knocker—in the shape of a Packers helmet—inside the screen door. He was reaching for the door handle when his cell phone rang.

He backed away from the door and walked around to the far side of the detached garage. He took off his glove, got his phone out of his jacket and answered it.

"Skarda."

"Sam! It's Gretchen! He's outside again!"

"Scott?"

"Yes! Yelling and pounding on my front door! I think he just fired a shot through my living room window!"

"Does he have a key?"

"No. I changed the locks."

"Get away from the door. Go upstairs and stay away from the windows. Call the police."

"Where are you?"

"Minocqua. I can be back there in two and half hours."

"I'm sorry, I'm really sorry . . ."

There was silence on her end of the line for a moment, but Sam could hear the pounding on her door.

"I'll call the police, but . . . could you come? Soon?"

"I'm leaving now."

"Thank you. Thank you."

Sam hung up the phone and ran down the driveway toward his car.

Inside, Jim Escher held the corner of the window shade away from the sill. He watched Skarda run back down the driveway and jump into his SUV. He waited until he heard the Cherokee's engine start, saw the headlights turn on, and watched it speed away down Bass Lake Road toward the highway.

Then he put the shotgun's safety back on.

ELEVEN

Two squad cars were still at Gretchen's house when Sam arrived. He'd been lucky to avoid a speeding ticket on the way back to Green Bay, but it turned out there'd been no need to hurry. Krebbs had left soon after Gretchen called Sam. Probably not because she'd called him, though.

Gretchen sat in an armchair in her living room, still wearing the Packers medical staff sweatshirt she'd worn home from work. She looked more restless than scared, as though she'd rather be out combing the streets for her ex-husband than sitting at a crime scene answering questions. The bay window had a bullet hole through it, with spider-web cracks circling the hole. Sam guessed a handgun from the size of the hole. A plainclothes cop sat across from Gretchen on a couch, as an evidence technician dug around a bullet hole in the living-room wall, and another cop out front searched for shell casings in the snow.

"You okay?" Sam asked. He sat on the arm of her chair and put his arm across her shoulders. She leaned into him and patted his leg.

"Yeah, I'm good. Thanks for coming."

"This the new boyfriend?" said the cop on the couch. He was a short man with dark razor stubble and bags under his eyes.

"Please stop that, Lieutenant VanHoff," she said. "I told you before, I don't have a boyfriend. My husband is jealous of everyone."

"Did you see him?" Sam asked.

"No. I just heard noise outside the door, and then the gunshot."

"Then you're not sure it was Scott."

"What do you mean? Who else could it have been?"

"I don't know," Sam said. "Neighborhood kids?"

That's not what he was thinking, but he didn't want to go into it with the cop sitting there. It looked like a clean-cut domestic, and it probably was. Best to keep everyone working on that premise, for now. If this was in any way connected to Mueller's efforts to undermine the team, Sam was going to find that out.

Sam asked VanHoff if they'd been able to find Krebbs since the last time they'd come out to the house. No luck, he was told. They'd keep trying. Sam was again advised to keep out of it. He'd only make things worse for Gretchen.

The technician eventually found the slug in the wall and put it in an evidence bag. The cop outside came in and said he couldn't find any shell casings. They'd take the bullet to the lab and see what they could learn. It would probably take a couple of weeks to get anything back. The lab was backed up, as usual.

When the cops left, Sam asked Gretchen if Scott owned a handgun.

"Not that I know of. I wouldn't let him have one around here, even if he'd wanted one."

"Hunting rifles? Shotgun?"

"No. He wasn't a hunter."

"Let's not take any more chances. I'm going to move in with you."

"But if Scott sees your car in the driveway, it will just convince him that I was lying to him. That we're . . ."

"No car in the driveway tonight when he shot a hole through your window. I was 150 miles away. If the cops can't find him, I guess I'll have to let him find me."

Gretchen sighed and put her arm around Sam's waist.

"This isn't going to end well."

"Don't think like that. I've seen lots of these. Most of them work themselves out. But in the meantime, you deserve to be safe. I've got my bag in the car. I'll bring it in."

He said it with a slight question in his tone, waiting for Gretchen to veto the idea. He was half-hoping she would. He'd have to call Caroline tonight and explain everything to her—that he was now living in Green Bay until further notice, in the home of an old girlfriend. That would be a fun conversation.

"Okay," Gretchen said. "You can use the spare bedroom. Take a right at the top of the stairs, last room at the end of the hall. Flip open the heat grate, or you'll freeze."

She got up from her chair and went into the kitchen. When Sam came back in from the driveway with his bag, Gretchen had a roll of masking tape and a piece of cardboard, covering the bullet hole in the living-room window.

Sam was up making coffee the next morning when Gretchen walked in, dressed for work. It was still dark outside.

"When do the players get there?" Sam asked.

"They start weightlifting around seven. Then there's a team meeting at nine."

"Any chance I can get some time with LaBobby Suggs this morning?"

"I don't see why not."

Gretchen put the tea kettle on the stove and got out a loaf of nine-grain bread for toast. She drank a glass of orange juice while Sam had coffee.

"I want you to know how much I appreciate this, Sam. I slept much better—I mean, I slept because you were here."

"You don't deserve to go through this."

"I don't know. Maybe I do. I chose Scott . . ."

Leaving unspoken the next part: instead of you.

"A woman should never blame herself when a guy gets abusive," Sam said. "It's not your fault. You can't think that way."

She gave him a thin smile and waited for the toast to come up, then put it on the table with some strawberry preserves. When the tea kettle started to whistle, she poured herself a cup and sat down at the table with Sam.

"Are you with someone now?" she said. "I feel bad that I haven't asked, but it's really none of my business."

"Yes. I called her last night and explained what was going on here."

"I'll bet she enjoyed that."

"She was . . . concerned."

"What's her name?"

"Caroline Crandall."

Sam told Gretchen how they'd met, and how distance and career issues were still in the way. It was all new territory. Sam had never anticipated discussing another woman with Gretchen. He thought it would be awkward, but he realized that enough time had passed for both of them.

"Is she . . . I mean, were there . . . I always wondered what you were doing after I went to Madison. I never heard from you."

"I never heard from you, either. I figured you'd made a clean break."

"I did. Eventually."

"What do you mean?"

"I missed you. Really missed you. If you'd called a month or two later and asked me to come back . . ."

"You wouldn't have. That's why I didn't call."

Gretchen smiled, looking into her cup. "You're right. But that doesn't mean I wouldn't have wanted to."

"And what good would that have done either of us?"

Gretchen looked up at Sam, her expression suggesting that she was trying to get a fix on who he was now.

"I know why you were a good cop. And why you're good at what you do now. You can really be cold when you have to be. You can shut things off."

"Sometimes it's the only way to get through something."

"What does Caroline think of that?"

"It scares her a little."

"Sensible woman." She got up from the table and put her teacup in the sink. Daylight had begun to brighten the backyard, though the sky was overcast. She said, "You're a good man, Sam. I hope she knows that."

"That's what I'm counting on."

T HEY TOOK THEIR OWN CARS TO LAMBEAU, and met in the parking lot outside the team entrance. Sam had already called Frank Janaszak for clearance to be at practice. He checked in with the guard, and they walked inside together. He followed Gretchen into the sprawling, brightly-lit weight room, where several dozen players in shorts and tank-tops were already working on the free weights.

"Ask the strength coach if he can spare LaBobby for a few minutes," Sam said.

"There's an empty equipment room down the hall to the right. You can wait for him there."

A few minutes later, the door to the equipment room opened and a massive man entered. LaBobby Suggs weighed at least 325 pounds, with a bulge above his waist that looked as though he'd stuffed a loaded trash bag under his shirt. His upper arms were as big as an average man's thighs, and his thighs were as big as the room's support pillars. He walked pigeon-toed, as though trying to force his knees to get within a foot of each other. Sam could hear the rasp of his lungs filling before he spoke.

"You wanted to see me?"

"Yes," Sam said. "My name's Skarda. I'm doing some security work for the team, and I want to ask you a few questions about the incident at the woman's house in West de Pere."

Suggs nodded and sat on a bench. "What do you want to know?"

He didn't seem embarrassed or reluctant to answer questions. He met Sam's eyes with a steady gaze. This was a man, Sam concluded, who'd seen all sides of life, and wasn't afraid of any of it.

"First, tell me how you ended up with the Packers," Sam said.

"I'd been in trouble with the Chiefs. My agent thought this would be a good fit."

"Who's your agent?"

"Michael Banks."

"What happened in Kansas City?"

"Drugs. I got caught with some coke at a traffic stop."

"Was it yours?"

"Would you believe me if I said it wasn't?"

"Maybe. Was it?"

"God's honest truth, no. Belonged to the other guy."

"Who was that?"

"Asshole. Punk I shouldn't have been with. Guy from my old neighborhood."

"And that's where?"

"East St. Louis. Shit hole I was lucky to get out of."

Suggs managed to avoid jail time because the asshole punk from East St. Louis had an extensive criminal record, and the cops couldn't prove who owned the dope, but the NFL made him sit out the rest of the season for violating the league's substance-abuse policy. Since he was also coming off knee surgery the previous year, and a separated shoulder the year before that, the Chiefs didn't think too hard before releasing him during the off-season.

"Michael talked the Packers into giving me a chance."

"You knew you'd be under the microscope here," Sam said. "How'd you end up getting in trouble with that woman?"

"I like to trust people—especially women. Know what I mean? I trusted the wrong woman."

Suggs told his side of what happened that night. He met the woman ("real good-looking, you know? The kind you don't see much around here") at a night club in Green Bay. There were drinks, there was some dancing, a few laughs, and then the woman invited Suggs to a party she was having back at her house. Suggs went—but there was no party. It was just the two of them. He didn't mind. He had a nice little buzz going, and assumed she did, too. Then she put the moves on him, and they ended up in bed. Suggs had practice the next morning, so he left at midnight. Sometime later that night he was awakened in his condo by cops banging on his door. Dellums had called the police, telling them she'd never met Suggs before he broke into her house, raped her, and stole money and jewelry from her.

"And none of that's true?"

"Hell, no. But they found one of her rings and a bracelet in my pants pocket."

"How'd they get there?"

"How do you think?"

"You were set up."

"Yes, sir."

"Why?"

"Money. I figure she'll drop the charges if I cough up six figures."

"Who's your attorney?"

"Peter McCullough. Chicago guy that Banks found for me."

"Has he heard from the woman's attorney?"

"No."

"No offense, but why not go after somebody making a lot more money than you?"

"Maybe she thought I was somebody else. Or maybe she thinks we're all rich."

"Any damage to her place?"

"Yeah. The cops found a busted door jamb. Some shit was smashed."

"But you didn't do it."

"Believe me, I didn't need to kick that woman's door down. Maybe to get out . . . but no, I didn't break nothing at her place."

"Did they do a rape exam?"

"Yeah. They found my stuff. We did it twice."

"Bruising? Bleeding?"

"Not when I left her. Not from me."

Sam had read the news reports about the case. Suggs had been released on bail the next morning, arraigned several days later, and was awaiting trail, likely in February or March. The judge had apparently decided that Suggs was not a flight risk, since he was a celebrity football player—a celebrity in Green Bay, anyway. The Packers had announced they'd take no disciplinary action until the case was resolved.

"Didn't McCullough tell you to stay out of strip clubs till your trial?"

"No, he never said nothing about that."

"How about the team? Didn't Horvath tell you not to be seen at a place like the White House?"

"Wish he had," Suggs said, shaking his head. "When that guy jumped Cornell, I knew I was fucked."

"Whose idea was it to go there?"

"Drabek's, I guess."

"The linebacker?"

"Yeah."

"How well do you know him?"

"No better than I know anybody else on this team. I've only been here since July."

Sam believed Suggs. There was no false bravado, and no attempt to deny his past. He knew he was damaged goods, and he knew he'd made some mistakes. But he hadn't ducked any of Sam's questions, and his answers were plausible. They could also be lies, but they fit a pattern taking shape.

"I'll let you get back to practice," Sam said. "Are Drabek and Johnson around?"

"Yeah, I saw them in the weight room."

"How about Truman?"

"He's here, too."

"How'd he get out of that club before the cops showed up?"

"Damned if I know. Maybe he's developed some kind of spider-sense about cops. If you find out, I'd like to know."

Sam spent about five minutes with Cornell Johnson, who was more guarded than Suggs, but insisted that he wasn't doing anything with the stripper that doesn't go on every night in strip clubs all over America. An innocent lap dance—and the next thing he knew, some redneck was throwing punches.

Johnson was another Packers reclamation project. He'd been All-Pro with the Jets, but he soon got caught up in Manhattan's fast lane. As his club-hopping increased, his production decreased. His name was in the gossip columns more often than on the sports pages. He tried to run with heiresses, actresses, and hip-hop stars, but ended up with a drug habit. He eventually put himself into a treatment program, but by the time he got out, he'd lost a step, and lost his position. The Jets cut him. He played a season with the Eagles. They cut him. He'd been released in training camp by the Jaguars, and then the Packers picked him up.

The Packers were his last chance, but the way the season was going, he didn't think it mattered much what he did after hours. When Drabek suggested the outing at The White House, he figured, what the hell. At the last minute, Johnson had asked Truman to come along—a chance to get to know the new QB away from football. He'd lost track of Truman when the fight broke out.

Drabek had a reputation as a brawler. He'd punched out an assistant coach when he was with the 49ers, just before the league suspended him for steroid use. When Sam approached Drabek to talk to him about the fight at the White House, the linebacker stood facing Sam with his sculpted arms crossed in front of his barrel chest, his legs apart and tensed, and said no.

"I don't know you. Talk to my lawyer," Drabek said.

"Who's that?"

"Peter McCullough. He's in Chicago."

McCullough again. Certain names kept popping up. Sam tried one more question.

"Who's your agent?"

"Michael Banks. Now get lost."

Truman was spotting for the team's backup quarterback on a free-weight bench when Sam approached. He eyed Sam warily, and told him he didn't have anything to say about the fight. Sam decided to take a calculated risk.

"Michael Banks told me you'd cooperate."

Truman looked surprised.

"You talked to my agent?"

"He doesn't have a problem if I ask you a few questions."

"Who are you again?"

"Sam Skarda. I'm working with Horvath on team security."

"Horvath, huh? Okay. I got some questions for you, too."

They walked into the equipment room. Sam closed the door behind them. They sat on the bench, looking at each other.

"How did you get out of the White House before the cops got there?" Sam asked.

"Hell, you oughta know that, if you're workin' with Horvath."

"What do you mean?"

"Horvath's everywhere, man. He was at the club that night. As soon as Drabek punched a guy, Horvath pops outta nowhere and tells me I need to get my ass out of there. How'd he know we were going to be there?"

Horvath hadn't mentioned being at the White House brawl when Sam had been introduced to him. Truman's question was a good one: How did he happen to be there? And why would he single out Truman to save from an arrest? Were the others expendable?

"When did you get out of prison, D'Metrius?"

"November 20th. Three days before Thanksgiving. There was a dozen news crews waiting for me when I walked through the front gate."

"And how many football offers?"

"None. I didn't think nobody was going to take a chance."

"So what were you going to do?"

"Go home. Work out. Write letters. I figured maybe I could talk somebody into giving me a tryout after the draft next spring. Maybe get invited to a camp as a free agent."

"Then the Packers called?"

"Not exactly."

"What do you mean?"

Truman hesitated. There was something he didn't want to talk about. He was choosing his words carefully.

"Horvath came to see me . . . at a . . . you know, kind of a party with some old friends. Over in Minnesota. Said Dick Jordan wanted to sign me, but I had to see him right away."

"Did you call Banks?"

"Yeah. He said it was all arranged. I just had to pass the physical."

"Did that surprise you?"

"Yeah, sorta. I mean, I knew I could still play, but I didn't know anybody else thought so."

"Why do you think Green Bay wanted you? Why would they take a chance on you?"

"I don't know. You tell me. You work for them."

"I don't know how they make their roster decisions."

"Well, look at this team. One win. What do they got to lose?"

Sam saw an opening, and wondered if it would be smart to go through it. Sam was now officially suspicious of Horvath, and he didn't need Truman relating this conversation back to the head of security. On the other hand, the only way to shake loose more information was to get somebody like Truman asking questions.

"Have you heard anything about the team being sold?" Sam asked Truman.

"No. I don't pay no attention to that kind of stuff. Besides, they can't sell this team—can they?"

"If things get bad enough here, they could."

Truman was silent for a moment, rubbing his chin. There were no dumb quarterbacks in professional football, Sam realized. Reckless, maybe. Selfish, and even egomaniacal. Possibly naïve. But not dumb. Truman was beginning to grasp the bigger picture.

"So you're saying they brought me in here to make a bad situation worse? So they could sell the team?"

"I'm not saying that," Sam said. "Let's see how things go on Sunday. Maybe you're the guy who's going to turn this thing around."

"I am," Truman said. He got up from the bench and walked slowly toward the door.

"D'Metrius."

"Yeah?"

He turned to look at Sam, who was holding out one of his cards, with his cell phone number.

"Keep your eyes and ears open. If something happens that doesn't seem right, let me know."

"Like what?"

"I don't know. But something odd is going on around here. Some people could go down. You don't want to go down with them."

Truman reached out and took Sam's card, then left the room.

TWELVE

Sam walked into Joe Horvath's office without knocking and sat down in a chair next to the man's uncluttered desk. The Packers' head of security looked up from his computer at Sam and said, "Have a seat."

"Thanks. What were you doing at the White House Tuesday night?"

"Watching strippers. Kind of a thing I have."

"Your wife doesn't mind?"

"She probably would, but I'm not married. What's this about?"

Horvath pushed himself away from his desk and swiveled his chair to face Sam. The eyes were piercing, and the moustache looked even more symmetrical than the first time they'd met. Sam looked around to see if the guy had an electric trimmer or a small scissors somewhere in the office. There were framed prints of pheasants, ducks, and hunting dogs on the wall. Aside from an oversized Packers schedule and a seating chart under an aerial photo of Lambeau Field, there was nothing that overtly said "football" in Horvath's space.

"I just thought it was kind of odd that you managed to get Truman out of there before the police showed up. Why not Suggs, or Johnson, or Drabek?"

Horvath laughed.

"There's a hierarchy in the NFL, Sam. You learn that when you've been around the league a while. 'Protect the quarterback' isn't just a rule on the field. Same goes for off the field. When that fight broke out, I knew I couldn't break it up, and I knew I couldn't get them all out of there. So I chose the most important guy in the room—our quarterback."

Horvath was such a ramrod-straight, no-bullshit type that almost anything that came out of his mouth could sound plausible.

"Did you know those guys were going to be there?" Sam asked.

"I had no idea. But pro football players have been known to show up in strip clubs from time to time."

"How many strip clubs are there in Green Bay?"

No hesitation. "Three."

"And those four guys just happened to choose the same one you were in?"

Horvath crossed his legs clasped his hands behind his head, and leaned back in his chair.

"Every business owner in Green Bay likes to have Packers come into their place, but Butch Grunwald really goes out of his way for this organization, and the guys like going there. Butch runs a respectable club. Usually, everyone behaves themselves."

"Usually."

"Hey, you mix tits and testosterone, every once in a while you're gonna get a little dust-up, y'know?"

This wasn't getting Sam anywhere. Sam needed to talk to someone outside the Packers family—someone whose first instinct wasn't to defend the home team at all costs.

"What's Doc Mueller's ex-wife's name?" Sam said.

"Sharon."

"Does she still live in town?"

"Yeah, far as I know."

"Do you have an address and a phone number for her?"

"I could look it up."

Horvath hesitated for a moment, as though hoping Sam would tell him not to bother. But Sam sat patiently, so Horvath punched a few keystrokes into his computer. He waited a moment for a file to come up, and then said: "Eighteen forty-nine Waukesha Drive."

He waited for Sam to take out a small notebook to write down the address, and then gave him the phone number.

"Anything else I can do for you?"

"That should do it, for now."

"Good. Because I've got quite a week going here. We got a game in ninety-six hours in an iced-over stadium. There's more snow on the way. Temperature's gonna be about zero at game time. What, exactly, is it Frank brought you here to do?"

"He explained it to you in his office," Sam said. "Maybe you were reminiscing about your favorite strippers. Mueller seems hell-bent on selling the team, and Frank wants to know why."

Horvath didn't like the crack about strippers—but then again, Sam hadn't met a lot of cops who were quick to laugh at themselves.

"Maybe the team ought to be sold," Horvath said. "We haven't been Titletown for quite a while."

"You want to see the Packers privately held?"

"I hate losing, and I hate working for the worst team in football. So does Doc Mueller. Green Bay used to mean championships. Whatever it takes to get out of the hole we're in, I'm for. Now, you'll have to excuse me."

Sam walked out of Horvath's office and took the elevator down to the club-house level. He cleared himself through the guard station again and found Gretchen in the trainer's room, working on a shirtless player's shoulder. It obviously hurt him to raise his right arm above his head. Gretchen was showing him a strengthening exercise in which he lay on his left side and lifted the arm to perpendicular, then lowered it again to his side.

"Try a set of fifteen, then another set of fifteen," Gretchen told him. "Do that three times a day, and the wall push-ups twice a day."

"Should I do any lifting?"

"No weights until I give you the okay."

She opened a wall cabinet and found sheets that had diagrams of the two exercises she wanted him to do. She handed him the two sheets.

"Think I can play Sunday?" the player asked.

"It's going to hurt. But I think you can play. I'll talk to Marv about giving you a shot before the game."

"Thanks, Gretchen."

The player hopped off the training table, looked at Sam with mild curiosity, and walked out of the room. Gretchen closed the cabinet door and turned to Sam.

"How many shots do you usually give on game day?" Sam asked.

"This time of year, maybe fifteen. Sometimes more. I'd rather not—these guys are hurting, and a shot just masks the pain. They could be injuring themselves even more."

"So why do it?"

"Because that's football. We couldn't field a team some weeks without shots."

"What's in the needle?"

"I'll probably give Justin Haugland—the wide receiver who was just in here—a shot of Toradol. It's an anti-inflammatory, and it's not addictive."

"What else do you use?"

"Some of the guys ask for Marcain. It's a local anesthetic and nerve blocker. Serious stuff."

"This happens all over the league?"

"Absolutely. The NFL knows all about it. They don't take a position one way or the other. It's up to the players and the team whether or not to use them."

Gretchen told him she had three more players to see before practice was over—assuming there weren't any new injuries to deal with. Sam said he was leaving the stadium to do another interview, and he'd meet her back at her house that night.

"Getting anywhere?" she asked.

"I don't know. I do know that Joe Horvath and I won't be going to the Packers draft party together."

"He's a no-nonsense guy, isn't he?"

"Most security types are, if they're any good. It only takes one mistake for a disaster to happen."

"I don't think Horvath is the type to make mistakes."

"We'll see."

SAM BOUGHT A GREEN BAY city map and found Sharon Mueller's house near Heritage Hill Park in Allouez, just east of the parkway that ran parallel to the Fox River. It was a sedate, moneyed old neighborhood with stone two-story homes, long sidewalks, and huge boulevard trees. No matter how long ago Doc Mueller purchased the house, it had to have been an expensive neighborhood to buy into.

Sam didn't phone ahead, figuring that it would be easy for Sharon Mueller to tell him not to come over the phone. He'd make it more difficult to get rid of him in person.

He rang the bell and admired the arched brickwork around the front door. The inside door was opened by a woman with glasses and gray-streaked dark hair cut short at the bottom of her ears. She wore a black sweater with a snowflake pattern on the front and gray wool slacks. Even through the storm door it appeared that she'd had some work done around the neck and eyes, but she hadn't spent a much time sitting at a makeup table that morning.

The woman looked both surprised and somewhat embarrassed to see a strange man standing on her porch. She pushed the storm door open a foot or so.

"Can I help you?" she asked.

"I hope so. My name's Sam Skarda. I work for the Packers. If you don't mind, I'd like to talk to you about your ex-husband."

"Doc? Is he in trouble?"

Sam smiled. "Not that I know of. But I'm new here."

"I didn't think I recognized you. I used to know almost everybody in the Packers front office, but . . . well, it's been awhile. Even the executives are getting younger. Come on in."

Sam walked into the foyer and handed his jacket to Sharon Mueller, who hung it in the hall closet. Sam wiped his boots on the mat and began to kick them off—common courtesy in the Midwest during the winter.

"Oh, that's all right," Sharon Mueller said. "A little water won't hurt anything."

Sam kept his boots on and followed her into the living room, tastefully decorated with a large Persian area rug over a gleaming hardwood floor, with a white sofa and a coffee table in front of the fireplace, and two white upholstered armchairs on either side of the sofa. There were no football pictures or souvenirs on the walls or the end tables. If a man had ever lived here, he'd left some time ago.

Sharon threw a switch on the wall, and a flame appeared in the gas fireplace.

"I was about to turn that on when you rang the bell," she said. "I was getting cold."

"It's a little raw out there."

"Coffee? Or . . . something else?"

"Oh, that's all right . . ."

"I'm thinking about having a martini."

That came out of nowhere.

"I'll take a couple of olives in mine. I didn't have lunch."

Sharon Mueller was in the kitchen for a couple of minutes and came back with two full martini glasses. She wasn't a bad-looking woman, if you could get past the sense that she didn't think so. She had nice, warm eyes and lips that still had some non-collagen life to them. Sam actually liked the lack of makeup, and the winter sweater couldn't completely hide what appeared to be a nice figure. He could imagine her being a head-turner when Mueller met her. Sam guessed that she was about fifteen years younger than her ex-husband.

Sam was sitting on the right side of the sofa, appreciating the fire and the drink. Sharon sat in the armchair to his right, raised her glass and took a sip.

"Now . . . Sam, is it? What did you want to talk to me about?"

"Did you know your ex-husband wants to sell the Packers to a private owner?"

Sharon cocked her head as though trying to recall having heard such a thing, and then turned her gaze—now becoming an appreciative gaze—back to Sam.

"No, I don't think so. But it's not his team to sell."

"No, it isn't. But if he can persuade the executive committee to go along with him, he could make it happen."

"Why would he want to do that?"

"That's what I'm—what we're trying to find out."

Sharon took another sip of her drink and absentmindedly began fluffing her hair with her fingers. In a dark cocktail lounge, she might still be trouble.

"I don't talk to Doc anymore. Not for over a year. What he does is his business."

"Were you friends with Ed Larson?"

That question scored. Sharon blinked, put her drink on the coffee table and settled back in her chair with her hands in her lap. Her eyes were glistening.

"Donna Larson is my best friend. I was with her this morning."

"I'm sorry," Sam said.

"I'm sorry, too. I don't mean this to sound as harsh as it probably does, but the world would be a better place if it had been Ed who survived that accident. He was a wonderful man."

"And Karl isn't?"

"Nobody calls him Karl. He's Doc. And he's . . . his own man. I don't hate him. But nobody tells him what to do. Ed would listen to you. Ed cared about people."

"Didn't Doc listen to you?"

"Not really. He had his boat. He had his snowmobile. He had his football team. He had his gambling trips. I assume he had his girlfriends. If I'd been willing to accept all that, we'd probably still be married."

"You said gambling trips. Doc likes to gamble?"

"Oh, my God. Does the pope wear a funny hat?"

Sharon told Sam that the Muellers and the Larsons used to go on all the team's road trips together as couples, and take side trips to tourist spots whenever they could. But in the last years of their marriage, Doc was increasingly drawn to locations that included casinos. He never missed hitting Atlantic City on East Coast trips, and it was either Las Vegas or Reno when the team went out west. Like most gamblers, he began having money problems.

"Maybe I could have put up with the girlfriends. We don't have kids, so it wasn't like he was hurting anybody but me. But when he started draining our bank accounts, that's when I pulled the plug. I wanted to get out while there was still something to get."

She was awarded the house in the divorce settlement, while Doc got the cabin in Minocqua. She also got half of the savings—which had been her savings; their joint account was empty—and half of his pension, which was enough to keep her in the house and wearing decent clothes. She was doing a little real-estate work now to keep some extra money coming in, to meet new people, and to have something to do. For a few years, Doc was in bad financial shape and seemed to get a grip on his gambling. He went back to practicing medicine to try to dig himself out of the hole. Then a couple of years ago he apparently came into another source of money.

"I don't know what he was up to," Sharon said. "He bought a Land Rover, tore down the old cabin and built a new house on our lot in Minocqua, bought a new boat and a new snowmobile, and got himself a nice condo downtown. I thought maybe the Packers gave him a raise. Or he started treating some very rich patients. Whatever it was, he started gambling again."

"How do you know?"

"Green Bay's a small town. If Donna doesn't tell me, somebody else will."

"What about the league? They don't like gamblers."

"They don't like the players gambling, or associating with gamblers. But it's a different story for the owners and executives."

"You mean, the league knows about Doc's gambling habit?"

"Of course. I've seen Doc at the craps table in Las Vegas with an NFL official. Do you think the league would have let the Oneida tribe sponsor part of the Lambeau Field renovation if they were worried about casino gambling?"

Sam had always assumed that the NFL had a zero-tolerance policy on gambling, which was why he had been surprised to see that the club had sold naming rights to one of the five entrances to Lambeau Field to the Oneida Nation—Oneida, as in Oneida Casino. It was the Packers who had sustained the league's harshest-ever penalty for gambling, when former league MVP Paul Hornung was suspended for the 1963 season—along with Alex Karras of the Lions—for betting on NFL games. The league had every reason to be wary of gambling, since there was probably more betting interest in the outcome of NFL games than any other sport in America. But Doc Mueller made no secret of his fondness for casinos, and he was one seat away from running the Packers.

"Any idea how steep Doc's losses have been lately?" Sam asked Sharon.

"None at all. He wouldn't tell me if I asked, and I wouldn't ask. I'm going to have another. Can I freshen that?"

She pointed to Sam's martini glass. The olives hadn't done much to counteract the effects of gin on an empty stomach. Sam held up his hand and said, "I've really got to be going. Thanks for the drink."

"Did you get what you wanted?"

Sharon was smiling shyly, with one elbow over the back of her chair, her winter sweater now pulled tighter across her chest. There was a loneliness in her eyes that almost made Sam feel guilty for running off.

"Yes, I did," Sam said. He walked to the foyer and put on his jacket. Sharon got up and followed him.

"I'm here most afternoons . . . evenings, too, if there's anything else."

"I'll keep that in mind. Thanks again."

Sam stepped out into the darkening afternoon. His car was just fifty feet away at the end of the sidewalk, so he didn't put his hat on, but his ears almost immediately began to sting from the biting wind. The forecast was for colder weather on the weekend. How did anyone play football in weather like this?

JIM ESCHER WASN'T COLD. His extended-cab Tacoma was parked at the end of the block, five houses down from Sharon Mueller's and across the street, where he could see Skarda when he came out of the house. The engine was running. Escher was wearing a black parka, unzipped. He'd been listening to the radio while Skarda was inside, maybe for an hour or more. What had he been doing in there all that time? Fucking her? From what Doc Mueller had told him about his ex-wife, Escher wouldn't be surprised.

His shotgun was wrapped in a blanket across the back seat of the Tacoma, along with his Remington Model 700 deer rifle with a Pentax scope. He also had a Colt Python revolver tucked inside his parka—a beautiful, expensive handgun that Escher had come upon after breaking into a cabin on Blue Lake a couple of winters ago. He had shot a few raccoons and a coyote with the gun, but it seemed designed for a more important purpose. Such as earning $100,000 of Mueller's money by finding and killing the detective from Minneapolis.

He'd been parked in the Lambeau lot when he received a call from Joe Horvath shortly after Skarda left Horvath's office: Skarda is headed over to Allouez to talk to Mueller's ex. Just thought you'd like to know. Here's the address.

Escher had arrived at Waukesha Drive just as Skarda was getting out of his car. Not that it would have mattered if he'd missed him this time. Horvath had promised to keep him informed about what Skarda was doing and where he went. He already knew where Skarda was spending his nights—in the home of that lady doctor. And Horvath told him killing Skarda would be easy to get away with. All the suspicion would fall on Gretchen Kahler's ex-husband, a stalker who was ignoring his restraining order. When the cops found Skarda dead, they'd assume the jealous ex-husband did it.

Escher wanted to know everything about Skarda's movements and habits. He hadn't made up his mind how he was going to do it yet—maybe a long-range snipe with the deer rifle, maybe a bullet in the head from the Colt revolver when Skarda was getting out of his car, or maybe blowing his face away with the shotgun when he came out of the lady doctor's house. There were options, and there was time— time for Escher to watch, to follow, to plan.

To hunt.

THIRTEEN

Sam kept his gun in his shoulder holster that night at Gretchen's house. She didn't like seeing it, but the patched-over bullet hole in her living-room window was all the argument Sam needed to make. The cops still hadn't found Krebbs. If this kept up much longer—hunkering down for the night in Gretchen's house, waiting and wondering whether Krebbs was going to attack her again—Sam would have to go out and find him. But for now, he'd let the police do their job. He'd do his.

Gretchen didn't watch TV. Krebbs had a thirty-four-inch screen in the basement, and there was a college football game on ESPN that night that Sam wouldn't have minded seeing, but instead they sat in the den off the living room—smaller windows—listening to CDs and reading. Gretchen's tastes hadn't changed since she and Sam had been together. She was still partial to Sheryl Crow, Rosanne Cash, Melissa Etheridge, Shania Twain, and Mariah Carey. The last three he could take or leave. He hadn't spent much time thinking about Gretchen since they'd parted—it was unproductive and pointless, Sam always told himself—but she always crossed his mind when he heard Mariah Carey singing "All I Want for Christmas Is You." When the song began to play from Gretchen's speakers—the slow-build-up intro followed by the pounding Wall of Sound piano and drums—he looked up from the magazine he'd been flipping through and glanced at her. She was looking back at him, with her book—a memoir about public health in Cambodia—turned over in her lap.

"I know you don't like Mariah Carey, but you have to admit, this is a great song," she said.

"I admit it," Sam said, looking back at the magazine. "It's a guilty pleasure."

"You want to talk?"

"About what?"

"About how we ended up . . . where we are. About where we're going. Both of us."

"As soon as we get a few problems cleared up here, I'm going back to Minneapolis."

He glanced again at Gretchen. The look in her eyes was not exactly pleading, but she seemed to be asking Sam to open up to her. About what, he couldn't be sure. Did she want him to ask her to come back to him? He didn't want that. Not anymore. Was she just looking for intimate conversation, or an arm around her shoulder, maybe a little physical contact on a cold, tense night? Sam didn't think he ought to do that, either. It made him furious that her out-of-control ex-husband was putting her through hell, and he wasn't going to leave until he was sure she was safe, but digging into the past had not been part of the agreement. Maybe he should have realized that old ground was inevitable when he agreed to come to Green Bay. But he'd have come anyway. He just had to figure out how to help Gretchen without hurting either of them.

"I'm sorry I brought it up," Gretchen said. She turned her book over. "It wasn't fair."

Mariah Carey was singing that she just wanted to see her baby standing outside her door, and Sam thought about the possibility that Scott could show up at any minute.

"Life isn't fair," Sam said. "You just have to get used to that."

"That's kind of glib."

"I suppose."

"Do you think Donna Larson is getting used to the idea that life isn't fair?"

"No. But nothing will bring Ed back. She's got to do what we all have to do: Face reality, and move on."

"Did I do this to you?"

"Do what?"

"Make you so callous? I remember a more sensitive guy."

"You helped, I suppose. But being a cop really teaches you how to shut down when you have to. I'm not as callous as you think I am, by the way."

"Really?"

"I miss Caroline, and I wish I could figure out how to make things work for us."

"You don't have to stay, you know."

"Yes, I do. I gave my word to you, and to Frank. I accepted a job. I can't walk away from that."

"What would Caroline want you to do?"

"I think she'd want me to come to Tucson now. But I'm not going to. Is that callous?"

"Yeah, but in a good way."

Gretchen smiled and went back to her book.

SAM SLEPT WITH HIS GUN on the nightstand. In the morning, he again had breakfast with Gretchen, and when she left for Lambeau, he followed her in his car, watched as she entered the stadium, then headed to Green Bay Memorial Hospital to talk to Stephen Kleinschmidt.

On the matter of selling the team to a private owner, Kleinschmidt and Mike Henderson were two of the three definite "no" votes—along with Frank Janaszak—remaining on the Packers' executive committee. Sam needed to find out what they were thinking now that Ed Larson was gone, and what they were doing to protect themselves.

He parked on the third floor of the ramp across the street from the six-story building, took the stairs down to the second floor, and walked through the skyway to the hospital. He introduced himself to the receptionist and asked to see Kleinschmidt. He wasn't sure a hospital CEO like Kleinschmidt would be able to make time for an unannounced visit, and the receptionist didn't look encouraging. But she put the request through, and was told to direct Sam to the executive offices on the sixth floor.

Kleinschmidt was on his feet in front of his desk, waiting for Sam to walk in. He was a clean-shaven man of about fifty with a ruddy complexion, curly gray hair, and an expensive suit and tie. He appeared to be in good shape, as would befit a health executive. His office was spacious, uncluttered, and antiseptic—the kind of place a benefactor would feel comfortable writing out a check with lots of zeros at the end.

"I'm glad to meet you," Kleinschmidt said, giving Sam a professional handshake. "Frank told me you'd probably be coming by. Have a seat."

Kleinschmidt sat down on a couch in the corner of his office. Sam took a chair on the other side of a marble table.

"Have you heard from Doc Mueller since he got back from Lake Minocqua?" Sam asked.

"No. Doc and I aren't on the best of terms these days."

"What's that about?"

"Mostly about this meeting coming up next week. I don't agree with him at all. The Packers should always be publicly owned."

"Is that all?"

"Well, we had a kind of falling out a few years ago, when he started practicing medicine again. He was using his celebrity status to cherry-pick some of our wealthiest patients. The other doctors didn't care for that, and I don't blame them. I mean, you could understand why a Packers fan would rather be seen by a former Packers team physician who once took Vince Lombardi's blood pressure. That didn't make it right, or ethical."

"How'd you resolve it?"

"I asked him to stop soliciting patients at the hospital. He refused—but awhile later he stopped practicing again. Sent his patients back to their original doctors. I asked him why, and he just said he didn't need it anymore."

"Did you know about his gambling?"

"We all know Doc likes to gamble. I couldn't say whether it was a problem or not. It's not really any of my business."

"You're on the executive committee of an NFL team. Doesn't gambling concern you?"

"The league policy covers the players and coaches. Not the executives. If I had any reason to think what Doc was doing was affecting the outcome of games, I'd have been concerned. But I'm sure that's not true. Why? Do you know otherwise?"

"No. But I'm trying to figure out why Mueller is so hell-bent on selling the team. Could he be in for a cut?"

"I suppose anything is possible. But I have to be honest with you—I think he makes some sense. My 'no' vote is basically emotional. I've lived here all my life, and I can't conceive of the Packers being owned by an individual or a corporation. I'm like Ed and Frank—it just wouldn't be right. But Doc has made some pretty convincing arguments. We're in terrible shape right now as a franchise, and we—those of us on the committee—have to accept a lot of the responsibility for that. We haven't met the challenges. Something has to be done, and the way I see it, Doc is just trying to find the answer. I don't agree with him, and I'm not going to vote with him, but I don't fault him for trying."

Sam figured Kleinschmidt for a clear-headed, conservative, bottom-line guy. He was responsible for two Green Bay institutions, and he understood how the real world worked. To make a hospital or a football team successful, you needed money and community support. The public still wanted the Packers to belong to them, not to an owner, so that's where Kleinschmidt was siding. But that could change. Not soon enough for Mueller, though.

"I'm sorry I have to ask you this, Stephen, but do you think Mueller might have . . . engineered that accident at Lake Minocqua?"

Kleinschmidt looked away for a moment. The idea had obviously occurred to him, but he wasn't eager to discuss it.

"I want to be careful here," he finally said. "Doc and Ed were friends for more than twenty years. Good friends. Their wives did everything together. As I've said, Doc and I have had our differences, but I don't want to think he could have . . . done something like that to a man I know he liked and respected."

"You don't want to think that. But do you?"

Another hesitation. Then: "Part of me does."

"I understand the committee is going to approve Boulanger at next week's meeting to take Ed's spot on the committee. He wants to sell. Mueller will have a four-to-three majority."

"I know. But he needs at least a five-to-two margin, or the board of directors—which basically means the public—will never accept it. He knows that."

"So how does that make you feel?"

"You mean . . . ?"

Kleinschmidt looked at Sam with something short of surprise. He knew what Sam was asking, but it was hard for him to hear it said out loud.

"Do you feel safe?"

"Not really."

There were too many balls in the air. Too many people who needed protection—whether or not they knew it, or admitted it. Sam's first instinct would have been to have Horvath orchestrate the necessary security to safeguard Janaszak, Kleinschmidt, and Henderson. Then he could continue his investigation and still be able to keep an eye on Gretchen. But Horvath was out. Not only did Sam not trust him, but according to Janaszak, Horvath had the Green Bay Police Department behind him, too. The GBPD was responsible for stadium security, and the local cops—at least eighty for each game—counted on the overtime they earned working Packers games. They would certainly be loyal to Horvath unless there was a strong case against him. Sam couldn't go in to the chief and expect him to provide protection for Packers executives. The chief would call Horvath, and Horvath would tell him it wasn't necessary.

"I don't think you'd be overreacting to hire a bodyguard," Sam told Kleinschmidt.

"And a food taster?" Kleinschmidt laughed weakly at his own joke.

"Just be careful. Park your car in a lighted place. Don't walk outside alone, if you can help it. Install a security system at your house. I'll do what I can to protect you—to give you a heads-up if I know something. But I can't be everywhere, and I don't have a staff. How about hospital security? Can you free up somebody here to stay near you?"

"How do I explain it to the board? We're understaffed here, too. God, what a mess."

"Maybe we're wrong—maybe I'm wrong about Mueller."

"I hope you are," Kleinschmidt said. But he didn't sound convinced.

Sam thanked Kleinschmidt for his time, gave him his card, and excused himself. When he left Kleinschmidt's office, he looked up and down the corridor. There were glass-walled suites on either side, several other office doors down a perpendicular hallway, and a half-circle receptionist/secretary's desk outside the elevator doors. It wouldn't be hard for a guy with a gun to come up the elevator, walk into the CEO's office, pop him, and walk back out before anyone knew what happened.

The good news was, that didn't seem like Mueller's style. Horvath's, maybe.

JIM ESCHER WAS WAITING on the third floor of the parking ramp, sitting in his Tacoma pickup ten spaces away from Skarda's Cherokee. He thought about the shotgun or the Colt, but getting out of the car seemed like a bad idea. Somebody could come up the ramp at any time. The Remington was the way to go. He was no more than thirty feet from the stairway door that Skarda had taken to enter the hospital. He wouldn't even need the scope. A ten-year-old couldn't miss from this distance. He rolled the window down about five inches and turned himself sideways in the truck cab. He put the barrel of the rifle out the window and aimed at the "THIRD FLOOR" sign next to the door.

Head high.

Perfect.

Skarda emerged through the stairwell door.

FOURTEEN

There was no one else visible in the ramp. Escher had the Remington in his hands, Skarda in his sights. A clear shot.

But he didn't pull the trigger.

Even in the ramp, the temperature was no more than five above, and the breath was steaming out of Skarda's mouth. A cloud of vapor enshrouded his head as he walked to his parking space. It made accurate aiming almost impossible, and Escher didn't want to risk a body shot. He couldn't afford to leave Skarda alive. He knew he'd have one chance at him, and it had to be money.

Skarda got in the Cherokee, backed out and headed down the curving exit. Escher put the Remington on the back seat and waited until Skarda's brake lights were no longer visible before backing out of his own space and following him down. He didn't want to have to pull up directly behind Skarda at the cashier's window. The guy was a detective, a former cop. He'd notice things. Escher didn't want to be one of the things Skarda noticed if he happened to glance in his rear-view mirror while waiting for change.

Yet he couldn't let Skarda out of his sight, either. He'd called Horvath, but Horvath didn't know where Skarda was going today, so Escher had to get up before dawn and park on a side street around the corner from Gretchen Kahler's house, waiting for Skarda's Cherokee to pull away from the driveway. He'd followed Skarda to the hospital, and when he saw the ramp, he thought he might be able to get a shot at him. Now he'd have to tail him to his next stop.

When Escher came around the curve in the ramp, he could see Skarda's SUV stopped at the cashier's window. Escher stopped, waiting for Skarda to get his change and pull out. That's when he noticed another car coming down the ramp behind him. Escher waited, hoping Skarda would pull out, but the cashier's window was still closed. What the hell was the hold up?

The driver behind Escher tapped his horn. Escher watched to see if Skarda's head turned, but he seemed to be looking straight forward. Then the driver behind Escher leaned on the horn. Escher turned on his emergency brake lights and turned to look at the driver behind him, a professional-looking man in a camel-hair coat. Probably a doctor, on his way to some big, important consult—or to catch a plane for a golf vacation. Escher looked at the driver and held his hands up in a helpless gesture, as if to say he didn't know what was wrong with his car. The driver behind him shook his head and got out. Escher didn't dare turn his face back to look at Skarda's SUV. Skarda had to have heard the long horn honk, and must have turned to see what was going on. Escher couldn't let Skarda see his face.

He covered the rifle on the back seat with a blanket, and rolled his window down as the man in the camel-hair coat approached.

"What the hell's the problem?" the man asked. "Stall?"

"I don't know," Escher said. "It could be the battery."

"Well, pop the hood. I'll take a look. I've got cables, if we need them."

The man walked to the front of the car, and Escher allowed his gaze to follow him. He could see the cross-arm raising in front of Skarda's SUV, and watched him pull out onto the street, taking a right. He couldn't lose him.

"Never mind," Escher said. He rolled up his window and accelerated quickly to the pay window, leaving the man standing on the ramp with his arms held palm-up at his sides. Another car was now waiting behind him, horn blasting away.

"What's the problem up there?" the cashier asked as Escher handed her a ten.

"Nothing." Escher ignored her and watched Skarda gain distance down the street. "Could you hurry it up?"

"Sorry," she said. A cloud of vapor escaped her mouth as she leaned toward the open window. "My fingers are cold."

Escher grabbed his change and blew out of the ramp as soon as the arm lifted. He could see the Cherokee two blocks away, talking a left. He managed to make up enough ground to see Skarda take the on-ramp to I-43 south. He was back within a few car lengths when Skarda exited on Mason Street. He headed east, took a left, and pulled into Henderson's Auto Plaza. Escher continued past, then turned around at the next corner, drove back and parked across the street from the dealership. The Cherokee was in one of the customer parking spaces outside the front door. He could see Skarda inside, through the showroom's two-story, floor-to-ceiling glass wall.

"Is Mike Henderson in?"

Sam was standing at a desk in the showroom where an attractive young woman wearing a thick green Packers sweater sat at a telephone switchboard. A nameplate on the counter above her desk said "Marcie."

"I think he's upstairs in his office," Marcie said. "Can I tell him your name?"

Sam introduced himself, and mentioned that he was with the Packers. Janaszak had said he was going to contact all the executive committee members about Sam paying them a visit, but it was possible Henderson hadn't gotten the word, or had forgotten Sam's name.

"Mike Henderson, you've got a visitor at the front desk," Marcie said into the intercom. Her voice could be heard echoing through the showroom. Sam took a seat by her desk and waited.

Escher HAD THE DEER RIFLE IN HIS LAP, and he could see Skarda sit down in a chair in the showroom lobby. He slid to his left in the truck cab until his back was against the passenger door. He bent his left leg up on the seat and balanced the Remington on his knee. The shot was about 200 feet—almost the same distance as when he'd nailed that tree-stand poacher. With the scope, Skarda's head looked as big as a basketball. The showroom window might alter the path of the slug slightly, but not enough to turn a center shot into a miss. Escher knew he wouldn't miss.

He put the rifle down. There wasn't much traffic—too cold for most people to be out kicking tires at an auto dealership—but he didn't want to take the chance that someone passing by, or looking out the showroom window, might notice him with the rifle. He'd decide when the time was right to take the shot, and get the hell out of there. Then he'd call Mueller and collect his hundred grand.

Sam STOOD UP WHEN HE SAW a big man in a dark suit walking toward him from the bottom of the stairway.

"Sam? Mike Henderson. Glad to meet you."

Henderson had a deep, resonant voice—the kind that suggested he did his own TV and radio commercials. He put out a large paw and shook Sam's hand. Up close, Sam could see that the suit had subtle green and gold piping.

"Like it?" Henderson said. He pulled open the lapels. On the inside right lining was the white Packers "G," outlined in green and circled in gold; on the inside left lining was the word "Packers" in green and gold lettering.

"The suit matches the socks," Henderson said, grinning.

He lifted his pants cuffs, and showed off a pair of gold socks with green-and-white "G" emblems in a checkerboard pattern.

Henderson looked like he had played college football, probably on the offensive line. He stood at least 6-4, with a nest of thick brown hair atop his round, cherubic face. A born glad-hander, Sam surmised. A guy you had to try hard not to like.

"Let's go up to my office," Henderson said. "That's where I keep the booze."

He winked at the receptionist, who smiled back.

Unlike Kleinschmidt's fastidious operating room of an office, Henderson's lair looked as if it had been decorated in Early College Dorm. There were plastic basketball nets on three walls, Packers schedules and player posters substituting for wallpaper, and at least a dozen bobblehead dolls with Green Bay jerseys and helmets lining the edge of his desk. On the wall behind the desk was a framed photo of Henderson shaking hands with Brett Favre at what looked to be a training-camp practice field.

"It's not gonna happen," Henderson said, after they'd both sat down.

"What's that?" Sam asked.

"The team is not gonna be sold. Not as long as I'm around."

"I think Ed Larson said that, too."

"Yeah, he did. Poor son of a bitch."

"After Boulanger's approved at next week's meeting, Mueller'll have the votes."

"Maybe so. But he doesn't have the fans, and he doesn't have the board. Not yet, anyway."

"Any idea if he's got a buyer lined up?"

Henderson looked around—a reflexive gesture, Sam realized, from days gone by when he'd been a mere salesman, rather than owner of his own dealerships. Pretend to check to see if the sales manager is listening, then shoot the buyer a number.

"You didn't get this from me, but the name I hear is Purdy McCutcheon."

"Who's that?"

"Black businessman from Atlanta. Played college ball at Georgia Tech, got a tryout with the Falcons, but got cut and went into business. Made a pile of money in real estate, from what I hear."

"Enough to buy an NFL franchise?"

"He's got investors. I don't know who they are, but one guy doesn't buy a team these days. You put a team of limited partners together. Purdy would be the front guy."

"Still, the minimum price of an NFL team now is around eight hundred million, right?"

"Yeah, that's about right. You can't smell the Cowboys or the Patriots for that kind of money, but you could buy a few clubs for eight."

"Including the Packers?"

"Definitely—if they were for sale. The shareholders would have to approve a change in the articles of incorporation to allow an individual to own more than two hundred thousand shares. The last hundred and twenty thousand shares sold were valued at two hundred bucks apiece, and we don't have to pay that much to buy them back. We don't have to buy them back at all, to be honest. But even if we did, that's just twenty-four million dollars. You throw in the value of Lambeau Field—unless the city decides to keep it—and you could still buy this team for a whole lot cheaper than the going price."

"So if somebody could buy the Packers, they'd be getting a steal."

"Better'n any deal I've ever given somebody."

Henderson gave out a belly laugh and leaned over to reach a drawer behind his desk. It turned out to be a mini-refrigerator. Henderson pulled it open, reached in, and came up with a pair of cold cans of Miller Lite.

"Want one?" he said to Sam. "I get 'em free from the brewery."

"No thanks—but go head."

"Don't mind if I do."

Henderson popped the top on his beer and took a swallow.

"Sellin' cars is thirsty work, I don't mind tellin' you. Especially on days like today, when it's so cold you might as well not have opened the doors."

Sam sat in his chair and watched Henderson take another sip of his beer. It was hard to imagine Mike Henderson having a problem with anybody in Green Bay, much less a fellow committee member. But he clearly understood what was going on, and had to have some reservations about Doc Mueller.

"How long have you been on the committee, Mike?"

"Seven years."

"Did you know Doc Mueller before that?"

"No, but I kind of idolized him, you know? He was the last link to the glory years, as they say. I mean, Bart Starr and those guys still come around, but Doc's been here every year, doing whatever it takes to make the team better."

"Do you like him?"

"Sure I do. Everybody does."

Not everybody. Sam decided not to bring it up his discussion with Klein-schmidt.

"What about the accident at Lake Minocqua? Were you at all suspicious?"

"Not at all. Doc and Ed have been friends for years. Sure, we lost a vote, and it looks like Doc is going to gain a vote. But those are separate deals. That's what I think, anyway."

"So you don't feel in danger, too?"

"Me? Hell no. What, you think somebody would try to kill me to get rid of my 'no' vote? That's funny."

Henderson actually did laugh at the idea, and then popped the top on the sec-ond beer.

"Sure you don't want one?" he said, wiping foam from his lip.

"No, thanks. I've got to be going. I do want to tell you, though, that you ought to be a little cautious until this is resolved."

"Cautious, how?"

"Don't go places by yourself. Install a security system at your house, if you don't already have one."

"Never had one. Don't need it."

"I know this sounds crazy, but there's hundreds of millions of dollars riding on your vote, Mike. Frank Janaszak just wants to be sure you're going to be around to cast it."

"Tell Frank to worry about himself. He could start by laying off the cheeseburgers. Hell, I'll tell him myself. I'll call him as soon as we're done here."

"That's all I've got," Sam said.

"Okay, then. I'll walk you out."

Henderson stood up, finished the second beer in two long swallows, and tossed the empty through one of his basketball hoops. It landed in a trash barrel underneath.

"That was definitely three-point range," Henderson said with a grin.

"Your toe was on the line," Sam said. "Two points."

"Awwww . . ."

They walked down the stairs to the main floor, and Henderson stayed with Sam as they crossed the showroom.

"What do you drive these days, Sam?"

"Jeep Cherokee. Just bought it a few weeks ago."

"I can get you into a Yukon for next to nothing if you're ready to move up."

"Thanks, but . . ."

The next sound they heard was the front window shattering, glass shards blowing inward from the impact of a bullet fired from somewhere outside. Sam instinctively dived for the floor, and saw Henderson falling next to him. Marcie the receptionist screamed, and a blast of frigid air gushed into the showroom. Sam crawled behind Marcie's desk, waiting to hear another gunshot. He looked out the shattered window and caught a glimpse of a truck pulling away, heading south. White, maybe off-white. Sam couldn't tell the make.

Salesmen ran to their fallen boss from their main floor offices while Marcie continued to scream "Mike! Mike!"

Sam saw Henderson lying face down, covered with pieces of broken glass, his hands around his face and blood dripping onto the floor. Then he slowly lifted his head.

"Is the fun over?" Henderson said.

He rolled to his left side and examined his hands. They were cut from the broken glass on the floor, but he hadn't been hit by the bullet.

"You okay?" Sam asked.

"You know, I don't mind a dissatisfied customer now and then, but I wish they'd just come and talk to me."

The salesmen began laughing. Henderson got to his feet and inspected his suit. There were a couple of tears in the sleeves.

"Gotta get me a new one of these," he said. "Dang. That's four hundred bucks right there. Marcie, would you call the police, darlin'?"

ONE OF THE COPS WHO CAME into the showroom fifteen minutes later was the same plainclothes detective who'd been sitting in Gretchen's living room the night someone fired a shot through her window. VanHoff. He recognized Sam immediately.

"What's going on here, Mike?" VanHoff asked.

"Looks like somebody took a shot at me, Bob."

"Everybody okay?"

"Just some cuts."

He held up his hands, bandaged with a first aid kit one of the mechanics had fetched from the garage. Marcie was still sniffling at her desk, but Henderson had never lost his bravado.

"Was this guy here when it happened?" VanHoff said. He jerked a thumb toward Sam.

"Yeah. We were standing right next to each other. Good thing these windows are an inch and a half thick."

"You might want to stay away from . . . Skarda, right?" VanHoff said. "He's mixed up in a domestic deal. I'm thinking the ex-husband is gunning for him. We pulled a bullet out of the wall at his girlfriend's place two nights ago."

Sam wasn't going to argue with VanHoff. He was sure the bullet had been meant for Henderson, but the cops weren't going to buy that, especially when they had the easier story in front of them: jealous ex-husband stalking the new boyfriend.

"Anybody see the shooter?" VanHoff asked.

"I saw a truck pull away," Sam said. "White or off-white, looked kind of dirty. I think it was an extended cab. I couldn't tell you the make."

"What does the ex-husband drive?"

"Chevy Trailblazer."

"What color?"

"Silver."

"Could be the same vehicle."

It wasn't. An extended-cab pickup wasn't an SUV, and silver wasn't white. But Sam was going to let VanHoff draw his own conclusions. Right now he was worried about Gretchen getting home safely, and being alone in the house. If the cops stepped up their efforts to find Scott Krebbs, so much the better.

VanHoff asked Sam what he was doing there, and seemed satisfied with the answer.

"If we're done here, I should be going," Sam said. VanHoff nodded.

"Thanks for coming by, Sam," Henderson said. "I'd shake your hand, but I'd get blood all over you."

"That's okay, Mike. Please be careful."

The car dealer gave him a serious look and a nod. He wasn't buying the cops' explanation, either.

FIFTEEN

Joe Horvath was walking the upper rows on the north end of an empty Lambeau Field, looking under the seats. The field below was indeed becoming a frozen tundra. The twenty-five-mile-per-hour winds that whipped across the combination of Kentucky Bluegrass and synthetic Field Turf had the effect of making three degrees Fahrenheit feel like twenty below. The Sunday forecast was one of the worst game-day outlooks Horvath could remember: light snow, gusting northwest winds, and a high of five below zero. Thirty miles of radiant heating pipe under the field would keep the turf playable, but the same could not be said for the open rows of metal bench seats. Under most of the seats, snow that could not be removed by the volunteers had turned to packed ice. It was a certainty that one unlucky Lambeau visitor was going to slip on the ice and hurt his back and neck on Sunday. With these conditions, there might be more.

His cell phone rang. He took his right glove off, put it under his arm and flipped open the phone, putting it under the earflap of his hat.

"Horvath."

"Hi, Joe. It's Bob VanHoff."

"Yeah, Bob, what's up?"

"Thought you'd want to know about a shooting at Henderson's Auto Plaza earlier today."

"Henderson? Is he okay?"

"Yeah, yeah, nobody was hit. One bullet through the showroom window. Looks like a .30-.06. We found the shell."

"Got a shooter? Or a motive?"

Horvath was audibly shaking when he asked VanHoff the question. His teeth had begun to chatter, and he couldn't tell whether the cause was the bitter wind or the possibility that VanHoff was on to something. He put his glove back on before his hand got frostbite.

"No shooter, but we think it might be that ex-husband of your team physician. Gretchen . . . uh, Kahler. They're recently divorced, right? She's got a restraining order. But, the guy's a nut case. We think he fired a shot through her living-room window the other night. She's got a friend visiting her, guy named Sam Skarda. He was with Henderson today. Says he's working for you. Is that right?"

"Yeah, yeah . . . he's doing some background checks for us."

"Well, he was standing right next to Henderson when the shot was fired, so we're looking at the ex. Scott Krebbs. We think he's trying to kill Skarda. Bullet deflected a little through that thick glass, or he probably would have got the job done."

"Where's Krebbs?"

"Dunno. Can't find him. I'll put a couple more guys on it. He's getting pretty reckless. But I thought you'd want to know Mike's all right."

"Good. Glad to hear it."

"You gonna need the usual number of cops on Sunday?"

"Yeah. With the weather, we could have some traffic problems."

"Okay. Well, if anything breaks on this Krebbs deal, we'll let you know."

"Thanks, Bob. Appreciate the call."

Horvath closed his phone, shoved it into his pocket and started walking to the nearest exit.

Escher. He was 100 percent certain. Why in god's name had Mueller ever trusted that stump-jumping hillbilly?

Of course, they had to trust somebody. Horvath couldn't do everything. He had to keep his hands as clean as possible until the ownership transfer took place.

Horvath had stumbled into his arrangement with Mueller. He hadn't been looking for more money or a better job, but he'd made a bad mistake one night and his circumstances had changed dramatically. It had turned out all right, though. He would come out of this better than he'd ever imagined.

He'd never cared all that much for sports, as a kid growing up in Fond du Lac. He loved to hunt and fish with his dad, but he came to realize that his dad's first love was brandy, and his second love was beer. He watched his old man knock the crap out of his mom, then desert the family when Joe was fourteen. Joe went to work when he was a sophomore in high school, doing whatever he could to help support his mother and two younger brothers. He tried college, but working full time and going to class was too much. Because he'd always loved guns—and because he'd been a hell-raiser himself, not unacquainted with the back seat of a squad car—cop work appealed to him. He got his first job in the little town of Augusta, Wisconsin, then caught on with the Green Bay PD. He decided to try for the FBI, so he began attending night classes at UW-Green Bay, studying criminal justice and finally earning his degree. The FBI hired him a year later.

He traveled constantly with the FBI, and never had the time—or the personality—to make it work with a woman. But he did want a house and some hunting dogs—so when the Green Bay security job opened up, he asked several of his old cop pals to put in a good word for him. The NFL liked FBI agents. He got the job. A year after he was hired, he bought a couple of acres out in Sobieski. There was plenty of grunt work running the Packers security department, and not as much time to time to hunt and fish as he'd hoped. He spent most of his off hours alone, training and exercising his dogs—and drinking. But he didn't do that anymore.

Horvath went up to the concourse level, walking around the curve of the bowl until he reached the doorway to the Atrium. He crossed the walkway to the elevators and went down to the parking level, exiting the stadium through the employee entrance. He got into the cab of his Tahoe, started the engine, and called Doc Mueller.

When Horvath explained to Mueller what he'd just heard from the Green Bay Police, Mueller told him to stay in his car and wait for a call from him. Ten minutes later, his phone rang.

"I called our friend in Chicago. He's furious. He thinks this will convince the cops we're trying to take out all the committee members."

"That's not what the cops think. VanHoff figures it's Krebbs gunning for Skarda."

"Then we caught a break. Listen to me: Call Escher and tell him he fucked up. We won't stand for fuckups. We have to convince the cops that they're right about Krebbs. Send Escher over to Gretchen's house tonight, and tell him he's got to kill both her and Skarda. He's got to make it look like a jealous ex-husband did it."

"How's he supposed to do that? Skarda's not dumb. He'll have the house locked tight as a drum."

"Don't worry about that. Escher can get into any place. He's been doing cabin break-ins around Minocqua for years. That's how I found out about him."

"Okay. If he does it right, it should work. He's gotta use an untraceable gun, leave it at the scene, and get the hell out of there. And no fingerprints. You think Escher can handle that?"

"Sure. Tell him we'll throw in another fifty grand for killing Gretchen. That should motivate him. But if it doesn't, tell him . . . tell him if he doesn't kill them both, we'll all get caught. If that happens, he's going down as an accessory to Ed Larson's murder."

"So we're promising him a hundred fifty grand, total?"

"Yeah. But you gotta figure out a way of getting rid of Escher as soon as he takes care of business tonight. Arrange to meet him somewhere up north to pay him off. Bury him under the snow. Or chop a hole in the ice and stuff him into a lake somewhere. No one will miss him."

"Got it."

Horvath closed his phone and shivered again. The heater just didn't work fast enough on days like this.

Sᴀᴍ ᴡᴀs ᴡᴀɪᴛɪɴɢ ɪɴ ᴛʜᴇ ᴅʀɪᴠᴇᴡᴀʏ when Gretchen pulled her car in and opened the garage door with her automatic opener. She waved to him as she drove past, smiling in a way that suggested she hadn't heard about the shooting at Henderson's Auto Plaza. He got out of his car and followed her into the house through the garage.

When he told her what happened, the color drained from her face.

"Was it Scott?"

"No," Sam said. He walked over to the living-room window and pointed to the patch over the bullet hole. "I'm pretty sure this was done with a handgun. The gunshot at Henderson's had to be a rifle. Nobody's dumb enough to use a handgun to try to kill somebody through a window from 200 feet away."

"Who, then?"

"I'm not sure. The cops think it was Scott, shooting at me. But I think the bullet was intended for Mike Henderson."

"Then . . . Mueller?"

"I doubt it. He's not going to risk getting his hands dirty."

"Horvath?"

"No. He's got to be accountable for his whereabouts. He can't follow somebody around Green Bay all day looking for a chance to take a shot with a rifle."

"Who, then?"

"I don't know. But whoever it is, he's in a hurry to get the job done. There's an executive committee meeting next week. Maybe Mueller wants to get rid of another vote. Force the committee to make a decision on the sale."

Gretchen stood near the stairs in the foyer, still wearing her heavy winter coat. Without speaking, she walked into the kitchen and picked up her car keys from the table.

"Let's get out of here," she said when she returned to the foyer.

"Where?"

"Anywhere but here. I'm not going to spend another night sitting around my own house, wondering if Scott's out there with a gun."

"Okay," Sam said. "It's Friday night in Green Bay on a Packers weekend. Show me Titletown."

Sᴄᴏᴛᴛ Kʀᴇʙʙs ᴡᴀs sɪᴛᴛɪɴɢ ᴀʟᴏɴᴇ at the End Zone sports bar in Appleton. No one knew him here. No one was likely to be looking for him in Appleton. It was a forty-minute drive south along the frozen Fox River from Green Bay, far enough to avoid the cops who were supposedly trying to find him, close enough to slip back into town anytime he wanted to.

Tonight, he wanted to.

He looked at the digital read-out on the Budweiser Packers clock above the row of schnapps bottles: 7:53. He heard the stew of sports audio coming from the projector TVs around the room—the NASCAR highlights on one, the Bucks-Cavaliers game on another, the NHL game across the room, and the Packers review and preview show from every corner of the bar. It was loud, warm, and anonymous in here. It was cold and dangerous out there. But he knew he had to go back tonight. Had to.

He finished his Newcastle and raised a hand at the bartender, a young guy with spiky hair, looking just out of college, or still working his way through. The bartender noticed him and drew another glass from the tap. He put the beer down in front of Krebbs and picked up the empty.

"Keep the tab open?"

"Yeah," Krebbs said. "Give me a shot of Johnny Walker Red, too."

He hadn't always been this guy, sitting in a bar forty miles away from where he belonged, drinking alone. He'd been going places once. Maybe the NBA, or at least coaching a college team. Or maybe a pro sports executive. The sky was the limit, back then.

Back when he'd first met Gretchen.

He took another long sip. She'd liked his physique right away. He could always tell. Girls looked at jocks differently than they looked at regular guys. And Krebbs wasn't dumb, like a lot of the guys he'd played with. When he first met Gretchen, she was impressed with his ability to talk about human kinesiology and nutrition. Most guys she met were intimidated by her medical knowledge, but Scott wasn't. He'd offered to help her study. She took him up on it.

Another swig, another memory of Gretchen floating through his mind: the first time they'd had sex. He'd been out running with her along Lake Monona in Madison. She was training for a 20K. He was helping her train, and trying to get into her shorts. He loved watching her taut ass bouncing rhythmically ahead of him, the ripple of her thighs as each stride landed and then pushed off again. She was a machine, so steady and compact, yet graceful. She could run all day, it seemed. But that day it rained, and they cut the run short, veering back to Krebbs's apartment. Her top was plastered to her chest. He could see her erect nipples through her shirt and thin running bra. It was a memory that never left him, a memory he never wanted to let go of. He'd taken his own shirt off, and noticed Gretchen staring at him. He took the chance of walking over to her and kissing her, then started to pull her wet shirt up from each side, telling her, lamely, that it would be best for her to get out of her wet clothes.

He expected resistance, as always. She wasn't ready for that, she'd told him several times. This time, she was ready. She held her arms above her head as Krebbs peeled the wet shirt up and off her. Her white sports bra might as well have been transparent. Soon that was lying in a wet heap on the floor with her shirt, and Krebbs's hands were all over her small breasts as she pulled him toward her with her arms around his neck, kissing him hungrily. They lay down on a nearby couch together, Gretchen tugging his shorts down to his knees. She pulled her own shorts off and straddled him, arching her back while he continued to envelop her breasts with his big hands.

He didn't know why Gretchen had chosen that day, but of all their times together, that was still the one that he came back to, over and over, remembering how good, how fresh, how overpowering it had been.

For some reason, and Krebbs could not understand why, it had never been quite that good again. It was as though he'd somehow disappointed her, and he always wondered what was going on in her head—what standard it was that he couldn't quite reach. Why the slow fade to complacency, to boredom, after that rainy afternoon? At first he couldn't believe there was another man. Then, he couldn't believe that there wasn't. She was not the type to let sex rule her decisions, but she was a woman, and he'd felt her craving that first time. Even before they were married, Krebbs sensed that he was barely hanging on to Gretchen. That made him doubt himself for the first time since he'd picked up a basketball. That made him hang out with his friends more often, looking for those pats on the back, those rehashed stories of how many points he'd scored that night against Germantown, or how he'd made that all-state guard from Stevens Point look like a JV player. That got him drinking more, because that's what you do when you and the other old jocks realize there aren't going to be any new stories; and that—he had to be honest—didn't bring him and Gretchen any closer together.

But that didn't excuse her. No, it did not. It *did not excuse her*. At some point that he couldn't quite recall, she'd given up on him. Now it was Packers this, Packers that, the new running back from Iowa State, the free-agent tackle from Boston University, the assistant linebackers coach, the ticket manager, the assistant general manager—the team president. She was getting the men she needed somewhere else. Maybe it was sex, maybe it wasn't—but in time, he knew it would be. She was through with him, through with their marriage. She was moving on without him.

It hadn't occurred to Krebbs at first that she might be moving not forward, but backward. Maybe she was still hung up on someone from her past. Like Skarda.

He'd heard about him, but not much. Gretchen didn't go into detail about who she'd known or what she'd done. He knew she'd worked in the Twin Cities as a paramedic before moving to Madison to attend medical school. He knew she'd dated a few guys. He knew the last guy she was with before starting med school was Sam Skarda, a Minneapolis police detective. Krebbs never thought he'd show up at their house, but damn it, he did. It explained a lot. Maybe it explained everything. He'd never really had a chance with Gretchen—not with Skarda still out there somewhere. Well, now he was here. In fact, he was staying with Gretchen, supposedly to protect her from her ex-husband. Well, fuck that. Fuck the restraining order. Fuck the cops. And fuck them both.

"Another one?" the bartender asked.

"No. They're finished. I'm finished."

SIXTEEN

Gretchen turned her Volvo off Lombardi Avenue onto Holmgren Way, then took a left on Brett Favre Pass, slowly creeping along with the other cars trying to find parking places somewhere near Brett Favre's Steakhouse. Sam knew they were in the heart of Titletown when they passed the ten-foot-tall kiosk with the black five-foot "4" on top, looking over the tangle of traffic the way the legendary quarterback once looked over a defensive secondary.

They squeezed into a spot in a parking lot two blocks from the restaurant and pulled on their hats and gloves for the brisk, windy walk. Despite the gusts of wind and the snow that glazed the pavement, there was a carnival atmosphere in the air. Lambeau Field was visible two blocks away. The bright brake lights of dozens of slow-moving cars lit up the surrounding snowbanks like little pink nightlights. Bundled bodies scurried into and out of the steakhouse, their breath creating a cloud of beer-flavored good cheer. The Packers might have been 1 and 12, but that wasn't keeping the hard-core faithful from enjoying one of only ten scheduled home-game Friday nights.

Inside the steakhouse, the foyer was a crush of well-insulated folks trying to work their way up to the harried young women at the reservation stand.

"Can you get us a table?" Sam asked Gretchen.

"Sure—in about two hours."

"What, the Packers team doctor doesn't have any pull at Brett Favre's?"

"Not yet. Maybe in ten, twenty years."

They moved slowly past the trophy case in the lobby, with the signed footballs, helmets, and one of Favre's MVP trophies. They passed the entrance to the gift shop, a narrow room decked floor-to-ceiling with hats, clothing, and autographed Favre merchandise. When they reached the front of the line, they were told it would be at least two hours for a table. There was no regret or sympathy in the young woman's voice. She'd been telling people the same thing all afternoon, and the place was still packed.

"What do you want to do?" Gretchen asked Sam.

"Is the food that good?"

"Actually, it is."

"Put our names in. We'll see how long I can last."

Sam glanced into the dining room on his right, a cozy, dimly lit wood-table, white-napkin area, the walls decorated with framed children's drawings of Favre, blown-up magazine covers, and a ten-foot-wide mural with the quarterback's face, superimposed over gold "MVP" lettering, staring coolly at the diners. Some of the customers were wearing coats and ties, nice sweaters, dresses. Others were wearing Packers sweatshirts, jerseys, and ballcaps.

To Sam's left was a crowded, noisy room with a mahogany bar that ran from one end to the other. There were tall bar tables in the center of the room amid the support columns, and there was a body occupying almost every square inch of sitting or standing space. Sam and Gretchen managed to squeeze inside, and while Gretchen worked her way toward the windows to find a place to stand, Sam slid, ducked, turned, and slithered to the bar. When he finally arrived, the couple in front of him offered to put in his order: two glasses of Leinie Red. Waiting for the bartender to get to his order, he watched as six buddies seated down the bar from him simultaneously chugged shots of Jaegermeister, slammed their empty glasses to the bar, and yelled "Go Pack!"

By the time Sam made it back to Gretchen's spot by the window, she was talking with the couple at the table next to her.

"They've been here since noon," she said, turning to Sam. "They come to Green Bay for a game once a year. They drive here to the steakhouse and have lunch, and stay all afternoon at the same table. Then they order dinner."

"I guess that beats waiting two hours for a table."

"Oh, quit whining. You won't starve."

"Did you tell them you're the team doctor?"

"No. They'd just ask me if I could introduce them to Brett Favre."

"And what would you tell them?"

"If I could introduce them, would we be crammed against this window?"

They eventually got a table, and Sam had to admit that the food and service were both excellent. He asked their server how much money she made in tips on a home-game weekend.

"Eight or nine hundred," she said.

"Has business fallen off at all the last couple of years?"

"Oh, yeah. The wait used to be three hours. The last year we went to the playoffs, I made twelve hundred in tips every weekend. Some people are still mad at Favre for leaving, but we're doing okay."

When the server left their table, Sam said to Gretchen, "Packermania can't last forever if the team keeps losing."

"I suppose you're right. When I was a kid, back in the eighties, it wasn't that hard to get Packers tickets. You could find a place to eat in Green Bay on a Friday night, no waiting. I suppose it could be that way again, one of these years."

"That's got to be Mueller's pitch to the committee."

"But so what?" Gretchen said. She gestured to the full dining room and the packed lobby. "We did fine as a publicly-owned team even before all this happened. It was a long, long time between Super Bowls. Nobody talked about selling the team."

"But that was before all this money came to town. Once you get used to this kind of an economy, it's tough to watch it slip away. Basically, Mueller is playing to the community's greed. It wouldn't be the first time that's worked."

"No, it wouldn't."

AFTER DINNER, GRETCHEN ASKED SAM what else he wanted to see in Green Bay.

"Where do the old players hang out? Some of the Lombardi guys must still be around."

"Let me call my uncle."

"Uncle?"

"Uncle Chet. He's lived here with Aunt Marilyn since the fifties. Knows everything there is to know about the Packers. You should see his basement. It must be the second-best collection of Packers stuff outside of the team museum."

"I didn't know you had an uncle here."

"Yeah, my dad's brother. You'll like him. He's a little nuts, but you'll like him."

"Does he know what's happening with you and Scott?"

"I don't think so. I didn't want to bother him."

"You should tell him."

"If I tell him, he'll want to help. If he knew about the restraining order, he'd insist that I move in with them. That'd just put him and Marilyn in danger. I won't do that."

She called Chet Kahler on her phone. While they talked, Sam gathered that she and Chet hadn't seen each other for a while. That was Gretchen: Go it alone, work it out by yourself. Asking for help shows weakness.

"Great. We'll meet you there," she said. She closed her phone and said, "He knows just the place."

She took Lombardi Avenue east to U.S. 41 and went north to West Mason—miles west of Henderson's Auto Plaza, which was on the other side of the river. She turned off on a frontage road and doubled back to a little one-story building near a strip-mall parking lot. Fuzzy's #63.

"Fuzzy Thurston?" Sam asked when he saw the sign, depicting a gold football going through a goalpost. Fred "Fuzzy" Thurston was one of the two pulling guards on Lombardi's famed power sweep of the sixties.

"Yes. Chet said the bar isn't much to look at, but Fuzzy usually stops by on weekends."

The bar was loud and smoky, onion-ring grease in the air and 1980s Southern rock and hair metal blaring from two giant JBL speakers next to the karaoke screen. Some loud, drunk, happy people sat around the center bar, which was decorated with license plates bearing Packers messages—PKR OWNR from Virginia, PACKRZ from Michigan, GB PACK from both Arizona and Hawaii. The walls featured the usual Packers photos, posters, pennants, and kitsch, definitely favoring the Lombardi years, and signed in bold Sharpie strokes by the players depicted—Starr, Hornung, Taylor, Dowler, McGee, Gregg, Wood, Adderley, Davis, Nitschke, Kramer—and, of course, Favre.

Chet Kahler was sitting at a table in the middle of it all. He saw Gretchen when they walked in, and waved her over with a big smile. Uncle Chet had a round face and chubby cheeks. He wore a green-and-gold Packers stocking cap and had a green Packers parka draped over the back of his stool. He stood up and hugged Gretchen, and shook hands with Sam. The family resemblance was not readily apparent. Chet was a soft oval of a man, while Gretchen was lean and firm. But the wispy hair that hung below Chet's cap was the same shade of strawberry blond as Gretchen's.

"Sam's doing some insurance work for the team," Gretchen told Chet before he could ask. "He's never been to Green Bay. I thought I'd show him around."

"Good-looking guy like this—you don't think Scott will get a little jealous?" Chet said, winking at Sam.

"It's not a problem," Gretchen said quickly and decisively.

A waitress with a missing tooth, a mullet, and a big smile took their order.

"This isn't exactly what I pictured," Sam said when the waitress had gone.

"What did you picture?" Chet said.

"Something wood-paneled, kind of dark and subdued, jazz or Burt Bacharach music, a few black-and-white photos of Fuzzy Thurston leading the power sweep. There'd be a couple of guys in a booth, wearing sport coats and turtlenecks, Super Bowl rings on their fingers, sipping martinis with adoring middle-age women in mink stoles."

"What decade are you living in?" Chet said with a hearty laugh. "If Paul Hornung walked in here right now, he'd be wearing an open-necked polo shirt and pair of jeans."

Sam noticed what looked like a bright yellow Packers helmet on the chair next to Chet, covered in a clear plastic bag.

"Souvenir?" Sam asked, pointing to the helmet.

Chet picked it up and set it on the table. The Packers helmet had two bold, black autographs on the yellow section above the green-and-white G. He carefully extracted the helmet from its protective clear plastic bag and showed to Sam and Gretchen. One of the autographs was Brett Favre's, and the other was Fuzzy Thurston's.

"Fuzzy just signed this for me a few minutes ago."

"Fuzzy's here?" Sam said.

"Yeah. He's in the gift shop at the back of the bar."

Sam hadn't noticed a gift shop. He glanced in the direction Chet was pointing, and saw a doorway at the end of the bar with steps leading down to a lower level. Sam had never been a Packers fan, but he'd always admired the organization's history and amazing fan support. Vikings fans could turn on their team at the drop of a pass, but Packers fans never gave up hope. Though he'd been too young to see those old Lombardi Packers play, there was an undeniable magic about their names and their accomplishments. They represented that last innocent, golden era of the NFL, before corporate arrogance and global marketing took over. Fuzzy Thurston had been one of their quiet cornerstones.

"I have to see Fuzzy," Sam said to Gretchen.

"Go ahead," she said with a smile. "I've seen him."

The gift shop was a modest, paneled room—almost like someone's rec room—with a basic selection of hats, shirts, and sweatshirts. A short line of fans waited to have their merchandise signed by the former All-Pro guard, who sat in a corner behind a table wearing a Packers jacket and ballcap. He was smaller now than during his playing days—days thoroughly chronicled by the photos around the bar of a square-jawed, sun-tanned strongman with a crewcut and a prominent nose. He was now somewhere north of seventy, with a white patch over his Adam's apple held in place by a strap around his neck, covering a tracheotomy hole. Life as an ex-Packers legend had apparently been a little hard on old Fuzz.

Sam bought a cap for Fuzzy to sign, and as the semi-legend smiled and scrawled his signature across the crown of the cap, Sam admired the massive Super Bowl ring on his gnarled finger. It was the symbol of ultimate football supremacy, but the Super Bowl need never have been invented for these Packers to be revered.

Sam thanked Fuzzy, returned to his table, and showed the cap to Gretchen.

"I'm going to wear this the next time I play golf in Arizona," Sam said. "There's Cheeseheads all over the place down there. They'll love it."

Chet actually gasped and said, "No!"

He was looking at Sam.

"No, what?" Sam said.

"Don't wear it! Put it in plastic! You saw Fuzzy—these guys aren't going to be around forever.'"

Chet put his own autographed souvenir, the Packers helmet, back in its plastic bag.

"I paid $400 for this. With Favre's and Fuzzy's signatures, it will be worth $800, easy, in a couple of years. I'm telling you, Sam, put that hat in plastic, or it's gonna lose value. Don't wear it."

"I hadn't thought of that," Sam said. "You're right. This is quite an investment."

"Don't laugh," Chet said. "Come over to my house tonight. I'll show you the stuff I've got in my basement. It's been appraised at over $200,000. When I go, Marilyn will be in good shape—if she decides to sell it all."

"What do you have?"

"Every Topps card for every Packers Player from 1956 to the present," Chet began, his eyes turning upward as though he were reading an inventory list on the back of his eyeballs, and his voice assuming the practiced drone of a salesclerk. "Signed game-worn jerseys by every starter on the first Super Bowl champs in 1966. Twenty-eight team-signed footballs. A complete set of Packers bobbleheads. Both the bronze and gold commemorative Super Bowl coin collections. Brett Favre and Bart Starr career wall plaques . . ."

"It's the little stuff that amazes me," Gretchen said. "He's got Packers bottle openers, salt and pepper shakers, beer steins, shot glasses, Christmas ornaments, towels, bedspreads . . ."

"An iPod case, an ice bucket . . ." Chet said.

"Even a toilet seat," Gretchen said.

"How about those yellow plastic cheesehats?" Sam asked.

Chet made a face.

"You can get those for twenty bucks at any gas station. I do have one, though. It's autographed by Doc Mueller."

Sam and Gretchen exchanged glances. If a Packer nut like Uncle Chet considered Mueller a hero whose signature was worth collecting, it was likely that Mueller could bring many of those fans with him if he managed to engineer the sale of the team.

"I'd invite you over to see it all tonight, but I don't want to wake Marilyn," Chet said. "She needs her sleep if she's going to make it to Packer Mass Sunday morning."

"Packer Mass?"

"It's a little over the top," Gretchen said, shaking her head slightly. "A lot of the local Catholic churches have a special mass at 6:30 a.m. on home game days, so season-ticket holders have plenty of time to get to their pre-game tailgate parties."

"It's just like any other mass, except that it's all green-and-gold in the pews," Chet said. "Everyone wears their Packers jackets and sweatshirts. No disrespect intended—and I'm sure none taken by the Lord."

"Speaking of getting some sleep," Sam said. He glanced at Gretchen, who nodded. They thanked Chet for meeting them, paid their bill, and got up from the table.

"We didn't get much chance to talk," Chet said to Gretchen. "Everything going okay at home?"

"Sure, fine," Gretchen said. "Same as always. Give my love to Aunt Marilyn."

Sam put his new ballcap on his head as they began to leave.

"Put it in plastic, Sam," Chet called to him.

Gretchen's ignition was balky in the increasing cold. She let the Volvo idle for a minute before pulling out of the parking lot.

"If Scott drives by tonight, your car in the driveway should keep him away," Gretchen said.

Sam was still smiling about Chet's urgent advice, but mention of Krebbs changed his mood to apprehensive. Would Krebbs stay away if he knew Sam was there? Or would it make him that much more determined to come in?

Scott Krebbs parked his Trailblazer around the corner from Gretchen's house. It was after ten o'clock. He knew Gretchen usually stayed home on Friday nights when the Packers were at home. She liked to get her rest, and she didn't like going out into the throngs of football fans crawling all over the city.

He guessed that the cops might have spoken to the neighbors about keeping an eye out for him. Gretchen wouldn't do that. She'd be embarrassed to admit she needed that kind of help and protection from her own husband. The neighbors were a nosy bunch. They all knew Gretchen worked for the Packers, and he was sure they were taking her side. It would be just like Jeff and Cindy next door, or Mrs. Schneider across the street, to be watching out the window for him and to call the cops if they saw him. There was a streetlight three lots away from theirs, and yard lights and porch lights on most of the homes immediately nearby—enough light for him to be seen from neighboring homes.

Light snow was blowing sideways, stinging Krebbs's face and making his eyes water. He got close enough to the house to see that Skarda's Cherokee was in the driveway. So they were home. In bed? He wouldn't be surprised. Not at all.

Across the street, he saw a figure halfway down the block, in a heavy parka with a dog on a leash. That would be Ted Betchell, walking his wife's yappy little

Maltese, Frida. Krebbs quickly stepped off the sidewalk and slipped behind a pine tree, waiting for Betchell and the dog to walk by. Frida must have noticed Krebbs's movement, because the dog began straining at its leash and barking in Krebbs's direction. Betchell glanced toward the pine, apparently saw nothing, and yanked twice, sharply, on the dog's leash.

"Shut up, Frida!" Betchell hissed.

Krebbs reached into his jacket pocket and put his gloved hand around the Smith & Wesson snub-nosed .38 revolver he'd bought from a newspaper ad last week. He was sorely tempted to blow away that fucking little dog. He'd always hated it—yapping at 6:30 every morning when the Betchells let it out on its chain, yapping for hours on nice summer days when Krebbs would be trying to take a nap with the windows open, yapping at midnight when the babysitter put it out of the house and then fell asleep on the couch.

A gun felt good. He'd never realized how it could make you feel like you could take care of things. He'd love to start with that yapping little piece of shit, but of course that wasn't what he'd come here to do. Maybe some other time.

When Ted and Frida were almost a block past him, Krebbs slipped into the backyard of the house with the pine tree. There were no fences between this yard, the yard next door, and Gretchen's house—just open space and a few trees. A good space for kids to run and play. The house already had a basketball hoop over the driveway when they moved in. It seemed to Krebbs that the neighborhood would be just what they wanted, the ideal place to raise a family. That's what Krebbs had thought when they bought the place three years ago—until he came to realize that there wouldn't be any kids. Gretchen might someday decide to put her career on hold long enough to have a baby, but it wasn't going to be with him. She'd made that clear.

After tonight, then, there wouldn't be any kids at all.

He stepped softly and slowly through the knee-deep snow in the adjoining backyards until he was standing at the corner of his former house. He crept along the foundation to the deck, trying to get a look through the sliding deck door to see if there was anyone inside. He could see the faint glow of a floor lamp in the living room, shining onto the kitchen floor.

He was about to put his foot on the first of the two wooden steps up to the deck level when he heard a tremendous bang.

Terrified, Krebbs scrambled awkwardly through the snow to the row of pine trees at the back of the yard, and dived face-first into a drift. He twisted around to see if anyone had come out of the house, or if another light had come on, but the upstairs was still dark, only the living-room light was on downstairs, and there was no visible movement in the house. What had made that noise? It sounded like some-body slamming a baseball bat against the cedar deck.

Then Krebbs realized what the noise was, and relaxed a bit. Every winter, when the temperature got below zero, the contraction of the house's wood frame made banging noises at night. He and Gretchen had been awakened by the noise many times. After seeing a story in the newspaper explaining the effect, they'd learned to ignore it. The fact that no lights had come on when he heard the bang didn't mean that Gretchen and Skarda weren't in there.

That noise had to wake them up, though. Krebbs waited in the snow drift for another ten minutes before approaching the house again. If he had to break a window to get in, he would, but he could always hope that Gretchen had made a mistake and left a door unlocked. Best to try that first.

The sliding door on the deck was locked, and there was no one in the kitchen or in the part of the living room that he could see. He stepped quietly off the deck and walked around the house to the garage side. He put his hand on the knob of the service door, and gave it a turn.

Locked.

Krebbs clung to the side of the garage and moved slowly to the driveway. He ducked next to Skarda's Cherokee, took off his glove and felt the hood. Ice cold. Skarda hadn't gone anywhere for at least an hour. He slid between the SUV's front bumper and the garage door, then quickly ran to the front steps, shielded from view by the two pine trees next to the porch.

The porch light was on. Gretchen usually turned it off when she went to bed. Even so, the neighbors couldn't have seen him, thanks to the trees. He gently eased the storm door open, reached in and put his hand on the front-door knob, turning his wrist to the right.

It opened.

Krebbs was almost disappointed in Gretchen. What a stupid thing to do. *This will cost you, my dear.*

He slipped inside and closed the door silently behind him. Then he took his gloves off, shoved them inside his jacket, and took out the Smith & Wesson. Reaching to his right, he found the wall switch for the lamp that was burning, and turned it off. Then he quickly walked across the living room and glanced into the den. No one there. They were upstairs.

Krebbs put his foot on the first step and tested his weight. No creak. Then the second—and a very slight sound of straining wood. The third step was silent. His kept his eyes on the railing at the top of the stairs, in the direction of Gretchen's bedroom.

He had to be ready to start shooting if anyone came out. Otherwise, he was just going to burst in and watch their faces as he ended their lives.

The stairs were cooperating. Krebbs made it to the top without making any sounds loud enough to rouse someone. With his back resting on the second-floor railing, he spread his legs and took one long, slow step to his left, then one more, until he was positioned in front of Gretchen's bedroom door. He paused just long enough to imagine the two of them together, naked, Skarda on top of Gretchen, or her curled against his side with her hair spread across his chest. Anger welled up from that place inside him that kept saying: *You were never good enough. Never good enough. Never good enough for you, was I Gretchen? Never good enough!*

He reached out, turned the latch, then kicked the door open with all the fury that had churned inside of him for months. He wanted to scream something coherent—"You cheating bitch!" "Fucking whore!"—something! But all that came out of his mouth was a strangled sob of despair and rage. Holding the .38 with both hands, he squared himself at the foot of her bed and began to pull back the heavy trigger— but there was no one else in the room. The bed was empty. He turned and raced into the hallway, turning toward the guest bedroom down the hall, when that door opened and the barrel of a pump-action shotgun emerged.

Using all the athletic skill he'd developed from years of basketball, Krebbs jumped over the railing just as the shotgun roared, obliterating the window at the head of the stairs. Krebbs landed hard in the middle of the stairway, badly turning his ankle, but the blast had missed him. So did the next one, fired at an angle that took out two of the spindles on the railing. Krebbs heard heavy footsteps pounding down the upstairs hallway, saw a dark figure aim the shotgun barrel down the stairs from over the second floor railing, and once again managed to hurl himself out of the way, sliding along the wooden floor of the foyer toward the front door as the shotgun shell blew a hole through the plaster on the stairway wall.

Three shots, Krebbs told himself. How many shells does a pump-action hold? Maybe he's out. I have to finish this.

Krebbs jumped to his feet, .38 in hand, and started to go back up the stairs. He saw the man charge down the stairs at him, pumping the shotgun, and Krebbs fired the .38. The recoil was much more severe than he'd expected from the small-barreled gun. His arm flew up in the air, and as he brought his hand down to steady it and fire again, he saw the man with the shotgun drop onto the stairs, with the gun still pointed toward Krebbs. He dived sideways and rolled into the living room as the shotgun went off one more time, splintering the front door. Krebbs saw the barrel of the shotgun drop, and aimed the .38 at the slumped figure on the stairs. Steadying his hand, he fired three times, hitting him at least once more. Then he turned and pulled the front door open, and limped out of the house. The gunshots had been loud enough that there was no doubt the neighbors had heard them. His ears were still ringing from the sounds, and he could smell gunpowder on his clothes. None of that mattered now. He'd killed someone back there. It must have been Skarda, though he hadn't gotten a good look at his face. Where was Gretchen? Had Skarda sent her somewhere else, then laid a trap? His mistake, then. Now he was dead, and wherever Gretchen was, he'd find her. He hobbled down the snow-packed driveway, his ankle throbbing, and started running as fast as he could, one short step on the sore ankle, two long hops on his good leg, down the street toward his car. One thought bounced wildly around in his skull:

I'll find Gretchen. I'll find her.

SEVENTEEN

Sam had been planning to give Gretchen's house a once-over before going inside, but as they pulled up to her driveway, he realized he wouldn't have to.

"Stop the car," he said.

"Why?"

Sam took out his phone, dialed 9-1-1, and reported a break-in at Gretchen's address. Gretchen looked more closely and understood what Sam had meant. She could see through the shattered storm door that the wooden front door was open, and appeared to have a hole smashed through it just below the doorknob.

"Scott was here," she said as Sam flipped his phone shut.

"He might still be here. I told the dispatcher that we'd sit in your car till the cops get here."

"He must have been furious. That hole in the door . . ."

"Don't let your imagination run wild. We'll figure out what happened soon enough."

"You really want to wait? Let him get away?"

"All I want to do is make sure you're safe. And you're safe right here."

The police arrived quickly this time—less than ten minutes after Sam called. Since the shooting at Henderson's Auto Plaza, the Krebbs case had taken on a higher priority. When the two squad cars arrived, Sam got out of Gretchen's car to meet them. VanHoff was in the second car.

"What happened here, Skarda?" he asked.

"We pulled up ten minutes ago and saw the hole in the door. That's all I can tell you. We called it in, and we've been sitting in the car since then."

The cops drew their weapons, one going around each side of the house to the backyard while VanHoff and his partner approached the front door. VanHoff reached the top of the steps and called into the house, "Police! Is anyone inside?" No response. The other officer took the opposite side of the door, and with their service weapons pointed skyward, they entered the house, again yelling "Police! Put down your weapons!" Within seconds, Sam heard VanHoff yelling, "I've got a body here!"

Sam walked up to the front door. He'd have preferred that Gretchen stay in the car, but he knew she wouldn't. She ran up behind him and pushed past him when he reached the front door.

"Hey, stay back," VanHoff ordered when Gretchen entered the foyer. She saw a pump-action shotgun lying on the foyer floor, a body on the stairs, the hole in the stairway wall, the broken railing spindles on the second floor, and blood spattered on the stairway railing and carpet.

"Who is it?" she asked, trying to get around VanHoff's partner to see the body.

"I don't know, ma'am. Please stay back."

VanHoff craned his head upward, looking at the damaged second-floor railing and the smashed window at the end of the hall.

"Anybody up there? This is the police!"

VanHoff got on his radio and called the two cops in the backyard to meet him in the foyer. When they walked in the front door, he told them to go upstairs and do a sweep.

"Nothing we can do about this one," he said, pointing to the body on the steps. "He's dead."

When the two officers had gone up the stairs, Gretchen switched on the foyer light to get a good look at the man on the stairs. He was white, wearing work boots, jeans, a black nylon snowmobile jacket, and a pair of black leather gloves. He was bare-headed, with tousled brown hair, and his face was covered with a growth of whiskers— short of a beard, but more than a couple of days of not shaving. There was a bullet hole in his forehead above his open left eye, and a dark blot of wet blood on his abdomen.

"I've never seen this man before," Gretchen said. She spoke in a way that re-minded Sam of the times he'd seen her doing paramedic work. There was no quaver in her voice; she was no longer in the foyer of her own home, now that the dead man on the stairway was not her ex-husband. She was merely at another crime scene.

"What about you, Skarda?" VanHoff asked.

"I don't know him."

VanHoff put on a pair of evidence gloves, then reached around into the man's back pocket and pulled out a wallet. He flipped it open and looked at the driver's license.

"James Alan Escher. Clear Lake, Wisconsin."

Escher. The guy who'd called in Mueller's truck accident up at Lake Minocqua. What the hell had he been doing here? Maybe he was the guy who'd fired the shot at Henderson's. Mueller's hit-man.

"The name mean anything to you?" VanHoff asked Sam.

Sam had to decide: Tell the cops what he knew, and hope they'd help him get to the bottom of the Escher/Mueller/Horvath/Truman connection, or assume that they'd brush it off as a fantasy. Most likely, they'd go straight to Horvath to get his take.

"No," Sam finally said. "Never heard of him."

He hoped his hesitation came off as an attempt to search his memory, rather than his conscience.

The officers didn't find anybody upstairs, but VanHoff did find a loaded Colt Python in Escher's jacket pocket, along with lock-picking tools that could have made the scratch marks they found around the lock on Gretchen's front door. One of the cops doing a neighborhood canvass found a white Toyota Tacoma parked a block away, with a Remington 700 on the back seat. When Sam heard that news, he was certain: Escher had been the shooter at Henderson's. But why? Which of them had he been trying to kill? Not both—that didn't make any sense. And since Escher could have gone to Henderson's at any time, it appeared that he fired through Henderson's window because Sam was there. So why had he broken into Gretchen's house? To kill Sam, and probably Gretchen, too. Horvath and Mueller wanted Sam out of the way. Horvath knew about Krebbs, and he and Mueller had probably decided it would look like the angry ex-husband had done the killing. If Krebbs had an iron-clad alibi, it wouldn't matter: Sam had no doubt that Mueller planned to have Escher killed as soon as he had done what he was sent to do.

And would the cops believe any of this? No.

VanHoff's wheels were turning too. He took Sam into the kitchen and sat down with him.

"Help me out, Skarda. We figured it was Scott Krebbs who took the shot at you earlier. Now we find this Escher character in your girlfriend's house—"

"For the last time, VanHoff, she's not my girlfriend."

"—with a couple of bullets in him, and a shotgun on the floor, with the serial number filed off. Looks like he came here to kill someone—either you or Ms. Kahler—"

"That's Dr. Kahler."

"—But somebody else killed him."

"Had to be Krebbs."

"Yeah, probably Krebbs. But what the hell was Escher doing here?"

"I don't know," Sam said. "Maybe if you guys could find Scott Krebbs, we'd find out."

"We're looking. But I think you know more than you're saying."

"I might. But I need to put a few more things together. Can you get me the name and address of the woman LaBobby Suggs was accused of assaulting?"

"What's she got to do with Krebbs, or this Escher guy?"

"I don't know yet. But if I'm right about her, I'll tell you all about it."

VanHoff stared at Sam, a lawman-to-lawman stare intended to search for the common bond between them. Sam had done that himself, working with cops from other jurisdictions. Sometimes you had to peel back the procedural bullshit and macho turf-protection to determine if you both really wanted to catch the bad guy. Sam had come to believe that he and VanHoff were both trying to do the right thing here, but Sam needed to produce more evidence before they would agree on what the right thing was.

VanHoff radioed in to headquarters for the information Sam wanted.

"Natalie Dellums, 4051 Creighton Street, West De Pere."

Sam wrote it down with the pad and White Bear Yacht Club golf pencil in his jacket pocket, then got up from the table and joined Gretchen in the foyer. A crime-scene forensics unit had arrived to catalogue evidence and take photos. Sam took Gretchen into the den. They sat together on the couch, and she leaned against him. He put his arm around her, remembering many nights when they'd sat together like this—happier nights. She curled her legs up under herself and rested on his arm.

"Who's James Escher, Sam?"

Her voice sounded weary, but not afraid. She deserved to know what he knew.

"I think he's Mueller's hired gun," Sam said in a whisper, in case one of the officers in the adjoining room was within earshot.

Sam told her about his conversation with the Minocqua police chief about Escher, and going to his house to talk to him—despite Escher's refusal. Sam hadn't thought of Escher when the shot was fired earlier that day at Henderson's, but it seemed pretty clear now that Mueller had sent Escher—through Horvath—to kill Sam.

"They probably thought it would look like Scott did it. But your ex showed up and spoiled the plan."

"I don't get it. What's in this for Horvath? He's got his dream job. Why get involved in all this?"

"I don't know. Maybe he's got money problems, like Mueller. Maybe he's been promised a more important job if the team is sold. Once I figure out what Mueller's up to, I'll have a better fix on Horvath."

"Do you think . . . they'll try again?"

"Horvath and Mueller are dangerous men."

"So's Scott."

"I know. But at least the cops are looking for Scott. Nobody's trying to do anything about Horvath and Mueller. Nobody but me."

"Can't you tell the police?"

"Everything I tell them will go straight back to Horvath. I've got to go over their heads."

"Over their heads?"

"Yeah. To NFL Security."

T̲HE NEXT MORNING S̲AM HAD TOAST and coffee in Gretchen's kitchen, and while she cleaned up the foyer, he placed a call to the NFL office in New York, asking to speak to someone in Security. Another voice came on the line and asked about the nature of his call. Sam explained that he was a private investigator from Minneapolis working on a case in Green Bay, and had some questions about Joe Horvath. After staying on hold for several minutes, his call was put through.

"Craig Botts," said the curt voice on the other end. "What can we do for you, Mr. Skarda?"

"What's your position, Craig?"

"I'm an agent with NFL Security. Now, what can we do for you?"

"I'd like some assurance that what I'm going to tell you stays between us. For now."

There was silence on the other end. Sam figured Botts had already had some-one key the name Sam Skarda into a database. The hit must have come back quickly, and to Botts's satisfaction.

"All right," Botts finally said.

Sam went through the recent events, including Ed Larson's drowning death, Horvath's manipulations with the players—bringing Truman to town, setting up the strip-club brawl, the shootings at Henderson's dealership and at Gretchen's house. He mentioned Mueller's gambling debts and the impending vote among the execu-tive committee members about whether to sell the team.

"We're aware of all those situations," Botts said.

"And . . . ?"

"We're monitoring what's going on in Green Bay."

"Through Horvath?"

"I'm not at liberty to say, Mr. Skarda."

"You've got a mess here, Botts."

"If that's the case, I strongly suggest you stay out of it, Mr. Skarda."

"Frank Janaszak hired me to look into it."

"That's unfortunate. Mr. Janaszak knows that we're always looking out for the best interests of our franchises, and we don't need outside help."

Sam felt his anger rising. It wasn't as though he was trying to harm the league. He'd discovered a potential scandal within the league's most storied franchise, and instead of being grateful about it, this Botts character was trying to scrape Sam off his shoe like a piece of gum he'd stepped in.

"Mr. Janaszak apparently doesn't have a lot of faith in your efforts," Sam said.

"Then why did you call us?"

"I'm wondering the same thing myself."

Sam hung up. There would be no help from the big boys in New York. His only hope was to convince the Green Bay cops that Horvath was neck-deep in all of this. It was time to visit Ms. Natalie Dellums.

GRETCHEN WAS DUE AT LAMBEAU at 10:00 a.m. for the Saturday walk-through and treatment sessions. Sam followed her to the stadium parking lot again, then turned south for the drive to Creighton Street in West De Pere. He plugged in his iPod, which randomly selected the 1950 Frank Sinatra recording of "Let it Snow, Let It Snow, Let It Snow!" The big-band arrangement of the Sammy Cahn/Jule Styne tune was almost absurdly cheerful. While Frankie was gloating about having brought some corn for popping, the Pied Pipers crooned in the background that he didn't care if it was ten below. The snow falling on Sam's windshield was the hard, biting kind that turned to tiny pebbles of white on the windshield. He turned on his intermittent wipers to brush them away, and switched off the music to get a forecast. It was eleven above, but the temperature was expected to bottom out at ten below overnight, with more blowing snow predicted for Sunday. *Let it snow, my ass,* Sam thought.

The block where Dellums lived wasn't a particularly desirable area. The apartment building was a two-story brick place with two units upstairs and two on the main floor. Dellums had one of the two main-floor apartments, according to the mailbox: Dellums, 2A.

He rang the bell. After waiting for a while, he rang it again. And again.

Finally an interior door was opened by a thick-necked, black-haired man with blue denim coveralls over a long-sleeved insulated undershirt.

"She ain't here, so quit leanin' on the doorbell," the man said. "Jesus Christ."

He started to turn away, but Sam put his hand on the door and held it open.

"You're talking about Natalie Dellums, right?"

"Yeah, I guess that's her name."

"Are you the landlord?"

"I own the place, and I live here. I rent out the other three units. Two guys upstairs, Natalie what's-her-face down here, across from me."

"When did you see her last?"

"Who the hell are you, anyway? Cop?"

Sam pulled out his private investigator's license and showed it to the man. Some people thought that gave him the same rights as a cop. He didn't mind if this guy was one of them.

"Okay, fine," the guy said.

"When did you see her?"

"I dunno. Yesterday, I think."

"You sure she's gone?"

"Sure, I'm sure. Her door's been open all morning. Nobody in there."

"Does she usually keep her door open when she's not around?"

"Between you and me, pal, I think she split."

"Why do you think that?"

"Come see for yourself."

He turned and walked inside, leaving the door open. Sam followed him down the hall, and he stopped in front of an open door.

"Mind if I go in and look around?"

"Knock yourself out."

Sam walked inside to a living room with cheap, worn carpeting, mismatched thrift-store furniture, lamps with crooked shades, and a bookshelf stacked with magazines, unopened mail, empty soda cans, and a glass bowl full of buttons, matchbooks, coins and paper clips. There was a Toshiba TV and DVD player on a stand facing the couch.

The owner remained in the doorway as Sam walked into the kitchen and found plates piled in the sink, drawers open, and plastic bags on the floor. In the bedroom, the dresser drawers were pulled out and empty; the closet was empty, too, except for a couple of wire hangers. Sam returned to the living room, picked up the remote and turned on the TV. The set was tuned to HBO. The picture was fine.

Natalie Dellums had left in a big hurry, taking all her clothes and leaving everything else behind. Sam doubted she'd be back. He'd hoped he could get her to admit knowing Horvath, and that she'd gone to the bar that night knowing LaBobby Suggs was going to be there. Instead, it appeared that Horvath had reached her first.

He gave the owner his card and asked him to call if he saw Natalie again.

"Whadya think I should do with her TV and stuff if she doesn't come back for it?" the man said.

"Keep it," Sam said.

"I ain't got room for all this crap."

"Sell it."

"Is that legal?"

"Maybe."

On the drive back to Gretchen's house, Sam decided LaBobby Suggs was right: Natalie Dellums had been involved in a set-up to draw one of the Packers into an ugly arrest. And who would have been behind it? Joe Horvath. Just as Horvath must have been behind the strip-club fight. He and Mueller were trying to make a bad situation worse in Green Bay by framing some of the team's notorious bad boys. That would turn the town against the team, and make the board of directors more likely to go along with a drastic change in the team's ownership. But Natalie Dellums had cleared out of her apartment sometime between yesterday and this morning—during the same time when Sam had asked VanHoff for her address.

There wasn't much doubt in Sam's mind that VanHoff had called Horvath after leaving Gretchen's house. Natalie had been ordered to get out of town.

With luck, she might still be alive.

G RETCHEN CAME HOME FROM LAMBEAU at 3:00 p.m. The players were headed to a Green Bay hotel for the night—common practice among NFL home teams on the eve of a game. The medical personnel, on the other hand, could stay in their homes.

"I'm not sure I want to," Gretchen said. She dropped her keys on the kitchen table and sat down, resting her chin on her hand. "I look around here and feel so ... violated. So unsafe. So pissed off."

"Let's take a look at this place and see what we can do," Sam said.

They found a hammer, nails, a saw, and some plywood in the garage. Sam cut one piece of plywood big enough to cover the hole in the front door and another for the shot-out second floor hall window, each of which they'd covered with sheets of plastic overnight. Gretchen nailed the plywood in place, and called a carpenter friend to ask if he could come over sometime next week to look at the broken railing spindles on the second floor. She'd bought some spackle on the way home, and still had a can of paint that matched the shade of pale blue in the hallway and stairway. Sam filled the buckshot holes with spackle, and Gretchen followed with a paintbrush. A window company was coming on Monday to do measurements on the hall window, the living-room window, and the front door.

When they were done, Sam put the tools back in the garage. He returned to the foyer and peered out the living-room window, wondering whether Krebbs would dare come back again tonight. Gretchen was in the upstairs hallway, staring blankly at the boarded-up window that had looked out at the backyard. He saw her turn and walk into her bedroom.

He went up the stairs and knocked softly on her half-opened door. She was sitting on the edge of her bed, hands on her knees, staring at the wall.

"I don't think I can do this anymore, Sam," she said. "I thought I was strong. I thought I could get through anything on my own if I had to. But I'm scared."

Sam walked over to the bed and sat down next to her. She took his hand and squeezed it. He squeezed back.

"You'll be okay. Scott made a bad mistake. Now the cops are really trying to find him, and when they do, he'll go to jail for a long time."

"Have I told you how glad I am that you're here?"

She looked up at him with her lips parted and her eyes glistening. She looked tired, uncertain, and beautiful.

Sam squeezed her hand once more, stood up, and went downstairs. There were a couple of Heinekens in the refrigerator. He got one out for himself and opened it. He was sitting at the kitchen table a few minutes later when Gretchen walked down the stairs and came into the kitchen.

"Want one?" he said.

"Thanks."

He got out a beer, opened it, and handed it to her. They sat at the table and looked at each other.

"I like having you back in my life, Sam."

"We can't go back."

"I know . . . but . . ."

"I understand something now. You didn't leave just because of your studies. If you'd really still loved me, you'd have found a way to make it work. And if I'd really still loved you, I'd have found a way to bring you back, or go with you. It wasn't going to work. You knew it before I did, that's all. No matter what's happened in the last few days, it still couldn't work."

The lines on Gretchen's forehead began to smooth out. She almost smiled.

"Maybe I was wrong to leave you."

"You weren't. And you know that."

"But you'll stay, won't you?"

"As long as it takes."

They clinked their bottles together, and both took long sips.

EIGHTEEN

They rode to the stadium together on Sunday morning, Sam driving the Cherokee. Gretchen became concerned about the weather before they pulled out of the driveway. The snow was coming down as hard and steady as it had earlier in the week, with the wind blowing at least thirty miles an hour. The plows were already out in her neighborhood. The intersections had begun to drift. The four-mile drive to Lambeau took forty-five minutes.

Kickoff was at noon. By the time they pulled into the players' parking lot, there were already hundreds of cars in the general parking areas, many fans already grilling bratwursts on hibachis and full-sized kettles set up on the snow-covered pavement. The flames from the grills flared and flickered in the wind—the sole burst of color to an otherwise slate-gray snowscape. The fans around the grills were bundled up in heavy boots, parkas, and snowmobile suits, with hoods over their heads and scarves in front of their faces. The snow continued to swirl in sideways from the bay, plastering the east-facing sides of the cars with a coating of ice and snow.

"It's one of those stalled fronts," Gretchen said to Sam after they'd gotten out of his car. "The worst weather for a game. The clouds just keep circulating clockwise, hitting us from the lake."

The temperature was near zero, and the wind-blown flakes stung Sam's eyes and face like tiny needles.

"I don't care enough about the Packers—or you, either—to sit outside for four hours in weather like this," Sam told Gretchen, who returned his smile. "Please tell me you've got me inside somewhere."

"Don't worry. You're going to watch the game in Frank's suite."

Sam took a last look at the huddled tailgaters before ducking through the players' entrance. If this weather kept up, they'd be drifted over by gametime.

Gretchen brought Sam up to the executive offices on the fourth floor, and walked with him down the hall to Frank Janaszak's luxury suite. It was empty, except for a busboy setting out serving trays, silverware, beer glasses, and tumblers. Down below, the field was being cleared by a four-wheel John Deere utility tractor with a spinning brush mounted on the front. The heating tubes under the field could not circulate enough warmth to prevent the snow from accumulating. By the time the utility tractor made its run down a sideline from one end zone to the other, the first twenty yards of sideline were nearly obliterated again. Two other vehicles were going back and forth over the yard-line stripes, trying to maintain a recognizable playing field. If the snow kept falling, it would be all they could do to clear the thirty-yard line for the kickoff.

Fans slowly found their way into the stadium, yelling to each other, throwing snowballs, and raising plastic bottles of beer in tribute to weather that promised to make normal football impossible. Packers fans assumed conditions like these gave them an advantage, but Sam recalled several big games at Lambeau in recent years when bad weather had not helped the home team—including their most recent NFC title game in sub-zero temperatures, which they'd lost.

Frank Janaszak came into the suite with his wife a little after eleven. He introduced Sam to Gloria, a happy-faced woman with round cheeks, lots of foundation, and a gray Polar Fleece cap with earflaps pulled down over her curly, platinum-blond hair.

"I get cold even sitting in here," she said. "I can't imagine how the players can stand it out there."

"They just put it out of their minds," Frank said. "Once the game starts, all they think about is football."

"I'm not sure that's possible today," Sam said.

The stadium lights were on, and there was nothing visible beyond the south rim of the stadium but swirling snow against a dense, colorless background. The snowplows on the field had been joined by men with brooms and shovels, trying to keep the yardlines visible until the plows returned to clear them again. The Minnesota Vikings came out onto the field first, almost invisible from the waist up in their white road jerseys. After the specialists futilely attempted to kick and throw the ball for a few minutes, their coaches decided little was to be gained by trying to loosen up in a blizzard, so the team retreated to the locker room. Then the Packers emerged from under the normally green canopy in the southwest corner of the stadium—a canopy now covered with at least four inches of white.

The players did calisthenics in the center of the field, kicking up tufts of snow with each step, and then broke into units to run practice plays. The home green uniforms looked black through the sheets of falling snow, and the gold pants and helmets were a muted pastel yellow. When the team's placekicker attempted field goals of forty yards through the north goalposts, the balls came off his foot as though he were kicking bags of laundry. They fluttered, veered hard to the left, and died in the snow, short of the goal line.

"Normally we do a series of fan-participation events," Frank told Sam. "Catching punts, kicking field goals, trying to pass the ball through a target. We called it all off today. No point."

"Is this the worst you've seen?" Sam asked.

"Yeah, I'd say so. We knew we might get one of these some year. Wouldn't you know, on top of everything else, we'd get it this year."

The Packers' offensive coaches gathered the quarterbacks, receivers, and backs for a passing drill. The receivers wobbled and slid while attempting to run their pass routes, while D'Metrius Truman and the other two quarterbacks struggled to see and hit their targets. Almost every pass that did find its way to the intended receiver was dropped.

"Marv'll have to keep it on the ground today," Frank said. "We should have an advantage. Truman was a hell of a running quarterback before his suspension. The fewer times we have to hand off the ball, the better."

Sam thought he spotted Gretchen on the sidelines with the rest of the medical staff, but he couldn't be sure. They were all wearing oversized green Packers parkas with hoods. At one point the shortest one—the one he assumed to be Gretchen—was talking to Truman, who had walked over to the sideline and seemed to be gesturing to the inside of his thigh, as though it were tight or sore. Sam picked up a pair of binoculars to get a better look. Gretchen was pointing toward the tunnel to the locker room, but Truman waved her off and walked back onto the field to rejoin the offensive drills.

Janaszak's wife called him up to the bar to one of the team sponsors. Sam settled into his seat and waited for kickoff. Looking through the Plexiglas at the swirling, wind-driven flakes made him feel as though he were in a reverse snow globe. All was calm inside. It was the outside world that someone was shaking.

From the opening kickoff, the game was a fiasco. The ball blew off the tee as the Minnesota kicker approached it, and he slipped and fell on his ass trying to stop himself. With a teammate holding the ball, the kicker managed to punch a twenty-five-yard line drive at the Packers' receiving team, which proceeded to fumble the ball back to Minnesota. Then Minnesota fumbled its opening handoff to the Packers.

The first quarter was scoreless. There were five fumbles, six punts for an average of 17.5 yards, three pass completions, and thirty-three yards of combined offense. The Minnesota head coach looked angry at first as the turnovers and lousy punts piled up, but it became apparent that neither team could move, or hold, the football for very long in the deteriorating conditions. D'Metrius Truman had one decent gain—a thirteen-yard scramble after dropping back to pass and seeing all four members of the Minnesota defensive line slip and fall in the snow on the pass rush. Truman's passing was less effective. He completed just one, a five-yard heave that started over the head of tight end Bo Lucas and ended up at his ankles.

It was late in the second quarter when Minnesota got its break. Truman dropped back to pass on his own twenty-eight-yard line, and the ball slipped out of his hands as he was bringing it up to throw. Replays confirmed that his arm was not yet coming forward, as Truman himself must have realized at the time. When the ball squirted loose, he tried to dive on it, but a Minnesota linebacker swooped in and tried to pick it up on the run. The ball slipped out of his hands, a Packers offensive lineman tried to fall on it, another Minnesota player knocked it out of his hands, and the ball kept skittering backwards toward the Packers goal line as wave after wave of snow-covered players attempted to land on it. Finally, Truman reappeared next to a pile of grasping players, and, seeing the ball rolling across the Packers goal line with several more Vikings stumbling toward it, he took three long strides and kicked the ball through the end zone. The nearest official immediately put his palms together above his head to signal a safety.

Marv Ackley turned to his assistant coaches, and, after a brief discussion, threw his red challenge flag. From his vantage point forty yards away, he had no idea whether the ball had ever changed possession, or who'd touched it last. The replays from various angles that were available in the luxury suite were conclusive, however: not only had Truman booted the ball across the back line, but his last lunging stride had aggravated something in his right upper thigh. While head referee Scott Harvey studied the replay monitor, Truman hobbled to the sidelines, where he was met by Gretchen and the rest of the Packers medical staff. They were taking him into the locker room on a cart when Harvey walked onto the field, switched on his microphone, and announced to the muffled howls of the crowd that the ruling on the field would stand. A "2" flashed onto the scoreboard next to Minnesota.

T WO MINUTES REMAINED IN THE HALF, but the scene in the Packers' training room was bordering on chaos. Gretchen had determined that Truman's injury was a strained groin muscle. Then a trainer brought in Bo Lucas, who appeared to have a broken leg. A minute later, still before the half had ended, safety Rashad Hakim came in with a dislocated shoulder, and center Ken Harycki hobbled in after him on a twisted ankle. It was all hands on deck, and one of the trainers put in a call to Doc Mueller.

"We've got bodies everywhere, Doc. We could use a little help down here if you're not doing anything," Gretchen heard the trainer say. Though she didn't want Mueller's help, or presence, it was too late for her to do anything about it.

"You gonna give me something for this?" Truman asked Gretchen.

"It's up to you, D'Metrius. If you want to try playing in the second half, I can give you a shot of Toradol."

"Gimme the Marcain."

"You sure you're comfortable with that?"

"I gotta play. This might be my last chance."

"On that field, you've got a real good chance of hurting yourself even worse. And with the Marcain, you might not even know it until after the game."

"Chance I gotta take."

Mueller arrived a few minutes later, hovering over Truman and asking if he was going back into the game in the second half. Gretchen told him she was going to give him a shot of Marcain, and went to the medicine cabinet to prepare the syringe.

Then Joe Horvath came through the door, accompanied by two Green Bay cops who were carrying a big, red-bearded man. The guy was moaning in agony.

"What do you have there, Joe?" Mueller said.

"Guy slipped on some ice in the stands," Horvath said. "Says he hurt his back. Can't feel his legs. We better look at him."

Truman glanced at the man as they laid him on a training table, then turned and looked harder at the man.

"I know that dude," Truman said. "He started that fight at the strip club on Tuesday. You remember him, Horvath. That's the dude!"

Horvath looked momentarily stunned, gaping at Truman without knowing what to say. Mueller glared at Horvath, who gritted his teeth angrily, then turned back to Truman.

"I don't have any idea what you're talking about. I wasn't there. I've never seen this guy in my life."

"You're lying, Horvath," Truman said, trying to jump off the table and approach him. Gretchen and one of the other trainers held him back. "You were there, and you saw this dude start throwing punches at Cornell Johnson. Let's get Cornell in here—and LaBobby. And Drabek. They all saw him. What's wrong with you, man?"

"Guy's fucked up," Horvath said to Gretchen. "You on something, Truman?"

"I see what's going on here," Truman said, shaking his head and getting back on the table. "Skarda was right."

Again, Gretchen saw Horvath and Mueller exchange glances. She administered the pain-killer shot to Truman's groin and told him to stay seated for a few minutes to be sure there weren't any adverse effects.

"Gretchen, he's all right," Mueller said. "We're stacked up in here. See what you can do for Lucas."

Gretchen gritted her teeth and moved to the table where Lucas was having his pants cut open by one of the trainers, to get better access to the possible break. Mueller had no business being in the room, much less giving her orders. But the rest of the team was now coming into the locker room for halftime, and a new flood of players had come straight to the training room for treatment. At least a half-dozen were complaining of frostbite symptoms.

Mueller walked up next to Truman and said quietly, "What did you mean, you see what's going on here? What's going on?"

"Horvath, man. He brought me here from a dogfight, just to get this team even more fucked up than it already is. That fight at the strip club—he sent us there. He set it up, with that dude with the beard over there. Skarda told me, man . . ."

"What about Skarda?"

"He said they're trying to sell the team. If enough shit goes wrong, it could happen. I gotta talk to him, tell him he was right. Hell, Horvath shot the guy who ran the dogfight. I ain't gonna cover his ass for that no more. I got to tell Skarda about that."

"Hey, let the executive committee deal with that. You're here to play football. You do want to play, don't you?"

"Hell, yes."

"What'd she give you?"

Mueller was keeping his voice low, while nodding his head toward Gretchen, who was attending to Lucas twenty feet away.

"Marcain."

"How much?"

"Hell, I don't know. One shot."

"One shot? That's not enough. Damn these incompetent . . . Look, Jerome Bettis took two shots of that stuff during a playoff game, and he was still in pain."

"You think I need two?"

"On a day like this, three."

"Whatever I got to do, man. Call her over."

"I don't need her. I was the team physician here for twenty years. I'll do it. But we've got to wait until just before the second half so the stuff will get you through the rest of the game."

"Yeah, okay."

Mueller cast another glance at Gretchen, who was trying to immobilize Lucas's left thigh. Every now and then she looked over at the red-bearded fan lying on an adjoining table. He continued to moan and complain about back pain, but it sounded fake even to Mueller. Why in hell had Horvath used that guy again? He could have ruined everything.

Marv Ackley stuck his head into the trainer's room, looked around at his wounded troops, and shook his head.

"Gretchen, who's out for the second half?"

"Just Lucas. Looks like a broken fibula. I'm sending him for x-rays. Rashad's shoulder popped back in. We re-taped Harycki's ankle. It should hold up. Everybody else just needs to get warm."

"What about Truman?"

"I gave him a shot of Marcain. He says he can go. Your call."

As the second-half kickoff neared, Gretchen and the trainers put their jackets back on, packed up their kits, and headed out into the main locker room.

"Are you good, D'Metrius?" she asked as she passed him on the table.

"Still a little sore, but I'll be out there."

Gretchen and Mueller exchanged unfriendly glances, and she left the room. When she did, Mueller slipped on a pair of latex gloves, found what he was looking for in one of the medicine drawers, loaded the syringe, and quickly injected Truman. Then he refilled the syringe and injected him again. He put the syringe back on the table where he'd found it, disposed of his gloves, and put a hand on Truman's shoulder. He tried to make direct eye-to-eye contact, but Truman's pupils were already dilated, and his eyeballs were glassy.

"You'll be fine in a minute, D'Metrius," Mueller said. "It just takes a while to get used to that stuff. Stay here until Gretchen can check back with you."

Then he walked past Horvath, glared at him, and left the room.

NINETEEN

Frank Janaszak got a phone call minutes after the Packers had taken the field for the second half. Backup quarterback Andy Radcliffe was in the game, and everyone in the suite assumed that Truman's leg injury had kept him from playing. The phone call told him otherwise.

"Oh, my God," Janaszak said. His mouth dropped open, his face turned pale, and the slightly drunken conversations around him ceased. "You're sure? You're absolutely . . . no, no. I'll be right down."

He shut his phone and looked around, speaking to no one in particular.

"D'Metrius Truman is dead."

"What?" The suite was suddenly abuzz with astonished questions from the guests: "When?" "How?" "Dead?"

"A few minutes ago," Frank said. "Gretchen Kahler gave him a shot of pain killer so he could play the second half. A few minutes later he collapsed. They couldn't revive him."

Sam jumped up from his seat.

"Let's go, Frank. Take me down to the locker room."

They went quickly out the door and down the hall to the elevator, and descended to the team level.

"How do you know it was Gretchen who gave him the shot?" Sam asked. "Who did you talk to?"

"Mueller. They called him back to the trainer's room . . ."

"Back?"

"I don't know why he was there. He said Gretchen gave him too much Marcain."

"No chance," Sam said. "Never. No Way."

He looked at Janaszak, who was sweating again, taking shallow breaths and looking as though the world was crashing down on top of him.

"Take it easy, Frank," Sam said. "We'll get through this. Mueller isn't as smart as he thinks he is."

"I'm worried about Gretchen. Mueller said he called the police."

It appeared Mueller had found a way to get rid of Gretchen. Sam figured he was next—and Mueller was smart enough to know that Sam knew it.

The scene in the locker room was as somber as a wake. Four uniformed Green Bay cops were there, one of them stringing yellow police tape in a wide area around the table where D'Metrius Truman's body lay, still clad in his wet green jersey and shoulder pads. From the waist down he wore only a jockstrap and his taped white athletic socks. His skin was beginning to turn a lifeless gray. Gretchen sat in a chair in the corner of the room while Lieutenant VanHoff jotted down her muted answers to his questions on a notepad. Mueller was pacing the room with a self-important urgency, as though he could somehow make this situation right if people simply paid enough attention to him.

Bo Lucas, who'd been fitted for a walking boot, sat on the edge of the training table next to Truman, with tears streaming down his cheeks. Horvath wasn't around. The other training tables were empty.

Sam and Janaszak walked over to Gretchen.

"Can we talk to her, VanHoff?" Sam said.

"I guess so. She needs to stay here, though. The medical examiner is on his way. We might have to make an arrest."

Gretchen looked up at Sam and spoke in a calm, steady voice. "I didn't do it," she said. "I know how to administer Marcain."

"Then what happened?" Janaszak asked. His question was desperate, the kind a man would ask if he came home and found his house had burned down.

Gretchen looked over at Mueller, who was staring back at her.

"Someone else . . . gave him something. I don't know who, or what. But Truman saw Horvath come in here with a fan who said he slipped and hurt his back. Next thing I heard was Truman saying he recognized the guy, and then he said, 'Skarda was right.'"

"Who was the guy Horvath brought in?"

"I don't know—a big guy with a red beard. They're both gone. I worked on Lucas and Hakim, and then I left the trainer's room. Five minutes later, a clubhouse attendant told me Truman fell off the table."

"Don't try to wiggle out of this, Gretchen," Mueller said, pointing a finger at her. "Your incompetence killed a great football player. I don't know why Frank ever hired you. Well, maybe I do know . . ."

The rest of the room fell silent, stunned at Mueller's accusatory tone. Sam left Gretchen and crossed the room to stand in front of Mueller.

"Shut your fucking mouth. I know what you're doing."

"You don't belong here, Skarda," Mueller said. Mueller turned to one of the cops. "This is a crime scene, isn't it? He's not part of your investigation. Get him out of here!"

"He stays," Janaszak said. The aging club president looked like he wanted to sit down before he fell down, but he summoned enough strength to confront Mueller. "I hired him, and I want him here."

The Brown County medical examiner and his team arrived a few minutes later. Two assistants removed Truman's jersey and shoulder pads, and the medical team did a preliminary exam. Then they put Truman in a body bag, hoisted him onto a gurney, and wheeled him out of the locker room to the loading dock, where a hearse was waiting to take him to the morgue. The medical examiner took Gretchen into an office next to the training room, and, along with VanHoff, questioned her for about fifteen minutes. When they emerged, Gretchen told Sam they were taking her down to police headquarters.

"Is she under arrest?" Sam asked VanHoff.

"Not yet. But we've got a problem here, obviously. She could use a lawyer."

"I'll call Stuart Fleischman," Janaszak told Gretchen as VanHoff led her out the door.

"Who's that?" Sam asked.

"Our corporate attorney."

"Too bad Stuart's not a criminal-defense lawyer," Mueller said. He smiled coldly at Gretchen and left the trainer's room.

VanHoff led Gretchen out into the locker room and toward the exit. Sam followed, not sure where he would go, or what he could do now to help her. The club-house doors opened, and a sodden, bone-chilled group of Packers clomped slowly past them into the locker room. Sam glanced up at one of the TV monitors in the players' lounge area and saw the final score—2 to 0, Minnesota—superimposed over a shot of NBC's sideline reporter interviewing the Minnesota head coach, who had several inches of snow piled on the brim of his ballcap. Apparently the media did not yet know that Truman was dead. Then Sam saw Janaszak huddling with coach Ackley and media relations director Liz Graczyk. They'd waited to make the announcement until the players could be notified first.

Ackley had a stunned look on his face after talking to Janaszak. Then he backed away, turned toward his players and asked for their attention. Bo Lucas had limped out of the trainer's room, and when the players saw his flowing tears, they realized something had gone terribly wrong. After Ackley's announcement that Truman had died, there were sobs in every corner of the room. Graczyk left to speak to the as-sembled media members outside the dressing room. Sam walked out after her, and as he elbowed his way through the reporters and camera operators, he heard Graczyk take a deep breath and begin speaking in a barely composed voice: "At approximately

2:37 p.m. today, Green Bay Packers quarterback D'Metrius Truman was pronounced dead by Brown County medical examiner . . ."

Graczyk's grim voice was overwhelmed by shouted questions as Sam walked down the corridor toward the elevators. Now what? Find Mueller? Find Horvath? Go to the cops and tell them everything he knew? Then what? He really didn't know enough. Not yet. If he tried to guide the Green Bay police toward Mueller and Horvath, it would look like he was just trying to throw up a desperate smokescreen to keep Gretchen out of trouble. He needed more proof. He needed help.

The only person he could think of was Craig Botts at NFL Security.

Sam took the elevator up to the executive offices, found an empty conference room, and called the NFL office in New York. He identified himself to the woman who answered the phone and told her he urgently needed to speak to Craig Botts. This time he was put through in less than a minute.

"Skarda, where are you?"

"At Lambeau. You've heard, I take it."

"About Truman? Yes, we know."

"The police took Gretchen Kahler, the team physician, in for questioning. She might be arrested. But she didn't do it. It was Doc Mueller and Joe Horvath. Truman found out at halftime that Horvath had been setting up Packers players for arrests. He was going to talk to me, maybe to the cops, but he never made it out of the trainer's room."

"Let me tell you something, Skarda. Joe Horvath has a distinguished record. He was with the Green Bay Police Department for eight years, and the FBI for fifteen. His record of service is impeccable. Why should I take your word that he's involved in this?"

"I know you had me checked out. You wouldn't have taken my call today if you hadn't."

"So?"

"So you know I'm solid. I'll put my record up against Horvath's, anytime."

"What do you want?"

"I'll give you something. A name: Purdy McCutcheon."

"We know who he is."

"Would he be the main money man if his group buys the team?"

"No."

"Who, then?"

"Michael Banks."

"The agent?"

"Yes. McCutcheon is the front man, but we've already investigated him and his partners. He needs help to pull this deal off. Banks brings more to the table than anyone else."

"Then he'd be the principal owner?"

"That's right. They could run the team any way they chose, but Banks would have controlling interest."

"How much do they need?"

"There's been no price set. We know the Packers' executive committee meets tomorrow to discuss it. But with the Packers' unique ownership, the committee could sell the team for far less than market rate."

"Does Banks have enough money to buy any team he wants?"

"No."

"But he could afford the Packers?"

"Depending on the price, yes."

"What about other bids?"

"They don't have to take bids. If they want to sell the team to McCutcheon and Banks, they can do it."

"What does the league think?"

Botts hesitated. Sam knew that his previous clients at Fenway Park and at Augusta National had stood up for him, or he wouldn't have gotten this much out of an NFL insider. It was clear that Botts was concerned about what was happening in Green Bay. But how much information was the league prepared to share with a private investigator who might be on the verge of exposing a scandal involving the NFL's most celebrated team?

"I'll say this," Botts said. "There have been . . . concerns . . . raised by other franchises that the Packers' ownership structure is unfair."

"Unfair? How? They're dead last in the league."

"True. But they've still got more championships than any other team. The other franchises worry that the Packers can always go to their fan base, sell more stock, raise more money, and use that for player acquisition. The other teams can't do that."

"So you're saying the league would go along with a sale."

"At this point, we'd have no objection. The league has been actively seeking an African-American owner."

"Even if he's not going to run the team?"

"That remains to be seen."

"Well, here's something anybody can see: Mueller and Horvath have been sabotaging the team from the inside."

"Can you prove it?"

"I'm trying to. I think Banks has promised Mueller that he'd be team president, with a big enough salary to take care of his gambling debts. You know Mueller likes the casinos, don't you?"

"We have information to that effect."

"And that doesn't concern you?"

"To our knowledge, all his gambling has been legal, in casinos. We don't have information that he's ever placed a bet on a game."

"But his wife told me he was in debt to his eyeballs."

"Our primary concern with gambling is players, coaches, and officials."

"Well, you might want to take a closer look at Mueller. Heavy gambling losses can make a guy do funny things. And while you're at it, run Horvath past your sources again. I'm telling you, he's dirty. And if he's dirty, somebody else out there knows it."

"We appreciate your concern, Skarda. Keep us informed. I'll give you my cell number."

Sam took down the number. Then Botts hung up.

SAM FOUND AN EMPTY OFFICE with a computer and did an Internet search for Michael Banks. After skimming a couple of articles about the mega-agent, he learned that the Banks Agency was based in Chicago. He used an online directory to find the address and phone number, and mapped a drive from Green Bay to Chicago. It was a little over 200 miles, and on good roads—if the plows were out all night—it would take him about four hours. He could leave first thing in the morning, see Banks, and be back in Green Bay around dinnertime.

It was dark when he walked out to the nearly deserted Lambeau parking lot, but the winds had abated, and he could see stars in the sky to the west. It would be very cold overnight as the high pressure moved in, but the forecasters were calling for a warm-up starting late Monday. Of course, a warm-up in Green Bay in December meant something in the twenties. He wanted to be in Arizona. He wanted to be with Caroline.

He started the Cherokee, turned the heater up full blast, and dialed Caroline's number. It had been a couple of days since he told her he was working in Green Bay on a case involving the Packers. By now, she'd have heard the news about Truman. He could hear the concern in her voice when she picked up the phone.

"Sam, they said on the news that they took the Packers team doctor into custody. Is that your . . . friend?"

"Yes. But she hasn't been arrested yet—not as far as I know."

"How did it happen?"

Sam explained what he knew about the first-half injury and the pain-killer shot, and about Truman deciding that he wanted to talk to Sam about Horvath's schemes. Then he told her about his call to NFL Security. "I'm going to police headquarters now. I'll have to go to Chicago in the next day or so. I wish I were flying to Tucson instead."

"What's in Chicago?"

"A sports agent named Michael Banks. He wants to buy the Packers."

"Banks. I just read something about him. He's merging his agency with another agent."

"Do you remember who?"

"Lassiter . . . Luther . . . Hollister. That's it. Arnie Hollister. The guy who represents that quarterback from Southern Cal. They say he's going to be the first pick in the draft this year—but he won't sign with the Packers."

"Last year's number one wouldn't sign with the Packers, either," Sam said. "He was represented by Hollister, too. Now Banks is merging with Hollister, just before putting in an offer on the Packers."

"Sounds fishy."

"I agree."

There was silence on the line for a moment, and then Caroline said, "I have to admit, it bothered me that you were seeing an old girlfriend."

"I told you, it's just business."

"But I wasn't sure she felt the same way. Now, I feel bad for her."

"I've got to get her through this."

"I know. Tell Gretchen I said to hang in there."

"I will. She'll appreciate that."

"Are you coming back here when this is over?"

"Eventually . . . yeah."

There was another moment of silence on the other end of the line. The issue of where, or whether, they would live together was always close to the surface. Sam felt he was a thousand years away from being able to decide where he really belonged, or what he and Caroline should do when this was over. Current events had to take precedence.

"Is there anything I can do from here?" Caroline asked.

"If she were in a Mexican jail, you might be able to help. I don't think Immigration has any pull with the Green Bay cops."

"You're almost in Canada . . ."

He laughed, and then had a thought.

"Wait, maybe there is something you can do. The head of Green Bay security is a guy named Joe Horvath. He once worked for the FBI. Truman told me Horvath picked him up and brought him to Green Bay after he got out of prison. Truman was in Minnesota at the time, but he didn't want to say why, or where. Can you find somebody to check with the feds and see if there was any kind of investigation going on with Truman, something Horvath might have found out about?"

"I'll talk to a friend of mine at Homeland Security in Washington who's pretty well connected."

"Horvath's no good, Caroline. If you ask enough questions about him, something's got to come up."

"Do you think he killed Truman?"

"No. I think his boss did."

"Where are those guys now?"

"Wish I knew."

S AM DROVE DOWNTOWN TO THE POLICE STATION, where he was told Gretchen had been transferred to the Brown County Jail, out by the University on Curry Street. That was not a good sign. They were holding her on probable cause and expected to file charges in the morning.

When he reached the jail, it was almost eight. Visiting hours ended at nine. The building had the antiseptic feel of a recently built junior high school—except for the gaggle of print and TV reporters in the lobby, hoping to snag an interview with anyone who could give them more information on the sensational story of a Packers team doctor in jail for killing a player. A bespectacled man in a gray topcoat was moving through them toward the exit, saying the Packers would have no comment. Sam assumed it was Stuart Fleischman.

"Stuart?" Sam asked as the man tried to shoulder past him.

"No comment. I'm sorry."

"I'm Sam Skarda. Frank hired me to investigate."

Fleischman stopped and looked at Sam, as the microphones and mini-cams pressed in close to them.

"We can't talk out here," Fleischman said. "Let's go back to the visitors' area."

They sat down behind the soundproof windows, and Fleischman outlined the situation: Gretchen would be staying in the lockup overnight. A judge had not yet set bail. That would be determined tomorrow morning, if and when the police filed charges. The Packers would consider providing her with a defense attorney, depending on the case that the police presented. If it appeared likely that she had, indeed, killed D'Metrius Truman, either through malfeasance or with intent, the team would provide neither bail nor defense.

"Intent?" Sam said. "You can't be serious. Why would your team doctor want to kill your starting quarterback?"

"She had no answer to that question when I talked to her," Fleischman said. "I'm sympathetic, Sam. She's in a hell of a mess. But saying that somebody else did it isn't much of a defense at this point. Besides, our interests cut several ways here. If we defend her, what about Truman's family? What about our loss of a potential All-Pro player?"

Fleischman gave Sam his card, and told him to call him if he learned anything that might help Gretchen's case. Then he went back out through the cluster of reporters, shouting questions they knew would not be answered.

Sam knew they were just doing their job, but it made him sick to think of videotape circling the globe, showing Gretchen doing a perp walk into a Green Bay jail cell and the team attorney refusing to issue a statement of support.

Sam was I.D.'d and searched by a guard, and then Gretchen was brought out wearing an oversized orange shirt over a white t-shirt, and orange pants. She looked battered, but not defeated.

"You've got to find a way to get to Mueller, Sam," she said as soon as she sat down across from him at the table. "He did this."

"I know. I'm working on it. But I have to go to Chicago."

"Why?"

"To see Michael Banks. I think he's the guy behind all this."

"And what good will that do? He won't admit anything."

Gretchen put her palm on her forehead and leaned on her elbow, blowing a loose strand of hair upward. She had never been one to sit and wait for her fate to be determined by others. It had to be killing her to be locked away, with no chance to help herself beat the charges.

"I'll just have to lay out what I know, and see how he reacts," Sam said. "If I can link him to Mueller or Horvath, this thing will unravel."

Sam's cell phone rang, and he looked at the guard standing at the door to see if it was all right to take the call. The guard nodded.

"Sam? It's Stephen Kleinschmidt."

"Hello, Stephen."

"I thought you should know. Frank Janaszak was admitted to the hospital an hour ago. He's had a heart attack."

TWENTY

T he entire executive committee had gathered outside the ICU at Memorial Hospital by the time Sam arrived. Janaszak was in critical condition, and could not have visitors. None, that is, except for Doc Mueller.

"I couldn't help it," Kleinschmidt said quietly to Sam when they walked down the hall to talk. "Frank's primary physician is Gretchen Kahler, and she's in jail. Doc asked Gloria if he could take over for Gretchen, and she said yes. I really can't override her wishes."

"He'll kill him."

Kleinschmidt shook his head emphatically, and looked over his shoulder toward the waiting area where the other committee members had gathered.

"Not if I have anything to say about it. We have our best cardiologist, Ben Richardson, monitoring the situation. I'll make sure Doc is never alone with Frank."

"Can you put a guard in the ICU?"

"That won't be necessary. I'm staying here all night."

"Then I'm staying, too. We can nap in shifts."

"Well, I wouldn't mind the help."

"What about the committee meeting tomorrow?"

"I suggested to the other members that we postpone. But they want to meet and install Tom Boulanger as Ed Larson's replacement. After that, we'll try to put off a vote until we know more about Frank's condition."

"If he dies, Mueller becomes president."

"That's right."

"Then the Packers are as good as sold to Michael Banks."

"Banks? The agent?"

"He's the money man behind Purdy McCutcheon."

"You know Michael Banks is originally from Milwaukee."

"No, I didn't. Looks like he wants to come home."

Outside the door to the ICU, the vigil of committee members eventually began to break up. First Sherwood Talley left, then Mike Henderson, then Jerry Pritchard. Only Gloria Janaszak and Kleinschmidt remained. Kleinschmidt went in to check on Frank's progress every five minutes or so, and came out with reports to Gloria.

Sam sipped a cup of coffee from a Styrofoam cup and listened, while keeping an eye on the medical people—nurses, orderlies, and the occasional doctor—who walked in and out of the unit. At two in the morning, Doc Mueller and Dr. Richardson emerged from the double doors.

"I'll check back every half-hour, Doc," Richardson said. He smiled encouragingly at Gloria and walked out of the waiting area and down the hallway. Doc Mueller approached Gloria and was about to speak to her when he noticed Sam sitting against the wall with a magazine on his lap. Sam was feeling a little sleepy, but the sight of Mueller was like a couple of slaps to the face. He fixed Mueller with a stare that said: Don't try anything with Frank. Don't even think about it.

Mueller returned his focus to Gloria, whose happy face had become red and streaked with dried tears.

"It's still touch and go, Gloria," Mueller said. "But that's good news. When Dr. Richardson and I first saw him, we didn't think he had a chance to pull through. With the medications Gretchen Kahler was giving him, I'm surprised this didn't happen sooner."

"What do you mean?" Gloria said. She pulled a wet handkerchief away from her nose, and her tentative smile evaporated.

"The woman's a menace. She had him on much higher levels of digitalis than was indicated by his condition. It almost looks like she was trying to kill him."

"I don't understand," Gloria said, in a voice that was trying to fight through a haze of sorrow and anxiety. "Gretchen was devoted to Frank."

"I know Frank liked Gretchen, but his loyalties were misplaced," Mueller said. "She killed one person today, and nearly killed another."

"That's enough, Doc," Kleinschmidt said. "Gloria, we don't know for sure what triggered Frank's heart attack. We'll have doctors checking on him through the night. I'm staying here, too. So is Sam."

"That's hardly necessary, Stephen," Mueller said.

"Oh, I think it is."

Mueller abruptly stood up, took his stethoscope from around his neck, and put it in the pocket of his white lab coat.

"Then I'll be going home to get some sleep. Dr. Richardson will call me if there are any changes."

"Thank you so much, Doc," Gloria said. "I don't know what I'd have done if you hadn't been here."

"Nothing but the best for Frank," Mueller said.

"Maybe there's no need for you to stay, either, Sam," Kleinschmidt said.

"I've got nowhere else to be."

"Then do you mind if I go to my office and catch a nap for an hour or two?"

"No problem. I'll come get you around three."

"Enjoy yourselves," Mueller said. He walked briskly down the hall and turned the corner toward the bank of elevators. Sam was tempted to follow him, but then had another thought.

When Kleinschmidt left, Sam moved over to the chair next to Gloria Janaszak. They were now alone in the room, a drab waiting area with sea-green walls, a few Naugahyde armchairs, a pile of well-thumbed magazines on an end table, and a white institutional clock on the wall, like the one in Chief Weston's office at Lake Minocqua.

"Do you and Frank have children, Gloria?" he asked.

"We have a daughter in San Diego. She couldn't get a flight out tonight, but I expect her here tomorrow afternoon."

"That's good," Sam said. "Someone should be with you."

"Gretchen has been like family to us. I wish she could be here. Frank was so upset when the police took her, I'm sure that's why . . ."

"It might have been a coincidence."

"Can you tell me what happened today? With Truman? "

"Believe me, Gretchen had nothing to do with it. She should never have been arrested."

"Then . . . it was an accident? Like with Frank's medication?"

"No, I don't think so. Gloria, I'm going to tell you something, and I hope you take my word, as a friend of Gretchen's. I don't trust Doc Mueller. Neither does Gretchen. Neither does Frank. That's why they asked me to come to Green Bay."

"I know Frank and Doc have had disagreements, but we're all family here," she said. She looked at Sam quizzically, as if challenging him to contradict her.

"Family members can do terrible things to each other. I was a cop for a long time. I saw it all. And what I've seen, and learned, since I've been here is this: You don't want Doc Mueller treating your husband."

Gloria looked away, and Sam knew there had been discussions between her and Frank about Mueller. Maybe not specifics, but enough that Gloria had reason to believe Sam was telling the truth. Still, with Gretchen in jail facing a murder charge, and her husband in critical condition, it was hard for her to face the idea of yet another betrayal.

She needed convincing, and Sam had an idea how to do that.

"Gloria, Doc said he was going home for the night. He left because Stephen and I are going to stay. He wouldn't have a chance to be alone with Frank."

"Uh-huh," she said, not yet following him.

"He wants Frank out of the way, permanently. He wants to be president. He wants to sell the team. The committee might vote to do that tomorrow, if Frank doesn't make it through the night."

Gloria's tear-reddened eyes began to open wider.

"I'm going to leave the hospital, get in my car, and drive around the block. If I'm right about Doc, he hasn't left the building. I think he'll be back within five minutes after I leave, and he'll go in to see Frank. Then will you believe me?"

"I . . . yes, I guess so. Are you coming back?"

"Definitely."

Sam patted her hand and stood, looking around. Richardson wasn't due back for twenty minutes. There was a large enough window for Mueller to get back into the ICU and finish the job that Sam suspected he'd started earlier in the day. Sam stopped at the nurses' station and said Gloria Janaszak wanted Dr. Richardson to return to the ICU immediately to look in on her husband. Then he left the hospital.

He'd been right about the temperature drop-off. It must have been well below zero when he walked across the street to the parking ramp. He hadn't looked around; he had no doubt that Mueller was some place well out of sight, but in a place where he'd know if Sam left—maybe by an upper-floor window that looked out on both the lighted skyway and the street. Maybe at the security guard's desk, watching the exit monitors.

Sam's Cherokee was on the first level of the ramp. He drove quickly to the heated pay booth, where he had to tap on his horn to wake up the young man inside, who was sleeping with MP3 ear buds under his stocking cap. The attendant opened the window, took Sam's cash, and closed the window again as quickly as possible, resuming his nap.

Sam was glad to see that the street in front of the hospital had already been plowed, and there were open meters close to the front door. He took a right out of the parking ramp, then made four lefts, driving around the block, and parked the SUV in front of the doors he'd just exited. The woman at the front desk looked surprised to see him but smiled perfunctorily as he punched the UP button next to the elevator. The ICU was on the third floor.

When the elevator doors opened, Joe Horvath was standing there, facing him.

"Forget something, Skarda?"

"What are you doing here, Horvath?"

"Doing my job—looking out for Frank. I don't think the family wants you here."

Horvath flipped open a cell phone, punched a button and said, "Skarda's back—at the elevators." Then he shut the phone.

"Looking out for Mueller, you mean," Sam said. "Get out of my way."

He pushed past Horvath and ran toward the waiting area. He saw Gloria Janaszak standing up, looking agitatedly back and forth from the doors to the ICU to Sam.

"He came back," she said when Sam got close to her.

"How long has he been in there?"

"No more than a minute. But Dr. Richardson was already there."

Sam walked through the ICU doors. A nurse noticed him immediately and told him he wasn't allowed there.

He walked past her and headed toward the first curtain in the unit. Doc Mueller emerged from behind the curtain of the farthest ICU bay with Richardson. Mueller looked outwardly calm, but Sam detected an effort to control the tone of his voice.

"No reason to get excited, Skarda," he said. "I just had a thought as I was heading home—something I wanted to check."

"Whether Frank was alone? So you could finish him off?"

"Frank's my friend, asshole."

"So was Ed Larson."

"Fuck you."

"You'll have to leave this area immediately," Richardson said to Sam.

"Yeah, I'm sorry. I just lost my way out of the hospital. It happens—right, Doc?"

He smiled at Mueller, who glared back at him. Then Mueller brushed past him and left the ICU. Sam and Dr. Richardson followed him out to the waiting area, where Gloria was still standing. She watched Mueller move swiftly past her and down to the end of the hall, where Horvath was waiting for him. She gave Sam a nod of concession, and then spoke to the cardiologist:

"Ben, I don't want Karl Mueller to get near Frank again. He's no longer our personal physician."

TWENTY-ONE

Gretchen's arraignment was scheduled for 9:00 a.m. Monday in at the Brown County courthouse. Sam felt trashed-out and disrespectful as he walked through the stone-arch front entrance of the refurbished, 100-year-old granite building with the stately clock tower. He was wearing the same clothes he'd been in the day before, after spending all night at the hospital with Gloria Janaszak.

He was ignored by the reporters who'd gathered for the arraignment, several of whom he recognized from the county jail the night before. He slipped into a seat near the defense table, where Stuart Fleischman and another man in an expensive suit—presumably a criminal-defense attorney—sat waiting for Gretchen to emerge from the secure doorway to the right of the witness stand. Sam took out his notebook and wrote a message to Gretchen—that Frank Janaszak had made it through the night. He passed the note to Fleischman, who read it, nodded, and put it on the table. A few minutes later a bailiff opened the door, and Gretchen walked in, still wearing her jail-orange shirt and pants. She walked steadily, with her head up, to the table where the attorneys were sitting. Television and still photographers in the press gallery recorded her every move. She smiled quickly at Sam and sat down. Fleischman showed her the note, and she turned around to offer Sam a look of relief and gratitude.

The news allowed Gretchen to keep her chin pointing straight forward while the distract attorney brought charges of involuntary manslaughter against her. The autopsy had revealed that, as expected, Truman had died of a massive and lethal dose of the pain killer Marcain.

The D.A. said that this was a classic case of "wanton disregard for the known dangers" of administering such a potent medication. The judge set bail at $100,000. Sam looked at the defense table to see if the Packers' attorneys were going to protest the figure, but they sat silent. A bailiff led Gretchen to the side door. She looked back at Sam and gave him a fleeting, hopeful smile, before walking out the door.

Sam and Gloria had chosen not to watch TV overnight in the hospital. He could only assume that the story was obliterating all other news in Green Bay, and he was right. On his way out of the courthouse, he bought a copy of the *Press-Gazette*. The three-deck headline screamed from above the fold:

TRUMAN DIES DURING GAME
PACKERS DOCTOR HELD
Pack drops to 1-13 in icy 2-0 loss to Vikings

And another headline below the fold read:

TEAM PRESIDENT JANASZAK
SUFFERS HEART ATTACK,
IN CRITICAL CONDITION

There was a photo of Truman on the snow-covered field, in the process of kicking the ball through the end zone, another photo of the gurney being loaded onto the hearse, and old head shots of Gretchen and Frank Janaszak. Gretchen was smiling, wearing a forest green Packers polo shirt. She didn't look like a killer.

Sam scanned the news stories for new information, but the Packers' media-relations team had done a good job of keeping a lid on the executives, coaches and players. They were all shocked and saddened, of course. They'd all thought Truman was a great guy, though they'd known him less than two weeks. Even the PETA and ASPCA spokespeople were conciliatory in their comments. It appeared that dying had been the magic move necessary to rehabilitate Truman's image.

Randy Joyce's column was predictably downbeat.

CAN IT GET ANY WORSE?

Just when we thought we'd bottomed out—hit the ground with a lifeless thud, like all those errant passes over the last three months—it turns out there's a sub-basement to this disastrous season.

It wasn't just a bad dream at Lambeau yesterday. Quarterback D'Metrius Truman really did die at halftime. Team president Frank Janaszak really did suffer a heart attack. Team doctor Gretchen Kahler really was arrested for murder. Oh, and the Packer really did fall to 1-13.

Only one thing can rescue this franchise now: Prayer.

Deeper in the column, Joyce made passing reference to yet another woe that had been heaped upon the Packers: a lawsuit that would be filed Monday on behalf of a fan named Brandon Feiger, who had slipped on a patch of ice under his seat during the first half of Sunday's game, severely—perhaps permanently—injuring his back. His lawyer wanted unspecified damages—which meant millions.

That must have been the guy Truman had been talking about—the guy Horvath brought into the trainer's room. It sounded like another part of the plan to destabilize the franchise—just in time for this morning's executive committee meeting.

Sam checked the time. The meeting was scheduled to begin at ten in the fourth-floor conference room of the Lambeau Field Atrium. Kleinschmidt had told Sam he wouldn't be allowed into the room, and Sam decided it was just as well—Mueller might not lay out his full proposal with Sam there. Kleinschmidt promised to meet Sam after the meeting and tell him everything that was said.

As he drove across town from the courthouse to Lambeau, Sam wondered where Horvath was. Now that he and Mueller had a four-to-two majority on the committee—Mueller, Talley, Pritchard, and the about-to-be-installed Boulanger, vs. Kleinschmidt and Henderson—Sam doubted that Horvath would be actively trying to improve those odds. Besides, Horvath's designated hitman—Jim Escher—was dead. But Sam still didn't feel safe. Horvath had looked at him with undisguised malevolence when he'd got off the elevator at the hospital. It was a look that said, *Your day is coming.* How long could Horvath and Mueller afford to wait? Sam didn't have the proof he needed to expose their racket yet, but he knew he was close enough to make the two plotters nervous.

Sam also wondered where Scott Krebbs was. He must have seen the story about Gretchen being arrested. Would that drive him underground, waiting to see what happened to his ex-wife—or would he take the opportunity to keep stalking Sam? Krebbs somehow had it in his head that Sam was to blame for Gretchen's dumping him, and unless the cops arrested Krebbs—or Sam was able to change his mind—he was still every bit as dangerous as Horvath.

H E WALKED IN THROUGH THE MAIN entrance, past the dripping icicles that clung to the statues of Lombardi and Lambeau. Inside, near the thirty-foot glass windows, a makeshift shrine to Truman was already growing. Mylar balloons, plastic and real flowers, cards, stuffed animals, and Packers trinkets were being piled up in honor of the late quarterback. Someone had left a sign saying "D'Metrius, a True Man," while others simply read "R.I.P." and "In Sympathy." One card, placed near the edge of the pile, said, "Say hello to the dogs for us." That one would be removed soon.

Sam walked across the Atrium lobby to the elevators and went up to the fourth floor. He saw a security guard sitting at a table in front of the door to the main conference room, and Stuart Fleischman signing in. Applause rippled inside the room. Sam walked down the hall and went into Frank's office to wait for Kleinschmidt to call him.

D OC MUELLER WAS SEATED AT THE HEAD of the table, waiting patiently as Tom Boulanger walked around the room and shook hands with the other committee members who'd just voted him in to replace Ed Larson: Henderson, looking affable as usual, and too large for the chair he was stuffed into; Kleinschmidt, who somehow had managed to pull himself together after his long night at the hospital to look fresh and businesslike; Talley, the banker, who was slender and studious-looking; and Pritchard, the contractor, who wore an ill-fitting sport jacket and looked like he had taken and thrown a few punches in his life.

Mueller had a stack of papers, folders, photos and charts in front of him, copies of which he began handing around the table to the other members. Then he stood up and addressed the group. He spoke without notes, and with a combination of technical authority and bedside manner that had won over many patients.

"Gentlemen, we face a crisis. You know the details: Our franchise value has fallen to twenty-fifth in the league. We're the smallest media market in the league, by far. We can't keep up with the Bears, the Lions, or even the Vikings anymore in terms of revenue. Draft choices and free agents won't sign with us. The best coaches don't want to work here.

"This problem isn't new, and we all know it. As far back 1968, Vince Lombardi asked for more power to run the team the way he saw fit. He wanted to be part-owner, but the bylaws wouldn't allow it, so he left for Washington—and what did we get? One division title in the next twenty-seven years.

"People keep asking why Brett Favre left. We know the answer to that. It was our inability to put enough talented players around him. He wanted another chance to win a Super Bowl, but he didn't believe this organization had the resources to put together the kind of roster it would take to get him there. We lost two legends because we didn't have money or the structure to give them what they needed.

"How bad are things now? Even the weather seems to have turned on us. There was a time when we always won games like yesterday's fiasco. Not anymore. And to top it off, our quarterback is dead, our team president is in the hospital, and we've just been hit with a lawsuit by a fan who may have permanently injured his back yesterday when he fell on some ice in our stadium. We can't go back to the public and ask for another bond issue. It's too soon since the last one. You know we'll lose.

"I've talked to all of you individually about our predicament, but I want to formally request that the committee vote on pursuing a sale of the team. Some of you have heard the name Purdy McCutcheon, a brilliant Georgia businessman and former player who has put together an ownership group that would like to buy the Packers. He's offering half a billion dollars."

"That's way under market value for an NFL team, Doc," Henderson said.

"I know that. But the community-owned stock certificates are worth considerably less than that. With half a billion dollars in the bank, we could pay our stock owners more than they paid for their certificates, even though we are not obligated by our by-laws to do that.

"In addition, McCutcheon will promise, in writing, to foot the entire bill to put a retractable dome on Lambeau Field."

Dome Lambeau? On the face of it, there were few proposals that would be more outrageous—turning Yellowstone into a paved skateboard park, perhaps, or filling the Grand Canyon with discarded electronic equipment—but indoor football in Green Bay came close. The idea did not move Kleinschmidt or Henderson in the slightest; Talley, Pritchard, and Boulanger, on the other hand, nodded their heads and looked at each other approvingly.

"The current estimate for such a project is somewhere in the neighborhood of three hundred million dollars. There are always cost over-runs, and the longer we wait, you know the more the price is going to go up."

"That's a fact, Doc," said Pritchard, speaking from his experience as a contractor—and as someone who surely would bid for the project.

"So you see, the total package would come in at just about market rate for a lower-end NFL team—which we certainly are at the present time," Mueller said.

"It kills me to hear you call the Packers low-end, Doc," Henderson said. "This isn't the Carolina goddamn Panthers we're talking about. Hell, we're still the Green Bay fucking Packers."

"I know, Mike, but the truth is we've slipped so badly in the last few years that even the Panthers are making more money than we are. You've seen the numbers. You know I'm not making this up. We could wait around, hoping for another Brett Favre to come along, or we can do the responsible thing and take action now, before it's too late. I honestly think this is the best way."

"It may be the only way," Talley said. "The league has never been happy with our ownership structure. They've put up with it for this long because we've been successful, even though the other franchises have squawked. But now, with our record, with this . . . suspicious death . . . with this lawsuit hanging over our heads— I can't see the league opposing a sale. I think they might even try to force one."

"I know the league office would be in favor of the McCutcheon offer," Mueller said. "And it doesn't hurt one bit that he's black. Green Bay has always been the whitest town in the NFL. This would allow the league to brag about its commitment to diversity."

"Better to get out in front of this now, rather than wait for something to be forced down our throats," Boulanger said.

"Tom's right," Mueller said. "This offer won't be on the table forever. Given our current situation, I would expect any future offers to be low-balls. Everybody knows we're not like other teams—we don't have a ton of cash invested that we need to get back. And I can guarantee you nobody else is going to offer to build a dome. Not with their own money."

"But why a dome, Doc? This team has built its reputation on playing outside— on the Frozen Tundra, for God's sake."

"I can answer that one, Stephen," said Boulanger, a handsome man with a thick head of dark hair and the demeanor of a congressman. "With a retractable dome, suddenly Lambeau becomes a year-round gold mine. We would hold huge conventions there. As head of the convention and visitors bureau, I can tell you for a fact that organizations would come from all over the country to spend three days at Lambeau Field. It would quadruple our hotel, motel, and restaurant revenues in an average year—and then there's the Super Bowl."

"The league assures me we'd get a Super Bowl within two years of completing our dome," Mueller said.

"No shit—a Super Bowl in Green Bay?" Henderson said. He whistled.

"A Super Bowl would bring in four hundred million dollars to Green Bay," Boulanger said. "I've seen the numbers."

"And the beauty of a retractable roof is that we could keep it open for games if we wanted to," Mueller said. "You know that within another twenty years, there won't be a northern-tier team that doesn't play indoors. With a retractable roof, the Packers could still be an outdoor team—not that it's given us much of an advantage lately. But with the roof, those draft picks who haven't signed with us because of the weather, those free agents who don't want to play here—we'd get those guys again. And we can keep the roof closed all week before a game, so we don't have to beg for volunteers to shovel out seats, and we won't have to worry about some doofus breaking his back and suing us."

There was silence in the room, but an obvious question hung in the air—one that Henderson finally asked.

"Doc, you keep saying 'we,' but the fact of the matter is, we—meaning those of us in this room—wouldn't be running the team anymore. We'd be out, and I have to say, I like being involved in running the Packers. I think we all do."

Mueller frowned briefly, than assumed his most patient bedside manner, as though talking to a man about his dying wife.

"Mike, what did we all agree to when we were asked to join this committee? To always act in the best interests of the Green Bay Packers. It's not about you, or me, or Woody, or even Frank. It's about guaranteeing that the Packers stay solvent and competitive. That's it. That's our job. Frankly, I'm a little surprised to hear you put your own interests ahead of the team."

"That's not exactly what I meant, Doc," Henderson said, in a wounded tone. "It's just that you keep saying 'we,' like we're still going to be part of this franchise. Are you still going to be part of the franchise? Has McCutcheon offered you a job?"

"No," Mueller said emphatically, but just a moment later than he should have if he were telling the truth. Henderson didn't believe him, and he wondered whether anyone else in the room did. Mueller didn't pause, but quickly went back to his prepared pitch.

"Gentlemen, people aren't beating a path to Green Bay—not football players, not convention planners, not residents of other states, and certainly not people with enough money to buy a pro football team. We love it here, but we know this isn't Las Vegas, or San Antonio, or Los Angeles—three places just dying to get an NFL franchise. For me, the kicker on this deal is that McCutcheon has promised to sign a permanent lease. He will never move this football team, as long as he owns it. No other buyer would be willing to do that."

Mueller described the handouts he'd provided: a chart Talley had developed showing gross revenues versus expenditures during the past five years; another chart comparing the Packers' revenues to those of the other thirty-one NFL teams, an estimate of additional year-round revenues available to the franchise; and the economic impact on the city and county, with a domed stadium, during an average season and a season with a Super Bowl; an estimate of the payouts necessary to stockholders in the event of a sale; and an architect's sketch of what a retractable dome would look like.

The committee members took fifteen minutes to look over the information. They were Mueller's numbers, obviously compiled and presented in a way to bolster his case. If he could swing either Kleinschmidt or Henderson, the lone holdout could be made to seem like an uncooperative crank. In any event, the sale recommendation would go to the forty-five-member board of directors, a body that rarely, if ever, vetoed a decision from the executive committee. Mueller's best chance was now, with Frank Janaszak indisposed.

"I'd like to call for a vote, gentlemen," Mueller said. "I hereby move that the Green Bay Packers be put up for—"

"Wait, Doc," Henderson said. "Why does this have to be done today? What's your hurry? Can't we at least wait a couple of days to see how Frank is doing?"

"What difference will a couple of days make?" Mueller said.

"Maybe all the difference in the world. If he recovers, he can rejoin the committee and vote on this."

"If he recovers, he won't be ready to come back to work for weeks," Mueller said, trying to sound concerned about Janaszak's well-being.

"But I'd sure like to know whether he'll eventually be coming back before I vote on this," Henderson said.

"So would I," Kleinschmidt said.

"This deal won't be on the table that long," Mueller said, maintaining his demeanor of calm persuasion.

"A couple of days—until we find out about Frank, one way or the other."

"All right. I can put McCutcheon's group off until Thursday. No later."

"We'll meet back here on Thursday, then, and vote on your motion," Kleinschmidt said.

"Thursday," Mueller said. "In the meantime, I'll be at my place up in Minocqua, if any of you have questions."

KLEINSCHMIDT PHONED SAM AFTER THE ROOM had emptied, and was still seated in his chair when Sam entered. He recapped the meeting, showed Sam the financial handouts that Mueller had distributed, and told him they'd managed to put off the vote until Thursday.

"The dome and the Super Bowl are the new wrinkles," Kleinschmidt said. "Even Mike Henderson seemed impressed."

Sam sifted through the papers Mueller had handed out, and was about to put the packet back on the table when he noticed that the last document was a copy of the lawsuit filed that morning in Brown County district court: Feiger vs. Green Bay Packers, Inc. Included on the cover sheet was Brandon Feiger's address, which Sam jotted down in his notebook, and the name of the law firm representing him: McCullough, Risebrow & Taylor, Chicago, Illinois.

McCullough. That name rang a bell. Sam flipped back through some notes he'd taken when talking to LaBobby Suggs. That was it—Suggs was represented by Peter McCullough of Chicago. Drabek, too. Sam went through the court document to see if there was a first name for McCullough. At the top of the first page of the complaint, there it was: Peter Joseph McCullough for the plaintiff. So McCullough was allegedly advocating for a couple of individual Packers players who were accused of crimes, and at the same time representing a fan who was suing the team.

The vote would be on Thursday. That gave Sam enough time to drive to Chicago. It was a long shot, but Sam was running out of ways to keep the Packers off the market, and Gretchen out of prison.

TWENTY-TWO

Michael Banks was born Michael Bankowski in Milwaukee, the son of second-generation Polish immigrants. Leo Bankowski, a city sanitation worker, and Mary, his wife, a waitress, worked hard to achieve a modest two-story house in a decent neighborhood on Milwaukee's South Side. Their original goal for Michael, their first-born, was to become a priest, but he showed little interest in the church or his catechism studies. If not a priest, then a lawyer, they decided. America was a harsh place for an uneducated man. There would be no sewer work for their son. He was smart. He ought go to law school, work in an office, keep his hands clean.

Like most boys his age, what Michael really wanted to do was play ball. He liked baseball, loved going to Brewers and Bucks games, but he adored football, and worshiped the Packers. He was not large or strong for his age, however, and his parents worried that something might happen to him on the football field that would prevent him from going to college and achieving more than Leo had.

When it was time to fill out the permission slip to play tackle football at school, Michael knew it was no use bringing the slip home. His parents would never sign it. His pals asked why he didn't come out for the team. Instead of telling them his parents wouldn't let him, he just waved them off.

"I don't have time," he'd say. "I'm going to get a job."

He was always tempted to follow that with "Someday I'm going to own the Packers," but he knew he'd be laughed at. Nobody owned the Packers. Not yet, anyway.

He started with a paper route, then became a stock boy at the local supermarket. When he was old enough, a vendor at County Stadium. That was the best. Twice each fall, the Packers played "home" games in Milwaukee. Michael sold Cokes, pretzels, and hot dogs, and still managed to see almost all the plays. On Sundays when the Packers were in Green Bay or on the road, he watched the games on television, dreaming of someday walking into the Packers locker room and chatting with the head coach or the star running back. If he owned the Packers, he could do that whenever he wanted.

Of course, a bright boy like Michael Bankowski would understand that the Packers were owned by the community, by thousands of stockholders. But Michael also understood that no business arrangements—particularly in sports—lasted forever. A good lawyer and a lot of money could get you anything you wanted in America.

Michael enrolled at Marquette University and breezed through his undergraduate work. He was already planning his name change. "Bankowski" was too old-world, too coarse. It wouldn't do for a young man who envisioned himself moving among the sports and entertainment elites. He knew it would hurt his parents deeply, but he was not going to attend law school as Michael Bankowski. He had his name legally changed the summer after his received his bachelor's degree, and by that fall, his classmates at the University of Chicago Law School knew him only as Michael Banks.

Nothing seemed to stop Banks on his rise to the top. His grades were outstanding, he made the law review, and he seemed to know and be liked by every student and professor at school. Most assumed that Banks was gearing himself up for a career in politics, but he never took his eye off his true goal: He was going to be a sports agent. The best, most powerful, and richest sports agent in America.

He started by simply hanging out where the athletes were. He knew he had no shot at representing the elite college players already projected as first-round picks in football, baseball, or basketball, but he made a habit of attending Big Ten games at Northwestern and introducing himself to freshmen and sophomores with potential, and to upperclassmen who'd been overlooked. He had professional-looking cards printed up. The phone of the Michael Banks Agency rang in his law-school dorm room.

His first break came on a bitingly cold March afternoon at Rocky Miller Park in Evanston, where Banks saw a big, raw, left-handed pitcher named Todd Whitley come in to pitch for the Iowa Hawkeyes and strike out four of the six batters he faced. Banks had been to enough games to know the family members from the scouts. He slid over one row and sat down next to a bald man with a long, bumpy nose, wearing a lined topcoat and holding a spiral notebook. The man was Art Burns, who'd pitched for the Phillies in the 1960s and now scouted high schools and colleges for them. Banks introduced himself and bought the older man a Styrofoam cup of hot chocolate. He wasn't sure if Burns would be willing to chat about his work, but he discovered that the old scout was cold, bored, and eager for some company and conversation. Burns poured a shot of Jim Beam from a pint bottle into his hot chocolate and gave Banks the skinny on Todd Whitley.

Whitley was coming off an elbow injury that had kept him sidelined for more than a year but had been a decent prospect in high school. He had grown considerably, and his fastball was better now than it had been before he was hurt. Major-league scouting directors were still wary of elbow injuries to potential prospects, however, and Whitley wasn't likely to pitch enough innings to move up on many draft lists. Thus, the big-time agents had stayed away from him, investing their time in players more certain to land hefty signing bonuses.

Whitley was exactly the kind of player Michael Banks had been looking for.

After the game, Banks waited for the Iowa players to file out of the locker room to the team bus, and pulled Whitley aside. In two minutes, he made an impression on the young pitcher as a real go-getter who believed completely in him. Whitley agreed to be represented by the Michael Banks Agency. He was drafted that June by the Cubs in the fourteenth round, made it to the majors the following year, made the All-Star team as a closer, and then signed a multiyear contract that gave up his first two years of potential free agency in exchange for a six-year, thirty-eight million-dollar deal. Banks got the standard ten percent—3.8 million dollars. He was off to the races.

With the money—and public attention—he accrued from the Whitley contract, Banks could travel, hire associates, entertain potential clients, and eventually land his big breakthrough signing: Devon Harrison, the Heisman Trophy-winning running back from Tennessee. Harrison was drafted third by the Chargers, behind a quarterback and a defensive end, but Banks rightly surmised that the Chargers were desperate for a young, powerful running threat and would do whatever it took to sign Harrison. Banks held him out of rookie camp, held him out of mini-camp, held him out of training camp, and held him out of the first six games of his rookie season. Eventually, San Diego caved in, as Banks knew they would, signing Harrison for more money than either the first or second picks in the draft had received.

The fact that Harrison blew out his knee five weeks later made the huge signing bonus look even better, from Banks's perspective. He'd protected his client from the catastrophe of having to actually go to work for a living if he couldn't play football.

It became Banks's standard M.O. to have his top picks hold out for the best contract in that year's draft, regardless of how many players had been taken earlier. Players who signed with Michael Banks understood that they were not likely to attend their first pro training camp, or play for the first month of the regular season. Increasingly, Banks was forcing teams to trade his clients to other teams when they balked at overpaying. Banks told his clients over and over again: Don't be in a hurry to sign. A great contract takes a long time, and there's really no rush. Your career might last fifteen years, or, like Devon Harrison's, five games, but either way, I'm going to get you the money you deserve for being the biggest, the fastest, and the strongest.

It became known as the Michael Banks Way: I represent only the best. If a team drafts one of my players, they'll pay for the privilege.

Some retired NFL greats began saying Banks was bad for the game, that no untested rookie deserved that much money coming out of college. Banks and his clients didn't care about the opinions of some broken-down old relics who hadn't been lucky enough to be born twenty years later. All they cared about were the zeros in the signing bonuses—the part of the contract that was guaranteed. And there were lots and lots of zeros. Banks became an extremely rich man.

The league hated Banks. Some teams refused to draft players that Banks represented. That was hard to do, however, when year after year, Michael Banks announced that he'd reached agreement to represent that year's Heisman winner, or the Outland Trophy winner, or the winner of the Davey O'Brien, Lombardi, or Butkus awards. Sometimes all of them.

In the past few years, however, another superagent had appeared to take a big slice out of the Banks empire. Arnie Hollister had picked off several high-profile college football players, including the last two Heisman winners. When both refused to consider signing with the Packers, it became clear that the Michael Banks Way was no longer exclusive to Michael Banks.

Team owners, general managers, and sports columnists wondered whether Banks was losing interest in his business. He'd been single-minded in his rush to the top of his field, so it was not like him to let players like Tyrone Givens and Dayne Collins get away to another agent. He'd held on to most of his existing clients—including some troublesome head-scratchers like D'Metrius Truman and LaBobby Suggs—but was no longer aggressively pursuing the game's top talent. No one knew better than Banks that you couldn't sit still in the sports agent business and wait for the blue-chippers to come to you. But that's what he appeared to be doing lately.

In fact, Banks was quietly preparing to clear his client roster.

He'd known Purdy McCutcheon since his college days. Georgia had played a non-conference game against Northwestern, and McCutcheon had had a good game at linebacker. Back then, Purdy was the kind of player who wasn't good enough to make the NFL, but too good to sign with a nobody agent like Michael Banks. Nevertheless, Banks made an impression, as he always did. And Banks stayed in touch, even when McCutcheon's pro career didn't pan out. Banks had seen something in the young linebacker that he liked—a combination of intelligence, ambition, and work ethic that made it clear McCutcheon was going places, in or out of cleats. When McCutcheon began succeeding in business, Banks would send him congratulatory notes from time to time. On scouting/recruiting trips to the south, Banks would try to get together with Purdy for dinner. Even then, the idea of owning the Packers was never far from Banks's mind, and something told him that Purdy McCutcheon could be part of that plan.

The more successful Michael Banks became, the more obvious it was to him that the NFL would never stand for him as sole owner of a franchise. He'd alienated too many in that highly exclusive rich man's club. Make that, rich *white* man's club.

While he knew the NFL would abhor a Michael Banks ownership, he also knew the owners were eager to sell a team—somebody else's team, of course—to an African-American. The league had a spotty record on race relations, as all pro leagues did, but a significant portion of its customer base was black. Purdy McCutcheon was a perfect fit. He had a football background, a spotless record, and a lot of money.

He had even more money, now that Banks had begun transferring large sums of his own money—through other corporations he owned or controlled—into the accounts of corporations owned or controlled by McCutcheon. It would not do for Banks to be seen as the principal money behind an ownership bid, even if he actually was. It would do, however, for him to be a minority investor. After the sale was complete, well, the cream would rise to the top. McCutcheon would eventually sell his shares to Banks. The roof would be completed, a Super Bowl would be held in Green Bay, another one would be scheduled, the team would be winning again, and the value of the franchise would have easily doubled from where it was today. Banks could then do whatever he wanted: Keep the team, if he still enjoyed the life of an NFL owner, or sell it at a profit of somewhere around a half-billion dollars. If the next owner wanted to move the Packers, that would be his call.

For several years, Banks had been secretly steering top draft picks and free agents away from Green Bay. There was no way he could even dream of prying his beloved franchise loose from its citizen owners unless it began to fail. He had to keep the best players from going to Green Bay, but he couldn't be the agent who did that, then turn around and expect to be allowed to own part of the team. That's where Hollister came in. Three years earlier, Banks and Hollister had reached a private agreement: Hollister would assume the entire roster of Banks Agency clients once Banks became owner of the Packers, if he agreed to keep studs like Givens and Collins from going to Green Bay. Banks knew it was a risky proposal. An ethical agent wouldn't touch it—in fact might rat him out to the league—but then again, how many agents were offered the world's most glittering stable of professional athletes on a platter? Hollister quickly agreed.

"I'm curious, though," Hollister had said to Banks after they'd each lit up cigars to celebrate the agreement. "Why would you give all this up?" He waved his lit cigar around, indicating the sumptuous office Banks occupied, with its view of the Loop through ten-foot windows, the world-class artwork, the four large-screen plasma TVs, and the glass trophy case that housed two Major League MVP plaques, a Bert Bell Award, two Super Bowl MVP trophies, and a dozen or more All-Pro citations, all presented to Banks by grateful clients.

"Because the games themselves don't mean anything to me now," Banks said. "I loved sports when I was a kid. That's why I got into this business. To me, the Super

Bowl was the ultimate achievement. Now, every year I've got at least six clients on both Super Bowl teams. I'm happy for the guys on the winning team, and sorry for the guys on the losing team. Either way, I get no sense of personal satisfaction out of the game. I'm a winner either way.

"I want to care about who wins, and who loses. I've got all the money I need, but I don't have that."

But it was more than that, Banks admitted to himself. More, and less. For most of his life, the goal of owning the Packers had driven him with a burning ambition that no other agent could touch. A potential client was like a loose ball rolling free at midfield, and Banks was going to get to that ball first, no matter what, as another small step toward his ultimate goal of amassing enough money to buy the team he loved.

But years in the business had revealed pro football to be just that—a business. He could no longer muster the same sentimental attachment to his boyhood heroes. He now saw pro athletes as interchangeable parts in an enormous money-making enterprise. He'd gotten to know too many of them; they weren't special. They were just men, like the guys who serviced his Bentley, or the brokers who managed his stock portfolio, or the repairmen who took orders from his wife at their Sheridan Road mansion. Professionals doing a job. And that was the way he saw himself, too— no longer a star-struck kid whose dream of owning his favorite football team was nearly within his grasp, but a professional businessman who'd tired of sitting outside the arena, and now wanted to buy his way in.

Owning the Packers would be another achievement no other agent could claim. To do that, he'd needed an insider. He'd needed Doc Mueller.

It had been easier than he'd figured. His insider had to be a member of the Packers executive committee, which left just seven possible candidates. After some discreet inquiries among friends and associates in Green Bay, he'd quickly realized that Frank Janaszak and Ed Larson could never be persuaded or bought, and that Mike Henderson and Stephen Kleinschmidt were Packers traditionalists with squeaky-clean backgrounds. Talley was more open-minded about the team's future, but as a prominent banker he had everything to lose and nothing to gain by getting involved in an under-the-table deal to sell the team. Pritchard stood to benefit if his construction company got the bid for the retractable roof, but he'd have to avoid any hint of a conflict of interest. They could count on his vote, but not his involvement.

That left Mueller, who was something of a folk hero because of his ties to Lombardi. He was also something of a loose cannon. It hadn't taken Banks long to find out about Mueller's gambling debts, his marital problems, and his ambition to run the team. He was in line to become president whenever Janaszak died or stepped down, but Mueller was in his sixties, and by all accounts an impatient man.

They met on a brilliant autumn day in San Francisco and flew down the coast together in Banks's private plane to the Cypress Point Club, where Banks was a member. The plan was to dazzle Mueller with the wealth and luxury that could be his if he helped steer the team toward Banks and his group. The plan worked. Banks paid for everything—the golf, the meals in Carmel, the lodging at an oceanfront home rented for the weekend—and Mueller lapped it all up like a starving cat. Over dinner and drinks on the second night, Banks told Mueller he would remain as club president, at a salary of a million dollars a year. Banks would pay off Mueller's gambling debts. He'd have a clean slate and glittering future. In return, Mueller had to help destabilize the franchise and steer the executive committee toward a sale. Banks said he would leave the means and the method up to Mueller, but he expected results.

Mueller had agreed, with one condition: He'd need help. He wanted Packers security chief Joe Horvath in on the plan. In return for cash up front and a promise of becoming director of Administrative Affairs—at five times his current salary—Horvath would be the guy to identify the worst thugs around the NFL, get their names to Mueller (who would in turn pass them on to Banks, who would steer the ones he controlled toward the Packers), and orchestrate their disruptive behavior when they arrived in Green Bay. It was a necessary component if the Packers were going to deteriorate to the point where the community would be willing to dump the franchise.

And Horvath would watch Mueller's back. Mueller knew he would, because Horvath already owed him.

It happened a few years back, while Mueller was checking on a patient late one night at Green Bay Memorial. Horvath was brought into the emergency room by paramedics—accompanied by two Green Bay police officers. He'd slammed his SUV into a telephone pole on a freezing February night, and the officers said they'd smelled alcohol in the car. One of them had worked with Horvath years before, when they were both young cops on the force, and Mueller knew the cop was conflicted about getting his old friend in trouble for DUI. It would undoubtedly cost Horvath his job as director of Packers security. The officers had been unable to administer a field sobriety test because Horvath had sustained a head injury and was lapsing in and out of consciousness. A blood-alcohol test was going to be necessary at the hospital.

Mueller didn't know Horvath well, but he did know that having indebted friends in positions of authority could pay off someday. Horvath could make trouble for Mueller about his gambling, if he so chose. Mueller took the opportunity to make sure that would never happen.

He told the cop that he would personally administer Horvath's blood test, and the young doctor in the emergency room, who was already busy with both an alcohol poisoning and a third-degree burn from a space heater, was happy to let Mueller lend a hand. Mueller drew his own blood instead of Horvath's, and of course it tested clean. Two days later Horvath was released from the hospital with a slight headache and no charges filed. Later that day, Mueller visited Horvath at his Lambeau office and made it clear that the only reason he still had has job was Mueller's involvement.

"You were at least point two-oh," Mueller told him. "You'd be cleaning out your office today if it hadn't been for me."

Horvath had stared back at Mueller, knowing a thank-you was not what the doctor was looking for.

"What do you want?"

"I'll let you know."

They'd been a good team. Even Banks had to admit he didn't think things would come together this quickly. He'd been prepared to wait at least another season or two, but the rapid decline of the Packers' fortunes made the time right to push for the sale. Especially now with Frank Janaszak out of the picture.

Banks was waiting to get an update from Mueller on Janaszak's condition Tuesday morning when his secretary rang his line.

"What is it, Gail?"

"LaBobby Suggs is here to see you."

"Did he have an appointment?"

"No, it's not on my calendar. He said they decided to drive down this morning. It's his only day off this week."

"They?"

"He's here with his bodyguard."

"Bodyguard?"

"Yes, sir. They're both waiting out here in the lobby."

"Fine, send them in."

Banks stood up and looked out his window at Lake Michigan, some thirty floors below and to the east of his suite of offices in the Sears Tower. He sometimes wished he had his own building, somewhere out in the suburbs, something like the compound Scott Boras had in Southern California. That way he could better control his clients' access to him. Now he had to gin up the cheerful, rah-rah demeanor of the sports agent who always had a positive word for even his most washed-up clients. He was tired of it, and he'd be glad when pathetic nobodies like Suggs dropped in on Arnie Hollister instead.

There was a knock on his door, and Banks said, "Come in."

LaBobby Suggs's enormous frame filled the doorway as he walked into Banks's suite. Behind him was a man Banks hadn't seen before, about five-foot-eleven, with sandy blond hair and the build of a hockey player, with a slightly bent nose.

"LaBobby, it's great to see you," Banks said. He walked around his desk to shake the nose guard's big paw.

"Yeah, same here, Mike," Suggs said. "This is my bodyguard, Sam Skarda."

TWENTY-THREE

Skarda . . . ? Where do I know that name?"

Banks had pulled up a couple of chairs for his visitors, in front of the gas fireplace that took up a good part of the north wall of his suite. He sat down facing them, the Chicago skyline and Lake Michigan spread out behind, eying Sam with the same critical eye he'd used to size up athletic prospects. He'd wondered what Skarda looked like. Now he knew. There was hard muscle under the jacket and sweater, that much was clear. There was almost certainly a gun, as well, perhaps holstered in the small of his back, despite the sign next to the entrance that said, "WE PROHIBIT FIREARMS ON THESE PREMISES." Banks could also tell from the way Skarda sat down that his left knee was not quite right. Everything else appeared to be in working order. The look in Sam's eye was all business. He was doing a similar inventory on Banks, coming up with the same conclusion: a dangerous adversary, not to be trusted.

"Skarda's a pretty common name in Chicago," Sam replied.

"What's that, Serb?"

"Czech."

"Plenty of those around. What makes you think you need a bodyguard, LaBobby?"

Suggs shifted in the chair, which was not quite big enough to comfortably hold him.

"Lotsa strange shit goin' down these days," Suggs said. "Home break-ins, guys gettin' punched in bars, hold-ups on the street—hell, you know how it is. If you're a pro athlete these days, you're a target."

"I understand," Banks said. "I know you get the memos we send out warning our clients to be careful about where you go and who you associate with. We don't want any of our athletes in trouble."

"Then we're on the same page," Suggs said. "I just figured I could use a little help—especially since I'm already in a jam up in Green Bay."

"Yes, that was unfortunate. Just a minute."

Banks got up, buzzed his secretary, and asked her to bring in a tray of coffee and soft drinks. He sat down again and looked at Suggs, then at Sam, and smiled.

"I'm sorry, I just find it kind of ironic that you've chosen a guy like Sam here to be your bodyguard. You're practically twice his size."

"I'm highly trained," Sam said.

Banks searched Sam's face for signs of humor, but found none. The door opened. Gail walked in with the tray and placed it on the coffee table between them. Suggs took a bottle of Coke out of the ice bucket. Banks poured himself a cup of coffee. Sam had nothing but kept staring at Banks in a way that he probably knew would make their host uncomfortable. Time to rattle the agent's cage and see which way he jumps.

"So, what brings you here today, LaBobby?" Banks asked. "Are you getting all the help you need from Peter McCullough's firm with your, uh, assault case?"

"Interesting that you bring up McCullough," Sam said. "Did you know he's representing a guy named Brandon Feiger, who's suing the Packers for a back injury he claims to have sustained at Lambeau on Sunday?"

"No," Banks said. "How would I know that?"

"Because Feiger is the same guy that Joe Horvath hired to sucker-punch Cornell Johnson at the strip club last week. LaBobby was there. He saw the guy. In fact, he's prepared to pick him out of a lineup."

"What's that got to do with me?" There was an edge in Banks's voice that even he recognized. He was disappointed in himself. He'd trained himself to remain totally calm and in control no matter how tense negotiations got. But this was a new challenge for him. He wasn't used to concealing criminal activity.

"Everything. I know you're the main investor in Purdy McCutcheon's bid to buy the Packers. I know you and Doc Mueller have been trying to sabotage the franchise so the town will be willing to give up community ownership."

"Now, wait a minute—"

"You've steered your most undesirable clients to the Packers, and then set them up with phony assaults and brawls, like LaBobby. No offense, LaBobby. When you knew you didn't have enough of the committee members to pass a sale vote, you and Doc decided you had to kill Ed Larson. When I started asking questions, you sent Escher to kill me. When D'Metrius Truman figured it out and was about to blow the whistle, Doc killed him. And then he tried to kill Frank Janaszak."

Banks made every effort to remain impassive, but hatred blazed from his eyes toward Sam. All had been going so well until this fucking detective showed up. But he still couldn't prove any of it. And there was still a very good chance that Skarda would turn up dead before he could convince anybody. Banks comforted himself with that thought, and allowed himself to take a couple of slow, relaxed breaths before responding. His chuckle actually sounded natural and unforced.

"That's the most amazing story I've ever heard," Banks said. He took another sip of his coffee, holding the cup with a steady hand for Sam's benefit. "LaBobby, where did you find this comedian?"

"I ain't laughin'," Suggs said. "You hear anybody but yourself laughin'?"

"LaBobby, I run a billion-dollar business. Why would I be involved in something as bizarre as this?"

"I got no idea. All I know is that I never broke into that woman's house, I never raped nobody, and that guy who started the fight at the White House is the same guy who says he hurt his back at Lambeau, and he's got the same lawyer as me—the guy you got for me."

"Coincidence," Banks said, inwardly cursing Horvath and Mueller for using the same guy twice. What, there weren't dozens of pliable stooges for hire in Green Bay?

"Maybe so," Sam said. "But I was a cop for a dozen years, and I never saw that many coincidences pile up in a year, much less in one case. You orchestrated this whole thing, Banks, and you're going down."

"Laughable."

"I'll bitch-slap the laughs right out of you," Suggs said.

Banks rose abruptly and said, "Get out of my office. Both of you."

He walked to the door and opened it.

"Suggs, find yourself another agent—if you can. I won't stand for having my character and reputation impugned. Certainly not by a broken-down ex-cop and a fat load of goo who's been a has-been for the last three years and is too dumb to know it."

Banks stood next to his open door, waiting for them to leave. Sam got up and walked out without looking at Banks, having gotten exactly the reaction he was hoping for. Suggs, however, stopped next to Banks and looked down at him, his nose hovering several inches above the agent's. There was deep hurt and anger in Suggs's narrowed eyes.

"You got the fancy office, the expensive suit, and the hundred-dollar haircut, and I may be a has-been," Suggs said, "but inside, man, you're worse than nothin', 'cause you never was nothin'."

Then he took Banks by the shoulders and pushed him backwards, the way he'd toss an offensive lineman out of his way—yet the lightweight Banks recoiled like a towel that Suggs had flicked into a laundry hamper. He reeled backward, knocking the coffee tray to the floor with a crash, and tumbled over the back of the couch. He landed hard against the window, and for a second Sam thought he might see the nation's most powerful sports agent fall thirty stories, ending as a glob of pavement pizza. The window vibrated but did not break.

"Get out!" Banks screamed. "I swear to God, I'll call the cops!"

"That's the last thing you'd do," Sam said.

Two athletic-looking guys in sweat suits had materialized outside Banks's office door, summoned by Gail when she heard her boss screaming. They took a step toward Suggs, who grabbed each with one of his hands and held them at arm's length, staring at one, then the other, with contempt.

"We was just leaving, gentlemen," Suggs said. "Unless you got something you want to say?"

They looked at each other and shook their heads. Suggs released them, and he and Sam walked out the door of the Michael Banks Agency and headed to the elevators.

"I don't think you're washed up yet, LaBobby," Sam said. Suggs laughed as they stepped into the open car and pushed the button for the lobby.

"Now what?" Suggs said.

"Now we go talk to Peter McCullough. And keep our heads up. Banks is going to send somebody after me."

"He better have somebody tougher than those two clowns back there."

"He does."

They walked across Franklin and got into Sam's Cherokee in the Sears Tower parking ramp. McCullough's office was a few blocks north on West Wacker Drive. It was getting close to noon, and the streets were clogged with slow-moving lunchtime traffic. The towering office buildings blocked out most of the low December sun, but the snow from last weekend's storm was melting and running in the streets. Sam guessed it might reach forty by midafternoon. The thaw was on.

The law offices of McCullough, Risebrow & Taylor were suitably subdued, wood-paneled, and old-moneyed. They probably didn't see a lot of clients like LaBobby Suggs. All heads turned when he walked into the lobby and asked to see Peter McCullough. Told that Mr. McCullough was with a client, and then had a lunch appointment, Suggs suggested to the receptionist that Mr. McCullough skip lunch, because Mr. Suggs of the Green Bay Packers was here to see him.

"I'll relay the message," the receptionist said. Her neck appeared to be cramping from looking up at the towering nose guard.

Five minutes later, they were escorted down a hallway to McCullough's office. He was a bookish, wiry man, somewhere around fifty, with thick, wavy hair graying at the temples. He wore tortoiseshell glasses, a gray three-piece suit, and the standard black wing-tips. Law books and a framed diploma from the University of Chicago Law School were the only prominent decorating touches in the businesslike office.

Suggs introduced Sam as a detective working for the Packers. McCullough invited them both to sit down.

"Did you get my message?" McCullough asked Suggs.

"What message?"

"Oh, I thought that's why you were here. I got word from the Green Bay police early this morning that the sexual-assault charges against you are being dropped."

"Dropped? Why?"

"Someone found Natalie Dellums' frozen body in a game preserve north of Green Bay last night. She was partially covered with snow, but with the wind on Sunday, some of it must have blown and drifted away. She'd been shot once in the back of the head."

"So that's it?"

"She can't very well testify against you now."

McCullough was studying Suggs to see how he reacted to the news. He certainly had to be thinking that Suggs might have shot Dellums himself, but Sam knew Suggs could account for almost all his time since Dellums had disappeared. The Packers were at practice Saturday, stayed in the team hotel Saturday night, and went to the stadium together Sunday.

"It was Horvath," Sam said. "He's covering his tracks."

"Horvath?" McCullough said. "Joe Horvath—head of Packers security?"

"That's the guy. You know him?"

"I talked to him about the slip-and-fall case at Lambeau. I'm representing Brandon Feiger, the injured party."

"And how did you end up with that case?"

"Feiger called me out of the blue. Said he'd heard I was good."

"Was Horvath cooperative?"

"Very much so. More than I expected, really. Normally, the employees of the company we're suing won't say anything unless they're officially deposed, or brought to court to testify. But Horvath said there was a lot of ice in the stadium that the volunteers couldn't remove. It was almost like he was helping us make our case."

"He was. He put Feiger up to it."

"How do you know that?"

"It's complicated—let's hold that for the moment," Sam said. "How long have you worked for Banks?"

"He's been a client for about five years. I represent some of his athletes. Not all of them."

"Not the big names? More the small fish, like LaBobby here?"

"Well, I wouldn't call LaBobby small," McCullough said with a polite laugh. "But that's right. He has someone else do legal work for his superstars."

"If I were you, Peter, I'd start distancing myself from Michael Banks altogether. I think you're going to be hearing in the next few days that he's connected to the death of Natalie Dellums, and a whole lot more."

McCullough pursed his lips and picked up a coffee cup on his desk, running his thumb along the lip. He looked like he wanted to tell Sam something. He did not look shocked at the news that Michael Banks might be in deep trouble. Finally, he leaned back in his chair and asked Suggs why he'd come to see him.

"We were just at Banks's office," Suggs said. "We told him what we knew. He threw us out. Now we'll tell you what we know. You can decide if you want to throw us out, too."

Suggs looked at Sam to see if he should go ahead. Sam nodded. He saw no reason to worry about McCullough going back to Banks with any of the information. For one thing, he believed McCullough was playing it straight with them, and didn't know about Banks's plan to take over the Packers. But even if he did—even if he called Banks as soon as they left McCullough's office—Sam had already confronted Banks, and told him everything he knew or suspected. He still had a long way to go to prove any of it, but he wanted Banks to realize how close he was to being exposed. McCullough couldn't hurt them. In fact, if he called Banks, it would reinforce the point that the circle was closing. Banks was bound to make a mistake—at least, that's what Sam hoped.

Suggs told McCullough that he and Truman had talked the night before the Minnesota game, and shared their suspicions about Horvath. When Truman had seen Feiger come into the trainer's room at halftime with Horvath, he knew the guy was working some kind of scam. Suggs hadn't seen Feiger that day—Horvath took him away somewhere shortly after Truman died—but he could easily identify him from the strip-club fight. Then Sam filled McCullough in on the rest: how Horvath and Mueller had sent a guy named James Escher to kill him, but had instead been killed by Gretchen Kahler's ex-husband; how he'd gone to see Natalie Dellums Saturday morning, but found that she'd left in a hurry a few hours earlier; how Mueller had returned to the hospital in the middle of the night, hoping to finish off Frank Janaszak. When Sam had seen McCullough's name on the legal brief at Monday's executive committee meeting, he decided to ask LaBobby to go to Chicago with him and confront Banks.

McCullough took it all in thoughtfully, interrupting only a couple of times to ask questions. When they were done, he said, "Isn't it time to go to the police?"

"I can tell them I suspect Horvath shot Dellums, but I'm sure he was smart enough not to leave any evidence that would tie him to the killing. Horvath still has a lot of pals on the force. And Mueller probably knows a hundred ways to make what happened to Frank look like an accident—or make it look like Gretchen's fault."

"Who's representing her?"

"The Packers, as of now. But their team attorney, Stuart Fleischman, said if it looks like she did kill Truman—their own player, after all—they can't defend her."

"We'll take the case, if she'll have us."

"I think she'd be grateful, but you've got a lot of conflicting interests going here, too," Sam said.

"Maybe not. I'm going to call a meeting with the partners this afternoon and recommend we drop Michael Banks as a client."

"I think that's a smart idea. We're heading back to Green Bay this afternoon. I'll call you when I know what Gretchen's status is."

"Please do."

McCullough stood up and shook hands with both of them.

"One more word of advice," he said. "Be very careful. Michael Banks does not accept defeat graciously."

Doc Mueller hoisted the twin-bladed ax high above his head and brought it crashing down on the maple log, splitting it in two with a satisfying *crunch*. He had all the firewood he needed, but it always made him feel good to add another couple dozen logs onto the pile under his carport. Besides clearing out the deadwood from the trees surrounding his house on Lake Minocqua, it was great exercise. It kept his muscles toned, burned calories, and honed his hand-eye coordination. He paused between logs to admire the view from the hillside on which his house was built. The sun was brilliant, creating sparkles on the snow-covered expanse of frozen water that stretched from his point near the country club to the homes on the other side of the bay. There were now half a dozen fish houses in the bay, including the simple old wood-sided house installed over the weekend by his nearest neighbor, Walt. Mueller had been in the house several times. Unlike the luxurious models that would go up on the lake in a few weeks—some with bars, bedrooms, furniture, TVs, sophisticated heating systems, and up to six holes in the middle of the carpeted floor—Walt's was a basic one-holer with a couple of folding chairs, a radio, a portable propane heater, and enough floor space for two guys and a case of beer. Walt cracked the same joke every year: "Next year I'm putting in a basement." Mueller kept hoping Walt would sell his rustic old cabin, and that it would be torn down by the new owners and re-placed with something new and classy, like Mueller's place. In the meantime, Mueller had a standing invitation to use Walt's fish house anytime he wanted.

Beyond the fish houses, Mueller's end of the lake was a trail of white that led all the way west through the wide part of the lake to the bridge that led into the town center. He laid the ax against the stump and mopped his forehead with his sleeve. Even 350 miles north of Chicago, the warm westerly winds had lifted the tempera-ture into the mid-thirties.

He set another log on the stump, end-up, but his cell phone rang before he could pick up the ax. He pulled the phone out of his jacket pocket and checked the number—Banks.

"Yeah, Michael."

"Sam Skarda just left my office."

"What the fuck was he doing there?"

"Throwing our plans back in my face. He knows everything—or at least, he's guessed it."

Mueller was silent for a moment. A downy woodpecker was going at a dead tree thirty feet away. Thin, wispy clouds hovered in the blue sky above the tops of the hardwoods. It was all so beautiful, so perfect. All the things that Mueller's asso-ciation with Banks had allowed him to have, and the things he would be able to have once Banks owned the team, seemed to be slipping through his fingers. All because Frank Janaszak had been too stubborn to realize that the eighty-year-old model of a little northern town owning an NFL franchise just couldn't work anymore. Mueller felt like picking up the ax and . . . and . . .

"What are we going to do, Michael?"

"We have to figure out how we're going to get rid of Skarda, Janaszak, and Kahler, and force that vote on Thursday. Call Horvath and tell him to meet us at your place in Minocqua. I'll be there by seven tonight—assuming the hicks up there have gotten around to plowing the roads."

"Driving's fine today. We're having a thaw."

"I want ideas, Doc. We let this thing go on too long."

Twenty-Four

The sun was setting when Sam pulled into the driveway of LaBobby Suggs's apartment building in Green Bay. It was a two-story stucco building with two units—upstairs and downstairs. Suggs had the upstairs. It wasn't a glamorous crib, by NFL standards, but Suggs was not a glamorous NFL player. His signing bonus out of college had long since been spent, and the free-agent contract he'd signed with the Packers was, like all other NFL contracts, not guaranteed—meaning if he were cut for any reason, his paychecks would stop. Banks was right: Suggs was looking at the end of the road, especially if he didn't play some eye-catching football in the season's last two games. He was already trying to save as much money as he could against the time when he'd be an out-of-work, 350-pound black man with a battered body and no job skills.

"Thanks for the help," Sam said as the big man eased out of the passenger seat of the Cherokee.

"You watch your ass," Suggs said. "You need me, call me."

The roads had been wet from melting snow, and Sam's Cherokee was a splattered mess. He was thinking of finding a gas station with a car wash when his phone rang.

"Sam, it's Stuart Fleischman. Gretchen wanted me to call you. She's being released on bail at 4:30 this afternoon, if you can make it over to the county jail to pick her up."

"That's great, Stuart. Who put up the bail?"

"Frank and Gloria."

"Not the Packers?"

"No, this was the Janaszak's doing, from their own bank account. As an organization, we're still officially neutral. But we're studying the case, and we may still decide to represent her."

"How is Frank?"

"He's doing much better. Dr. Richardson is letting him go home tomorrow."

"That means they won't vote on Thursday."

"I would think not."

"Thanks for the call."

"No problem."

Sam put the Cherokee in reverse, backed out of the apartment-house driveway and headed for the Brown County Jail. He arrived just as darkness began to descend on the city, leaving a band of orange in the western horizon beneath the layers of pink and then deepening blue. Stars began to shine overhead, standing out boldly against the near-blackness of the eastern sky over the bay. This didn't feel like another cold front coming in. The breeze felt warm, almost spring-like.

Sam walked into the building and found some of the same reporters and photographers waiting for Gretchen to come out of the holding area. When the door opened and Gretchen emerged, wearing the same Packers game-day shirt, pants, and green parka she'd had on when she was arrested, Sam quickly walked up to her, put his arm around her and led her out the door and down the jailhouse steps.

"Ms. Kahler, did you kill D'Metrius Truman?" a reporter shouted after her.

"Was it an accident?" another yelled.

"Were you angry because of the way he treated those dogs?"

"Did you hate him?"

Sam tried to lead her away to his car, but she stopped and turned to face the trailing reporters.

"I didn't kill D'Metrius Truman. I didn't hate him. I barely knew him. He seemed like a decent person. He was injured in the game, and I treated him professionally. I don't know how he got an overdose of Marcain. I gave him a safe, approved level. That's all I have to say."

She turned and walked with Sam to his car and got in while the cameras continued to flash and whir and the reporters continued to shout inane questions that she had no intention of answering.

As Sam pulled away, he looked at Gretchen to see how she was holding up. He was surprised to see her smiling.

"I've always wondered why people try to duck away from those jailhouse questions," Gretchen said. "They look so guilty if they're not willing to stand there, face the cameras, and say they didn't do it."

"You didn't look guilty," Sam said.

"I don't feel guilty," she said. "Jail really sucks, and I'm sorry Truman died, but I feel great to be out. Frank's going home tomorrow, and I think I know how we can get Doc Mueller. Can you drive me to the hospital?"

Sam nodded and turned west on University Avenue. On the way to the hospital, he told her about his trip to Chicago with LaBobby Suggs. She listened without interrupting as Sam described confronting Michael Banks, watching Suggs manhandle the agent and his two security guards, and having some of his suspicions confirmed at Mc-

Cullough's law office. He told her about McCullough's offer to represent her, but she said Frank had arranged for a local defense attorney named Karstens to take her case.

"Frank really came through for you," Sam said. "He must think pretty highly of you."

"It's mutual," she said. "He's one of the finest men I've ever met."

The way she said it, Sam had a feeling she was including him in that select group. He glanced over at her in the passenger seat and saw that she was smiling at him. He grinned back, and returned his eyes to the road.

"How are you going to trip up Mueller?"

"I have to look at Frank's chart, and talk to him and Richardson about the medications he took, beginning Sunday afternoon after I was arrested. I'm sure Gloria was in a panic when she found out Frank had had a heart attack, and when Doc Mueller offered to help—well, why wouldn't she let him? He was part of the Packers family."

"Mueller said something at the hospital about the medications you were giving him—that they almost killed Frank."

"That's what he would say, to set me up. Frank was fine on Sunday before and during the game. You saw him—he was agitated about Truman, but that would be normal. I'm betting we'll find that something went into his system after I was arrested that shouldn't have been there—and I'm betting he got it from Mueller."

Dr. Richardson was not at the hospital when they arrived, but Janaszak had been moved out of the ICU into his own room, and was awake and alert. Gloria was sitting in a chair next to the bed, working on some crocheting, and a huge smile crossed her face when she saw Gretchen and Sam walk into the room.

"Oh, thank God you're out!" she said. She stood up and rushed to Gretchen, giving her a hug as though she'd just returned from a six-month expedition to the North Pole.

"Thanks to Frank," Gretchen said. She looked over Gloria's shoulder at the pale man who was lying in the bed, a patterned hospital gown tied around him and a suspended IV drip attached to his right arm. Janaszak smiled, too, and gestured for Gretchen to come to him. She walked over and kissed him on the forehead, while Janaszak put his hand up to her face and patted her hair.

"I'm so sorry, Gretchen," he said. His voice sounded weak, but Sam could tell by looking at his eyes that he was mentally up to speed. "What a terrible thing to have to go through."

"Me? Don't worry about me, Frank. I was worried sick about you. How are you feeling?"

"Fantastic. I wanted to go home today, but Richardson wants to run a few more tests tomorrow morning before he lets me go."

"No sign of Doc Mueller?"

"None. The murdering bastard."

"I wouldn't let him come in the room if he tried," Gloria said, losing her smile.

"When are you going to see Richardson again?"

"Tomorrow morning around seven."

"Good. I want to take a look at your workup and your chart. I'll compare the medications I was prescribing for you with what they found in you when they brought you in."

She asked Janaszak to think back to Sunday and try to remember what happened before he fell ill. In slow but steady words, Janaszak described feeling "a little overwhelmed" after the medical examiner's team took Truman's body to the morgue, and then having to tell Marv Ackley, the team, and the media about Truman's sudden death—all the while worrying about Gretchen being in police custody. Then he remembered Mueller looking at him with a concerned expression and saying it appeared he was in trouble.

"He said I needed to sit down and relax for a few minutes. We sat in my office and he got me a cup of tea."

"Tea?"

"Yeah, I thought it was odd. I don't drink tea, but he said he had an herbal tea that was very relaxing. I remember drinking some of it, but . . . well, next thing I knew, I woke up in the ICU."

"Foxglove."

Sam looked at Gretchen.

"What?"

"Foxglove," she repeated. "It's sometimes used in herbal teas. It's the original source of digitalis."

"Well, that's what you had me taking," Frank said. "That shouldn't have hurt me."

Gretchen shook her head.

"A therapeutic level of digitalis isn't far from a lethal level. Mueller would know that. All he had to do was get you to drink some foxglove in an herbal tea, and it would combine with the digitalis you were already taking to push you right into a cardiac event."

Frank sighed, let his head fall back into the pillow, and stared up at the ceiling.

"I remember thinking, 'I wouldn't let this guy stick a needle in me, or give me a pill, but what could a cup of tea hurt?'"

"Maybe the cup is still in your office," Sam said. "If we find it, we can have it tested for foxglove residue. We can also search Mueller's office. Maybe he got careless and left the unwashed cup or some of the tea lying around."

"Another cup of that stuff would have shut off your lights for good," Gretchen said. "Richardson can run a test on you in the morning to see if they can find any traces of the tea still in your system."

Gretchen turned to look at Sam, and he nodded. If they found traces of foxglove leaves in Frank, or in the office, then—combined with Frank's testimony—they had him. Mueller must have been sure Frank wouldn't survive to talk about it—and any suspicion, therefore, would fall on Gretchen for overmedication. Just like with Truman. Except Janaszak lived.

"Frank, Mueller said he was going up to his place at Lake Minocqua until Thursday's meeting, but I don't know where Horvath is, and I don't trust either one of them. I'm going to arrange with Kleinschmidt to have a guard posted outside your room tonight, just to be sure."

"Not necessary, Sam. Stephen has had a guard out in the hall since you and Gloria were here all night. Now, Gloria needs to go home and get some rest."

"And get the house ready for your homecoming," she said.

"We'll meet you back here tomorrow morning at seven," Gretchen said. She patted Janaszak's hand. "I want you to know how much I appreciate your putting up my bail money. Once we nail Mueller, you'll get it back."

"I couldn't stand the thought of you spending one more night in that jail, Gretchen," Janaszak said.

"After we meet with Richardson tomorrow, we'll go to the cops," Sam said. "Then it will be Mueller's turn to be the guest of Brown County."

GRETCHEN WAS SILENT AS THEY WALKED back to Sam's Cherokee in the parking ramp. When they got into the SUV, he turned and saw a tear rolling down her cheek.

"Hey, come on. He's going to be fine," Sam said.

"I know. But he almost died. That son of a bitch Mueller almost killed Frank. God, Sam, I want that bastard to pay for this. For everything."

"He will. I can pull this all together now. VanHoff will have to arrest Mueller and Horvath after he hears the whole story—especially after Frank tells him what happened Sunday."

Sam paid two dollars to the parking-ramp attendant and turned the car toward Gretchen's house. He couldn't imagine that she'd slept well the past two nights, and the truth was, he hadn't caught up from the night at the hospital.

His cell phone rang when they were a few blocks from the house. He pulled it out of his jacket pocket and checked the number. It was Caroline calling.

"Hey," he said. "What's up?"

"Hi, Sam." Caroline's voice sounded refreshed, untroubled—a welcome relief from the strain everyone around him had been feeling. She was a warm desert breeze that filled his heart. He was almost done in Green Bay. He might be in Arizona in a couple of days.

"I got some information for you, from the feds."

"About Joe Horvath?"

"Yes."

Through her Homeland Security contact, Caroline had found out that the FBI had been working on busting a dogfighting ring in Minnesota. Some of the participants were the same guys that D'Metrius Truman had been associated with before he was arrested. An agent named Donald Meacham had infiltrated the group under the name of Reggie Clark, and had gotten a tip from some of the guys in that group that Truman might be attending a dogfight near Harris, Minnesota. Meacham used to work with Horvath in the FBI, and when Horvath had contacted Meacham to find out if the feds had a problem with Truman signing with the Packers, Meacham had told Horvath about the upcoming dogfight. Since Truman hadn't broken any laws after being released from prison, Meacham and the feds didn't mind Horvath interceding to get him out of there before the bust.

"So that's where Truman was when Horvath picked him up," Sam said. "If Truman had been there during the bust, he'd never have played another down in the NFL."

"That's right. But there's more. Horvath and Truman were gone by the time the bust went down, but the guy who owned the farm—a guy named Wesley Dillon—was shot and killed that day. There were no witnesses, and they haven't found the gun. It could have been anybody there—but the feds haven't ruled out Horvath or Truman."

"Thanks, Caroline. That really helps."

"Do you think you've got these guys nailed?"

"Absolutely. There's no way the executive committee would vote for a sale now."

Sam had turned into Gretchen's driveway and parked the car in front of her garage door. Gretchen started to get out on her side when her door was suddenly pushed shut from the outside, throwing Gretchen against Sam. He dropped the phone and started to reach for his gun, which was still holstered in the small of his back, but then he saw Krebbs's face, twisted in hatred, pressed against the passenger-side window. His wet breath fogged up the glass, but Sam could still see the barrel of what looked to be a snub-nosed Smith & Wesson pointed directly at Gretchen's head.

"Open the fucking door or I'll blow your heads off!" Krebbs hissed.

Gretchen reached over and pulled the door handle, pushing the door open a crack. Krebbs reached in with his free hand, and, keeping the gun pointed at Gretchen's head, unlocked the back door. Then he pushed the front door shut again and got into the back seat, closing the door after him.

"Hands where I can see them, Skarda!" he yelled. He waved the gun back and forth between Sam's head and Gretchen's.

"What are you going to do, Scott?" Gretchen said in the calmest voice she could muster. She tried to make it sound like she was asking him what he planned to buy at the grocery store.

"You know, that's a damn good question," Krebbs said.

Sam could see him in his rear-view mirror, illuminated by the yard light outside Gretchen's house. He was bare-headed, and sweaty strands of hair clung to his forehead, as though he'd had a cap on and had been running. He hadn't shaved in days. The cop-killer goatee now nearly blended in as beard. Sam had expected his eyes to be wild and white with the crazy anticipation of shooting two people, but there was actually a look of cold calculation in his glare. Sam could smell alcohol on his labored breath.

"When I went to your house Friday night, I didn't know for sure what I was going to do, babe," Krebbs said. "I brought a gun, but—I don't know. Maybe I would have changed my mind. It's not that easy to kill somebody you love. At least, I didn't think so—not then.

"But I killed that guy here Friday night. I thought it might have been Skarda—and you know what? It didn't bother me. Not a bit. All I cared about after that was finding you. When I heard you were arrested, I was pissed off. Pissed off, because I couldn't get at you. I knew you couldn't have killed that player, but I didn't know whether you'd ever be able to prove it. Then I heard on the news today that you'd made bail, so here I am. And look who you're with."

"Scott—"

"Like I said, I already killed a guy. Now it doesn't matter if I kill two more people."

"It's not what you think, Scott. I told you—Sam is a friend. That's all. He's here on business."

"I don't believe you. I think you never got over him, you got tired of me, you asked him to come here so you could get back together. Now he's living with you. But not much longer."

He put the nose of the gun up to the base of Sam's neck. Sam had to try to twist around and somehow throw Krebbs off balance, but he knew there was no way the shot could miss—no way Sam could avoid getting a bullet in the head. But at least it might give Gretchen a chance to survive, a chance to grab Krebbs's gun. He knew she'd do that. One dead was better than two.

Sam could hear Caroline's faint voice on the phone that now lay on the floor by his feet, calling his name—a tiny electronic echo coming from the world a million miles beyond the confines of the SUV. It might be the last sound he'd hear: the sound of his lover's sweet voice, wondering why he wasn't answering her, before the roar that would take his life. Sam tensed his leg muscles, determined to spin around fast enough to create some chaos when Krebbs pulled the trigger.

He was about to whirl when Gretchen said, "All right, Scott! I'll admit it. I was having an affair."

Sam's eyes darted quickly to Gretchen. She held his gaze for a second, with a look that seemed to say, *Go with me on this.*

"I knew it," Krebbs said. "I knew it. You bitch. You goddamned fucking bitch."

He shoved the barrel of the gun up the side of Sam's head and pointed it directly into his temple.

"But it wasn't with Sam!"

"What?"

Krebbs let the gun slide down again to the base of Sam's neck.

"It wasn't Sam."

"Who? Who were you fucking?"

"Doc Mueller."

TWENTY-FIVE

Mueller?" Krebbs said. "Mueller?"

"Yes."

"No way. I don't believe you. You said you hated the son of a bitch."

"What would you expect me to say? I didn't want you to know."

"I'll kill him. First him, then you."

"Why don't you forget about killing anyone?" Sam said. He could feel that the pressure from the gun barrel was no longer sticking into his neck. "You're not in as deep as you think you are. Not yet."

"What do you mean?"

"The guy you shot here on Friday was a hired killer. He was hiding in the house, waiting for us to come home. He tried to kill you instead. You shot him in self-defense."

"Who hired him?"

Now Sam had to do some quick calculations. He was sure Gretchen had thrown out Doc Mueller's name to try to buy some time. If he told Krebbs that Mueller had sent Escher to kill him and Gretchen, would it destroy her ruse? He thought about Horvath, but Krebbs wouldn't have the patience to listen to the explanation, and besides, Horvath's involvement didn't make sense without Mueller.

"It was Mueller," Sam said. "You're not the only one who gets jealous. He thought the same thing you did—that I was picking up again with Gretchen. He wanted me dead. But I don't think he'd have killed Gretchen. He loves her. When you really love a woman, you don't kill her."

Sam was hoping that would snap Krebbs out of his murderous mindset, but he seemed to ignore Sam's last words.

"You know, I always wondered if the guy you were screwing was somebody on the Packers executive committee. But I thought it would be Frank Janaszak."

"Scott, Frank's almost eighty. I adore him, but not that way."

"Yeah, well, Mueller's not exactly a kid, either. What is it about those old guys, huh? You get off on the wrinkles? I don't get it."

"I can't explain it," Gretchen said quietly. "I'm sorry."

"You keep saying that—you're sorry. What the fuck does that mean? You screw some Packer big shot, then you toss me out in the street. If you didn't want to ruin my life, you wouldn't have done that. Then you'd have nothing to be sorry about."

"I—I'm just sorry, that's all."

"Yeah, well, I'm sorry, too. Sorry that I can't let Skarda live. After I kill him, I'm going to blow Mueller's goddamn dick off, then his head. And I'll make you watch before I do you."

"You know where Mueller is?" Sam asked.

"No, but I'm sure Gretch does."

"I don't," she said.

"I do," Sam said.

"Where?"

"He's at his house on Lake Minocqua. It's about three hours north of here. I've seen it—but you'll never find it without me. I don't think Gretchen's ever been there."

"I haven't."

Krebbs was silent for a minute, his breathing still coming in deep, excited gulps. Sam prayed that he would come to only conclusion that would keep him and Gretchen alive for at least three more hours.

"Okay," Krebbs finally said. "You're going to drive us there. Now. I'll be back here with a gun aimed directly at your skull. If I even think you're going in the wrong direction, or tying to get somebody's attention, or any fucking thing at all except driving straight to Mueller's place, your brain is going out the windshield in little globs. Same for you, babe. A hand signal to another car, anything I don't like, and I'll end it right now. I'd love to see the expression on your face when I start pumping bullets into your boyfriend, but it doesn't have to be that way. I can do you first, and him later.

"So, drive, Skarda. I always wanted to see Lake Minocqua."

Krebbs settled back in the seat, and Sam could see the gun in his rearview mirror. He backed out of the driveway and turned the Cherokee to the west. He drove slowly through the neighborhood, glancing at the homes along the street, with their lighted windows, families finishing their dinners or sitting in front of their televisions, kids in upstairs bedrooms doing homework, maybe staring at their Green Bay Packers posters and dreaming of someday playing for the hometown team. Much the way Sam had grown up, and Gretchen, too. Probably even Krebbs, though Sam knew nothing about his background.

And Caroline . . . was she still on the line? Had she heard any of Krebbs's rantings? Sam didn't want Krebbs to know about the phone on the floor.

"It's a long drive, Scott. Can I play my iPod?"

"Keep your hands on the wheel."

"Gretchen can do it."

"Fine. Put some music on and shut up."

Gretchen plugged the mp3 cord into the iPod that rested in the cupholder between the two front seats. The screen lit up. She turned the volume switch on the car radio, and got the news station that Sam had been listening to on the trip back from Chicago.

". . . posted bond late this afternoon, and told waiting reporters that she did not kill Truman."

Then they heard Gretchen's voice:

"I treated him professionally. I don't know how he got an overdose of Marcain. I gave him a safe, approved level."

"Brown County prosecutor William Daubach said Kahler's involuntary-manslaughter trial will likely begin sometime in early February. In the meantime, Green Bay police are investigating a possible connection between Truman's death and the near-fatal heart attack suffered by Packers president Frank Janaszak, for whom Kahler acted as personal physician . . ."

"Turn that shit off," Krebbs said.

Sam told Gretchen to push the "source" button on the tuner to switch to the iPod.

"What do you want to listen to, Scott?" Sam asked.

"Hey, I don't give a shit, okay? Pick something, and shut up."

"Just hit the pause button . . . bottom of the wheel," Sam said.

The Christmas playlist resumed. Nat King Cole sang his first version of "The Christmas Song," from 1946. The languid, jazz-club arrangement of the sentimental song was so incongruous, given the nutcase with the handgun in the backseat, that Sam hoped, desperately, the music might make Krebbs see how absurd his intentions were.

"You like this old-guy shit?" Krebbs said.

So much for improving his mood.

"Yeah, I do."

"Don't you have anything new, like this century? Got any Foo Fighters?"

"Yes. Gretchen, go to albums. Click 'The Colour and the Shape.'"

Soon the pounding drums and driving guitar line of "Everlong" filled the car. At least it would be impossible to hear Caroline's voice if she were still trying to get Sam's attention on his phone. Dave Grohl's edgy, insistent vocals on the chorus made it hard for Sam to feel hopeful about how this was going to turn out. He tried not to let himself get swept up in the urgency of the music—in this setting, it sounded like a desperate, murderous outlaw soundtrack. He had to keep his head, keep his optimism, to somehow think of way to get them out of this alive.

Sam went through many scenarios as he drove through town, heading for the interstate that looped around the city. Swerve off the road, roll the SUV and hope, somehow, that he and Gretchen would be the ones who emerged alive? Krebbs wasn't wearing a seatbelt—but neither was Gretchen. She'd unbuckled and started to get out of the Cherokee when they arrived at her driveway. Pretend to get lost somewhere along the way, drag the trip out, hope Krebbs lost his concentration, or maybe even fell asleep? No, he'd threatened to start shooting if he tried something like that. Dive out the door at a stop sign? He couldn't do that—even if Krebbs didn't shoot him immediately, Sam did have his seatbelt on. And that still left Gretchen.

Sam had given a number of public-safety talks in his years on the police force, and there was one thing he always emphasized to parents and kids: If somebody tells you, even at gunpoint, to get into his car, don't. Ever. Chances were extremely good that the perpetrator would not shoot you right there on the street, but as soon as you got in his car, where he was in control, your chances of survival decreased by about ninety percent. And yet here he was, held at gunpoint in a car. With Gretchen next to him, his options had been severely limited. Talking on the phone to Caroline had been enough of a distraction that he hadn't been as alert as he should have been. He'd temporarily forgotten about Krebbs. He and Gretchen were likely to pay for that mistake with their lives. There were no tricks that would work here. The best thing he could do was switch to hostage-negotiation mode and try to talk him out of it.

That usually didn't work, either.

They were on the approach to the I-43 bridge that crossed the mouth of the Fox River where it emptied into the bay.

"What are you going to do after you kill us all?" Sam said. "Drive my car back to Green Bay and park it in your driveway? Move back into the house, put a pot of coffee on? Bring in the newspaper and look for a job?"

"I haven't thought that far ahead."

"No, psychos never do."

"Fuck you."

"What I can't figure out is, why don't you suicide killers shoot yourselves first? Save everybody else a lot of grief."

"Who says I'm gonna commit suicide?"

"Hey, I'll put money on it right now. After you kill Gretchen, I got twenty that says you blow your own brains out. So why not just do that first? After that, you won't care what happens to her anyway."

"You think you're being pretty clever, don't you? I'm going to kill Gretchen because of what she did to me. She cheated on me. Then she kicked me out of my own fucking house. She should never have shit on me like that. I loved her more than any man will ever love her. And I'm going to see to it that no man ever gets the chance to love her."

"Sure. If you can't have her, nobody can. That old bit."

"That's right."

"You know how these things always end, don't you? With thousands of people reading about you in the newspaper and hearing about you on TV, thinking, 'What a jerk-off. Too bad that poor women ever married him in the first place.' They'll hate you, and feel sorry for her."

"I don't care."

"If you don't care what happens when this is all over, put the goddamn gun in your own mouth and pull the trigger."

"Shut up, I told you."

"Do it."

"Shut up!"

"Do it, Scott."

"No!"

"Do it!"

Then there was the awful, familiar roar of a gun being fired, so close and so loud that Sam felt his eardrums were bursting. His shoulders hunched involuntarily, but when he knew he hadn't been hit, he quickly turned to Gretchen, who was staring into the back seat, her eyes wide open in terror. Sam adjusted the rear-view mirror and saw that Krebbs was still alive, still glaring straight forward. Then Sam noticed a whistling sound, and realized that Krebbs had put a bullet hole in the roof of the Cherokee.

"The next one is for Gretchen, if you don't shut your fucking mouth," Krebbs said.

"I just thought a little conversation would help pass the time."

Sam felt a painful blow against his right ear. Krebbs had hit him with the revolver, not hard enough to send the car off the road, but hard enough to get his point across.

"Hey, it's kind of hard to stay between the lines when you do that."

"Last warning, smart guy."

Krebbs hit him in the ear again. This one broke the skin, and Sam felt blood trickling down the side of his neck.

They were in the middle of the bridge. The music had momentarily stopped between tracks, and Caroline's voice from Sam's phone was now unmistakably audible.

"Hey, what's that noise?" Krebbs said.

"My cell phone," Sam says. "I was talking to my girlfriend. I dropped it when you jumped into the car."

"Yeah? Give it to me."

Sam reached down to retrieve the phone, wishing he'd worn his Glock in an ankle holster. He could still hear Caroline calling his name as he handed the phone to Krebbs, who put it up to his ear and listened for a few seconds.

"Nice voice," Krebbs said. "Bet you wish you'd stayed wherever the hell she is."

"No," Sam said. "I came here to help a friend. I'm not sorry I did that."

"Well, you can't help her now."

Krebbs put his mouth to the phone and said, in a demented falsetto, "Sorry, Sam can't come to the phone right now." Then he rolled down the window and pitched the phone over the railing and into the river below.

"That's one way to make your problems go away," Sam said.

"Shut up and drive."

Twenty-Six

A warm wind—warm for December—made the tops of the pine trees sway and the bare branches of the hardwoods rustle against each other outside Doc Mueller's lake home. He could see a few lights around the lake as he looked out his kitchen window, but there was no moon tonight, and the lake itself was a vague suggestion of gray beyond his shorefront.

He could hear the splats of water hitting his deck from the dripping icicles that clung to the edge of his roof. His Arctic Cat snowmobile was parked next to the deck, where he'd left it after a late-afternoon run out onto Lake Minocqua. The open water under the highway bridge into town had grown in the warm daytime sun, stretching maybe seventy-five feet on either side of the abutments—though it had not spread close to any of the fish houses. There was no snow in the forecast, so no need to put the sled under the lean-to roof tonight. He'd do that in the morning before heading back to Green Bay.

There was much to do in Green Bay, before Thursday's meeting. First on the agenda was to make sure Frank Janaszak never returned to his seat as committee chairman. There would be no vote on Thursday if the committee members had any hope of Frank's extending his run as team president. Mueller knew that Frank was being released from the hospital in the morning. He didn't know what Frank remembered about Sunday afternoon, and he couldn't take a chance that he wouldn't testify about the foxglove tea. It was time for the frail Packers boss to take a permanent turn for the worse.

Then there was the Skarda problem. When Horvath arrived, they'd have to think of a way to get rid of him. It didn't have to be immediate—Mueller didn't believe Skarda had enough provable information to go to the cops—but the longer he hung around, the more trouble he'd make. What worked for Natalie Dellums could just as easily work for Sam Skarda: a bullet to the back of the head, his body dumped somewhere in the frozen countryside.

Mueller was pacing. He was worried, nervous—but he didn't mind feeling that way. He'd learned that from hanging around pro athletes for forty years: If you weren't nervous before a big game, you didn't belong there. It was the way he felt in a high-stakes poker game, or at the craps tables in Vegas. Slightly scared that he'd lose, but far more excited about the prospects of winning. If you weren't willing to take big risks for even bigger payoffs, you really weren't living, just existing. He was now just two days away from becoming Packers president, and a few months from a million-dollar salary, free use of the team's executive plane, and the power to hire and fire anyone he wanted. He'd be Vince Lombardi—all-powerful, and answerable not to a seven-man committee of contractors, hospital administrators, and car dealers, a forty-five-member board of directors, and 112,000 stockholders, but to just one man: Michael Banks. They could then begin undoing all the damage they'd done to the franchise, get the retractable roof put on Lambeau, get All-Pro players to come to Green Bay again, host their Super Bowl, and play for another championship. The Packers would quickly return to the top of the league, where they belonged, and this time it would be Doc Mueller's doing.

Maybe they'd build a third statue in front of the Atrium: Lombardi, Lambeau, Mueller.

He walked through the living room to look out the front window, expecting either Horvath or Banks to pull up at any time. Banks had said he'd be leaving Chicago around mid-afternoon. Mueller had then called Horvath, who told him he couldn't leave Green Bay until he'd met with a group of NFL Security officials from New York about emergency evacuation procedures at Lambeau. A pain in the ass—everybody was worried about terrorism these days. But Horvath said he'd leave as soon as he could.

Mueller's place in Minocqua was not convenient, but nighttime in the north woods was the ideal time and place for the three of them to get together. They couldn't all be seen together before the committee vote.

At a few minutes past ten, Mueller saw headlights pull into his driveway. He couldn't make out the vehicle until the headlights were extinguished. Then he recognized Banks getting out of his BMW and walking up the steps to the front door. Mueller opened the door and stood aside as Banks entered, stamped the wet snow from his Ferragamo loafers onto the carpet, and kept walking through the living room to the kitchen.

"What have you got to drink?" Banks said, skipping the pleasantries.

"There's gin, vermouth, vodka, Scotch and bourbon in the cabinet above the sink," Mueller said. "Beer in the fridge."

Banks poured himself a bourbon, and Mueller made a Scotch on the rocks for himself.

"Directions easy to follow?" he asked the agent.

"Yeah, they were fine. I just had trouble getting out of the Loop. As soon as I take over the Packers, I'm moving my office."

Mueller heard the "I" and wished he'd said "We." He thought of himself and Banks as a team, but Banks had the annoying quality of assuming Mueller was willing to do all the heavy lifting to make this happen with no recognition. It was true that Mueller wasn't bringing any money into the deal, but he'd done everything else. The extra money would be nice, but Mueller wasn't going to remain in the background after the ownership change. He didn't like it there.

Banks took off his topcoat and hung it over the back of a kitchen chair. He was wearing a dark blazer and a blindingly white shirt with no tie, though he'd probably had one on when he left the office. Obviously, he hadn't taken the time to change clothes before driving north. He carried his drink back into the living room—a man's room, with a stone fireplace, trophy fish mounted on the wood-paneled walls, and a felt poker table next to the fifty-two-inch liquid crystal TV in the corner. Banks picked out the most comfortable leather armchair and sank into it, bringing the drink to his lips twice before speaking again. Then he sighed and looked at Mueller, who was still on his feet.

"You look nervous, Doc."

"A little, maybe."

"You should be. This deal is hanging by a thread. Everything we've worked for. Skarda's this close to going to the cops."

"What's he got, Mike? Tell me there's a cop anywhere in Wisconsin that wouldn't laugh him out of the station house if he went in and told this story."

"You sure you covered your tracks on the Truman thing?"

"Positive. Gretchen Kahler's going down for that one."

"And Dellums?"

"Horvath used an untraceable gun, and threw it in the Fox."

"How about Janaszak?"

"Here's my thought about that. We need him out of the way for good, or the committee will keep stalling. I'm going to have Horvath go over to his house tomorrow night after he and his wife have gone to bed. I know they sleep in separate rooms. Horvath will give Frank an injection that will stop his heart for good."

"What if he wakes up?"

"He's already weak. Horvath can cover his mouth until the stuff works. There won't be a problem."

Banks swished his drink glass, making the ice cubes clink against the sides. Then he held it out to Mueller. *So that's how it's going to be,* Mueller thought. He might only be answering to one man, but that man was going to treat him like hired help. Mueller's hands were dirtier, but Banks was certainly not clean. Mueller knew he could always find a way to get rid of Horvath if things went sour, but he'd make Banks understand that he would take him down, too, if necessary.

"I'm still worried about Skarda," Banks said loudly while Mueller poured two more drinks in the kitchen.

"Don't be. I've got that figured out, too."

Mueller came back into the living room and handed Banks his drink. He opened the fireplace screen and tossed on three more split logs from the pile on the hearth, then sat down on the couch. He stared at the famous sports agent, who wore a thousand dollars' worth of clothes wherever he went. He was small but handsome, self-assured, barely into his forties, and rich beyond all normal definitions. Yet what he had wasn't enough—that's what he and Banks had in common. That's all they had in common. Mueller had saved lives, saved careers. He'd been in cancer wards, ICUs, emergency rooms, and he'd been on the sacred frozen tundra of Lambeau Field, caring for fallen warriors. All Banks had ever done was watch from luxury sky-boxes while real men sweated and bled in the arena. The only instruments Banks knew how to use were the TV remote and the fountain pen.

"You ever hunt, Michael?"

"No. God, no."

"Fish?"

"No. When I want walleye or snapper, I go to Catch Thirty-Five."

"You never played sports, did you?"

"Not varsity. My parents wouldn't let me. Said I was too small."

"What do you weigh?"

"One-forty-five. Same as the day I graduated from law school."

"So you work out?"

"I don't have to. I watch what I eat."

"When I'm up here, I catch what I eat. Or kill it."

"Congratulations. Where the hell is Horvath?"

"He'll be here soon."

"Good. I'm giving him till the weekend to kill Skarda. If he can't get it done by then, I'll turn the job over to you."

Mueller had exhausted everything he wanted to say to Banks. They sat in silence, listening to the rustle of the wind through the trees until another set of head-lights flashed through the window from the road outside. They both heard the car pull into the driveway and assumed it was Horvath.

"GET OUT, BOTH OF YOU," KREBBS SAID, pointing the gun back and forth from Sam to Gretchen. "And don't slam the doors."

They got out of the car and closed their doors softly. Krebbs got out the driver's side. Sam was tempted to tell Gretchen to run into the woods, but there was no guarantee that Krebbs wouldn't simply shoot her in the back from where he stood, just a few feet from her. Better to take their chances on what might happen inside.

Sam took a quick look at their surroundings. Mueller's Land Rover was in the driveway. So was a dark-colored BMW with Illinois plates. Could be Banks—Sam assumed he'd called Mueller as soon as he and LaBobby Suggs walked out of his office. They would be plotting their endgame tonight. Sam glanced under the overhang of the outbuilding and saw that the snowmobile wasn't parked next to the boat. Could Doc be out riding? There were lights on in the house.

"Give me your car keys," Krebbs said to Sam. "You won't be needing them."

Krebbs stood just beyond arm's reach from Sam. He put his hand in his pocket and took out the keys, tossing them to Krebbs, who caught them in his free hand without taking his eyes—or the .38—off Sam.

"Now your gun."

Sam reached behind his back and started to take the Glock out of its holster, but Krebbs told him to stop and turn around. Sam turned his back to Krebbs, who reached under his jacket and extracted the gun.

With a gun in each hand, Krebbs told Sam and Gretchen to walk up the stairs to Mueller's door.

Sam considered one last appeal to what was left of Krebbs's rational brain, but decided to keep his mouth shut. If Mueller and Banks were inside, Krebbs couldn't shoot them all before someone took him down. With any luck, Mueller would go first. It would be a brutal end to the Packers' ownership issue, but better that way than having Gretchen and Sam take bullets.

When they reached the front door, Krebbs put his hand on the knob, gave it a twist and pushed it open. Mueller and Banks were sitting in the living room, both staring at the door in surprise. Krebbs shoved Sam and Gretchen through the door and then screamed, "Down on the floor, everyone!"

Sam and Gretchen did as they were told. Mueller and Banks had stood up, their mouths hanging open and their hands starting to rise in defensive positions.

"On the fucking floor!" Krebbs screamed. He pointed Sam's Glock at Mueller and his own .38 at Banks. Both slowly sank to their knees, then put their palms out in front of them and stretched out on their stomachs.

"What the hell is this, Skarda?" Mueller said. His eyes and Sam's were both just inches off the floor, no more than five feet from each other.

"Shut up, Mueller," Krebbs said. "Gretchen told me all about the two of you. I came here to kill you."

"The two of us? What? You're crazy—who are you?"

"I'm the guy Gretchen divorced because she was fucking you."

"You got some bad information, pal," Mueller said.

"It comes right from her mouth!"

"Listen to me—"

"After I shoot you, she goes next. Then Skarda. Then—who's this guy?"

He waved the gun pointing at Banks.

"Put the goddamn guns down," Mueller said. "You've got this all wrong!"

Sam's right leg was splayed out behind him about two feet from where Krebbs was standing, just inside the doorway. With a quick sideways whip, he might knock Krebbs off balance, but he couldn't take him down. Gretchen was on the floor to Krebbs's right. Sam tried to catch her eye to see if they could coordinate something. If she watched him and reacted as soon as Sam made contact, they might have a chance. Someone would get shot, but maybe not killed—and maybe it wouldn't be Gretchen or Sam. But he knew he had to act before Mueller convinced Krebbs that he hadn't been sleeping with Gretchen. If Krebbs believed him, Gretchen would be the first to die.

JOE HORVATH STEERED HIS TAHOE around the corner of the muddy gravel road that led to Mueller's house, and his headlights caught the reflection of a set of tail lights on a car that didn't belong in Mueller's driveway. He immediately cut his engine, turned off his lights and waited until his eyes adjusted to the darkness. He recognized Mueller's Land Rover, and the BMW had to belong to Banks. The other vehicle looked like a Jeep Cherokee. Skarda drove a Cherokee. Something was very wrong here.

Horvath took his handgun from the glove compartment, knowing he'd already racked a bullet into the chamber. He slid out of the Tahoe and gently pushed the door closed. Mueller would have called him about Skarda being there, if he could have. Was Skarda crazy enough to drive up here and confront Mueller? It didn't make sense, but Horvath knew he had to kill Skarda sooner or later. Might as well be now.

He ran to the driveway, where he could see into the lighted living-room window. He couldn't see anyone inside. Horvath moved quickly around the side of the house, taking long, sloshing strides through the soft, shin-deep snow until he reached the deck off the kitchen. He peered through the window into the living room. One person was standing, an unshaven man holding two guns, his mouth moving, uttering muffled, agitated words. On the floor Horvath saw heads and legs. One head moved upward—it was Mueller. He was talking to the man with the guns. Who was it? Could that be Gretchen Kahler's ex?

At this point, Horvath decided, it didn't matter who the guy was. He looked crazy. He looked like he could start shooting at any moment. There was no way to get through the kitchen door quietly enough that the guy would not hear it open or see Horvath enter. His only move was to come in fast and hard. Crouching, he slowly eased the screen door open, then let it rest against his shoulder as he put his left hand on the knob of the kitchen door. He slowly turned it until he knew the door was unlatched. He raised his gun in his right hand and then pushed through the door.

Krebbs's head snapped to the left at the sound of the kitchen door crashing open. He turned both guns in that direction. Sam saw the guns swing, and put all his strength into a hard kick at Krebbs's left leg. Krebbs stumbled sideways as a gunshot from the kitchen crashed into the paneled wall behind his head, and Krebbs returned fire with his .38. Gretchen kicked at Krebbs's right leg, and Krebbs fell to his knees as another shot whizzed from the kitchen and embedded in the wall. Krebbs fired back three times at the figure crouching behind the stove in the kitchen. Sam couldn't tell who it was, but he had to take sides with the new arrival. He knew what Krebbs's intentions were. With the new guy—more than likely Horvath—they'd find out soon enough.

Once again, Krebbs's balance and athleticism kept him from harm. He dived behind an armchair near the front door as one more gunshot exploded from the kitchen, then he jumped up and fired once more as he simultaneously opened the door and scrambled outside. Horvath came running out of the kitchen with his gun in his right hand, supported by his left. He rushed to the doorway. Horvath with a gun was bad news for Sam and Gretchen. If he got a clear shot at Krebbs from the doorway, his years on the FBI firing range would pay off. Now that Krebbs was in retreat, Sam couldn't see how his death would help the situation.

He rolled to his right and bumped hard into Horvath's leg, then kicked the door shut. He tried to tackle Horvath, but the ex-cop slammed his free hand into the side of Sam's head. He shook a leg loose and kicked Sam in the ribs, causing Sam to lose his grip. But Sam did manage to keep his body curled up in front of the door so Horvath couldn't pull it open. Horvath kicked Sam again, this time in the back, and managed to open the door wide enough to extend his gun hand through it. Then he got his head and shoulder into the opening, and scanned the driveway for Krebbs. The engine on Sam's Cherokee was revving. Horvath fired two more times, but Krebbs had backed the Cherokee out of the driveway and was speeding away on the narrow road.

TWENTY-SEVEN

oc Mueller pulled himself up off the floor and looked around at the scene in his living room. Horvath stood panting in the doorway, his gun at his side, staring off into the darkness. Sam was still on the floor, holding his ribs. Gretchen was kneeling next to Sam, asking him if he was all right. Banks—where was Banks? Mueller saw a pair of shaking Ferragamos, toes down, protruding from behind the couch.

"He's gone, Michael," Mueller said, not attempting to hide his disgust. "You can come out now."

Banks slowly raised his head from behind the couch. The fear in his eyes looked as though it might not recede for days. He started to stand, then looked down at himself and groaned. When he walked out from behind the couch, he kept his legs together, but it was plain to see that his pants were wet from the crotch to the knees. He sat on a wooden chair at the poker table, hands between his legs, with his shoulders shaking.

Horvath, who had closed the door and walked to the center of the living room, looked down at Banks and laughed.

"It's easy to give orders, isn't it?" Horvath said. "Not so much fun when the shooting starts."

He popped the nearly spent magazine out of his Smith and Wesson and inserted a new one, racking a round into the chamber.

"Anybody want to tell me what that was all about?"

Mueller told him about Krebbs bursting in and accusing him of having an affair with Gretchen, and threatening to shoot them all. When Horvath asked where he got that idea, Mueller glared at Gretchen.

"She fed him that bullshit."

"He ambushed us at Gretchen's house tonight," Sam said. He had managed to get into a sitting position on the floor, despite the ache in his ribs and back. "He was going to kill her right there. She had to tell him something."

Mueller crossed the floor and picked up Gretchen by her arms and lifted her until his face was an inch from hers.

"You almost got me killed tonight," he said, barely containing his fury.

"Better you than anyone else I can think of," she said.

Mueller threw her back down to the floor, and Sam started to get up, but Horvath aimed his gun at Sam's head. Sam eased back down to his sitting position. It would be hard to make the case that they were any better off now with Krebbs gone. He was nuts—but, in their own way, so were Horvath and Mueller.

And they had far more to lose than Krebbs did.

"You want me to go after that punk?" Horvath said. He looked at Mueller, then at Banks—who was looking at Mueller. Doc was now calling the shots.

"No need," Mueller said. "He won't be back, and he won't go to the cops. He's already wanted for murder. Now they can add kidnapping."

"What should we do with these two?" Horvath said. "Shoot them?"

"No. That's the gun the Packers issued to you, right?"

"Yeah."

"The bullets could be traced back to your gun. And you can't lose that gun without a lot of questions being asked."

"What if nobody finds the bodies?"

"They'd turn up eventually. We can't bury them—the ground's been frozen since mid-November. I'm not going to spend all night trying to dig through the snow and frost."

"What, then?"

"Go get the duct tape. It's on the top shelf of the closet next to the dishwasher."

Horvath came back with a full roll of duct tape. While Mueller held the gun on Sam and Gretchen, Horvath tied Sam's hands behind his back and then tied his ankles together, wrapping on layer after layer until he was immobilized. Then he moved over to Gretchen and started pulling a long piece of tape off the roll.

"Not yet," Mueller said. "She's still wearing her Packers game-day stuff."

"So what?"

"She was arrested in those clothes. Got out of jail in them. A dozen cops would have seen that. She wouldn't wear that stuff here voluntarily. We don't want them to find her like that."

Mueller handed the gun to Horvath and went into one of the bedrooms. He came back with a gray sweatshirt and a pair of blue jeans.

"My ex-wife left this stuff here. It should fit."

He threw them at Gretchen and told her to put them on. She took off the green parka, threw it on the armchair next to her, and started to put the sweatshirt over her Packers medical staff shirt. Mueller shook his head.

"Uh-uh," he said. "Take off the shirt."

Mueller held the gun on Gretchen as she reluctantly pulled her polo shirt over her head, revealing flat, muscular abs and soft mounds protruding from her white sports bra. None of her captors averted their eyes. Gretchen quickly pulled the on the sweatshirt.

"Now the pants," Mueller said.

Gretchen took off her white running shoes and pulled off her dark khaki pants. She sat on the floor in her white panties while she unfolded the blue jeans and put her legs into them. She pulled them up to her waist, zipped them, and put her shoes back on.

Then Banks and Horvath went into the kitchen with Mueller while he explained what they were going to do next. They poured themselves drinks and spoke quietly, but Sam could make out the gist of what Mueller was proposing. About 400 feet offshore was a fish house that belonged to Mueller's next-door neighbor Walt, who wouldn't be back till Saturday. Mueller had the key. There was a portable propane heater in the fish house. The neighbor was always careful to keep it well-ventilated. This time, he would not be so careful.

Mueller would tell this story: He'd invited Gretchen and Sam to come up to his place for a couple of days, to talk and mend fences. They wanted to do some ice fishing, so Mueller gave them the key to the neighbor's fish house. They were gone all day, and when Mueller went to check on them, he discovered that something had gone horribly wrong. The house had been improperly ventilated. Sam and Gretchen were dead of carbon monoxide poisoning. It would actually only take an hour or two. They'd put them out there tonight, lock them in, and Mueller would go back out in a couple of hours to cut the duct tape off their hands and legs. Then he'd pretend to discover them sometime the following afternoon. He'd call the cops, of course. Maybe there'd be some suspicion, but nobody could prove anything.

"What about Janaszak?" Horvath said. "He'd know these two would never come up here on a social visit."

"He'd know if he weren't dead," Mueller said. "As soon as we get them into the fish house, you're driving back to Green Bay to put Frank Janaszak out of his misery. I've made up a special injection for him. You stick it between his toes, and next thing you know, Frank's poor, abused ticker gives out for good."

The three men came out of the kitchen and pulled Sam and Gretchen to their feet.

"How do we get them out there?" Banks asked.

"Joe and I will drive them," Mueller said. "Just help us get them into the Land Rover."

Horvath picked up Gretchen in his arms while Mueller opened the front door for him. When he got her outside, she started to scream. Horvath brought his left arm under her neck and covered her mouth with his big palm.

"Why don't we just tape their mouths shut?" he asked Mueller.

"I don't want any duct tape residue on their faces," Mueller said. "We'll take the tape off their legs and arms when we go back later."

Mueller nodded and began walking down the steps to the driveway.

"Besides," Mueller added. "Once we get them out there, the more they scream, the faster they take in the carbon monoxide."

"And the faster they die," Horvath said.

He carried Gretchen down to the car with her mouth covered, while Mueller and Banks managed to pull and drag Sam behind her. From the looks of the neighborhood, screaming wasn't going to help. The nearest cabin belonged to Walt, who owned the fish house, and he wasn't around. There were no lights on at the houses and cabins farther away.

They got Sam and Gretchen into the Land Rover, and Banks went back up to the house while Mueller got behind the wheel and Horvath slid into the passenger seat. He turned and pointed his gun at Sam.

"Try anything funny, and it ends right here," Horvath said. "Doesn't matter to me."

Mueller started the engine, backed around Banks's BMW, and drove through the snow beside the house to the backyard. He flicked on his headlights and found an open area of lakefront to the right of his dock. The four-wheel-drive SUV had no trouble making its own path out onto the lake, and within about a hundred feet they were on well-packed snow, thanks to hundreds of snowmobile tracks.

"This where you and Ed went through?" Horvath asked Mueller.

"Close," Mueller said. "There's a car and truck landing on the other side of the bay. That's one of two places you can legally drive onto the ice. The other's downtown. I drove out over here because I figured some do-gooder in town would try to stop us from going out. Besides, I was pretty sure the ice was thinner here."

That settled that. Sam had been sure Ed Larson's death was no accident, but now Mueller was admitting it. Why not? Horvath wouldn't tell, and Sam and Gretchen weren't going to be around.

"Is it safe to be doing this?" Horvath asked.

"You mean, is the ice thick enough? Sure it is—now."

"I mean, will anybody see us drive out here and bitch to the cops that we didn't use a legal point of entry?"

"People mind their own business around here. Besides, it's midnight. Nobody's around."

They reached the fish house and parked as close as they could, to reduce the strain of carrying the two bound captives. Sam saw no signs of activity anywhere around them. The other fish houses were dark, and there were no snowmobilers out for midnight rides on this end of Minocqua. Mueller used his key to open the padlocked door of the fish house, which rested on a kind of wooden pallet that had been mostly covered by blowing and drifting snow. He stepped inside and started the propane heater. Then he and Horvath carried first Gretchen and then Sam into the windowless, five-by-ten wooden hut. It would have been pitch black inside, except for the glowing burner of the heater.

"Make yourselves comfortable," Mueller said. He made an elaborate show of unfolding two plastic armchairs and brushing off the seats, then put Sam and Gretchen into them.

"You never should have asked Skarda to come here," Mueller said to Gretchen, shaking his head. "Things didn't have to go this way."

"And let you keep killing people?" Gretchen said. "You make me ashamed to be a doctor."

Mueller walked up to Gretchen and slapped her across the mouth as hard as he could. She cried out quickly, then choked back any further sound. She wasn't going to give Mueller the satisfaction of knowing how much it had hurt.

"You could have kept your job after Banks bought the team. You know, it's funny you told your ex we were lovers. I've thought about that. Thought about it a lot, actually. You've got a great ass. I'll bet you're a real handful in the sack."

"You're disgusting."

"And now look what I have to do."

"You don't have to do anything," Sam said. "You're enjoying this. You and Horvath are a couple of sick bastards."

Horvath kicked the side of Sam's chair so hard he fell over sideways and hit his head against the side of the fish house. The hiss of the propane heater was close to his ear, and he tried to inch away from it.

"That's exactly what I'm talking about," Sam said. "We'll be dead in an hour, but you just had to get in a last stomping. Did the FBI kick you out because you're a sadist?"

"Give it up, Skarda," Mueller said. "You had your chance at us."

He now sounded lighthearted as he ran his hands along the bottom of the wall, to see how tight the seal was between the wall and the floor. Then he ran his hand along the upper edge of the wall where it met the roof.

"Look, Mueller, you can still get out of this," Sam said. "You know, I know, and Gretchen knows that you killed Truman with extra shots of pain-killer, but the truth is, I didn't go to the cops because I couldn't prove it. You're already in the clear on Larson—the local cops here never even considered an investigation. Frank Janaszak's still alive, so you've got nothing to worry about there. If you kill us, that's the one that's going to nail you."

"If I don't kill you, Banks doesn't buy the team, I don't become club president, Joe here doesn't get his promotion and raise, Lambeau doesn't get a dome, the Packers continue to suck —you see what I'm saying, Skarda? I'm going to kill you because of all the good that will come of it."

Mueller started whistling as he continued to check the seals at the corners of the fish house. Horvath held the gun on Sam and Gretchen, and Sam had no doubt that Horvath would like to use it.

"You killed that guy in Minnesota—didn't you, Horvath?" Sam said.

"What guy?" Mueller said, stopping his inspection. "What's he talking about?"

"Damned if I know," Horvath said. He glowered at Sam, and adjusted his grip on his handgun as though trying to keep himself from pulling the trigger.

"Sure you do. Wesley Dillon. The farmer who ran the dogfights, up by Harris. You know, the day you picked up Truman. Why'd you kill him? Afraid he'd talk?"

"Shut up."

"Do you suddenly get morals when it comes to dogfighting? Or did you just do it for kicks?"

"You killed a guy that day?" Mueller said. "Christ, Joe, is there anybody else I don't know about?"

Horvath was silent. It was instantly clear to Sam that, whatever Horvath had been promised, Mueller and Banks couldn't afford to keep him around after the sale went through. He'd be the fall guy. He was either too compromised, too loyal, or too stupid to figure that out. And Horvath didn't strike Sam as loyal or stupid.

"What does he have on you, Joe?" Sam said to Horvath. "Photos of you diddling little kids? Did he catch you stealing from the gift shop? Come on, Joe, you're smart enough to know Mueller and Banks are going to push you in front of a snow plow as soon as they get the team."

"That's enough, Skarda!" Mueller bellowed. "Get in the car, Joe."

He took a blanket from the wooden bunk and stuffed it into the vent hole. He'd make sure to put the blanket back where it had been when he returned in an hour or so.

Before padlocking the door, he stuck his head inside and said, "Remember, shout all you want. Use up that precious oxygen. How long do you figure it will take, Gretchen? Twenty minutes, maybe a half-hour, if you regulate your breathing?"

"Shut the goddamn door," she said. "I can't stand to look at your face anymore."

Mueller laughed shrilly and pushed the door closed. They heard the padlock click shut, and heard some kind of thumping and brushing noises outside the door. Eventually they heard Mueller's footsteps recede to the SUV, heard the driver's-side door open and close. The engine started, and they heard the Land Rover back up, then pull up next to the shack. It sounded like either Horvath or Mueller got out and climbed onto the roof of the SUV, then leaned onto the top of the fish house. There was a noise coming from the area where the vent protruded outside the shack. Sam realized that the bastards were making sure the outside part of the vent was plugged, too. After a while they heard the man on the roof lower himself back into the Land Rover and shut the door. Then they heard Mueller and Horvath drive away over the snow-covered lake.

Twenty-Eight

Scott Krebbs sat behind the wheel of the Jeep Cherokee, sniffling and wiping the tears from his eyes.

For nearly an hour, he'd been parked in a private driveway on Country Club Road, fifty feet from the highway that led across the bridge into Minocqua. The house where he was parked looked like a seasonal cabin, closed up for the winter. No one would bother him there while he waited for the self-loathing and shame to work its way through him.

He could turn north on Highway 51, drive into town, find a bar, have a few drinks, get control of himself, and try to figure out what to do next. He could turn south on 51 and head back to Green Bay, or Neenah, or as far south as he could get in Skarda's Cherokee before he ran out of money.

Neither idea addressed the rage he was feeling. *I'm such a fucking loser!*

Skarda had been right. He didn't care what happened next. He might as well shoot himself. But then his cheating bitch of an ex-wife would win. He'd be dead, out of her way forever, and she'd be free to keep screwing Mueller . . . or maybe it really was Skarda. Or maybe it was someone else entirely. How could he know anymore? How could he trust a word that came out of her lying mouth? No, Scott, I'm not having an affair. Why don't you believe me? It's just over between us—there's no one else. Well, yes there is someone else. No, it's not Sam. I've been sleeping with Doc Mueller.

No, Krebbs didn't care what happened next—not to him, not to anyone. But he did care about letting Gretchen live out the rest of her life, having sex with other men, forgetting all about what they'd meant to each other. She'd played him for a fool. Maybe it was Mueller, maybe it was Skarda, maybe somebody else, maybe the whole Packers team, but the only way to be sure that no other man ever touched her again was to kill her.

Driving into Minocqua for a drink wouldn't accomplish anything. Driving out of Minocqua wouldn't accomplish anything. He'd come here for one reason, and he'd run away like a sniveling coward when that guy with the gun showed up. What must Gretchen think of him now? Was she laughing at him with Mueller and Skarda? Scott was all talk. Deep down, a wimp and a failure. He never was much of a man.

He wiped his nose with his sleeve. Next to him on the seat were the two hand-guns. He'd show her how much of a man he was.

He was at least a mile from Mueller's place, and no one had followed him. Who would be there now? Skarda didn't have a car. Gretchen would still be there—and Mueller, of course. There had been two other guys—one little runt who looked ter-rified, the other a big, tough guy with a gun. Where was the tough guy now? Krebbs knew he should turn around, go back to the house, no matter what, and settle this—even though the guy with the gun seemed to know what he was doing. They wouldn't expect him. They thought he had no guts. But he did. He'd show them. He just needed to get ahold of himself, somehow . . .

A set of headlights illuminated the road and the trunks of the tall white pine trees, coming from the direction of Mueller's place. Krebbs sank down in the seat, hoping he'd pulled the Cherokee far enough into the driveway. He peered over the top of the seat and saw that the approaching vehicle was an SUV, maybe a Chevy. It looked like the one that had been in the driveway of Mueller's place when he'd run away. As it got closer, he was sure: a green Chevy Tahoe, the same one that had arrived at Mueller's place after they had. He could see that there was only one person in the vehicle, and though there wasn't enough light to see his face, it must have been the same guy who came through Mueller's kitchen. He was wearing the same kind of black fleece hat with earflaps.

The Tahoe slowed when it came to the highway, then took a left, heading south—out of town, back toward Green Bay.

So the tough guy with the gun had left. Krebbs felt a surge of adrenaline pump-ing through him. Now it was a fair fight—he had two guns. Maybe they had none.

He searched Skarda's glove compartment for extra ammunition, but didn't find any. He climbed into the back seat and found an overnight bag in the rear storage area. Unzipping that, he found two extra magazines for Skarda's Glock. He reloaded the .38 with the extra bullets he'd brought with him, put the Glock clips in his pants pocket, and got back into the driver's seat.

T HE PROPANE BURNER GAVE OFF A HELLISH red glow inside the fish house.

"How do we know when it starts to get to us?" Sam asked Gretchen. He spoke quietly, trying to conserve oxygen.

"First, a headache," Gretchen said. She also spoke softly. "Then tired. Then stomach pain. Then dizzy and confused. Then . . ."

She didn't have to say any more. Sam's head was beginning to hurt. He'd read stories about ice fisherman who'd been found dead in their shacks from CO poisoning, but since there were never any witnesses left, he didn't know how long it took. The heater wasn't very big—but it didn't need to be, in such a small space.

"Should I try to kick this thing down?" he said.

"You'll die faster."

"I'll die trying."

"I'm so sorry, Sam."

"Don't give up."

Gretchen's hair was plastered to her forehead, her face was dripping sweat, and perhaps tears. The heater was cranked way too high for comfort. No doubt Mueller would turn it back to a reasonable setting before their bodies were discovered.

Sam rolled toward the door, swung his duct-taped legs around and kicked at the door. He was too far away to make any kind of impact, and the effort made his head hurt more. He rolled his shoulders back and forth until they were closer to the door, and his knees were bent at a ninety-degree angle, with his feet just a few inches from the wooden door. He put all his strength into four powerful kicks, but the lock held and the door did not open. The pain in his head was becoming severe. He was panting now, and he knew he wouldn't last much longer if he didn't get his breathing under control. He swung his legs behind him and tried to get his nose and mouth as close to the bottom of the door as possible. There was the faintest hint of cold air coming through, but not as much as he'd hoped. That must have been the brushing noise they'd heard: Mueller had pushed snow up against the bottom edge of the door to seal it from the outside air.

Still, it was better than nothing.

"Gretchen, can you roll yourself over here?"

She saw what Sam was doing and dropped to her knees from the chair, then to her side. She used her bound legs to slide forward sidewinder-style, eventually getting her face in front of the door crack. She took several breaths, then looked at Sam, who'd moved to the side to make room for her.

"I'm not sure how much good this does. Deep inhale . . . means deep exhale."

"How's your head?"

"Hurts."

"Shit."

Gretchen rolled her shoulders away from the door so Sam could get another breath through the crack. It didn't seem to help, and the effort to move into place was exhausting him. He knew he was losing the energy to try, and he knew he couldn't let that happen—but he was getting so tired. He glanced over at Gretchen —smaller than he was by a good sixty pounds—and saw that her eyes were closed.

"Gretchen!"

Her eyes flickered open.

"Move over here. There's room for both us. Come on—you've got to."

Gretchen managed to slide herself forward again, and she and Sam contorted their legs in a way that they could both get their faces next to the door's bottom edge. She took in a breath and then Sam heard her sigh—a long, tired, melancholy sigh.

Not like this, Sam thought, dreamily, as the sense of danger began to slip away. Not like this . . . he hadn't expected it to be like this. When he and Gretchen had been together, he'd once thought that they would eventually grow old together . . . die together . . . but not on the floor of a Wisconsin fish house . . . in the dark . . . in the cold. . . . Now it just seemed funny, that they'd be here, like this, fading away . . . where was Caroline? Arizona . . . where he should be . . . what was that pain in his stomach? Had he eaten something bad? Head was all right now, but the stomach . . . should keep breathing through that crack, right? It just took so much effort . . . See Caroline soon . . .

"I DON'T SUPPOSE YOU'VE GOT AN EXTRA PAIR of pants around here . . . in a smaller size," Banks said to Mueller.

Horvath had left for Green Bay. Mueller was just waiting to go back out on the ice, unlock the door to the fish house, untie Sam's and Gretchen's hands and feet, and come back to the house for some sleep. The relationship between Banks and Mueller had changed dramatically in the last hour. Banks had revealed himself as a coward—useless in a crisis that took more than a checkbook to solve.

"Just the ones Gretchen took off," Mueller said. He didn't try very hard to suppress a smug grin as he stared at the dark urine stain on Banks's pants. "They're small—should fit you just fine. Try 'em on."

Banks scowled as he removed his own pants and boxer shorts and pulled on the Packers-issue khakis that Gretchen had worn. They were a little tight, but Banks was able to zip them up.

"I was going to burn those, and her shirt and parka," Mueller said. He pointed to the pants Banks was now wearing, a smile still playing on the corner of his lips. "You want me to burn your stuff instead?"

"Might as well," Banks said. He avoided making eye contact with Mueller. "I'm getting another drink."

Mueller opened the fireplace doors. He picked up Bank's pants and shorts with a fireplace poker and tossed them in. The flames spurted and sizzled as the stench of urine wafted from the blaze. Next he tossed Gretchen's shirt into the fire. He picked up her parka, lying on the leather armchair, and realized the fabric would melt in the fireplace. He'd have to find someplace else to get rid of it.

"You want this?" Mueller said. He walked to the kitchen entrance and tossed it to Banks, who had a fresh drink in his hand. Banks put his drink down and slipped the parka over his head. It was a good fit.

"These are nice," Banks said, rubbing his hand on the opposite sleeve.

"Consider it a souvenir. Just don't let anybody know where you got it."

Neither he nor Banks would ever forget this night—Mueller was confident of that. The night Banks had pissed his pants when the bullets started flying. The night Mueller had taken care of the last of their problems. The night Mueller had established himself as the alpha male in their partnership.

Mueller checked his watch. Maybe half an hour from now, he'd head back out to the fish shack. He didn't want to get there too early. He didn't particularly need to watch their dying moments.

He heard and felt the bullet simultaneously—the one that crashed through the living room window and tore through the skin of his upper right arm, spinning him to the side. The pain was not as great as the shock. Now what—who? Jesus Christ!

"What was that?" Banks yelled from the kitchen. He wouldn't come out to look. Mueller had dropped to the floor and was crawling toward the kitchen when three more shots were fired through the window. One ricocheted off the fireplace, one embedded in the back wall, and another chipped a chunk of antler off a mounted deer head.

From the front yard, a voice screamed, "I'm going to kill you, Gretchen! You hear me?"

Mueller recognized the voice—it was that crazy son of a bitch Krebbs. He'd come back, and now Horvath wasn't around to save them.

"It's Krebbs!" Mueller yelled to Banks. "We've got to get out of here!"

"Don't you have a gun?" Banks's voice was shrill and panicky.

"Deer rifles and a shotgun. They're not loaded. We have to go! Out the back!"

Four more shots were fired from outside, breaking another window. Mueller slithered on his belly into the kitchen, then got up and ran for the door to the deck.

"Where are you going?" Banks screamed. "Don't leave me!"

"If you're coming, move your ass!"

Mueller grabbed a jacket off the hook next to the door and ran across the deck to the back of the house where his snowmobile sat. He jumped on, turned the ignition, and cranked the throttle. Banks leaped on behind him and pulled the parka's hood over his head as Mueller set out toward the lake. Banks cringed when he heard the door from the kitchen to the deck bang open, and heard several more gunshots whiz past them. He was fully exposed to Krebbs, and there was no doubt in his mind that the next bullet would hit him squarely between the shoulder blades, or in the back of the head. He felt his bowels loosen. Another pair of pants was about to go.

"Move this thing, goddamn it!" Banks screamed in Mueller's ear.

"Shut the fuck up!" Mueller replied. "I can't hit top speed until we get out onto the lake!"

*B*ANG! BANG! BANG!

Sam was back in Minneapolis, still a cop, testifying at a killer's trial. The judge kept pounding his gavel. Sam was curled on the floor of the courtroom, waiting to be called to the stand. So tired today . . . maybe if he put his head down, caught a quick nap . . .

BANG! BANG! BANG!

"Is anybody in there? I'm going to open this door!"

Why would the judge want to open the courtroom door? Where was the bailiff—wasn't that his job? Maybe Sam wouldn't have to testify. Just get to his feet, go back to the office, maybe take some Pepto for this terrible stomach ache . . .

Then, a gunshot, accompanied by the sound of metal being broken. No mistaking the noise a gunshot makes. Somebody had a gun, shooting up the courtroom. . . . Sam lifted his head and realized he wasn't in a courtroom. He was lying on the floor of the fish house, on Lake . . . something. Mueller and Horvath—had they come back to shoot him and Gretchen?

The door swung open, and cold, clean air exchanged with hot, poisonous air. Sam looked up into the black sky and saw a man with a pistol in one hand and a flashlight in the other. His face took on a faint pink glow from the burner on the propane heater. Sam thought he recognized the man . . . there was a badge emblem on the front of his black knit cap. A cop. Where were they again? Minocqua, that was it. Sam tried to focus on the face, and then he recognized the man. The chief. He'd sat in his office. What was his name? Weston. Chief Weston.

Gretchen.

Sam turned and saw Gretchen lying next to him, eyes closed. She hadn't heard the banging or the gunshot—or if she had, she was too out of it to respond. Sam knew she didn't have much time left. He was still helpless to do anything for her, with his own hands and legs bound with duct tape.

"Get her out of here," Sam said.

Weston was already pulling Gretchen's legs. He slid her fifteen feet from the open door of the fish house, then came back for Sam. When they were both well clear of the doorway, Weston took a utility knife from his belt and sliced the tape from Sam's ankles and wrists. Sam tried to stand, and fell once, but the cold night air was pumping energy back into his system. His head and stomach still hurt, but he knew he was going to be all right as long as he kept gulping oxygen. Never had cold winter air been so welcome.

"Why . . . how did you find us?" Sam managed to say.

"Got a call from your girlfriend."

Weston was kneeling next to Gretchen. He cut her bindings, then gently slapped her cheeks. He picked up a handful of snow and began rubbing her face with it. Gretchen's eyes fluttered and finally opened. She held her stomach with her arms and curled into a ball, rolling to the side. But she was moving.

"Caroline called you?"

"Yeah. She said she was talking to you on the phone a few hours ago in Green Bay, and she heard someone break into your car. You must have dropped the phone, but she heard the guy say he was going to kill both of you. Then she heard him tell you to drive to Minocqua. To Doc Mueller's."

Sam kneeled down to Gretchen and gently turned her toward him. She put a hand up to her forehead and grimaced, then looked at him. She took several deep breaths, and then managed a small smile.

"She cut it . . . a little close," Gretchen said.

"I'll speak to her about that," Sam said. He smiled back at her.

Weston dialed 9-1-1 and asked for paramedics to meet him at Doc Mueller's place, and gave the address. Then he closed his phone and helped Gretchen into a sitting position. She still looked dazed and ill. He told her to keep taking deep breaths, then turned to Sam.

"I decided to take the snowmobile over—faster that way," Weston said. "When I got to Fishers Island I saw a vehicle driving away from this shack. I was going to drive over to talk to him, but something didn't seem right. Why would somebody be out here after midnight? Why would they drive? I know Doc has a sled, so I thought maybe it was the guy who jumped you in Green Bay. I figured I'd better stop here first to take a look. I knew right away that the heater was on—I could hear it. And the door was locked, so I shot the padlock off. Who did this to you? That guy who made you drive up here?"

Sam steadied himself by putting a hand on the snow-covered ice, and then stood up to face Weston. The chief had frozen iceballs in his goatee from the ride across the lake, and his cheeks looked raw and wind-burned. He hadn't believed Sam that Mueller was dangerous when they'd talked last week—would he believe him now?

"It was Mueller, and a guy named Joe Horvath," Sam said.

"Come on," Weston said. "Why would he do that? What about the guy who car-jacked you?"

"I don't know where he is," Sam said. "Horvath chased him off with a gun. Now—"

Both Sam and Weston turned their heads suddenly when they heard what sounded like gunshots. The shots appeared to be coming from the other side of Mueller's house. They heard a window break, more shots, then a door banging. The next sound was a snowmobile engine firing up, followed by several more gunshots. The headlights of a snowmobile could be seen bobbing in the darkness behind Mueller's place, heading for the lake. More shots were fired, though they couldn't see where the shooter was. The snowmobile hit the lake at high speed and then veered sharply to the left, heading west on the lake toward town.

"Jesus, what's going on here?" Weston said. "Get on the sled."

Sam helped Gretchen to her feet and guided her to the seat of the chief's snowmobile, then got on the back. It was a snug fit for three people, but Weston couldn't leave them in the middle of the frozen lake. He made sure they were seated securely, then turned the ignition and eased the throttle open. Gretchen clung to Weston, and Sam put his arms around her. Weston reached down to his hip with his right hand and loosened the thumb snap on his sidearm.

As they started off for Mueller's dock, another set of headlights emerged from the wooded lot around the house—this set belonging to a fast-moving automobile that was sending up sprays of wet snow as it swerved through Mueller's yard to the lake. Weston slowed his sled and drew his weapon as the vehicle charged onto the ice and took off after the first snowmobile.

"That's my Cherokee," Sam said. "That's gotta be Krebbs—the guy who jumped us. He's going after Mueller."

The Cherokee did a rear-wheel skid as Krebbs tried to make a high-speed turn to the left on the snow and ice, but eventually the four-wheel-drive began working its magic and he got the traction needed to move forward. He quickly gained speed as he pursued the receding black form of the snowmobile ahead of him.

Krebbs stuck his head out the window and screamed something at the fleeing sled. Then his left arm emerged, gun in hand, and he squeezed off a shot while the Cherokee continued to gain speed.

"I gotta go after them," Weston said. "You two get off."

Sam lifted Gretchen off the sled.

"Go up to the house," he told her. "Wait for the paramedics. I'm going with Weston."

Gretchen was still too groggy to put up a fight. Weston turned and looked at Sam.

"You sure you want to do this?"

"You don't even know who who's shooting at who, or why," Sam said. "Let's move it."

Weston gunned the throttle and the snowmobile shot forward, leaving Gretchen standing in the dark. She slowly turned and walked to the shore, taking deep breaths and shaking her head.

TWENTY-NINE

"J esus Christ, Doc, he's following us!"

Michael Banks had turned his head as far as he could to look behind them as Mueller's Arctic Cat raced across the lake in the dark. He had to grab the edge of the parka hood and pull it to the side so it didn't obscure his view, and when he did, he saw the Jeep Cherokee come crashing out of Mueller's backyard and skid onto the lake. It was a long way behind them, but the headlights were turned in their direction, and Banks could hear the Cherokee's engine revving as the vehicle gained speed. He then heard what sounded like a gunshot, coming from behind them.

"What the fuck is wrong with that guy?"

"He wants to kill me—and he thinks you're his ex-wife."

"What?"

"He thinks you're Gretchen! You're wearing her pants and parka!"

"Shit!"

Banks wanted to pull off the parka, but the temperature had dropped since the sun went down, and he didn't think he could stand to ride on the back of the speeding snowmobile in just a shirt.

"Can you outrun him?"

Mueller didn't think so. On packed snow, an SUV should be able to get up to highway speed in a matter of a minute or less, topping out around eighty-five, maybe ninety miles an hour. Mueller's Artic Cat wasn't a racing sled; he'd never taken it much above fifty, but he figured he could push it to sixty-five or seventy if he had to. They were already losing ground to Krebbs, and eventually he'd catch them.

"We don't have to outrun him," Mueller shouted back to Banks.

"What do you mean? He's got a gun!"

"I know. But we'll be at the highway in a few minutes. The water under the bridge isn't frozen."

"You can't go over open water!"

"The hell I can't!"

Mueller cranked the throttle full out. He could veer to one side of the lake or the other and try to go up into the trees, through somebody's property, and try to lose Krebbs that way. But if he made a mistake, ended up blocked by a fence, or hit something, like a swingset or a clothesline or a backyard barbecue pit—any dumb thing at all that he couldn't see in the dark—Krebbs would have them. It was safer to just stay on the lake, keep the speed as high as he could, and count on getting to the open water before Krebbs caught up with them.

It wasn't going to be all that easy—the highway bridge into town was supported by eight concrete abutments, with openings of about twenty feet between each of them. And the town fishing pier extended out from the north shore of the lake, blocking the gaps between the first four abutments. Mueller would have three open channels under the bridge to choose from, and he'd have to get lined up properly, or they wouldn't make it. He'd never skipped open water before, but he knew that maintaining speed was only part of the problem. There was the weight of the sled and keeping a straight line, too. Stunt drivers and lake racers did it all the time—if you kept your speed and your line, you could skip over hundreds of feet of open water. If you had to brake or change course, you'd lose momentum, and the sled would sink.

He quickly tried to calculate how far the open water extended away from the sides of the bridge. He'd last driven across the bridge into town Tuesday afternoon, and he had seen water on both sides. The opening might be even wider now—maybe two hundred feet—since the recent thaw. Most winters, the water under the bridge never froze, because of the salt dumped on the bridge by the highway department. The county plow would come along and blow the ice, snow, and salt over the bridge railings to the lake below, and the salt would melt whatever ice had begun to form. Meanwhile, the rest of the lake froze at a normal rate, and nobody thought twice about bringing their trucks and heavy fish houses out onto the middle of Lake Minocqua, even though the water under the bridge was still open.

Two hundred feet. If he could maintain a speed of sixty miles per hour, he could do it—a straight shot over the open water between the abutments to the ice on the other side of the bridge. If Krebbs caught them before they reached the water, he'd surely kill them both. If Mueller made it across the water before Krebbs got there, only two things could happen: either Krebbs would see the open water in time and manage to stop the SUV before skidding into the water, or he'd keep going until it was too late. Either way, Mueller would be free of him.

But then what? With Skarda and Gretchen dead, he'd bought some time. Horvath was taking care of Janaszak. When that was done with, Horvath could track down Scott Krebbs and kill him before Krebbs had a chance to come after Mueller again. And maybe the news that his ex-wife was dead would make him forget about revenge. If Krebbs wanted to disappear to another state so the Green Bay cops couldn't arrest him for murder and kidnapping, that would be fine, too.

But what about the Packers? Was there any way their plan could work now? Even if the committee somehow found a way to ignore everything that had happened, was there a chance in hell they'd vote for a sale now? Skarda had spoiled everything—Skarda and that maniac behind them. Mueller was a gambler, but he knew when to fold a bad hand, and that's what he was holding now. Too many questions, too many deaths—and then there was the realization that he and Banks could never work together. Banks would find a way to get rid of him, just as they had planned to get rid of Horvath. A deep sadness suddenly descended on Mueller as the dim outline of the bridge began to come into focus, far in the distance. It was over. He'd played for the jackpot, and come as close as a man in his situation could have hoped, but it wasn't going to happen. Maybe Banks—clinging to his back like a screaming, hysterical woman—didn't realize that yet, but nothing had ever been so clear to Mueller. He could survive this, but he couldn't win.

KREBBS HAD NO TROUBLE GAINING SPEED in the Cherokee. The surface snow on the lake was packed firm by hundreds of snowmobile tracks, mostly in a straight line from the town center to the far eastern bay of Lake Minocqua where Mueller's place was located. He got the SUV up to fifty, then sixty, then seventy-five, occasionally feeling a slight wobble or skid, but constantly accelerating. He knew he was gaining on them. He fired out the window a couple of times, and he could see Gretchen turn to look at him from under the hood of her Packers parka.

What could she be thinking? Running off with Mueller on a snowmobile wouldn't save her. He'd follow them wherever they went, even if they tried to leave the lake. The four-wheel-drive Cherokee could go almost anywhere through the foot of snow now on the ground. He was faster than they were. He'd either catch them or corner them—Gretchen and Doc Mueller. There was no doubt now. It had been Mueller all along. She'd jumped on that snowmobile with him with no hesitation. If that's the way she wanted it, they could die together. He would empty Skarda's gun into the two of them, and leave the gun with their bodies. Maybe the cops would think Skarda did it—wherever he was. It really didn't matter. Gretchen and her lover would be dead. He'd have won. What happened to him after that was of no consequence.

He was close enough now that he could see a word on the back of Gretchen's parka. He knew it said "Packers," but he wasn't close enough to actually read the letters yet. But he'd be almost on top of them in another half mile, at most.

He fired another shot at them, but he knew he had not been accurate while shooting from the window of the Cherokee with his left hand. He decided to save the rest of the bullets, so he'd have enough when he caught them.

"Who's the asshole in your car?" Weston yelled over his shoulder to Sam as the chief's Polaris sped after the Cherokee's taillights.

"Jealous ex-husband of the woman," Sam yelled back. "He wants to kill her."

"Why?"

"Thinks she's having an affair!"

"With you?"

"Not anymore. With Mueller!"

"Is she?"

"No—but we had to tell him something!"

Sam knew Weston still hadn't changed his mind about Doc Mueller, but that didn't matter now. Weston had prevented two murders, and he believed he was on the trail of the would-be killer. If anything, Weston was probably furious at Sam for setting Krebbs after Doc Mueller, but all that could be straightened out eventually. They had to try to catch up to the Cherokee and take Krebbs down before anyone else died.

"How fast can this thing go?" Sam asked.

"Eighty, maybe eight-five."

"We're not gaining on him."

"He can't go much farther."

"Why not?"

"Bridge coming up in less than a mile!"

Sam tried to get his bearings, and then remembered the bridge on Highway 51 that led into town from the south. Lake Minocqua was like a butterfly, with two enormous wings of water that met at the butterfly's body—the four-lane highway bridge. When he'd driven into town last week—when it had been colder—the water under the bridge was open. Maybe Mueller could get through. Krebbs couldn't.

Even in the dark, Mueller knew he was approaching the water. He couldn't see it yet—just a vague darkness that could have been the shadow of the bridge on the white lake. But he knew what it was, and he knew it was time to position the snowmobile so he was perfectly lined up with the center opening. A quick thought flashed through his mind, almost amusing: It was like running a third-down play toward the middle of the hash marks to position the ball for a field-goal attempt.

He heard another gunshot from the racing SUV. Behind him, Banks fidgeted and twisted in his seat, making it hard for Mueller to line up the speeding sled with the opening and hold it on a steady course.

"Sit still!" Mueller yelled.

Still Banks continued to shift his weight from side to side, as though he were trying to slow them down.

"What the fuck are you doing!" Mueller bellowed.

"Trying to take this goddamn parka off!"

Mueller risked one more look behind him, and saw that Banks had the Packers parka halfway over his head, with his right arm extended upward and his left hand frantically trying to pull the loose jacket off his head and arm. The effect was like hoisting a parachute behind them, catching air and slowing them down. The miserable coward thought he could save himself if Krebbs realized he wasn't Gretchen.

The water was fast approaching, and Mueller was beginning to panic. They didn't have enough speed. He needed another ten miles an hour if they were going to make it—and the fool on the seat behind him was doing everything possible to slow them down. Time for one last roll of the dice: He didn't need Banks waving and flapping that parka. He didn't need the extra 140 pounds Banks added to the weight of the sled.

He didn't need Banks.

Mueller reached behind him with his right arm and shoved Banks to the left of the sled. Because Banks was no longer holding on to anything, he had no chance to stay seated. His body lurched to the side, and he toppled onto the hard-packed snow and tumbled over himself at least half a dozen times.

Mueller felt the lighter sled shoot forward as he gunned the throttle, desperately trying to adjust his course as the tips of the skis came in contact with the water.

KREBBS SAW GRETCHEN FALL OFF THE SIDE OF THE SNOWMOBILE at almost the same instant he realized that the dark patch ahead of him wasn't the shadow of the bridge, but open water.

"No!" he screamed.

He jerked the wheel of the Cherokee to the right and slammed on the brake as hard as he could. The vehicle lurched to the right, skidded on the ice under the snow, and then the weight of the Cherokee shifted hopelessly to the left. The two right wheels lost contact with the ice, and as Krebbs tried to turn the steering wheel back to the right, he felt the Cherokee start to roll. His last look at the person lying directly in the path of the out-of-control SUV brought a shock to him: That wasn't Gretchen. It was a man.

The Cherokee landed hard on its left side, then rolled onto its roof. Krebbs was not wearing a seatbelt, and he bounced around the interior of the Cherokee as though he were weightless. The Cherokee banged off the ice on its roof and continued to roll toward the water, its windows smashing and its doors popping open.

When it landed hard on its wheels, there was a cracking noise that could be heard up and down the lake.

Banks barely had time to look up after landing on the ice, and when he did, he saw the tumbling Cherokee blotting out the stars in the night sky above him. The underside of the SUV was the last thing he ever saw as it landed where he was lying, broke through the ice, and took him to the bottom of the lake.

"HE BROKE THROUGH!" WESTON YELLED when he saw the Cherokee flip and crash, then disappear.

"Mueller's still going!" Sam said.

Beyond the bobbing ice chunks and the rapidly disappearing roof of the Cherokee ahead of them, they could see a plume of white water, headed under the bridge. It looked like Mueller had enough speed to make it through to the other side, but he wasn't going through at a straight angle. He would hit one of the abutments if he didn't turn the sled. Mueller knew it, too, and tried to gradually adjust his course, knowing that a sharp turn would slow him down too much. But he cut it too close. Trying to ease the sled to the right, he grazed the wall of the abutment, and the left ski made a metallic scraping noise as it bounced off the concrete and threw the Arctic Cat to the right. Mueller's right knee dipped into the water as he frantically tried to regain speed and straighten his course. The turn back to the left proved too much to overcome. As he emerged from under the bridge, his sled slowed down, tipped on its side, and started to sink.

"Doc's going down!" Weston yelled. Seeing no sign of life near the bubbling water where the Cherokee went under, Weston turned his snowmobile to the right and raced toward the public fishing dock. He drove off the ice and up the hill to the parking lot of the condominiums that overlooked the dock at the north side of the bridge. Then he turned to the left, onto Highway 51, and gunned the sled to the middle of the bridge. Sam and Weston jumped off and ran to the railing, trying to spot Mueller in the icy water.

The sled was submerged, but Mueller's head was still above water, perhaps fifty feet from where the open water ended and the ice began.

"Hold on, Doc!"

Weston ran to his Polaris and got a plastic braided rope from under the seat. He clipped one end to the frame of his sled and threw the other end over the railing. It landed in the water a couple of feet away from Mueller.

"Grab the rope, Doc!"

MUELLER SAW THE END OF THE ROPE splash in the water near him. He looked up at the bridge railing, some twenty feet above him, and saw two figures staring down at him. One was Gary Weston, his buddy, the local police chief.

The other was Sam Skarda.

"Grab the rope!"

Grab the rope? Then what? Skarda was alive. He was going to prison for the rest of his life.

He'd played for the highest stakes he could imagine. He'd gone all in. He'd led a fantastic life—most of it, anyway. There'd been bad times, but his guile, his resourcefulness—and sometimes his sheer good luck—had always allowed him to bounce back. When he'd been at his lowest, Michael Banks came into his life. Hooking up with Banks had led to another good run. It had almost given him the spectacular payoff he'd always dreamed of. It had been worth the gamble—worth going all in. He'd never second-guess himself about that.

"For God's sake, Doc, grab the rope!"

It was cold in that lake—unbearably cold. He wished he'd had another chance to shoot between those abutments. Goddamn that pussy Banks—he'd ruined it. What a spectacular getaway it could have been. But Skarda and Gretchen had lived, so it really wouldn't have mattered. Awful cold—and tiring just to tread water. The float suit he'd worn when he and Ed broke through the ice would have come in handy now—if he'd wanted to live.

"The rope, Doc. The rope! To your left!"

No, he wouldn't grab the rope. What was the point? There was no ace coming down the river. Nothing left worth playing for. He opened his mouth and let the cold lake water rush in.

There were worse ways—and times—to die.

THIRTY

Joe Horvath pulled up to a meter outside Green Bay Memorial Hospital at 4:00 a.m. The street was deserted, and Horvath was dead tired. He'd been fighting to keep his eyes open for the last hour of the drive back from Minocqua. He wasn't as young and tough as he still pictured himself. Two three-hour drives that night, plus the shooting at Mueller's place and the trip out to the fish house to asphyxiate Skarda and Gretchen Kahler, had taken a lot out of him. But there was one more vital duty to perform before he could go home, feed his dogs, and sleep for twelve hours.

Doc had prepared a syringe, wrapped it in a white napkin, and placed it in an ordinary brown paper sack. He'd shown Horvath how to administer the shot: Spread the big toe and the second toe apart, insert the needle at least an inch, push the plunger, and then, if necessary, cover Frank's mouth until the stuff took effect. It wouldn't take very long. Horvath didn't ask what was in the syringe. He didn't want to know. Didn't care. All he cared about was eliminating the last person—a sick old man to begin with—who stood in the way of Banks and Mueller buying the Packers.

Director of Administrative Affairs. That's the job Mueller and Banks had promised him. It sounded important enough, yet vague enough, that he could do almost anything that wasn't directly football-related. It would be a huge step up from director of Security, in both prestige and in salary. He considered it a lucky break for him that Mueller had been in the emergency room the night those cops had brought him in on a DUI. He'd had to do some unsavory things for Mueller in exchange for holding onto his job, but the way things were playing out now, he was going to end up with a much bigger role in the new administration than he could ever have hoped for otherwise.

Still, he kept hearing Skarda: "They're going to push you in front of a snow plow." He had no reason, no evidence, to think that was true—but what if it was? He'd done things, and he knew things, that could put Mueller and Banks in jail for decades. Maybe they would decide they'd be safer with Horvath silenced. But then who would do their dirty work? Guys like Banks and Mueller would always need a hatchet man, and who better than the one they already had? The one who had proven he could get the job done, keep his mouth shut, and cover their asses when they made mistakes.

And what a mistake they'd almost made, letting that lunatic Krebbs get the drop on them. Horvath was still uneasy about not going after him when he fled Doc's house. Maybe Mueller had it right, that the punk was scared out of his mind and wouldn't dare make trouble for them again, with murder and kidnapping charges hanging over his head—not to mention the likelihood that his rage would dissipate when he found out that Gretchen was dead. But Horvath would feel a lot better when he could track Krebbs down and do a Natalie Dellums or Wesley Dillon on his ass.

First things first. Frank was supposed to be getting out of the hospital and going home in the morning, after a few final tests. Depending on what the security situation was at the hospital, it might be easier to do it here, right now, than wait to sneak into Frank's house later on and do it with his wife sleeping down the hall. He didn't want to have to kill Gloria, too, if he could help it.

Horvath put on his lightweight leather gloves and got out of the car. He walked to the main entrance, prepared to wait for a good opportunity to enter, and saw that there was no one at the reception desk. He walked casually past the desk to the stairway. If someone was standing guard over Frank's room, they might be watching the elevator doors. Besides, a little climb might be just what he needed to clear his sleepy brain.

He carried the paper sack in his left hand, keeping his right hand free to take his Smith and Wesson out of his jacket pocket. He'd reloaded when he stopped for gas in Rhinelander, and had a round in the chamber. You never knew.

When he reached the fourth floor, he slowly pushed the fire door open and peeked into the lobby by the nurse's station. He didn't see anyone there, and the lights were dimmed. He expected to see a couple of nurses on the floor, but they weren't likely to be moving up and down the halls as often as during the daytime. The patients were getting the sleep they needed.

Mueller had told him Frank's room number, and where to find it. He would simply walk down the hallway, turn to his left and proceed to Frank's room. If he didn't see anyone, he'd give Frank the injection, wait to make sure it worked, and leave. If someone did see him and asked what he was doing there, he'd tell them, as head of Packers security, that he was checking to make sure his boss was all right. Then he'd leave, and wait to use the syringe when Frank got home. Simple as that.

No one was sitting at the nurses' station. Maybe she was on break. Horvath followed the numbers down the hall to 417, saw the open door, saw the drapery pulled around the bed for privacy, and walked into Frank's room.

He was asleep. There were flowers on every available surface, with get-well wishes on the cards, most in green and gold. The television on the wall in the corner was tuned to ESPN, but the sound was turned low. Frank looked pale, but that wasn't unusual. There was no IV attached to his arm or oxygen hose under his nose; the doctors must have felt he was about ready to go home.

Too bad Frank was about to suffer a terrible setback.

Horvath put the bag on the chair next to the bed and gently reached over to take the edges of the sheet and blanket that were pulled up to Frank's chest. He drew down one side until his right leg and foot were exposed. Frank was still sleeping soundly, making it all much easier for Horvath. He opened the brown paper bag, took out the napkin, unfolded it and picked up the syringe in his right hand.

"Dr. Horvath, I presume."

Horvath's head snapped around to the edge of the curtain on the other side of Frank's bed. He was staring at Craig Botts, who had a semi-automatic pistol aimed at Horvath's heart.

"What are you doing here?" Horvath asked.

His mind spun. He'd just seen Botts, not more than nine or ten hours ago. Botts said NFL Security had sent him to Lambeau to study evacuation procedures. They'd toured the stadium together, looked at seating charts, inspected entrances and exits, and then Horvath had driven up to Minocqua. Botts had said he was flying on to Minneapolis.

He hadn't.

"I could ask you the same question, but the answer is pretty obvious," Botts said. "Put the syringe down. Now."

Frank's eyes opened. He smiled at Botts.

"Nice work, Craig. He never guessed."

Horvath tried to guess what they knew. How had they known? Should he go for the gun in his pocket, try to make a run for it? He knew Botts—he was ex-FBI, too, and he was good. Real good. Botts would drop him in the blink of an eye. And why should he take the fall for Mueller and Banks? Everything he did, he'd done because they told him to. Well, not the dogfight guy. But they'd never be able to prove he did that, anyway. He'd used Truman's gun, and the only two witnesses were dead.

Dellums? They couldn't prove that one, either. That gun was at the bottom of the Fox.

The fog was beginning to clear from his head, and he realized that something had gone very wrong up in Minocqua.

"Skarda? Kahler?" he asked.

"They're alive," Frank said. "Sam called a couple of hours ago and told us you were on your way."

"But how . . . ?"

"Seems someone made a midnight visit to that fish house," Botts said.

"I knew that asshole would outsmart himself. Where's Mueller?"

"Not sure. The divers should find him by sunup."

"Banks?"

"Same deal."

So now, Horvath realized, he was the one holding the bag. It wasn't supposed to turn out this way. He had plenty of dirt he could spill on Mueller and Banks, and had always been prepared to use it, if necessary. But if they were dead . . .

"I want to talk."

"That's a good idea," Botts said. "First things first. Hand me your gun."

Horvath used his right thumb and index finger to slowly pull the gun from his pocket. He laid it on the bed by Frank Janaszak's feet.

"Frank, if you would, call the Green Bay Police Department," Botts said. He handed Janaszak his phone, while he held the gun on Horvath. "Tell them there's been an attempted murder at the hospital."

THIRTY-ONE

Sam was on his way up the steps to the main entrance of the Green Bay Police headquarters when he passed a square-shouldered, balding man with a sharp, thin nose, and humorless eyes. The man crushed out his smoke and spoke to him.

"Too bad about your Cherokee, Skarda."

Sam stopped to look at the man. He didn't recognize him.

"Craig Botts. NFL Security."

Sam stopped and shook the man's hand.

"No big deal about the car," Sam said. "We hadn't had enough time to get attached to each other."

Botts lit another cigarette. Sam remained outside with him, his hands in his pockets. It was almost noon on a day that was turning sharply colder, and white winter clouds drifted across the brilliant blue sky. Sam couldn't tell if the cloud escaping Botts's mouth was cigarette smoke or the vapor of his breath in the frigid air, but he wasn't inclined to go inside to get out of the cold just yet. The fresh air still felt wonderful.

Sam's nausea was gone, but he still felt the lingering effects of the minutes he and Gretchen had spent breathing the noxious gas. She was in good condition at St. Mary's Hospital in Rhinelander, recovering from her near-fatal dose of carbon monoxide. A few more minutes, and it might have been too late.

No items of lasting value had been lost when Sam's Cherokee broke through the ice on Lake Minocqua: a Glock 23 that could be replaced, plus his key ring and an overnight bag with some clothes, which would eventually be salvaged when they pulled the vehicle out of the water. But Scott Krebbs was somewhere under the ice, too, no longer tortured at the thought of Gretchen moving on to lead a happy life without him.

When Sam heard that Horvath had been apprehended at the hospital, he knew he had to get back to Green Bay to tell Lieutenant VanHoff what he knew. He'd already spent the early-morning hours with Gary Weston, describing what had led up to the chase across the frozen lake. Weston was skeptical that Mueller could have been a murderer, but he eventually accepted the story when Botts called to tell him about Horvath's arrest and confession.

Weston arranged for an off-duty officer to drive Sam to Green Bay. They stopped in Rhinelander to look in on Gretchen. Then Sam had called Kleinschmidt, who told him the committee had decided to put off its next meeting until Frank Janaszak was well enough to attend. The first order of business would be to find a replacement for Doc Mueller. Selling the team would not be on the agenda—either at the next meeting, or any other time.

According to Botts, Lieutenant VanHoff had begun interviewing Horvath shortly after sunrise. By midmorning, VanHoff had heard enough to recommend dropping the involuntary-manslaughter charges against Gretchen for the death of D'Metrius Truman. Horvath wasn't offering any information on Dellums or Dillon, but he volunteered that Banks had ordered Mueller to send Jim Escher to kill Sam and Gretchen at her house. The rest of the plot was being revealed in slow, painstaking detail in an interrogation room.

"What changed your mind about Horvath?" Sam asked Botts, who had put both his hands inside his overcoat and was letting the cigarette dangle from his lips. "I didn't expect you to be in Green Bay when I called you last night."

"I made some calls to a few of my FBI friends. We became concerned enough to come out here and do some more investigating."

"Was one of the contacts Donald Meacham?"

"Yes. Horvath's trip to Minnesota to pick up Truman raised some flags. Whether the police can nail Horvath for killing Wesley Dillon is another story."

"Doesn't matter. They've got him on three counts of attempted murder. He'll go away for a long time."

"What's next for you, Skarda?"

Sam would have to wait around a day or two longer. VanHoff had questions for him, and he'd promised Gretchen that he'd pick her up from the hospital in Rhinelander and take her back to her house as soon as she was released. He'd have to rent a car for that, and to drive back to Minneapolis. There was also the matter of his fee, but he had no doubt that Frank and the executive committee would prove grateful when it came time to write the check.

"Back to Minneapolis. Then to Arizona—maybe for a long time."

"What's there?"

"A beautiful woman who saved my life."

Botts nodded, and tapped his growing ash. He again let the cigarette hang from his lips and thrust his bare hand back into his coat pocket.

"If you're interested in getting into a slightly different line of work, I would put in a word for you with the head of NFL Security. We're always looking for good people.

You've got the police background. You know sports. You're fit. And I think your instincts are excellent."

Sam turned the idea over in his head, briefly. It would be steady work, perhaps more interesting than the small-time cases that came his way in Minneapolis. He'd be investigating players, their friends, family, and contacts, and might be asked to poke into organized crime, drug gangs, and gambling—anything that had the potential to make the NFL look bad.

But he didn't have to think about it very long. He'd left the Minneapolis Police Department so he could be independent. Working for the NFL might eventually turn him into a robot like Botts—obviously an outstanding officer, but the perfect embodiment of what was often called the No Fun League. Sam had a quick image of the mundane side of life as an NFL Security agent: peering at players standing on the sidelines during a game, and writing down the names and numbers of the ones whose socks weren't pulled up high enough.

"I appreciate the offer, but I don't think it's a good fit," Sam said. "I'll bet you don't have an NFL Security Force band, do you?"

"No."

Sam thanked Botts for stepping in to save Frank Janaszak. Then he excused himself and walked into the lobby of the police department. He asked to see Lieutenant VanHoff. The desk sergeant told him to take a seat; VanHoff would see him as soon as he was free. Sam asked if there was a pay phone, and the sergeant pointed to a hallway, saying there was a wall phone around the corner.

Sam entered his credit card number, and as he dialed Caroline, he started humming "I'll Be Home For Christmas"—a hit for Bing Crosby during World War II, when millions of battle-scarred guys just wanted to get home to the women they loved. Sam smiled. He was pretty sure he knew where home was, now.